Conversations Among Butterflies

Mike Mitchell

This work is completely fictional, but is informed by the author's extensive experience and research in Latin America. He has lived in Argentina, Panama, and Honduras, and has worked and traveled in nearly every country in North and South America. A central topic of this novel comes from his book entitled *Transitions from Military Rule in South America: The Obligational Legitimacy Hypothesis*, which won the Top Thesis Award at Naval Postgraduate School for National Security Affairs and was also selected as a Defense Institute of Security Assistance textbook for Latin American Area Studies. He has also published peer reviewed journal articles on Gramsci and other topics of minor mention in this work. It has always been the poet that has captured the heartbeat of Latin America and some poets are briefly noted in this work. The author has provided references for the poems and poets mentioned in this novel in the last pages of this book for the reader's convenience and to further honor these artists.

Byblos Media
Newark, Delaware

ISBN13 978-0-9746003-7-6
Kindle Edition ASIN 0-9746003-7-7

Printed in the United States of America

First Edition

Cover artwork by Mike & Vicky Mitchell
Design and layout by Tom Mitchell and Rosey Hansen

More by this author check out www.mike-mitchell.com

Contents

Prologue

THERE ARE MANY BUTTERFLIES IN THIS LUSH VALLEY. Some show off and are very visible while others seem to disappear when they are chased or threatened. Some play dead. Some seem to dance and love to grab onto things, or thoughts, floating in the breeze. Some are fast. Some are slow. Some are devious, and some are simply simple. One species of butterflies that has long made its home among the river banks has been named by man the Heliconius Charitonius. Neither this butterfly nor its pre-winged caterpillar form know this name or care about its classification. As a caterpillar it cares about the passionflower plant that it gorges on day and night. As an adult butterfly it cares about the passionflower blossom. It is unique among its butterfly cousins for the ability to eat pollen and sip nectar. This dual feeding ability contributes to its energy, health, and longevity, with adults living up to six months. The few butterflies that feed on pollen are also typically brightly colored, show superior mimetic diversity, and are not a popular meal among predators because of their acidic taste.

Heliconius is also a social species as butterflies go, but fairly solitary as caterpillars. Adult butterflies sleep in large clusters and typically return to the same place every night. They retain warmth together—they cannot fly unless they are warm, and these groupings deter predators. It is also during the night that they digest the pollen they collected during the day. They use visual, olfactory, tactile, and auditory cues in their social communication and mating rituals. This specific Heliconius is called the Charitonius in honor of the Charites, or Graces, of Greek mythology. These Charities were the personifications of charm and beauty in nature and in human life. They love all things beautiful and bestow talent upon mortals. They were fountains of inspiration in poetry, philosophy, and the arts of life. They could also have a dark side and were sometimes associated with the underworld, secret organizations, and power. No one ever suspects the butterfly.

The Heliconius caterpillar has many long black spikes protruding from its body and is generally a solitary fellow. After the caterpillar's life of self-absorbed consumption, it enters its cocoon, also called a chrysalis. Emerging only a few days later, completing its metamorphic transformation, the butterfly is in its full glory. It attracts mates with its boldly striped black and white wing pattern, but this coloration is also aposematic—conspicuously challenging and warning off enemies.

There are thirty nine known species of the Heliconius genus. A few people wonder if there may be a closely related fortieth species called the Madrugada. It has evolved from tasting acidic and warning its predators with coloration, to yet another form of protection.

Chapter 1
Digno Evento

"…AND AS A SERVANT, SOLDIER AND PROTECTOR of this sacred banner that represents all that is good about the country of my birth, I pledge my honor, my undying loyalty, and my life to protect her from all who would harm her in any way, in the name of God our maker. *¡Viva la patria!*" Captain Diego Peña always felt a deep exhilaration that touched a place in his soul that the rest of his being didn't even know existed except at times like these when he performed this annual ritual of wrapping himself in the flag of his country, as if in a cocoon of duty and obligation, and reciting the Oath of Brotherhood. He found it somewhat sad and telling that this ceremony was almost unknown to the general populace and that his fellow soldiers had been reciting this very same oath since his forefathers had discharged the Spanish back to the Iberian Peninsula just over 150 years ago. The tradition actually dated back to the Roman practice of the Sacramentum—the oath of office that Roman officers took upon receiving their commission from the Emperor. At least that is what he had been taught at the military academy.

Captain Diego Ibarra Peña y Lopez was a fourth generation officer who had dedicated his life to the service of his country. Some of his military academy classmates had entered the service of arms out of pressure from family tradition, some for economic reasons, but most because of a sincere love of country and a youthful lust for adventure and glory. A few became disillusioned or disappointed at some point in their chosen profession, but Captain Peña knew of only three classmates in that unfortunate situation. Nearly all came to crave the feelings of brotherhood and camaraderie of the officer corps and those bonds became as accepted and essential as air to breath and water to drink were for the body. Captain Peña could not remember a time in his life when he did not want to be a soldier. Now at the age of 32, he could not imagine any other existence.

The officer corps brotherhood, catalytic events like taking the Oath, actual combat and the rigid military lifestyle, brought a level of meaning to his life that he doubted the majority of his country's populace ever experienced, even once. It wasn't the adrenaline rush that ignorant journalists pointed to as an explanation for this lofty feeling. It wasn't their fault they couldn't explain something they probably never felt. Captain Peña did not see himself as elitist. He wasn't better than his countrymen, but he did feel set apart in both meanings of the word: separated and called. As he stood before his men, feeling the early morning sun begin to warm the earth beneath his highly shined black shoes, he had no doubts about his place in the world. As his baby brother, who was a medical doctor, often observed, Captain Peña's synapses were hardwired military. For a split second while standing there in front of his command, he wondered whether he had been born hardwired, or whether it was a process like today's event that created a militarized junction between the billions of neurons in his body. It never entered his thoughts to consider whether that was good or bad. It simply was. He understood from the joking banter with his brother that neurons acted according to an all or nothing rule. If a neuron responds at all, then it must respond completely. That pretty much summed him up, he thought.

The all or nothing demands of military service had left Peña single, although he had to admit to himself that most of his academy classmates were now married and many had children. He had noticed an intriguing local young lady at his present post, but he knew nothing about her and thoughts of her would have to wait. Today held a very full schedule. "All or nothing neurons," he thought with a melancholy smile.

"Sergeant Hernandez!" he bellowed a little too exuberantly. His heart was still bathed in adrenaline from the ceremony he had just consummated in front of his command. "Post the colors and put the company at parade rest!" he ordered to officially conclude the ceremony.

"Yes, my Captain!" returned Sergeant Hernandez with equal pomp and a sharp salute.

Captain Peña returned the salute and half a smile. He appreciated this mestizo non-commissioned officer who seemed to have the same respect and love of country that he did. Sergeant Hernandez was also the most efficient Company First Sergeant he had ever met, and that significantly lessened the professional demands on his time here in Mariposa. 'So why have I not found time to search out the local beauties?' he asked himself for the hundredth time. 'Hernandez's tight ship won't hurt my chances for promotion either,' another part of his mind added.

Captain Peña turned from the company of soldiers as Sergeant Hernandez barked out the orders of the day. The young conscripts held almost a filial love for Hernandez and feared the Captain. 'As it should be,' thought Peña.

Within three steps Captain Peña's thoughts were on his first event of the day. He was to travel to the small airport near Mariposa, the largest town in the sector of the country under his responsibility. He both detested and looked forward to this part of his duties. As the ranking officer in the Mariposa sector, he had the obligation to meet any visiting dignitaries and occasionally the tourists that came into the airport on the twice weekly flight from the capital. Officially these duties were designated as good will ambassadorial responsibilities. Unofficially, since the military coup four years earlier, this was a way for the local commander to keep track of who was coming and going from his sector of responsibility. From either perspective he didn't mind this break in his schedule of more mundane activities. He liked the pomp of this digno evento at the airport, but not so much being part of the center of attention. What he really didn't like were the comments from first time visitors who were disappointed with the rundown look of Mariposa that didn't match the color glossy travel brochures and travel agent hype that brought these foreign visitors here.

"What do they expect for $35 a day hotel rooms anyway?" he muttered as he inspected himself. His face seemed glossy in the mirror like those ridiculous travel brochures. 'Humidity of this inland valley and my ceremonial uniform are conspiring to drown me in perspiration,' he noted with a fleeting concern of potential hypocrisy, but no complaint about the obvious mismatch of uniform and environment. Peña stood at sixty nine inches tall, with a lean, but muscular build, short black hair, and dark brown eyes. He had never had problems with whiskers and in fact only had to shave every other day. He was also humble. He had no idea that he was the personification of what most other officers either thought or wished they looked like. Normally he would not travel to the airport in his best dress uniform. 'Why waste that on these tourists?' he thought. He was running a little late today, however, because of the ceremony and he didn't have time to change. He grabbed the keys to the stockade's best jeep and he was on his way.

The drive was uneventful and the breeze from the open jeep felt good. Even the decaying foliage that cluttered the edge of the road and marked the border between the unruly jungle and the civilization of the road smelled like perfume today. Twenty minutes later he was at the airport chatting with the National Police lieutenant, who was in charge of airport security. 'I really don't like this man. He is old enough to be my father and with that age should come wisdom, and he has less dedication to selfless duty than a stray dog,' Peña thought to himself. He tried to think of an appropriate exit as he listened to the lieutenant babble about some goats that had gotten loose on the runway just as the plane was taking off on a return flight to the capital last week.

"I could have lost my job!" the lieutenant was saying.

"Not to mention losing the plane and the people on board," Peña added half under his breath.

His words were drowned out as the loudspeaker announced the arrival of Flight 125 from the capital. Captain Peña looked out the window and could just make out the twin engine turbo prop aircraft descending out of the clouds and already perfectly lined up with the runway. Aviation amazed him and he wondered if he should have chosen the Air Force instead of the Army for his career. That thought lasted less than one second. He knew he had chosen correctly. Flying may be more adventurous, but in his country the power was held by the Army. The Air Force and Navy were secondary services at best. They didn't even have a seat at the table of the ruling Junta.

"Please excuse me, lieutenant, I am going to walk out to the tarmac today and meet the plane."

Usually by this hour in the morning it would be raining this time of year, but today was partly cloudy. The sun shining through picked up his spirits once again as he walked out the door. By the time he had positioned himself near the parking spot, the plane was just touching down.

Captain Peña was watching a butterfly fight against a light breeze to get to some flowers across the tarmac when he heard, "What will the plane bring today, my Captain?" a voice from behind him asked. It was the airport custodian who stepped out of the shadows of the terminal.

Captain Peña thought the man looked as old as the hills that surrounded the Mariposa Valley and just as wise except for always surprising him from the shadows. "Ayyy, Alejandro, you gave me a start! I didn't know you were behind me," Peña said, trying to cover the fact that he really had been startled.

"I am sorry, my Captain. I am old, but I am still as nimble as a cat," Alejandro Costa joked

"And obviously as ornery as one I see," Peña retorted. "Any more scares like that and you will wish you had as many lives as a cat," Peña continued with joviality he hoped masked his annoyance that this old man could always catch him unaware.

The plane pulled up to the only marked parking spot on the tarmac and shut down its engines. The door opened and out came the only stewardess. She looked like she could have been Alejandro's mother and with enough makeup to hide a decade or two. She was quick on the stairs, even with a knee length uniformed skirt and high heals. "That has got to miserable to wear those shoes all day in her type of job," he silently commiserated. He felt his own feet begin to float in the collected perspiration in his dress shoes. Next came several government bureaucrats that Peña recognized. He would have to meet with them sometime this week to discuss the progress of the power plant that was being built just below the new Dam, located about fifteen miles from here at the north end of the Mariposa Valley. He could actually have met with them that morning and they could return on the afternoon flight, but he knew the game and didn't want to cause undue contention. He would wait until they contacted him, which would be after at least a day. They would then schedule a meeting the following day after that. This way, these bureaucrats would get three or four days of *viaticos* which was a sort of living expense for being away from home.

The plane only held fifteen passengers, but he wouldn't be surprised if no one else deplaned. Tourist season officially ended two weeks earlier and the rainy season would soon be upon them with a vengeance. Just as he was about to turn and catch up with the bureaucrats to greet them, he noticed movement again at the door of the plane. At first he thought it was one of the pilots, but then he glimpsed the flowing long hair. He said, "Oh, maybe I should have considered the Air Force," thinking it was a female pilot, but then realized it was a female passenger who was evidently struggling with something in the doorway. As Peña approached the plane he could smell an intoxicating perfume and then reminded himself that any perfume was pleasing to someone who lived in an Army stockade with two hundred and fifty soldiers.

Captain Peña reached the aircraft door. "May I be of assistance?" he asked in Spanish without thinking.

The person in the aircraft turned and looked out the door. She was stunning and exotic. Her blonde hair was shoulder length and stylishly curled. Her eyes were hazel and her complexion was…, bright red.

"Thank you sir," she answered in apparent frustration and perfect Spanish. "The flight attendant said she was going to help us with our bags, but evidently she had more important things to do!"

'From the look of her, she might have gone for oxygen so she could make the return flight before her retirement,' Captain Peña quietly thought. "I would be glad to help you with your bags," he said out loud. "Alejandro, bring the baggage cart to the plane!"

Turning back to the aircraft Captain Peña was struck anew with the beauty of this visitor. Her slender smooth hand of manicured nails gave him two large suitcases and a hang-up bag before he could ask her a question. He carried the bags to the cart Alejandro had just delivered. When he turned back to the aircraft, he got a second surprise. She was not alone. A man about Peña's age or maybe a little older was deplaning. It was hard to tell with *gringos*.

"Of course she wasn't alone you fool," Peña mumbled to himself. The man was muscular, also with blond hair though darker. He was well tanned and had gray, nearly light blue eyes. He wore loose fitting tropical clothes including a typical North American tourist shirt, white pants and tennis shoes with no socks. He was carrying a tennis racket and an attaché case. The man squinted when he stepped from the aircraft into the sunlight and he almost missed the first step down the stairs. He did bump his head on the top of the door, the Captain noted with guilty amusement.

"Don't over tax yourself," Captain Peña mumbled, certain the breeze would carry away his verbal thought.

"He's not used to carrying his own bags," the young lady answered from just behind him.

For the second time this morning he was startled. He turned with a jump and began an apology.

"That won't be necessary, he doesn't speak Spanish, and although we were only recently married, I partly share your sentiment," this intriguing visitor retorted.

"Well, I do apologize for my rudeness, if just to you then," the flustered Peña added.

"Oh, just to little ol' me, then," she mimicked condescendingly.

"I am sorry miss, I mean Mrs. I didn't mean it that way," Captain Peña explained, feeling a trickle of sweat roll down his back. "I only meant that I would apologize to you because he doesn't … Well you know what I mean."

"It's Mrs. Farnsworth, Louise Farnsworth. That's Harold," she said with a twinkle in her eye.

She had obviously been baiting him with this banter and with some success Peña admitted to himself. These were strange *Norteños*.

"It is an honor to be the first to welcome you and your husband to Mariposa, a jewel on the necklace of my country," Captain Peña responded in English, shifting into his official greeter role for protection. He came to stiff attention and announced, "My name is Captain Diego Peña, Commander of the Mariposa Stockade and legal authority of the Mariposa Sector."

"We are pleased to meet you Captain Peña," Mrs. Farnsworth responded in English as her husband joined them.

"From your accent, I take it you are from the United States?" Captain Peña answered effortlessly in English, but with a slight British accent.

"Very good Captain," Mrs. Farnsworth answered with an approving smile.

"Yes, we are Americans." Mr. Farnsworth added.

"Ah, but we are all Americans in this hemisphere," Captain Peña replied a little too competitively.

"Oh, yes... Well, of course. I didn't mean that you weren't...." Mr. Farnsworth stammered.

"What do you say we get out of the hot sun and continue our detente in the air conditioned building?" Mrs. Farnsworth interjected.

Here it came, the part of this duty that he detested the most. The rich *Norte Americanos* will now discover the rustic nature of Mariposa.

"I am sorry Mrs. Farnsworth, there is no air-conditioning in the terminal. Actually, there is no air-conditioning in this valley, except what God provides."

Instead of the shock he expected to see registered on her face, he thought he saw some embarrassment quickly covering up real hurt.

"No, it is I who needs to apologize," she replied with formality. "I already love your butterfly valley, and I am sure God will provide a sufficient breeze to keep unintended sharp words from reaching unintended targets," she added and then turned and walked toward the building.

Mr. Farnsworth and Captain Peña watched her enter the building. "What in the world is she talking about?" Farnsworth asked.

"Sir, I only just met your wife. I am not sure what she meant," he answered unconvincingly.

"Well, I suppose that is one reason I fell in love with her. She is like a new sunrise every minute," Mr. Farnsworth mused and headed for the door, leaving Captain Peña with the baggage cart loaded with the Farnsworth luggage.

Chapter 2
River Currents

"THIS IS THE BEST HOTEL IN OUR HUMBLE VALLEY, *Señora* Farnsworth," Captain Peña announced as they stepped from their vehicle. The smell from the car's exhaust was mixing with the wet and decaying foliage around the hotel—which didn't smell as good as it had earlier on the drive from the airport. The hotel seemed even more rundown and drabber today than usual to the Captain. He immediately raised his defenses.

"Please, call me Louie," Mrs. Farnsworth intoned. She hopped from the 1962 Chevy Impala. "I love the car, it's a classic!" she added.

The hotel had sent the older, but adequate sedan to the airport to transport the Farnsworths. Despite his better judgment, Captain Peña had decided to escort the sedan into town. He wasn't sure why and actually he hadn't given his decision a second thought. He looked at the sedan again, wondering what made it a classic.

The ride had only taken about fifteen minutes. The Captain walked to their sedan a bit too briskly for the mid-morning humidity and heat and he was curious what the Farnsworth's thoughts would be of Mariposa now that they had traveled the dusty road and were face to face with the rundown buildings and sleepy atmosphere of the town. He steeled himself for the typical rebuff others had offered once arriving in town.

"Pretty much what I expected," Mr. Farnsworth commented to no one in particular after he stepped from the sedan.

Captain Peña stiffened and felt his blood pressure rise. He was surprised he also felt a disappointment in this couple.

"I agree Harold. This is the perfect destination!" Louie announced and stepped through the doorway to the Hotel *Otra Vez*.

As she disappeared into the shade of the hotel lobby, one of the nicer buildings in the city, Peña wondered again at the apparent differences between these two *Norteños*. He chuckled at the thought. He knew there definitely was a difference. She was gorgeous and he was an idiot. He believed he was making allowances for her because of her beauty, her ability to speak Spanish, and her apparent intelligence. Then he reconsidered that all this might have been because she was simply a pleasant person.

"Right, that was my thought, Louie," Harold added with enthusiasm, or was that sarcasm in his voice? "Captain, could you watch our bags for a minute while I catch up with Louie and sign in? Thanks!" and Harold was off.

"I off-loaded their bags, and now the commanding authority for this entire sector of the country is left to guard them? I really don't like this *Norteño*," Peña said out loud, this time hoping Farnsworth heard him. 'I think I have at least judged him correctly. If he tries to tip me I will make sure the hotel re-assigns them the room with no windows, then he can really enjoy the famous Mariposa heat and humidity,' he added in his mind. The thought made him smile.

"You enjoy this kind of work I see Captain," Louie said as she passed through the hotel entry walking directly for the baggage. Peña dropped his smile as fast as Louie seemed to change direction. "I apologize for the second time this hour for Harold," she added. "As soon as I realized Harold had left you with our bags I asked him to check us in so I could help out with the bags."

"Yes. Well, I am not sure I will accept your apology this time. It is he who should apologize and I don't think he even realizes his poor manners," Peña answered with some indignation in his voice and then immediately afterwards felt some embarrassment for speaking his mind to a complete stranger.

"Harold is not the uncultured oaf, nor the spoiled, insensitive brat that you may be thinking he is," Louie said almost soothingly.

"That may be *Señora*, but I have no interest in nurturing my eternal patience in order to discover the real Mr. Farnsworth," Peña added and shifted into a formal stance. "I must take my leave of you now, as I have other business that demands my attention. I sincerely hope your stay in Mariposa is pleasant. Good day, *Señora*." With a slight stiff bow he turned to leave. His mind captured the picture of the *Norteña's* face glistening in the humidity and eyes with, what? Hurt? Possibly it was just weariness from her travels.

"Thank you for your welcome and your kind assistance, Captain," the lovely lady said graciously. "I am certain our visit will be everything I expect. I also hope your meetings with those government bureaucrats are uneventful," she added with a slight smile.

Peña turned back to Louie trying to clear the surprised look off of his face. "Do you make it a practice to insert yourself into everyone's business, *Señora* Farnsworth?"

"Really, please, call me Louie. And, no, I don't. It was a quiet flight from the capital and I don't think those men knew I spoke Spanish. I couldn't help but overhear their conversation in that small aircraft. Let me just say, you're in for a busy week and they came loaded for bear."

"Loaded for bear?" Peña asked, momentarily forgetting his irritation with her.

"Just a North American saying. Your English is excellent, but then, your accent sounds like British English, so I shouldn't have used that expression. In this case it means something like, they have some big guns aimed at you. Shifting the blame from the distant bureaucrat to the man in the arena is obviously a game played all over the world, and they are prepared to shoot if necessary. By the way, how do you get to the river from here?"

"Are they here to talk about the river?" Peña asked, completely confused.

"No, they are here to tell you the bad news about the power plant, or something like that. Their entire conversation during the flight was how your administration here, and you in particular, have impeded the scheduled opening of the plant. I want to go to the river, because that is why Harold and I chose Mariposa for our honeymoon."

Peña's thoughts raced through his head: bears, the power plant, the river, a rude *Norteño*, and a honeymoon. This had really been an enlightening conversation, about as enlightening as the Campaña Caves with no torch! He had been frustrated with Harold, and now the bureaucrats were eroding his emotions. "You passed the turn-off for the river two blocks back on your way from the airport. Good day," he snapped.

"Captain Peña," Louie responded gently. "Captain Peña, I would like to have a pleasant conversation with you and I think you will find I am not a blond joke in the flesh and that Harold is really not as crass as he seems. Would you be our guest for dinner tonight? It would really mean a lot to us," Louie asked with sincerity. "That is, if your schedule allows it. And please bring your..." She stopped, unsure how to complete her request.

Against his better judgment, Captain Peña heard himself interrupting her invitation, accepting, and telling this beguiling *Norteña* that he was not married, would come alone, and to call him Diego.

Captain Peña drove slowly back to the stockade. Although his mind kept returning to thoughts of the *Norteño* visitors, he finally succeeded in bringing his concentration around to the bureaucrats from the capital. 'Of course this should not be a surprise,' he thought. 'They are more interested in their careers and not being questioned for their ineptitude by the Junta council than getting to the truth of failure to open the power plant on schedule. Fortunately I have sent monthly reports to General Cruz detailing the problems and my own prediction that the plant would not open as planned. The General's replies and the fact that the planned news announcements were postponed is proof that someone in the capital is listening to me. I wonder what these *servants of our country* have in mind?'

He turned into the stockade entrance, saluted the guard who stood at rigid attention when his jeep passed and pulled up to his reserved parking spot. He would have Sergeant Hernandez detail someone to drive it back to the motor pool. Peña was anxious to get out of his ceremonial uniform, but wanted to see if there was any urgent business waiting for him at his office first.

"Celia, good morning," he said to his secretary. "Could you have Lieutenant Mendoza and Sergeant Hernandez report to me as soon as they can break away from their duties?"

Celia was an efficient and friendly person. She had served the previous two commanders of this post and had worked at the stockade before the coup that placed the Army in command of the government. Just as with Sergeant Hernandez, he wasn't sure what he would do without her assistance. It was Celia, in fact, that had suggested he begin a regular correspondence with the capital on the slow progress of the power plant.

"As you wish, my Captain," Celia answered. "You have two messages on your desk. Our visitors from the capital would like to meet with you this evening for dinner. It seems they are going to visit the Dam and the power plant first. Not a very courteous way to begin their visit to our valley. They seem to be in a hurry. Didn't they just get here today?"

"I saw them at the airport, so I assume they felt that was enough introductory pleasantries. These are servants of the country and they have no interest but to do their job," he added with a sarcastic chuckle.

With a smile of understanding and agreement, Celia added, "The other message is from General Cruz warning you that the bureaucrats, I mean servants of the country, were on their way to Mariposa. It seems he only learned of their travel this morning in his daily situation briefing. So how did you know they were coming, if the General only just found out?"

"Know? I didn't know. I went to meet the plane as usual and when they stepped off the plane that was the first I knew."

"Oh, I see. So only your keen intuition told you to wear your ceremonial dress uniform this morning to meet a plane that could have possibly arrived without any passengers?"

"Celia, you are of my mother's age and you have her wisdom, but I do wish you wouldn't treat me like your errant son. I am supposed to be the commander here, you know," he said in mock reprimand. "This is the anniversary of my graduation from the Academy. I took the Oath of Brotherhood this morning. That reminds me. Please prepare some notes for me to send to a few of my classmates. Say, seven copies expressing my best wishes to them. I will personalize the salutation and write each a note."

"And about the invitation to dinner?"

"Tell our humble servants from the capital that I have already accepted a dinner invitation from the *Norte Americanos* that traveled with them on the flight this morning. I would be happy to meet with them before or after dinner, or first thing in the morning. It would be rude to change my plans at this time."

"North American visitors? Dinner? You? That is not the Captain Peña I know. Are they important?"

"Important? Not that I know of. They are here for their honeymoon, although they are not all that young. No, we didn't get off to a good start this morning and I thought it was the proper thing to do."

"So you invited them to dinner?"

"Actually, she…" Peña stopped abruptly and thought carefully about the implications of what he was saying. "They invited me. What could I say?"

"I see," said Celia with amused understanding. "I assume they are staying at the *Otra Vez*? I will make sure you get a good table tonight," Celia added. She turned back toward her desk.

"Yes, the *Otra Vez*. Thank you," Peña answered. "And yes, she is pretty and her husband is an idiot, but what do you expect for *Norteños*. Oh, and let's plan on having the meeting with our servant friends tomorrow morning. They aren't going to want to meet right before dinner and risk the meeting breaking into their dinner hour since I won't be joining them. After dinner they will be too tired. They aren't here to nurture our friendship and mutual respect. They will want to be fresh, so I expect tomorrow morning it will be. They came loaded for bear you know," Peña added, chuckling to himself at the literal translation into Spanish and Celia's quizzical look. "Now, I will be back in twenty minutes. I am going to get out of this uniform before I shrivel up like a new conscript meeting Sergeant Hernandez for the first time."

When Peña stepped out of his office, he could hear Celia ask her desk, "They brought a bear with them?" Peña smiled broadly and suppressed an audible laugh.

A half hour later, Captain Peña was back at his desk in a more comfortable uniform. He was wearing green uniform slacks and a light green shirt. His award ribbons were proudly displayed on his right chest and a black name tag on his left chest, just above the pocket. His Captain's rank was neatly attached to his shoulders. His belt buckle and black shoes were shining. He was in his environment, understood his role, and was confident he could handle his responsibilities. Within minutes of his return to his office he heard a brisk knock at his door. Lieutenant Julio Mendoza and

Sergeant Hernandez stepped into the office and reported with a brisk salute. Peña returned the salute and said, "Julio, have Celia come in and close the door."

This was not uncommon as this small group often met as a sort of executive council to discuss sensitive matters that Captain Peña did not want to bring up with his whole staff. Celia soon stepped in with her note pad and all made themselves comfortable.

"When we are through here, Sergeant, could you detail someone to return the jeep to the motor pool? Thank you. Now the matter at hand is the surprise visit of some bureaucrats from the capital. When I saw them get off the aircraft I thought their visit was routine. We barely greeted each other. Now I understand their visit to be a less friendly hunting trip to find a scapegoat for their failure to bring the power plant on line as scheduled." Peña didn't elaborate and let the group assume his information came from General Cruz and not the beguiling *Norteña*.

"Are you saying they are going to blame their failures on us?" Julio Mendoza asked with a little too much emotion.

"Not exactly. They are going to blame it on me," Peña answered. "This is a big enough problem that they must have a big enough target to point at. No matter. Julio, they know you, so I can't ask you to be present at their visits to the Dam and the power plant today. Could you have two of our engineers present? Send one to each site. These should be people who are not unwelcome or unexpected at the Dam and the plant. Do not send the same person to both locations. That would be too obvious that we are keeping an eye on them. Have them report to you with whatever information they can glean. I will be dining with two tourists tonight. I will expect their report in my quarters tonight after dinner. Say twenty-two hundred hours."

"Excuse me, my Captain, but I have another suggestion," Sergeant Hernandez said.

"Yes, what is it?" Peña asked.

"They have presented an order from General Cruz' office for a vehicle and driver. I could hand pick the driver. He may not hear anything, but you never know."

"From General Cruz' office? Interesting. When was it signed?" Peña asked.

"It is today's date, but it would have to have been prepared at the latest yesterday because their plane left very early this morning."

"And who signed it?" Celia asked.

"A Major Horta. I don't remember the first name. Why do you ask?" Hernandez asked Celia.

"No reason," she said and glanced at Captain Peña with warning in her eyes.

"Very good, Sergeant. Make sure we provide them with a good driver. We will meet here tomorrow at zero eight hundred to go over our game plan for the day with our visitors. Any questions?"

"No sir, not yet anyway," Lieutenant Mendoza answered.

"No sir," Sergeant Hernandez said.

Before Celia could answer, Peña said, "Celia, please stay for a few minutes. I want to go over those notes you were preparing for my classmates. I need to get them in the mail today." Peña stood to signify the meeting was over. When they were out the door, he turned to Celia and asked, "So what do you think? Is there a conspiracy in the works? The note from General Cruz that you left on my desk, was it the General who called or someone from his office?"

"No, it was the General. I know his voice," Celia assured him.

"He didn't warn of anything except their visit was a surprise to him. Could he or someone in his office be in on this visit and its true purpose?"

Celia answered followed by a cautious question. "You know exactly why they are here and indirectly suggested you received that information from the General. I didn't say anything in the meeting, but I know he didn't offer any reason for their visit other than routine business. Is there something I should know, or is it none of my business?"

"The *Norteña* on the plane overheard their conversations. They evidently didn't know she spoke Spanish. She gave me a warning of sorts. Could you call the headquarters and confirm the car and driver request orders. Confirm that we are here to support our important guests, but the copy they gave us isn't a very clear copy and we want a copy of the order for our records. If they press you, drop it. I don't want to raise any suspicions. I trust General Cruz with my life. In better days I would trust his staff as well. Unfortunately, politics have entered our ranks and I am not sure what agenda is playing out here. Either way, let me know what you find. Thank you, Celia, and let's keep this part of our research between you and me."

Chapter 3
Dinner Tables

ALEJANDRO COSTA WAS RETELLING THE NEWS FROM the airport while his wife Emma completed the preparations for dinner. The beans smelled very good and Alejandro was hungry. Even though they had some sort of beans almost every night, only sometimes spiced with meat, he didn't complain and he was grateful for Emma's creative skills in the kitchen.

"I think I really surprised the Captain today, Emma. He tried to hide it, but I really got him!"

"Don't be so boastful old man. You are lucky he didn't put you in jail for your little trick. Then you wouldn't be laughing," Emma said. She added the last of her spices to the tired pot of beans.

"He wouldn't do that. Captain Peña is a thoughtful Commandante. He is not at all like Captain Zarro."

"I thought we agreed never to mention that name in this house again, Alejandro?" Emma said with sadness in her voice.

"I am sorry my *media naranja*," Alejandro said, trying to comfort his wife of thirty seven years. Both Alejandro and Emma still felt the pain of the rumored arrest of their son Gustavo at the hand of a zealous Captain Zarro in the North of the country. Gustavo had been in the wrong place at the wrong time, and although his parents knew him to be a good young man, rumors suggested that he was arrested as a possible guerrilla fighter. They had never heard from Gustavo since. There was great pain in the Costa home when this same Captain Zarro was posted in Mariposa. There was melancholy happiness in the humble Costa home when Captain Zarro was transferred to the capital. The Costa family had made a resigned peace with Captain Peña, Zarro's replacement. Peña seemed like a good person, but he still represented the Army that had taken their oldest son. Now their only other son, Francisco (known to most as Paco), was staying away from home first for weeks at a time and then disappearing altogether, leaving the small Costa farm for his parents and his baby sister Diana to deal with. They could use Paco's strong back, but they didn't raise the subject because they strongly suspected he actually was working with the guerrillas, and that subject was just too painful to talk about.

"There are times when my daydreams let me forget that Gustavo is gone from us Emma. I can almost see him in the shop working just out of my view. I think if I turn my head quickly, he will be there, if only for a second. A few times I have obeyed my desire to see him once more and I have rapidly turned my head, only to get dizzy from the quick movement," Alejandro admitted with a melancholy he regretted, because he knew it would only add to the burden Emma carried.

"*Daydreams have endlessly turning paths going over the bitter earth,* old man," Emma shared.

"Is that from one of your poets Emma, or your own thought?" Alejandro asked. When Alejandro met and courted Emma, he had assumed she was a simple woman with simple interests, like most of the people of this quiet valley. Soon after their marriage, however, she disclosed the secret she had kept hidden, even from her parents. She had a passion for poetry. Her passion went far beyond a hobby, unless you consider breathing a hobby, Alejandro mused. He had supported her interest over the years with small purchases, torn pages from a magazine a passenger had discarded at the airport where he worked part-time, and a few times with books of poetry that mysteriously found their way to the Mariposa Valley. Often, when Emma could not find the words to express herself, she used one of the hundreds of poems she had memorized over the decades. As their years and family grew, their conversations became rich with thought, perspective, and insight that also rubbed off on their three children, but in interestingly different ways.

"Yes, Antonio Machado was a poet from Spain I believe. The poem is *Sobre La Tierra Amarga* (Over the Bitter Earth). When we speak out loud of Gustavo it is like walking on bitter earth for me. It is interesting the poet's thoughts define your own Alejandro. He says *"these daydreams are sad playthings for an old man."*

"That they are, my love; especially now that Paco is also gone. Thank goodness we still have Diana with us," Alejandro admitted. With these sad thoughts, he realized he had lost his appetite.

"Dinner is ready Alejandro," Emma announced. "Could you go get Diana from the garden and we will eat?" she added, bringing them both back to the world of their day-to-day survival.

On the other side of Mariposa, Sergeant Enrique Hernandez was in the non-commissioned officer's mess at the stockade, and was just sitting down to his dinner. He loved the comradery of the mess hall. As a senior non-commissioned officer, he had a set place at the center table. His place setting was always ready for him. His hat was hung on a wooden peg in the hallway that was reserved for him. When the junior non-commissioned officers entered the mess, they first reported to him and asked permission to join the mess, before sitting down to eat. Altogether, the order, the tradition, and the daily practice of the mess in part defined his world. Sergeant Hernandez was married, but had no children. His wife Consuelo was his best friend and the joy of his life, but oh how he loved the Army! If he had been asked at that moment why he had decided to make the military a career, he would have said, "the food is good." He didn't like sharing his deeper feelings about his chosen profession, even with Consuelo. She understood his feelings, perhaps even shared the same sense of loyalty and dedication as he, but it was not something they had ever discussed. Sergeant Hernandez did not think deep thoughts and rarely pursued the reasons behind actions. He knew what he liked and he knew how to get things done. That combination had taken him to the top of his career path. He was content, or at least he would be if the food ever got to his table, he thought. Consuelo was working this evening assisting the local medical doctor, so tonight he would enjoy the company and the food provided by his chosen profession.

"Ramirez, is this a forced diet you have planned for me or is the food going to arrive sometime yet this evening?" Hernandez bellowed to the waiter who was one of the conscripts unfortunate to get this evening duty for the month.

In the center of town, Captain Diego Peña was trying to concentrate on the conversation. Mrs. Louie Farnsworth was speaking in English so that her husband Harold could participate. Peña wasn't sure if his English was so out of practice, or if it was his irritation with Harold Farnsworth that was causing his thoughts to wander. The Farnsworths had chosen the best restaurant in town either by luck, or research, or a quiet call to the hotel front desk from Celia, he wasn't sure. For a relatively small city, Mariposa was replete with many good and several excellent restaurants. The industry and natural resources of this valley had brought businessmen (and the resultant political entourages, Peña thought) to this valley over the past fifty years, spawning a humble theater, a small opera house that was presently closed, restaurants, and a Gentleman's Club of sorts. The Army detachment was small enough that there were not sufficient officers to warrant an officers club at the stockade. Instead the Army paid the membership fees to the Gentlemen's Club, which had an excellent sports facility, a bar, a members-only dining facility, and a library that rivaled the best in the capital. Peña usually dined at the Club, but tonight he was enjoying the better food at the Brooklyn Bridge Restaurant. The locals had a hard time pronouncing the foreign name, so they just called it "El Puente" because of the bridge painting on the front of the building.

"So why is this restaurant called the Brooklyn Bridge?" Harold Farnsworth had just asked.

"About one hundred years ago," Peña explained, "just after the turn of the century, a U.S. businessman from New York arrived here looking for raw material opportunities to exploit. He had heard that a deposit of Jade had been discovered that looked to rival the mines of Guatemala. He was frustrated with the lack of culture," Peña said with derision in his voice, "in the village of Mariposa, so he decided to build a restaurant that would rival the best in this part of the world. As the story goes, before arriving in our country, this man had spent time in the Amazon region. There is a bar in Iquitos, Peru where the Amazon officially begins, which is built from the extra pieces of Paris' Eiffel Tower. The idea intrigued him. As with many from the North, I think he felt obliged to bring a piece of the developed world into the wilderness of the developing world," Peña editorialized with more negative feeling than he really felt. "Since this man was from New York City, he contacted associates there and arranged to ship the misfit pieces from the Brooklyn Bridge that had been built some twenty years before that. The beams you see in the ceiling are from that bridge. So is the steel cable that surrounds the bar. The jade mine failed, so all his energy went into this restaurant. He married and raised his family here. He passed away about 40 years ago the locals tell me. The restaurant has maintained its quality and traditions, mainly for the tourist trade now. By the way, the Coney Island hot dog does not exist. It's just a tradition to leave it on the menu. The Chef isn't even sure what it is."

"Hmmm, paradox of the periphery. I was in the Philippines some years ago," Harold Farnsworth interjected. "There was a restaurant near Angeles City north of Manila called the New Birth Soul Food Kitchen that seemed very out of place, but the food was excellent. I wonder how many restaurants have been started by Americans…, sorry Captain, North Americans, or any expatriates who missed home, that there are in the world?"

"At least this restaurant isn't the result of our most prolific export, fast food burger joints," Louie Farnsworth added.

"There are some parts of your, how do you say…, pop culture that I do not care for, but I must admit I became addicted to pizza during my only visit to the States," Captain Peña claimed. "You mentioned a paradox. I know that word, but I don't understand your statement."

"Oh, I read a book recently about a young man and his grandfather," Harold began. "The author discusses a phenomenon that he named the paradox of the periphery. It goes something like, there seems to be a need by some who move from the geographic center of a culture, for example, to hold even tighter to that culture than those still at the center. Those at the center are more at liberty to continue to evolve as they define the culture. Those on the periphery either tend to merge with other cultures, or react to this dilution and feel an obligation to hold even faster to the cultural as it was when they left it. After a time, the center can't even recognize these peripheral pockets of orthodoxy, perhaps because these pockets often choose just a vein of the center to hold on to and not the whole. It appears this Brooklyn Bridge Restaurant may have been created for similar reasons."

"I think we over analyze sometimes. It takes away the freshness and creativity of the actual action," Louie added, to lighten the conversation.

Captain Peña appreciated Louie's insertion, but not for her intended purpose. He found himself understanding and even agreeing with Harold's comment and how it might apply to the Army, but he did not want to agree or find anything in common with him. Almost in surprise he heard himself saying, "No, I agree with your husband *Señora*. It is important to understand why we make certain decisions or we may find ourselves the slaves of unconsidered habit. Is that a proper way to say that? If we don't understand ourselves and our actions, we are not much above the animal in the forest."

The dinner conversation was going much better than Captain Peña had expected. Ironically, he wasn't even sure of the real reasons why he had agreed to dine with them. He liked the opportunity to stretch his understanding of *Norteños*, but he chafed at their lack of understanding of his culture and his country. He wondered how many actually arrived in his country and still would not be able to mark it on a map of the world. He could name the last five presidents of the United States, but was certain most if not all the *Norteño* tourists could not pick out the present leader of his country on a multiple choice question. It wasn't that knowing a name is all that important, but most *Norteños* and Europeans he had met assumed they had all the answers and with that so-called greater understanding, came the requirement to share it with whoever would listen. And they have no idea....

"Captain, Captain, where did you go?" Louie was asking him.

"I'm sorry, *Señora*. It has been a very busy day and I am afraid I have not fully cleared my mind of those duties. I truly apologize," Captain Peña said, somewhat flustered.

"That is how Louie got me to come on this trip. The lure of clearing my mind," Harold explained.

Captain Peña glanced at Louie and back to her husband. "Clearing one's mind is an interesting reason to put at the top of the list for a honeymoon," Peña noted with amusement, but was immediately sorry he had said what he was thinking.

Harold nearly choked on his *agua con gas*. Louie laughed with a little embarrassment and said, "Now you had better explain yourself, sweetheart, or risk our subscription to the Victoria Secrets catalogue."

"Louie, we don't have a subscription to…" Harold paused. "And anyway, why we are here is certainly of no interest to the Captain, but you are right, I did bring up the subject." Turning to Captain Peña, Harold explained, "This is really our second honeymoon, Captain. Our actual honeymoon was a disaster and…"

"You're digging a deeper hole sweetheart," Louie warned her husband with a big smile on her face. It was evident she was enjoying this.

"OK, let me start over," Harold offered. "We were married five months ago. Our honeymoon was a gift from Louie's parents. To San Diego, California. No sooner did we arrive at our hotel, than I received several phone calls from my business partner. I spent the first day of our honeymoon in the hotel's business suite trying to keep our investors from bailing out on us, while Louie worked on her tan. Let me just say, things went down hill from there. I don't want to bore you with all the details, but my company was undergoing a very important transition, something we didn't foresee when Louie and I set our wedding date. Anyway, one of the reasons I chose this valley for our second honeymoon was because it is off the beaten path. And it seemed, at least from the brochures, like the perfect place to adjust my priorities to where they should be. To make some life changes and clear my mind as I said, and most important to dedicate that newly cleared mind one hundred percent to Louie."

"Excellent recovery, sweetheart," Louie said. "Besides the coincidental name of the hotel which still brings a smile to my face. Maybe we should share the main reason we chose Mariposa over the other places we considered. The good Captain might be able to help."

Chapter 4
Heat and Hiding

"Did you know the Monarch Butterfly travels over two thousand miles every season between Canada and Mexico?" Harold asked without waiting for an answer. "These small insects can correctly navigate and find the same spot every year. I was in the Oyamel Forest in Michoacán, Mexico researching these phenomena…, well that's where I met Louie. She was there visiting some ruins farther south and heard about the annual event and came to see them before traveling home. The name of your beautiful valley is another reason we decided to 'retry our honeymoon here.'"

Captain Peña was amazed. This *Norteño* had just talked for a full minute without seeming to take a breath. "I don't see the connection," Captain Peña admitted out loud. "I understand that mariposa in English is butterfly, but we don't have Monarch butterflies here, at least I don't think so." Peña was suddenly unsure of himself and feeling frustrated that this *Norteño* knew something about his valley that he didn't.

"The Monarch butterfly navigates by the sun, but it is more complex than that, of course," Harold confirmed. "The path of the sun effects chemical levels in the butterfly. They can correctly orient themselves after seconds of a storm abating, or the darkness of early morning…"

"Now that is something I can relate to," Captain Peña said to himself, not realizing he had said it out loud.

"What's that?" Louie asked.

"What?" Captain Peña and Harold asked in unison.

Harold had been so engrossed in his own story that he hadn't quite heard Captain Peña's statement.

"You just said that is something you and butterflies can relate to," Louie answered.

"Oh, are you a butterfly fan, Captain?" asked Harold with some increased interest.

"What? No. I was thinking about being able to navigate by heading toward the heat. Not a bad attribute for anyone in the Army, no?" the Captain suggested with open honesty. "But I still don't understand what all this has to do with our little valley here, far from Mexico."

"The Madrugada Butterfly, of course!" answered Harold with full enthusiasm now. "What is the translation of Madrugada again Louie?"

"Early morning, or dawn," Louie answered.

"Yes, that's right. The Dawn Butterfly. I like the Spanish version better. Sounds more exotic," Harold said.

"I see," the Captain said and nodded with some understanding. "So you are a, what is the word? He who studies insects?"

"An entomologist?" Harold suggested. "No, no, not at all Captain, but I am honored you would think that. No, at best I am an amateur in the insect world, but I am entomophagous in a manner of speaking," Harold added with a chuckle at the joke that only he understood.

"What I think Harold is joking about," Louie interrupted, "is he has found ingenious ways to harness the power of insects. Well only butterflies to date. For commercial purposes. Very lucrative purposes actually. Captain, you are looking at a person who holds eleven, last time I counted, international patents on the replication of butterfly based navigation systems."

"I see," the Captain said for the second time in less than a minute, but completely baffled and not sure at all who these two people were. He was simultaneously intrigued and lost which amounted to extreme frustration in Captain Peña's military trained mind.

"Well, if you do, you are much smarter than I was when Harold first tried to explain all this to me in Mexico amongst the Monarchs. Harold has an understanding of two worlds: that of butterflies and that of modern technology and its capabilities to copy what Mother Nature has gifted our winged friends with. And so far the butterflies have not bothered to sue for patent infringements."

"I am afraid Louie makes this all sound very complicated," Harold said with embarrassed humility that struck the Captain as genuine, the first quality in this *Norteño* that he found likeable. But that might also be a possible sign of weakness. "Da Vinci watched birds and put a workable airplane on paper. He was just too far ahead of technology at the time. I simply have the technology, so the challenge is really quite simple. I started a company whose basis for innovation is Mother Nature. So far, we are doing some exciting things, but I don't want to bore you with those details."

"Oh, right Harold. You love to tell the details to anyone you meet," Louie chided good-naturedly. "But thank you for sparing the Captain. We should at least get to the issue of why we are here. Remember? The Madrugada Butterfly?" Louie added.

"Right," Harold agreed. "I'm sorry Captain. As you get to know me, you will discover that I am a bit of a scatterbrain.

Please forgive me. The Madrugada Butterfly is perhaps one of the most amazing creatures God has put on this earth. I am here foremost for a second chance at a honeymoon with my bride, but also I admit, to learn more about your butterfly. I have a dear friend who once lived in this valley for several months as a young man and who recently told me about the amazing properties of the Madrugada. According to him, the Madrugada Butterfly under the right conditions has the capability to disappear."

"I see," the Captain said. Then he suddenly realized how funny this was in English and started laughing. The joke was partly from the unintended and not really funny play on words, but more so because this *gringo* was not really scatterbrained. He didn't seem to have a brain at all. "Mr. Farnsworth," the Captain said after he had stopped laughing. "I have lived in this valley for some time and in this country my entire life, except for several military courses I have attended in Great Britain. Not only have I not seen this phenomenon, but I have never heard a single local person talk of this. I believe your friend was not telling the truth, or he had too much to drink and dreamed the whole thing up."

"Captain, I assure you he was not lying, nor was he drunk," Harold responded with annoyance. "He was a Mormon missionary here about 17 years ago. He said he saw it happen early one morning near the river. I have spent the last three months studying the possibilities of such a phenomenon and there is a slight chance of this type of polymorphism in this genus."

"I did not wish to offend you Mr. Farnsworth. It just seems quite impossible. And I am afraid I do not understand your explanation of the genius of polyism. We are fighting the dark side of polyism. Anarchistic guerillas. I don't see any genius in their form of terrorism!"

"Now it's me who doesn't know what we are talking about," Harold admitted, taken aback by the sudden burst of passionate anger from the Captain and this talk of anarchism and terrorism.

"Captain Peña, I think we have a major communications breakdown here," Louie offered. "As usual, it is left up to the gentler sex to sort things out. I think Harold is talking about the capability of a specific genus or category of butterflies to morph, or change their attributes. Harold, your use of complex and scientific language is not only baffling the Captain, but it has me lost as well. I studied political science in college, remember?"

Captain Peña was not sure he liked being defended by this or any woman and even more that she had said he was baffled, even if he was.

Louie continued. "Captain, I can assure you of one thing; Neither Harold nor I have an opinion on the internal politics of your country or the insurgency your government is facing. That does bring up a good point though. Is there any danger of our wandering outside of the city?"

"There has been some detected movement of the enemy, but we have not had an encounter in many months. I see no great danger. And I apologize for my misunderstanding your explanation Mr. Farnsworth."

"Again, I am the one that needs to apologize," Harold said and shook his head. "Please, let me try one more time." Harold took a drink of his *agua con gas*, took a thoughtful breath and began again. "I really didn't mean to say that it is possible for something to actually disappear, but only that it might be possible for one of your local butterflies to camouflage itself in some unique way so that it is nearly impossible to see. This does sound like a pretty crazy idea, but then again, Louie and I are here for a vacation. The disappearing butterfly act is only a side show. If it doesn't exist, as you suggest, that is fine with me."

"I have also learned a lot from the butterfly," Louie added. "Butterflies are delicate creatures, with lots of enemies, not unlike people. Like the butterfly with its exoskeleton, people can appear very tough, but have weaknesses that make us all fragile in some way or another."

"I have often thought that my little country had much to offer the world in its natural diversity. I never would have thought an interest would come by way of a common butterfly that can disappear. Maybe I don't have as much in common with the butterfly as I indirectly suggested earlier. Only the terrorist hides in my world." As the Captain shared these last thoughts he had glanced at Harold to connect their earlier exchange about going toward the heat of battle. He had a thought. "*Señora* Farnsworth, on second thought it may be wise to have an escort if you and your husband were to travel outside the city searching for your disappearing butterfly. I can have Sergeant Hernandez and a few of our men accompany you, not that there is any danger. If there was I wouldn't allow you to travel. But it would be good to get the men out of the stockade and for the locals to see them in a more…" He paused to think of the most appropriate words. "…friendly way than on a regular patrol."

"That is very kind Captain," Harold responded. "We have been too much of a bother already. If it isn't dangerous, then we would be happy to chase the Madrugada on our own."

Captain Peña smiled. "This is your honeymoon and you should chase the Madrugada, definitely on your own," he said. "But it is no problem to have some of my men accompany you to the river, if for no other reason than to have a guide of the local area with you."

"I am sure there was something there that I missed," Harold said. "Camouflaged butterflies and camouflaged conversations..."

"I will explain it to you later in detail, Harold," Louie interrupted. She smiled coyly and blushed. "Now let's try the flan," she added, quickly changing the subject. "Is it good here Captain?"

Chapter 5
Chasing Windmills

"Sergeant Hernandez, after you dismiss the men, please report to my office. I have a small task for you today," Captain Peña commanded quietly at the completion of the routine morning formation.

"Yes, my Captain." As Hernandez turned to the men he tried to manufacture a scowl of displeasure at the sight of the soldiers and growled, "Company! Attention! Dismissed!" Sergeant Hernandez had tried to sound gruff, but he loved his men and his men knew this and once they got to know him, never felt anything but loyalty toward him.

The Captain was another story. They didn't fear him in the same way they did Captain Zarro before him, but he was an officer and that was enough. They would do their duty and follow his commands, but few of them harbored any thought that he saw them as anything but the tools of his trade. Most of them would complete their mandatory enlistment, leave the Army and go back to their own lives and their own dreams. Perhaps a few of their rank would choose the path of Sergeant Hernandez, but probably not for the patriotic reasons the Sergeant had made the Army his life. Today's conscripts were less interested in service to their country and more interested in making money and getting a job that would take them to the capital, or perhaps out of the country altogether. No, most of those that might make the Army a career would do so because they had no immediate prospects elsewhere.

Sergeant Hernandez made his way to the headquarters building, smiled at Celia, entered the Commandant's office with a brief knock of the open door and saluted the Captain who was seated at his desk. "Reporting as ordered, my Captain."

"As you were, Sergeant," Captain Peña said, suddenly frustrated that he was sending Hernandez out on this detail while he was trapped at his desk with the preparations for the meetings with the bureaucrats later in the morning. His thoughts began to ramble. *Señora* Farnsworth was right. They had come... How had she said that? Loaded with bear? Such is the duty of command. He stood and walked around the desk to a map on the south wall of his office.

"Sergeant, I would like you to take a few soldiers and accompany a couple of *Norte Americanos* to this area of the river." Peña pointed to where the two branches of the Rio Cambalache converged at the North end of the Mariposa Valley. For a moment he looked at a thumbtack on the map, on the East branch, nicknamed the Elazar Branch by the locals, where the dam was being built. He thought of all the questions he had to answer yet this morning. More frustrated than he meant to sound, he said, "You will find this couple pleasant enough. They are looking for the Madrugada Butterfly habitat, if there is such a thing. The roads are not clearly marked in that area and they need a guide. It would be good for the people in that area to see you and some of the soldiers in a peaceful activity there. The last time a patrol went through that area there were signs of the MNS rebels. Keep your eyes open for any further movement by the so called Comandante Helicon," Captain Peña said with disdain, although he wasn't sure if the disdain was more for the paperwork on his desk or for the rebel leader. Both represented different enemies and both reminded him of the duty he felt to simply serve his country when so many were simply out to ruin it either from callous commerce or thoughtless terrorism.

"Thank you also for meeting earlier this morning. The report from the driver you selected to accompany our out-of-town friends was particularly interesting. Enjoy your day in the campo," Peña added, partly to take away the bite he felt his earlier words carried and partly because the driver really did bring back some interesting information.

"It will be a pleasure to accompany the *Norteños* to that area. I know it well. I must admit I feel guilty in that pleasure, as I will be leaving you and Celia to deal with the visitors from the capital alone."

Peña chuckled at the implied compliment and the unspoken barb. That Hernandez grouped Celia as Peña's key support and purposely didn't mention Lt. Mendoza was not a surprise. It would be very unprofessional for a non-commissioned officer to speak directly to an officer of his negative feelings about another officer, even a lieutenant of whom the non-coms' typical quip is: 'Lieutenants, you never know whether to burp them or salute them.' On the other hand, most wise lieutenants in their first postings usually found a senior non-commissioned officer to mentor them in the things the Academy didn't teach them. Lieutenant Mendoza had rebuffed the Sergeant's helpful advice early on in his assignment as the deputy commander of the stockade, a relatively new position that was created to give the stockade commander more time to handle his other principle responsibility as administrator of the political sector each stockade oversaw. Mendoza was proving to be a capable officer, but not very teachable and much more interested in the political power of the sector commander that Peña held, than his own duties within the stockade.

"I will pass on your suggested promotion of Celia to the proper authorities and struggle to endure with our lieutenant," Peña replied.

"Sir I didn't mean anything of the kind by my statement. I was only thinking of your sector duties and Celia's understanding that comes from many years of service to the commanders of the chair you presently occupy. I hadn't thought of Lieutenant Mendoza," Hernandez replied with no apology in his voice.

"Yes, I see. Of course," Peña said as their eyes communicated volumes of interchange. 'How difficult it would be to explain this conversation and what really just happened to a person unfamiliar with military professionals,' Peña thought. Proper command lines, authority, and decorum were maintained. They were required for the efficient execution of orders in the heat of battle or to accomplish unsavory duties, yet open exchange of wisdom between a commander and his most important link with those he commands was accomplished nearly effortlessly. "We are lucky, you and I, Sergeant. We have found our place in the world and revel in it. Dismissed."

"By your leave, my Captain," Hernandez answered with what might have been a slight misting in his eyes, something both also acknowledged but would never speak of. They both turned to their duties with zeal, brothers in arms with a high responsibility that came with holding a virtual monopoly on the coercive power in their delicate society.

Their mountain camp air felt brisk and the smell of breakfast had drifted into Antonio Martín's tent. Antonio Martín—better known to his rebel troops as Comandante Helicon—felt invigorated and ready for the day. He had grown to enjoy the coolness of the mountains and the lack of the stilted humid air of the valley below and of the futile busyness of the capital where he had grown up and more recently attended college and worked. He had heard rumors through his lieutenants that some of the men were getting restless and felt that maybe their leader was getting too comfortable in the mountains. Antonio stepped out of his tent and called to a young man standing by the fire to bring him some salted fish. He would not eat the fresh breakfast prepared for the rebel troops he commanded. He wanted them to know he could sacrifice too. Comandante Helicon was a young man at thirty. He looked older because of the scruffy beard he kept short and ill trimmed, and his thin build and face always appeared deep in thought—almost disconnected from the distractions of daily life. He was born old he told himself often to bolster his confidence in leading the *Movimiento Nacional de Hegemony Socialista*, known by the locals simply as the MNS. It chafed Antonio that the H for hegemony was conveniently left out of their name. Antonio often lamented that such a key descriptive of who they are and what it stood for was not publicized. Yet he also knew these were simple people and the concept of hegemony and its lack of presence in their vocabulary relegated it to a conversation topic by armchair intelligentsia in the capital. Someday it would be applied by the visionary leaders of the revolution and understood by all.

Just three and a half years earlier his young wife, Carmen, and he had marveled at the bright career ahead of him as a university professor and entomologist. Then only three years ago, a freak accident had killed his wife who was pregnant with their first child.

Pushing those bitter thoughts aside, Antonio called to his most trusted lieutenant and de facto second in command, "Cesar, it is time. Bring the maps to the table when you finish breakfast. We have an attack to plan." As he walked away, he could feel the electricity pass through the group of men who were standing close by Cesar. He knew that within minutes the whole camp would know they would soon go into harm's way in another step toward a final victory to create a new country and new hope for those left on the side of the road of the so called progress the Military Junta of his country was constructing. The metaphor brought him back to his morose memories surrounding the death of his wife. "To avenge your death and to make meaning of your sacrifice I will not give up the fight," he told the mental image of his wife.

Professor Antonio Martín had dropped out of his position at the university during his legal battle with the military government. Toward the end of his losing litigation with the tribunal reviewing his petition, one of his ex-students approached him with a pamphlet that had changed his life. He had been aware of several fringe elements at the university that had bristled at the military coup nearly two years earlier. Now those fringe elements and many others had experienced nearly five years of brutal repression, especially in the capital. The pamphlet was from a group calling themselves the *Movimiento Nacional de Hegemony Socialista*. The pamphlet had excerpts from Antonio Gramsci's Prison

Notebooks. Antonio had only opened the pamphlet because he shared the same first name with this hitherto unknown author. What he read filled his heart with something other than grief. Perhaps he was developing an emotional tool to fight against the Army that not only killed his wife, but did so without remorse or responsibility.

"...*Dominant groups in society, including fundamentally but not exclusively the ruling class, maintain their dominance by securing the 'spontaneous consent' of subordinate groups, including the working class, through the negotiated construction of a political and ideological consensus which incorporates both dominant and dominated groups...*" Antonio recited from memory the words in that first pamphlet. He had joined the small group of students and soon became their natural leader because of his relative age and his position as a professor. Where most of the students simply pushed for anarchy, Antonio guided and channeled their rage and energy into a lethal and powerful weapon against the military junta he hated. The MNS attacked a few logistics depots early on, partly to gain notoriety and partly to put the military government and the civil populace on notice that they existed. These small acts of violence garnered new members—many older than himself, and soon they were large enough to become a real threat to the military. It was not safe for most of the MNS to stay in the city, so they moved to the mountains to establish their operational headquarters. They were initially very successful, but were brutally put down in almost every open confrontation with the military. They had retreated to their present location to lick their wounds and to redirect their efforts. Today would be a start in that new direction for guerilla tactics against the country's infrastructure.

Louie noted that it looked like another lazy day for the bureaucrats from the capital as she finished her breakfast in the hotel cafe. They were quietly devouring enough eggs to make chicken magnate Frank Perdue smile from his grave. She had gone jogging this morning while Harold slept in. They had been up late, but were both asleep by the *Madrugada*. Louie chuckled at Captain Peña's comment the night before. She loved to watch Harold while he slept, but she had felt restless and decided to see the city as it was awakening. Mariposa really was a beautiful place. She could see why Captain Peña took such pride in it. Then she reconsidered. Perhaps it was pride in ownership like a farmer and his land, or a trainer of a young race horse.

"Do you think those gentlemen ever worked a full day in their lives?" she asked Harold to break him away from the notes he was reviewing while munching on his eggs and some sort of fried meat.

"I have never had much use for bureaucrats Louie. I suppose they are necessary and I know my feelings are unfair to many who keep the wheels of civilization turning, but some seem like leeches and where one will suffice you often find five." Harold gulped down his fresh squeezed orange juice and added, "And these specimens of the homo lethargis group seem especially prone to those attributes."

"I can't wait to get out into the countryside this morning!" Louie exclaimed. "I am so glad you chose this little valley for our vacation. I hope you find your butterfly, but if you don't, that may prove your theory. If you can't find one that is invisible, couldn't that mean it really has disappeared?" Louie teased.

"I am all for disappearing back into our hotel room. After all, this is the Hotel *Otra Vez*, which means again, right" Harold added in his own teasing voice. "I can look for the butterfly later."

"Yet another use of the hotel name," Louie added conspiratorially. "Maybe when we get back from our trip this afternoon we can find someone that knows why it is named that. Don't let me forget."

"So you are asking the absent minded professor to remind you of something?"

"Well, first, you aren't a professor anymore, and second, since we've been married, I have noted there are some things you are very good at remembering. I doubt you will forget. Now, on to our butterfly safari! Where did the Captain say his sergeant was going to meet us?"

"Celia," Peña called to the outer office where his secretary's desk was located. She had placed her desk nearly in front of his door several commanders ago, so anyone entering had to physically pass by her. Peña was not the first to consider asking her to move it to a more convenient location, and also not the last to reconsider once he got to know this wise matriarch of a long line of successful stockade commanders. "Do you have the report completed for the meeting with our visitors? I would like to read through it one more time before their visit."

"Yes sir. It is on the left corner of your desk in the gray folder," she called from the outer office. He could almost see her grin from the other room.

"Thank you," Peña called back with joking annoyance.

The quick handwritten reports Peña had asked for yesterday were sitting on his desk in his quarters when he returned from dinner. The visit to the Dam and the power plant appeared routine. They spoke with no one in private. They took pictures of the infrastructure, but made no negative comments. All three Mandarins (as he had begun thinking of them) seemed pleased with the progress and the personnel. On the drive back to Mariposa, however, the conversation became telling. 'Thank goodness for Hernandez' suggestion to supply just the right driver,' he thought.

The driver had reported: "They seemed to be in a very good mood, joking about something to do with a shipment that was cancelled by the short-sighted Army. One of them, I do not know which, said something like, 'If they would just leave this work to the professionals, this power plant would already be in operation! Now they will see how difficult this work really is and how important we are to the country.' Another one of them added, 'Just because they have guns, they think they have the right and the know-how to run everything else.'

"The third passenger was very quiet most of the day and I rarely heard his voice. In reaction to the last comment, however, he spoke up and said with much energy, "Victor, that is enough! Do you want to get us all tossed in jail, or killed? We are here to ensure we keep our jobs and are able to continue serving the government, whoever is in power. We are not a second revolutionary front, so keep your emotions and your stupid comments to yourself." They all became more subdued after that. As they were leaving the vehicle at the hotel, I noted they had left the camera they had taken with them lying on the floor of the backseat. I could see it because I had been holding the door open for them. I grabbed the camera and called to them. One of them, the one with a mustache, became very flustered and ran back to grab the camera from my hands as if I had planned to steal it. He then began complaining to the other two gentlemen that they were not taking this assignment with the seriousness it deserves. He was saying something about, 'this is a lot bigger than just the three of us and some Captain in a forgotten corner of the county' when they walked into the hotel lobby. That is all I can remember."

The morning meeting produced little new information, but it had given Peña the chance to sort things out, and his team was aware of the problem on their hands. Peña had asked Celia to attend the meeting to take notes, both of what was said and more importantly what was not said.

"Celia," Peña called out after reviewing the notes, "did you ever hear back from headquarters on who ordered this trip and when the orders were actually prepared?"

"Nothing yet sir," she said. "I don't want to push too hard. I'm trying to keep it routine as you suggested."

"This entire visit is anything but routine, I am afraid," Peña said, mostly to himself.

Chapter 6
Heliconius Madrugada

Sᴇʀɢᴇᴀɴᴛ EɴʀɪQᴜᴇ Hᴇʀɴᴀɴᴅᴇᴢ ɢʀᴀsᴘᴇᴅ Lᴏᴜɪᴇ's ʜᴀɴᴅ and helped her out of the Viet Nam era military jeep.

"Thank you Sergeant Hernandez," Louie said.

"Please *Señora*, call me Enrique. It will make the soldiers jealous, and soon my wife will hear the story of my duties escorting the beautiful North American and I will be treated with more care and respect," he said jokingly. He was old enough to be her father and he had treated her like his daughter since they met at the hotel. He had been very relieved she spoke Spanish and delighted when she proved to be an interesting traveling companion. She was not demanding, expectant, or ignorant of his country or the culture. Her husband was quiet, but also seemed easy-going, although he hadn't said much since the conversations had mostly been in Spanish.

"OK, Enrique. Please call me Louie. I don't know about making your soldiers jealous, but when your wife hears about you spending the day with a difficult *Norteña*, she may take pity on you, or she may clobber you with a frying pan."

"Either way, if the soldiers are jealous, it will be worth it. Here is the spot the Captain suggested you start your search," he said and pointed to a jungle marsh near the river. "I am not an insect expert, although I have swatted and killed my share in this valley. I have noticed mariposas at the edge of the swamp near the road many times. You are looking for the black and yellow striped ones that this valley is named for?"

"I think so. I really never thought to ask my husband what this butterfly looked like," she admitted. Switching to English, she asked Harold, "Enrique, the Sergeant, wanted to know if we were looking for the black and yellow striped butterfly. I told him I never thought to ask you."

"So it is Enrique now?" he teased. "Yes, Heliconius Madrugada. Its cousin looks very similar. Heliconius Charitonius, the state butterfly of Florida is quite common in many parts of the southern United States, Mexico, Central America, and the West Indies. The specie we are looking for is only found in this valley as far as I know. It is not very colorful. Here is a picture." He handed her a blank piece of paper and watched for her reaction.

"There's nothing... OK very funny," She said. She then wadded up the paper and threw it at him. "Lead on Harold, let's find your invisible butterfly."

"If you see one," Harold began explaining, "don't chase it. They seem to fly very slow and graceful, but if disturbed they can fly very fast. If you are patient they almost come to you. They tend to stay near the edge of trails, roads, and rivers according to my research about their cousin butterfly. They tend to avoid places where they have been disturbed, so we probably won't find many near that village we passed about a half mile back. They tend to roost at night in large groups of up to seventy butterflies. I suppose that is some kind of protective instinct like their rumored disappearing act. I think it is probably too late in the day to find their roosts. The Heliconius is the only genus of butterfly known to eat pollen, so we should probably be looking for flowering plants. Does the Sergeant know what a Passion Vine looks like? That is supposed to be their favorite plant."

"Enrique, Harold says these butterflies like to eat the pollen from the Passion Vine. Do you know what that looks like? I am not sure what the local word would be for that plant."

"I am sorry Louie. I have only seen them as I have driven by this area on patrol. The only reason I look at the vegetation is to make sure there are no guerilla fighters in them. Wait, there, is that one?" he asked excitedly.

"A guerilla or a butterfly?" Louie asked jokingly.

"There, in that group of plants nearest to the road. It looks like there may be more than one. They blend into the shade. And, don't tell the Captain, but my eyes aren't what they used to be."

"I think I see some butterflies!" Harold shouted off to Louie's and Enrique's left. "There must be twenty or thirty of them!"

"We see a couple over here also. Maybe two or three," Louie replied.

"That's great," Harold exclaimed. "Now as you approach them, don't frighten them. Let them come to you."

Louie quietly walked forward. Harold walked toward the bush he was focused on. Enrique stayed back by the road partly to watch this scene, partly to watch for MNS rebels that he didn't believe were anywhere near, but mostly because it didn't seem like a macho thing for the First Sergeant of soldiers to be doing. The three soldiers that he brought with him stayed back at the jeeps wondering what was going on.

"Oh nuts," Harold whispered. "I forgot the little boxes I brought along back in the jeep. I don't want to touch them if we can avoid it. Could you ask one of the soldiers to bring them down to us?"

"Harold, I don't think we have to whisper. Do they react to sound?" Louie asked.

"No we don't have to whisper, it just helps me be calmer in my movements," Harold answered. "Let's get those boxes."

"Enrique, could you have one of your men bring down those little white boxes we left in the jeep. We want to capture a couple of those butterflies to look at closer," Louie explained.

"Of course," Enrique said. "Carlitos! You will find two small white boxes about the size of your hand in the back of my jeep. Bring them here to the *Norteño*."

The soldier sprang to action and was soon on his way down the shallow embankment. "*Aqui estan, señor*," he said to Harold and handed the boxes to him.

"Gracias," Harold said in his best Spanish. He held open one of the boxes and with a steady hand moved the box lid over to the butterfly on the closest plant. It flew a small distance away, but then came back and landed on the box lid. Harold slowly closed the box, hoping the butterfly would stay on it. It did and soon they had one captured Heliconius Madrugada or Charitonius, he wasn't sure. He did the same thing with the other box. "Easy as..." He paused and snapped the second box closed. "That!" he exclaimed.

"The Dam construction was completed nearly two months ago," Antonio Martín, known as Comandante Helicon to the guerrilla fighters and their enemies, explained to his lieutenants. "We have stayed quiet and out of sight most of that time. I wanted enough movement to let them know we weren't too quiet and raise suspicions that we were up to something big, but I wanted to be quiet enough that they might convince themselves that we had been severely wounded in our last confrontation."

The MNS soldiers nodded in understanding and began to think of what Comandante Helicon was saying. Were they going to blow up the Dam?

Antonio looked at these trusted soldiers of the revolution. He wondered again if they were willing to do what he now was going to ask of them. "The new government of the revolution will need the infrastructure of the power and communications lines that now supports the repressive military junta." He noted an almost imperceptible relaxing in the faces of his men. He wondered if it was the lines by their eyes that gave away their thoughts? How odd to think about issues of body language at the very moment the revolution fully became a war, and not just the irritation of a buzzing fly in the room.

"This construction will continue to be of only marginal propaganda use until the Elazar Dam and power plant are completed," their comandante continued with additional force in his voice. "Then the electrical generation will bring new power to a decadent regime and prolong our country's agony. It is our task… No! It is our duty to blow up that Dam and bring them to their knees."

Antonio believed he could read the eyes much too easily. He resolved to work on that so that they could not read him so easily. "I have asked Cesar to brief you on the plan of attack. Cesar, please." Antonio motioned for Cesar to spread the maps out on the makeshift table and stepped back to watch his men from a less central position. "Do not spare any details Cesar. We must do this right, as we will not get a second chance."

"As our Comandante has explained our target is the destruction of the Elazar Dam. We have several secondary targets as well, to cause as much confusion as..."

Antonio watched closely and thought to himself, 'Yes, they will do it. They have their doubts, but they will do it for the revolution and for me.' He knew they would do it for Comandante Helicon, but questioned if they would do it for Antonio Martín. Antonio had chosen this *nom de guerre* on a whim to separate his past from his future. He believed the Army probably knew who he actually was, but for some reason they played along. Perhaps it was the media that liked the sensationalism. Perhaps it made the Army feel bigger, measuring themselves against an enemy with a name rather than fighting a young college professor. As an entomologist, he had studied and admired the insects of this quiet valley, which had more diversity than most countries. When it became obvious that his destiny, the destiny of the revolution, and this tranquil valley in a forgotten corner of this country were tied together, he had chosen a variation of a butterfly's name. Afterward, he had enjoyed many an inward laugh at the additional meanings this name stood for in this revolution for control of the entire country.

Thoughts of an entomologist entered his mind involuntarily. Heliconius was the genus of this interesting butterfly. It was the longest living of any of its kind, probably due to its curious pollen eating habits. No matter that the butterfly's or his longevity were important to this revolution. Today the revolution was a caterpillar with long black spines that were lethal to the touch. Tomorrow it would be a butterfly, a symbol of freedom, lightness, and detachment. How this genus of butterflies had come to hold this name he was not sure. Perhaps it was its curled tongue. What he knew for certain was that the root of the name came from the Greek: Mount Helicon in Boeotia, the mythical home of the Muses and the Graces of ancient Greece. That was also the second home of Zeus himself, after Olympus. Mount Helicon was a place of enlightenment and understanding. The metaphor was crystal clear to Antonio. These mountains surrounding the Mariposa Valley had become Mount Helicon. The capital was Olympus. He was the commander of the destiny of his country. He alone could bring enlightenment and understanding to his country. And yet there was still more. He knew that helicon also meant spiral, as in the coiled energy of a watch spring. "I, Antonio Martín, and this revolution, will unleash the potential energy of this country that so long has been suppressed by the ruling class and the military. It is a pity that this must start by ending the very habitat of the Heliconius Madrugada."

Chapter 7
Scientific Studies

"ALEJANDRO, OLD MAN, WHERE ARE YOU?" Emma Costa called out, but she was sure she knew where he was. She would have sent Diana to have him come in for supper, but she also knew Diana was with him. Emma smiled when she recalled how Alejandro dedicated so much time to their only daughter. Their son, Gustavo, had been born with an insatiable desire to prove himself to his father. That may have played a part in his decision to join the MNS guerrilla fighters, and for his probable death. Emma shuddered and quickened her step, shifting her thoughts to Paco. 'My second son is old enough to have a family of his own, but he worries about his parents in our old age and about the turmoil in the country, in our little valley. Paco worries about his ability to support a family.' Paco worried and thus worried his mother almost to tears.

There were days when it seemed Emma must carry this worrisome load about her children alone. Alejandro only wished to see the positive and count blessings. Then there was Diana. Twenty-two years old just three months ago. She should also be married and bring the grandchildren her parents desired almost more than life itself. 'Ah, that hotheaded Geraldo,' Emma thought and reprimanded the ground as she stomped a little harder when she approached Alejandro's makeshift workshop. Diana had been informally engaged several years ago, but her *novio*, Geraldo, had also chosen the path of the guerrilla fighter and also died at the hands of the terrible Captain Zarro. Emma suspected that it was Geraldo who had talked Gustavo into his involvement. Emma begrudgingly remembered that at least Geraldo's parents were able to recover the body for a Church burial.

"There you are my darling," Alejandro said with a smile when he saw Emma enter the small shack. "Diana and I were just talking about you." Before Emma could scold him, he continued. "I was just saying how talented you are at noticing the little things. *Quien no comprende una mirada, tampoco no comprenderá una larga explicacion.* The person who doesn't understand a quick glance, will not understand a long explanation."

Diana was quietly laughing, knowing her father was deflecting a complaint from her mother, yet also knowing the real reason for the complaint was that he spent so much time with Diana and also that he dearly loved his wife. Even for all her gruffness, she deeply loved him.

"So you see my dear," Alejandro was saying, "you are our example of quiet seeing and understanding what you see."

Despite herself, and knowing what he was doing, Emma broke into a smile, happy to push the frustrations about her family back into the dark cellar in her mind where she kept the deepest worries. She let her heart open to the love she had for this wise old man. "I think you two have been out here long enough," Emma scolded. "The beans are ready and if you don't get into the house this instant, they will warm your outside because you will be wearing them, rather than eating them to warm your stomach."

"Mama, honestly it was my fault," Diana explained. "I asked Papa a question and we were just coming to a conclusion when you stepped in."

They left the shack where Alejandro carved wooden figures to sell in the market and at the airport, but where mostly he carved at ideas and Diana collected the shavings.

"And what was this question that kept you from helping your mother with dinner, *Mija*?" Emma asked, not really curious but wanting to be a part of their lives and interests.

"Trees are large and hard to understand in one quick glance," Diana replied. "So, can you know the *Pau d'arco* tree by cutting it up into pieces and studying those pieces?" she asked and looked over at her father.

"That is what you were talking about? Even cooking beans is more important than chewing on that question. *Mija*, you have such big thoughts. We are poor and simple people. It is enough to know that the bark of the *Pau d'arco* when made into a tea can cure some sicknesses. That is knowledge you can use as a mother of children," Emma delicately reprimanded.

"It is my fault Emma. Diana asked why I never carved anything out of *Pau d'arco*. I told her the wood is very hard and more like sculpting stone than carving wood." Alejandro explained.

"So then I asked papa how he knew so much about trees. Was it because he had cut up so many? And he told me it is impossible to understand life by slicing it into pieces. When you cut the tree you kill it. How can you understand the living tree when it is dead?"

"I don't know if I understand," Emma answered, "but I do know that life is a sacred thing and the mind cannot fully understand the sacred. Only the heart can decipher that mystery, *Mija*. The most important decisions in life must be made with the heart, not the mind. My mind sees an old man with foolish thoughts, but my heart sees a father who loves his daughter. I suppose it is my responsibility to fill your stomach with beans and his to fill your mind with ideas."

"And the both of you to fill my heart with love," Diana answered, suddenly remembering the many poems that her mother had memorized to express deep thoughts while her father used the simple tools of his trade and nature as his metaphors. Neither of her parents were simple people, yet they simply lived for their family and even daily survival brought them meaning beyond physical sustenance.

"Harold, these butterflies look so delicate," Louie said. "Are you sure we can do this without injuring them?"

"Pin that one out rigid on the Styrofoam mat so it can't move," Harold requested with excitement. "I want to take a closer look at the wings with this magnifying glass."

"Oh, I am so sorry!" Louie exclaimed when the wing broke off from their first specimen. "Do butterflies have feelings? Did that hurt?"

"I am certain they don't have the same feelings as we do," Harold speculated. "Here let me put that wing under the pocket microscope I brought. This might work out better anyway."

After a lengthy and very careful study, Harold had to admit this was just a simple butterfly wing with nothing special about it. Disappointed, he asked, "Louie, could you bring me the other box? I am not sure what the other one may show us, but let's take a look anyway. Maybe only males or females can camouflage themselves."

Louie handed him the box and he opened it. To his surprise, it wasn't there. "Louie, did we already open this box?" he asked with amazement.

"No. Are you sure you caught it when you shut the lid? We were all excited. It could have slipped out I suppose, or even on the bumpy ride back to the hotel," Louie said trying to console him.

Antonio Martín could not escape his scientific paradigm of the world, both as an entomologist and in his role as the dedicated revolutionary Comandante Helicon. He saw the destruction of the Elazar Dam as a cause and effect situation. This was not a *War of Manoeuvre*, such as the Bolshevik Revolution of 1917. The MNS had tried the frontal attack and failed. "No," Antonio told himself for the hundredth time, "this is a *War of Position*. The struggle will be long and the suffering great, but our means will justify the ends. Again to bolster himself, he took out a well worn pamphlet and began to read the words of his mentor and self-claimed namesake, Antonio Gramsci:

> *A crisis occurs, sometimes lasting for decades. This exceptional duration means that incurable structural contradictions have revealed themselves and that, despite this, the political forces which are struggling to conserve and defend the existing structure itself are making every effort to cure them, within certain limits, and to overcome them. These incessant and persistent efforts... form the terrain of the 'conjunctional' and it is upon this terrain that the forces of opposition organize.*

Antonio hoped it would not take decades. Fortified in his beliefs once again, he turned to the small group of men who had been hand picked to accomplish one last reconnoiter of the Elazar Dam and the Army security emplacements. "You are to verify our maps one last time and confirm the accessibility to the points on the Dam that I have shown you in the photographs, where we will need to place the explosives. We are at a critical juncture. I must warn you once again that no one is to see you, and no one must know you have been there. That means you must not be discovered and you must not kill any soldiers or do anything to raise the enemy's concerns. They are decadent and have grown lazy, but we cannot take any chances. Do you have any last questions?" their Comandante asked. He had chosen these men for their stealthy skills, but also for their willingness to execute his orders without questions. As expected he met silent stares. "Good then, off you go. Be cautious. I will expect you back by tomorrow afternoon."

After his soldiers of the revolution had disappeared into the jungle below their mountain roost, Antonio pulled out his pamphlet again. He flipped the pages until he found the passage:

So one could say that each one of us changes himself, modifies himself to the extent that he changes the complex relations of which he is the hub. In this sense the real philosopher is, and cannot be other than, the politician, the active man who modifies the environment...

"And modify the environment I will do very soon!" Antonio assured himself loud enough for the camp of soldiers to hear.

Chapter 8
Heliconian Captures

HAROLD HAD BEEN LYING THERE WIDE AWAKE FOR ABOUT thirty minutes. Usually it was Louie who was already up and dressed when he struggled to open his eyes. This morning he instead feasted his eyes upon his beautiful bride. "Louie, are you awake?" He waited for an answer and questioned in his mind how such a scatterbrained geek could interest such an angel? 'What does she see in me?' he wondered. 'Does she realize what an inspiration she is to me?'

Louie's blonde hair almost glistened in the morning sun that made its way through the protective canopy of mahogany and teak trees just outside the open window of their hotel room. Strands nearly covered her face and Harold wondered again how women can stand such an irritation.

Harold thought back to the first time they met in Mexico. He had been struggling to collect the data for another navigation patent based on the Monarch butterfly and had already booked passage home in frustration when he literally bumped into her at a bend in a jungle trail. He had escorted her to see the Monarchs and they had simply talked. He had never been much of a conversationalist, but she was so easy to talk to and so full of surprises. Her conversations seemed like the jungle path they met on; so many turns, pleasant surprises, and beautiful foliage along the way. She had taken immediate interest in his work. Without consciously realizing it, he cornered the ideas he had been chasing for weeks and had gone even farther. Louie had become his muse and then much more: his best friend and the love of his life. They were married after just three months of courtship in Louie's hometown of Tacoma, Washington. Harold had grown up as an only child. Louie had three older brothers and two younger sisters. Harold immediately felt like a part of the family. Louie was born a member of the Church of Jesus Christ of Latter-Day Saints—the Mormons. Harold had discovered the Mormons in his last year in college at Cambridge in England and had joined the Church there. This shared understanding was another early bridge that helped span the gulf of their differences.

Harold grew up in Boston to a stable, but boring (relative to Louie's dynamic family) household. He had no complaints. He loved his parents and they seemed to be content with each other, but not nearly as demonstrative in their affection for each other as Louie's mom and dad. Harold had a hard time being demonstrative about anything and thinking of others. It was not that he was self-centered, but rather that he had yet to fully escaped the rut of habit as an only child. Louie was observant, focused on others and very much the peacemaker and the pacemaker of their relationship. That may be because of being a middle child, Harold had conjectured. Her name was chosen because her parents had expected another boy and had already selected the name Louis. Without missing a beat, her parents named her Louise and the nickname Louie came from her older brothers.

"Hey you handsome hunk of man" Harold heard from a corner of his consciousness, which quickly brought him back from his daydream. "Where are your thoughts?" a sleepy Louie continued.

"Well good morning sleeping beauty," Harold joked, trying to mask his emotions of wonder but almost getting lost in her amber eyes still partly covered by strands of hair. "I've already been up, ran a few miles and..."

"Yeah, whatever," Louie interrupted. "You sir are the epitome of the high tech geek. Your mind does not shut down until two AM at the earliest, and will not fully function again until it thinks there is a reasonable chance of some junk food in the near future. Your idea of exercise is limbering your fingers on a computer keyboard," Louie continued with a light laugh.

Harold bent over and kissed her, wondering for the hundredth time why she never got morning breath like he did. They eventually got up, got dressed and wandered into the hotel café for breakfast. "Well, let me see," Harold said aloud while he scanned over the menu in Spanish that he could not read. "We can have eggs, or we can have..." He paused and slapped the menu down on the table in disgust. "Eggs. I think I will just have some juice this morning."

"*Dos jugos de naranja, por favor,*" Louie said to the waitress near the counter and then shifted her attention back to Harold. "So what is on the agenda today, my great hunter of butterflies?"

"Do you think we could get someone to take us back out to the area where we found those butterflies yesterday? I would like to give it another try. Then maybe we could continue the drive up into the hills for a hike, if you would like."

"I hate to bother Captain Peña and I am not sure we can ask Sergeant Hernandez without checking with the Captain, so let's see if we can find another way out there. Let's see how the butterfly safari *part duex* goes. If we are successful and you discover any secrets, we can celebrate with a hike and a little flirting in the jungle," Louie said with a wink and half smile.

Harold gulped down his orange juice that had just arrived at the table and said, "In that case, no time to lose!"

The small band of Comandante Helicon's revolutionaries had scoped out the Dam and the Army security. They had discovered a gaping hole in the security perimeter and were confident they would bring good news to their leader.

"Hold it!" the point man whispered and raised his right hand to stop the group behind him. They were just about to cross the road when an unexpected line of Army vehicles passed by. Five vehicles and a troop truck heading for the Dam site was not good news. What if they were about to change the security perimeter, or simply add soldiers to the security detail? Cesar knew they had to find out before returning to camp. Their entire night's study of the area was now possibly obsolete. He conferred with his men and they reversed their course. "Hopefully we will be back on the trail within an hour or two," he told the weary men.

"You have been to the power plant construction site many times but this will be your first visit to the Elazar Dam?" Captain Peña asked the bureaucrats after they stepped from the cars that had just arrived at the Dam construction site. He wasn't sure if they had been there before he had replaced Zarro as the sector commander. He still didn't know why they had decided on this surprise visit to the Dam. The power plant was only two-hundred meters from the base of the Dam, yet they had never bothered to even inspect its progress. There hadn't been any insurgent activity for quite some time, but he was a cautious man and didn't like these spontaneous plans with government officials providing tempting targets.

"Sergeant Hernandez, keep the soldiers with the vehicles, but send two with me and our guests," Peña ordered. "We won't be gone long." He started up the incline to where one could view the entire Dam site. He purposely walked rapidly on the dusty trail because a couple of the bureaucrats seemed out of shape and all but one were wearing white suits.

"Yes, I think it is just around this bend," Louie explained to the driver they had found through the front desk attendant at the hotel. "We are here, this is the spot!" she exclaimed in Spanish and to Harold in English. "Stop the car over by those large trees. We shouldn't be too long."

Before long they were out and walking toward the plant growth between the road and the river bank. Only minutes later they had two more butterfly specimens in their boxes and they rechecked through a peep hole Harold had fashioned before they left that morning.

"Well that wasn't too complicated," said Harold with satisfaction. "Still up for the hike Louie?"

"I am getting a little hungry since breakfast was so light. Let's enjoy the picnic lunch we brought and then go on the hike," Louie suggested.

"Good idea. How about we check out the higher terrain farther down the road. It might be a little cooler for a relaxing lunch." Moments later they were in the car and traveling farther up the road, following the river on their left.

"Harold, this is beautiful! How about that spot in the shade?" Louie suggested. They spread their lunch on a blanket borrowed from the hotel and laid back to enjoy the peaceful scenery.

Cesar and his men were relieved to see this was just an inspection tour and the soldiers and their leaders were rejoining and preparing to leave the site. "Now is our time to get in front of them so we can cross the open road and the river before they depart," Cesar told his team. They quietly backed out of their viewpoint and hurriedly walked down the trail.

"This is really good chicken," Harold claimed, "but my fowl products full level light will be on for quite awhile by the time we finish this vacation." As he reached for a drumstick, he heard a noise behind him to his right. He expected it to be a bird, or perhaps a farmer coming down hill. Instead he caught a glimpse of what he thought was a rifle he surmised to be an AK-47. He'd seen plenty just like it on TV. He wasn't sure there was any danger. Captain Peña and Sergeant Hernandez hadn't mentioned anything about problems, or had they? Despite his forced calm, he instinctively tried to duck, even though he and Louie were sitting in the open.

"I'm already getting tired of chicken," Louie was saying. "I..." She paused, puzzled. "Harold what's the matter? Did you swallow wro... Ahhhg!" Louie screamed when she saw four men step out of the brush with weapons pointed at them.

Harold quickly stood up and tried to place himself between Louie and the intruders. From behind him he heard the door to the car that brought them there slam and the engine rev. He turned slightly to his right and could see the car do a quick turn and speed off down the road. As he began to think what that meant he faced back around and his nose was smashed with the butt of one of the AK-47's he had just identified. He crumpled to the ground with a muffled cry blocked by his own hands that now had blood streaming through them and his eyes filled with tears so badly that he couldn't see.

Just as Cesar came through the brush to see what the commotion was, Louie attacked the guerrilla that had flattened Harold. She had moved quickly enough that the man with the rifle hadn't had time to bring it around to protect himself. Louie was on fire with rage and not thinking straight. She went straight for the man's eyes with her finger nails. He backed away just enough that she missed her target. His unwillingness to drop the rifle, however, to better block her attack allowed her nails to find flesh. Part of her mind was repulsed by the feeling of her nails sinking into a human face, even the face of the person that had just hurt her husband. Almost like a third person watching this encounter, Louie could hear herself screaming incoherently. She could feel the warm blood of her target trickle through her hands turned claws as he pulled away with his own screams of pain.

"Get control of her!" Cesar shouted to the man nearest to this cat fight. Cesar glanced up the hill and could see the dust of vehicles approaching. He only had a split second to make a decision. "Get both of them and pull them back into the bush, NOW!"

The MNS guerrilla that had approached Louie grabbed her roughly around the waist from behind and began to pull her away from the scene. He had taken some of the air out of her, but before they were more than ten steps away she was able to scream Harold's name.

Harold forgot his pain momentarily, but still couldn't see clearly. As the next closest guerrilla approached, expecting an easier time with this subdued *gringo*, Harold exploded upward with all the force he could muster and caught the man right under his jaw with both hands clenched together in a move that would make a champion volleyball player proud, knocking him into Cesar.

Sergeant Hernandez was the first to see the encounter just down the road to his left. He recognized Louie because her *Norteña* clothes did not fit the picture. Then he realized something was happening. He wasn't sure whether these were common thugs or something worse until he was out of the vehicle and saw the AK-47s. He pulled his revolver and aimed at the guerrilla farthest from his new friends. He missed because he was running, but it alerted everyone of the new complexities.

"Grab them both and let's get back into the trees." Cesar commanded, wishing he had waited until after the Army caravan had gone by to make their way back to camp. "They will be useful in case we need to bargain our way out of this mess!"

The man holding Louie continued to retreat into the forest. It was all the guerrilla with Louie's fingernail marks in his face could do to help up his fellow freedom fighter that Harold had flattened. Cesar grabbed the shirt of the next closest of his men and pulled him past the retreating injured men and then pushed him toward Harold. At that moment, Sergeant Hernandez had taken time to aim at the man who seemed to be the leader and squeezed off another shot. It hit the MNS rebel soldier as he was being pulled past Cesar. The man let out a short cry and his forward momentum caused him to fold on top of Harold. The situation was worsening by the second. The next shot would surely find Cesar as he realized he was the last of his squad in the full open. "Retreat!" he called out to no one but himself.

Seconds later Sergeant Hernandez was at the scene. He commanded the soldiers coming up behind him to continue on in pursuit of the guerrillas. "*Señor* Farnsworth, OK?" he asked in his broken English, expecting to find him dead. When he pulled the guerrilla off of Harold he heard a groan. He checked the guerrilla and found him still breathing and only wounded in the shoulder. "You will live, you scum!" he said and then roughly shoved the man onto the picnic blanket.

Harold attempted to stand up and attack Sergeant Hernandez, not knowing what was going on.

"*Tranquilate, Señor*! Friend! Friend!" Enrique exclaimed, using one of the very few words he knew in English.

Captain Peña had been in the second to the last vehicle with the bureaucrats. They had turned the same color as their white suites as soon as they heard the gunshots. Captain Peña told them to stay in the car and commanded the soldiers in the last vehicle to stay and protect their guests. When he got to the scene, Harold was on his feet and holding a hastily ripped piece of the hotel blanket on his nose. As Captain Peña began asking Harold what had happened, the soldiers sent to chase the guerrillas returned fifteen minutes later with the news that there was no sign of the insurgents. "Where is *Señora* Farnsworth?" Captain Peña asked the returning soldiers.

"We saw no sign of her, sir," one of the soldiers said between deep breaths.

"How could you lose them so quickly? It looked as if at least two were injured and still another was dragging a kicking *Señora* Farnsworth!" Sergeant Hernandez bellowed. "Now, let's try this again with me leading you sorry excuses for soldiers."

"As you were, Sergeant," Peña commanded. "At best you would discover them as you were being ambushed and at worst they would kill or injure *Señora* Farnsworth so they could move quicker. They took her as a bargaining chip. She is of no intelligence or military value. Her best chance is to let this settle down and she will probably be released," Captain Peña surmised. "If the soldiers couldn't find them earlier, they surely won't now. Let's get our friends from the capital safely back to the stockade because they are valuable targets."

Chapter 9
Into the Pit

LOUIE HAD QUIT FIGHTING. SHE WAS EXHAUSTED. Twenty minutes after the encounter with these guerrillas, they had stopped when they were sure the Army had lost their trail. "Get her tied up," Cesar commanded. "Bind her hands together tightly in front of her so we can pull her from the front. Shackle her ankles with another cord so one of you can hold it from behind. Move, quickly!"

Cesar was concerned about what Comandante Helicon would say. This encounter may have cost them the mission. He had considered releasing the *Norteña* after he was sure that the Army was not an immediate threat. After all, at this point she would just slow them down and complicate their stealthy return.

"Also, tie her mouth shut. We don't want her to make any noise during our return," Cesar added. This was a new scenario he hadn't faced before. Unlike their enemy, kidnapping was not something the revolution had yet exhorted to. He had decided to bring her back to their camp and had blindfolded her some distance away from it. He would let Comandante Helicon decide what to do with her.

"Wa-er," Louie said as clearly as she could with her mouth gagged. She was parched and hoped that this would also provide her with a short break. "Wa-er," she repeated. During their forced march she had thought through this as much as her mind allowed. She had told herself she wouldn't speak

Spanish so possibly they wouldn't realize she understood what they were saying and that would possibly aid in her escape.

"Wa-er," she said for the third time.

"*Cállate!*" her captor said and pulled hard on the cord, cutting into her ankle and causing her to stumble. As she fell, the cord tied to her hands grew taught causing the man in front to tug hard also. Without thinking, she pulled back with both her arms with the remaining strength she had. This caused the man in front to fall sideways. He wasn't hurt, but the men behind snickered and that embarrassed him. He whipped around with the loose end of the cord and slashed her across the shoulders, cutting her blouse sleeve and leaving a welt on her left bicep.

"That's enough!" Cesar commanded. "We need to deliver her in one piece. It will be the Comandante's decision what will become of her." He was now having his doubts about bringing her this far toward their camp, but it was too late to let her go. His fate was in the hands of Comandante Helicon's mood. "Let's take a couple minutes break. I think she was asking for water. Give her some and be more of a gentleman about it. We are not animals."

'Oh yes you are,' Louie thought. 'So I am to meet their boss. Hopefully he will see the folly and the danger in holding on to me,' she hoped silently and decided not to cause any more trouble, at least for the time being.

The rest of the trek was miserable, but uneventful.

"We can't just wait to see what some terrorist is going to do with her Captain!" Harold shouted. "What is the use of patience when every minute may be her last." Harold was feeling good enough that he was now fully angry at the lack of action being taken to rescue Louie. Somewhere they had found what must be the only piece of ice in the Mariposa Valley to help take down the swelling in his face. Even under these circumstances he had briefly considered putting it in his mouth instead.

"I understand your feelings *Señor* Farnsworth. I do not want to put her in any more danger than she already is faced with. A clumsy, ill thought out attack, at a location we don't know, and at an enemy whose size and armament we haven't a clue about, will only escalate the chances of fatalities," Captain Peña explained for the sixth time according to his memory.

"No, you don't understand Captain. This is my wife! This is our honeymoon. Those are killers that have her. I am very glad you got your important visitors back safely to the fort. At least your career is still in tact," Harold said with as much sarcasm as he could muster.

"*Señor* Farnsworth, that is enough! I will have you removed, or perhaps better, put in the stockade jail for your own protection if you do not cease with your whining and let us carefully plan our next step. What will it be?" Captain Peña asked with the last measure of patience in him.

Exasperated, Harold wanted to let out another scream. Instead he heard himself saying, "Perhaps I should leave you for a few minutes to collect myself. I am sorry for my rudeness. I know this is not your fault. Is there somewhere I can go to be alone for a few minutes?" Harold knew what he needed to do and pleaded with a contriteness that was overcoming him now, along with a strong wave of nausea.

"Sergeant Hernandez, please escort *Señor* Farnsworth to my personal quarters," Captain Peña ordered with a firm voice. "He is free to stay there as long as he would like. Also, please post a guard outside my quarters in case he would prefer to return here to the Command Post. Also make sure he doesn't try to leave on his own."

"*Señor* Farnsworth," Peña said in a gentler tone of voice and turned to face Harold. "Sergeant Hernandez will take you to a quiet and safe place. Feel free to make yourself at home and clean yourself up."

Harold almost lost it again when Captain Peña said safe place. He didn't want to feel safe when Louie obviously wasn't. He kept quiet because he feared talking would take his nausea to a new level.

It was when the Sergeant opened the door to a set of rooms that Harold realized he had been taken to Captain Peña's quarters. Once the door was closed Harold rushed to the bathroom and vomited up the blood from his nose that had collected in his stomach. He still felt a little dizzy, but the nausea was almost gone. After trying to wash his face and inspecting his nose, he went back to the small front room and attempted to kneel, but almost collapsed onto the hardwood floor. He bowed his head, feeling a little vertigo, and began to pour out his soul to his Heavenly Father. He wept for only the second time since he had met Louie. The first time was for joy as he knelt across the altar when they were married. There was no joy in the tears he shed this afternoon. He felt as if he had been thrown into the darkest of pits and there was no way out. He felt powerless or worse, useless, to do anything that would help the most important person in his life. The only thing he knew to do was to pray, and pray he did like he had never prayed before from the depths of his soul that matched the depth of the pit he felt himself to be in. He felt terrible for feeling terrible, knowing that his Louie was the one to feel terrible about.

In the very depths of his misery, he felt guilt, even though he didn't know what he could have done better. That made him even more frustrated. He was deeply worried about Louie. A tiny measure of peace, like a dot of light in a dark room, entered his heart. He knew the feeling of this gift, but it was never as profound as it felt this time. A thought entered his mind. *Let the Captain do his job.* He is a good man. Within a few minutes he was asleep on a couch in what must have been Captain Peña's living room.

"Emma, have you heard the news?" Alejandro breathlessly asked and tried to balance the feelings of peace as he entered his humble home with the dark cloud of warning he felt the moment he heard the news of the kidnapping.

Emma stepped out of the kitchen. "Old man there is always gossip to share in this little town," she said. "Leave other people's business outside our doorstep and we will all be happier."

"This isn't gossip Emma. I heard this from one of the soldiers that was there."

"Soldiers? There? What are you talking about Alejandro?"

"I am trying to tell you. There was an attack on the two *Norteños* that came in on the plane from the capital the other day. Revolutionaries from the mountains the soldier guessed. He said there were twenty or thirty of them. They tried to kill the man and they took the lady with them!"

"*¡Santo cielo!*" Emma exclaimed, immediately feeling the tension in her throat almost blocking her air passage. "Are these people important? Why would revolutionaries take the woman? Are they rich? Do they want money?"

Alejandro sat down on their worn couch which looked as tired as he suddenly felt. "I don't know any more than I've told you. To be honest, I wasn't thinking so much about the *Norteños*. I was wondering if Paco might have been a part of the attackers. They seemed to know the area pretty well. The soldier said the group disappeared within minutes of the attack. They just vanished," and continued his words only as thoughts, 'like our sons and butterflies.' He then added out loud, "That would be quite a trick with that large of a group and the woman to keep quiet."

"I thought you told me everything you heard. This is something new. What else should I know? Why do you think Paco was a part of this?" Emma asked, now feeling her husband's concern.

"I have no more information, I really don't. Maybe it is just my imagination again, running wild with the possibilities," he mumbled while he rubbed his stubble face which distorted his words. No matter, Emma had retreated into her own world of thoughts and fears.

Breaking the silence, she quoted in a painful monotone, "*Aquela triste leda madrugada, cheia toda de mágoa e de piedade, enquanto houver no mundo saüdade quero que seja sempre celebrada.*" Then, she repeated the quote in broken English as was her habit. "The dawn rises lovely but ill-fated and full of grief. For as long as heartbreaks prey upon our tragic world, this dawning day should be forever famous and celebrated." She paused and shook her head sadly. "I felt something evil was on the horizon. This is the start. Life has simply been too pleasant and peaceful. I have come to expect the balance of tragedy in our lives."

"Now it is your imagination that has grown beyond rationality. Emma, I said I *wondered* if Paco was among the group. I didn't say he actually was. In fact I think there are many reasons why he wasn't a part of the group. People would have easily recognized him for one, which would have put us and him in certain danger. He may not fear for his own life, but he knows what his brother's disappearance... has already done to this family." Alejandro could not bring himself to say the word death that hung in their minds and thoughts constantly.

"I suppose you are right Alejandro. My fears for Paco are like a sore that never fully heals. Just a little bump and it is opened up again. '*Estoy vivo...*' I am alive in the center of a still fresh wound, as the poet said."

Alejandro knew that Emma leaned on her poets in her times of greatest joy and greatest grief. He asked, "So which of your poets are speaking with you today?"

"I don't know. They just come out of my mouth without me thinking about it. Yes, Luís de Camões, the great Portuguese poet, and Octavio Paz, one of my favorite Mexican poets. I am sorry you have to put up with such a strange wife," she said in her soft, but unapologetic way.

"You ought to be teaching at the university in the capital, not cooking beans for a poor woodcarver who must clean up other people's messes at the airport just to put those beans in the pot."

"I like cooking beans for you old man," she shared and then gave him a kiss on the cheek before getting up to prepare the eternal pot of beans once more.

"Captain, may I ask you a question?" Harold uttered after he re-entered the Command Post.

Captain Peña turned to see a man whose clothes and face still looked disheveled, but whose countenance was different—energetic, almost glowing? There was a confidence and a peace about him that caused Captain Peña to stare for a few seconds longer than was comfortable for either of them. "What is it *Señor* Farnsworth?" he asked finally.

"Could you tell me your first name?"

"Diego."

"May I call you by your first name?"

"Certainly sir," Diego answered, but wondered why.

"Thank you. My name is Harold. It is kind of a stuffy name and I have no nickname, so if Harold is alright with you, I would appreciate it if we could start anew, and on a first name basis. This will not be an easy time for me, but I trust you and appreciate your effort on behalf of my wife. If there is anything I can do, please let me know because I feel completely helpless. Otherwise I will try my best to stay out of your way."

Diego Peña was speechless. He had seen men on the doorstep of death turn almost saintly, but even those most heartfelt pleas for remission paled in comparison to how *Señor* Farnsworth, Harold, looked and talked and how Diego felt about him. "There is something you can do for us. Do you have any pictures of your wife?"

"Yes, at the hotel."

"Good. May I have a few soldiers escort you to your hotel to retrieve the photo? I don't believe you are in any danger. The soldiers are for your convenience."

"That would be fine. I will return immediately."

"Put her in the cave," Cesar said as they arrived at the camp. "I will go find the Comandante. Oh, and Julio, get your face cleaned up."

Julio spit with a meanness and disgust that caused the hardened men around him to shiver inwardly. His face had red encrusted streaks on it from Louie's attack. He turned and did as he was commanded.

The cave was a small enclave in the hillside that Comandante Helicon had used for any of the men who became drunk and disorderly during the weeks of boredom following their last battle with the enemy of the people. It was cramped, damp, dark and smelled of vomit and men who had not bathed in a very long time.

Louie discovered almost immediately the only two blessings she would ever find in the pit that would be her dwelling place for what would come to seem like a lifetime. First, she could take off the cords that bound her hands and her ankle. Secondly, she was alone. That could have frightened her, but she had feared worse being paraded through the camp and incarcerated in a public place. Here she could pray, sleep with a certain level of peace, and at least there was a bucket where she could relieve herself. "Funny what you fear most in situations like this," she tried to joke to herself. 'Like anyone I Have ever known finds themselves in a situation like this,' she thought. She tried to smile, but her face remained solemn. "You can handle this Louie," she told herself in a whisper. She lightly ran her fingers across the welt on her arm and the cuts on her wrists. She knelt on the cold rock that provided a cold and uneven floor in this overheated jungle. She was grateful to be healthy and strong, and that her captors had not treated her any worse than they had. She felt the rocks she was kneeling on push back. Everything around her was cold, dark, and void of light. She collapsed on the ground, but remained undefeated.

"Bring her out here in the light," her mind registered as that command mixed with a dream she was having about her childhood on her grandfather's farm in Eastern Washington. Louie woke shivering when a rough hand grabbed her sore wrist and pulled her to her feet. She was led out into the fresh air and the sun felt good. Louie felt the eyes of many surveying her. She could also almost put faces to the thoughts behind those eyes. Some were fearful of her because surely the Army would be looking for her. Some felt more powerful, being able to measure their strength against this powerless woman in their midst. A few obviously felt sorry for her. 'Bless them,' she thought. Some felt an animal lust, and the saddest, the most frightening, a few felt absolutely nothing at all.

As her eyes adjusted to the brightness of the early morning, they met the dark and worrisome eyes of a man not too much older than Harold. His features and dark complexion were actually handsome, but Louie knew in an instant that these eyes were some of those that registered a lust for her, yet mixed with something else. Was it rage?

"I am so sorry for the inconvenience *Señora*," his voice was saying. Was it in English or Spanish? She wasn't sure. It was not a difficult act for her to register incomprehension.

Within seconds all went black and she felt herself crumpling to the ground before she lost all consciousness.

Chapter 10
Introductions

"Diego? Are you here? Captain Peña? Anyone?" Harold called out as he walked from the office/den that now doubled as a guest bedroom in Captain Peña's quarters at the Army stockade. After some wrangling last night, Diego had talked Harold into staying at the stockade, more for military convenience than any concern for his safety. Just the paperwork and reporting requirements, along with any follow-up questions due to the dynamics of the situation were reasons to keep the *Norteño* close by. It would be convenient for Harold in case they heard anything from the patrols Peña had set up around the valley. What finally convinced Harold to move from the hotel to the stockade, however, was Peña's suggestion that this way his small medical staff could make sure there were no complications from his up close and personal introduction to the butt of an assault rifle and he would be one of the first to hear of any news about his wife.

Harold fumbled for his wristwatch that he had stuffed into his pocket the night before. "9:20! How could I have slept in with Louie who knows where?" Disgusted with himself, he began to dress quickly, then slowed down as his head began to pound to the beating of his heart and vertigo set in. He rationalized that if there was anything at all to report, he knew someone would have awakened him. He felt as if he was in the way at the Command Post, but concern over that was quickly outweighed by his need to be where he felt like he was doing something—anything. He finished cleaning up, checking the cuts on and around his swollen nose, and recalled the events of the previous night.

"Surprisingly, your nose isn't broken *Señor* Farnsworth," the physician from Mariposa had reported last night after a painful examination. "We have no X-ray equipment here. You would have to travel to the capital for that," the doctor had explained. Harold's quick glance and concerned eyes had caused the doctor to continue. "But I don't think that will be necessary. We will want to keep an eye on you for a few days to watch for any possible complications from the contusions and cuts, internal sinus ruptures and so on. But it looks like you will be fine in a couple weeks."

'Fine in a couple weeks!' Harold thought. 'My wife, kidnapped by obviously brutal terrorists, taken into the jungle to who knows what conditions, and I will be just fine?' Harold reviewed the situation silently again, feeling completely helpless. He noticed a picture on the fireplace mantel of Captain Peña ('maybe he was a lieutenant then,' Harold thought) and a young woman. Diego looked younger in the picture, perhaps just graduating from military school. 'Looks like a West Point uniform,' Harold thought to himself. 'The girl is pretty, but with a sad countenance. She wears a smile, but behind the smile is grief.' He was surprised at himself. He was never good at seeing beyond the façade. That was one of Louie's gifts. Maybe it was the feeling of the vacuum created by her absence that added to his present sensitivities, or, 'maybe I'm just imagining it because I need to feel more of a human connection,' he told himself.

"Ah, you are awake," Diego said when he entered his quarters. "I hope the bed was comfortable and that you feel a little better this morning. The previous sector commander brought his wife and his wife's mother to this valley. You are the first since their departure to sleep in the mother-in-law room. I keep my books and a desk there, but never use it. No time. And to be honest, no interest to sit around this place alone. So I go to the club downtown and sit alone," he added with a half laugh gilded by an almost imperceptible loneliness.

"I slept more than fine. In fact I have just been beating myself up about how long I actually slept. And feeling guilty all over again; first, for not being able to protect her and then for not being able to do enough to find her."

"We will find her, *Señor* Farns..., err, Harold. I have five patrols searching for possible trails. We know they are in the mountains somewhere, probably within just a few days of here. Unfortunately, once into the jungle we could walk within forty yards of them and never find them." Immediately he was sorry he shared that last statement with Harold and it showed on his face.

"Captain, you can talk to me straight. If we spend any amount of thought or energy trying to act on stage with each other, that is taken away from our abilities to find and rescue Louie."

"First, it is Diego, please. They couldn't have been that far away," Diego continued. "I have also talked with the wounded insurgent, but so far he is not saying anything. He will however," Diego added cautiously. "I have some additional reports to fill out for my commander. I can accomplish that from the information you gave us last night. Could you look this over and see if it is correct, especially your identification information? There is some concern about the fact that you are foreigners—foreigners from the United States. That is a very sensitive subject for our government.

The ruling junta is not on the friendliest of terms with your government, but we are not enemies either. Your Embassy has been notified of the incident. They of course registered their concern. It seems it plays well in the capital that it was communist insurgents that attacked innocent tourists."

"First of all, this report is in Spanish," Harold observed, "so again I find myself worthless to help, and secondly, I don't follow that this tragedy plays well."

"I apologize for my callousness, and I am sorry about the report. I will translate out loud the key parts to you. I am not thinking as clearly as I should. Our military had to take control of this country due to the unrest in the streets of our major cities, as well as the inability of our civilian government to deal with that and the economy, industry, and agricultural reforms. The elected government was completely ineffectual. We have the know-how, the organization, and the vision to get the country on its feet again before sinking into the abyss of chaos that would have taken decades to climb out of. It was, you might say, a pre-emptive strike on apathy and chaos." Diego paused to see if Harold was following his explanation. "Taking power from a democratically elected government is not looked upon with much understanding by most countries, in particular yours. That the challenges we face reached out and touched a U.S. citizen is seen by our government as a bridge of potential understanding about the complexities of security and rule in our crumbling society. Your relatively new sensitivities due to your own tragedies in New York City, your Pentagon, your own fight against terror, and of course your wars in Iraq, Afghanistan, and elsewhere, may also be ingredients in our government's rapprochement with yours. I hope this doesn't make you feel like a pawn in a bigger game. I want you to realize that I know the only game, if I can use that word, of importance to you, is to find your wife. This is also good for your situation, however, because our government would like nothing more than to rescue your wife and look the hero. They have told me to expect every support to aid in finding and rescuing your wife."

"I am not sure all these politics and power plays make me feel any better, but thank you for explaining them to me. Your vocabulary and understanding of these matters is surprising, I mean uhm, impressive."

"You mean not expected for a humble Captain of Infantry in a small third world country in a lonely and nearly for-gotten valley, until recently?" Diego chided good naturedly, but with a trace of his old defenses.

"Well I think you are exaggerating my under expectation, but since we are trying to be open with each other, yes. You strike me as uncommon for a career military man."

"And you Harold, from the moment I saw your wife trying to deplane with all those bags without your help, you struck me as thoughtless and spoiled like many *Norte Americanos* that visit this valley."

"Louie makes quite a first impression. I am painfully aware that I make quite the opposite impression. That isn't an excuse mind you. Alas, I am imperfect and trying my best to improve. I am really quite capable on my own and not as absentminded as I appear. But when I am around Louie, I become a little baby, with all the helplessness that suggests. That is my story. What's yours?" Harold quickly added to deflect any more attention on himself and calm the sea of inadequacy that was crashing on his shore.

"I am assigned to manage this situation personally. I have assigned the day-to-day sector administration duties to Sergeant Hernandez, who already takes care of most of those responsibilities anyway. And I will be given the increased support of a Major Zarro who will arrive here this afternoon from the capital. He was the commander of this sector before his promotion and has face-to-face experience with this rebel group."

"Great information Diego, but hardly the answer to my question. Maybe you do have a future in politics. Seriously, tell me about you. Education, family, future plans. Are your married?"

Taking a deep breath and letting it out slowly, Diego started with clipped words, "I think another time would be better for a personal conversation." Seeing the pain in Harold's eyes and the slump of his shoulders, Diego quickly added, "But here is the short story: generations of military family, military academy, military life, retire, die." He smiled at Harold hopefully. "Oh, and no."

"No?"

"No, I am not married."

"So do they teach you this interrogation deflection technique in the Army? Name, rank, and serial number, and all that? I will give you a second to recapture my confidence while I tell you about me, whether you want to know or not. I am from a small family. Just my parents and me. I grew up mostly in Boston. That's on the Atlantic Coast in the Northeast."

"Yes, I know that," Diego interjected, a little too pridefully.

"Well yes, of course. Sorry. Anyway, no more interruptions, even if I blaspheme your culture, religion, country and make you out to be a dimwit, or I will never get through this."

"You have done most of that already—that is except for religion and my favorite fútbol team, so I will be quiet," Diego said with a slight chuckle.

"Why I need to tell you, I am not sure, but I feel so stinking helpless to change the reality of things. I am hoping this fills that void a little, I suppose. Anyway, I am not without my diplomatic talents," Harold said. He tried to remember the feeling he experienced about this foreign military Captain in whose hands his wife's future was held. "I finished high school in two years and finished college in two more years. I don't say that to brag, but more as an excuse for my poor social skills. I was 17 when I got my Bachelors Degree and I had never been on a date. I was too young for all my classmates and too nervous around girls my age because I was used to being around girls much older than me. I guess I just sort of set that part of my life on a shelf and tried to bury myself in studies and then my research and then later, my company. Until Louie came along, that is. I swept her off her feet with all my stored up charm and personality."

"So you are some sort of genius?" Diego asked, but for some reason not surprised.

"Hardly. I just learn things quickly and remember them. I think genius creates. I am simply good at imitation," Harold said with true humility. "Because of my accelerated schooling, I was put in a few classrooms with people we would term as geniuses, and I promise you, I am not in their class of intellect. And I am glad, really. With their brain power comes a high expectation and maybe even a responsibility that the rest of us don't carry on our shoulders. I am not saying most carry that stewardship well, if at all, but it is there all the same."

"So in other words you are saying the dumber you are, the less social responsibility you have, the less obligation you should feel to produce?" Diego asked skeptically.

"Well, you said it yourself. The Army took control because no one else in your society was capable. Did I get that right?" Harold asked earnestly.

"I am not sure a group principle translates to individuals so cleanly. Just because someone is born really smart doesn't place them at the threshold of great responsibilities. Some of the best commanders I have served were just above average intelligence. Their true talents were hard work, loyalty and willingness to sacrifice."

"Actually I sort of agree with you. Being born a genius doesn't give anyone the responsibility to become President of a country, nor the right to great power. I would shudder at the thought of one of those geniuses I knew in school running a company, let alone a country. On the other hand, I didn't mean their responsibility was to exercise great leadership. I was trying to say that they were born with God given talents and that they had the responsibility to develop and multiply those talents for the good of others. But that goes for all of us. We all have something to give. I simply meant that Beethoven was driven to give us his symphonies. Newton was driven to give us physical theories and Einstein was driven to turn them on their head. Pelé set the bar higher for professional soccer and Tiger Woods may yet someday do the same for golf. Jim Ryun had it within his potential to run a four minute mile as a junior in high school, and he did it. Sadly, others have had the potential and they let it pass, or didn't work hard enough and just coasted"

"I do not know this *Señor* Ryun, but you had it within you to finish high school in two years and you did it."

"There is a difference between completing and creating, surviving and setting the standard," Harold tried to explain. "Anyway, I am not sure how we got on this subject. I was just trying to explain my social shortcomings. A poor excuse no matter what the explanation, however," he added, becoming uncomfortable with the direction of the conversation. "That's enough about me anyway. I've given you enough time to provide a slightly expanded story of your life, at least past the single syllable answers you tried to pass off on me just now."

"To be honest, no one has ever really pushed me to tell them more. My classmates from the military academy are my only friends. I haven't been in one assignment long enough to make good friends outside of my professional circle," Diego stalled.

"You can make a life-long friend in five minutes," Harold injected, "but I do assume being an officer and spending most of your waking day with enlisted personnel, where a distance must be maintained, is a lonely life sometimes."

Diego had been looking out the window and glanced around to look at Harold. He was surprised at this non-military *Norteño's* insight. "How did you deduce that? Do I look lonely?"

"No. Leadership carries a certain mantel and you have that look. I am pretty unfamiliar with the military culture, but my father led a large company and I remember seeing that same look sometimes. So you said you are not married. Any female friends?" Harold prodded. "Who is in that picture in your living room?"

"My baby sister, Carmen. That picture was taken shortly after my graduation from the academy. She died about a year later of cancer. I was in Great Britain in training at the time and was not able to return home for the funeral. I have a brother just 18 months younger than me who is a doctor. Both of my parents lived in the capital where I grew up. My uncle, my father's brother, is a retired Colonel working in civilian status for the military provisional government. He may actually be sent out here to handle the public relations if the news agencies decide to descend on this valley. Hopefully they will be convinced that it is too dangerous here and they can get all the information they need from their traditional government contacts."

"Would it be best for everyone if I moved back to the hotel?" Harold asked, assuming up to this point he would be staying with Diego. "With the Major this afternoon and possibly your uncle?"

"No," Diego interrupted. "Both will be housed in the guest quarters that are being vacated today by our bureaucrat guests who moved on the post last night and have quickly decided that their important work here is complete and it is best that they get back to their duties at home where they are urgently needed. I expect by the time they arrive in the capital, they will be the experts on rebel attacks and will humbly explain how things could have been much worse except for their courageous leadership during the crisis," Diego explained with an acidic mix of sarcasm and amusement. "I expect Major Zarro will want to talk with you after I pick him up at the airport. Perhaps we could have dinner together. His English is not as good as mine. He completed an advanced infantry course in Germany I believe and has not been abroad except for that one experience."

"Whatever will help move this effort forward I am all for it," Harold stated flatly.

"*¿Señora? ¿Señora?* Are you hearing me?"

Louie could hear a thickly accented voice speaking in English, but she still hadn't opened her eyes. She vaguely remembered leaving the cave, but wanted to gain a little more control of her faculties before starting this process again. "Yes, I hear you," she said and slowly opened her eyes. It was not as bright as she remembered, but then realized she was in a large tent. It smelled of oiled canvas and cigarettes. She tried to sit up but her head began throbbing when she moved. Louie slowly laid her head back down as the feeling of nausea came back.

"Drink," the voice said.

Louie allowed the cool water to slide down her throat. It felt like the first rivulet of water across a parched desert landscape. She could physically feel the flow of the water all the way to her stomach. She craved more.

"*Tranquilete*, slow," the same voice said. "Go get the Comandante. She is awake," the voice said in Spanish to someone outside the tent.

Within seconds the man she remembered as Comandante Helicon from seemingly a few minutes before was standing at the foot of whatever she was laying on. "I hope you are feeling better *Señora*. You did not have a very restful day I am afraid. I thought it best you stay in my tent instead of the cave. My men were careless in their travels with you and I am afraid you were quite dehydrated. You will need to drink plenty of water, but do it slowly or you will get sick and lose the badly needed fluids. What you really need is a... Ahh. What do you call it? *Intravenoso*. A hook up with liquid into your blood. No matter. That is impossible, so we must help you this way."

"Who?" Louie asked and immediately paused. "Where am I?" she stammered, trying to get better control of her swollen tongue.

"I am sorry *Señora*. I have forgotten my manners," Helicon said gently. "You are our…" he paused. "Guest. Allow me to introduce myself. I am Commandante Helicon. These men are the courageous freedom fighters of the *Movimiento Nacional de Hegemony Socialista*. We are the true protectorate of the people of our country. And your name, *Señora?*"

"Louisa Farnsworth. Innocent bystander and unhappy guest of your freedom fighters," Louie answered with all the courage she could muster.

"Ah, you are feeling better. I detect a little courage, a little humor perhaps. I do apologize again for bringing you into our country's little family feud. First we must see to your health, then we will decide what the best course of action is for you and for the Movement. Please rest. We can talk after you have more water and a little to eat. Please feel at home, but do not leave the tent. That would be very unwise." The Comandante turned and left as quickly as he had appeared.

"Cesar, let us take a walk," Comandante Helicon suggested as a quiet command. When they were out of earshot of the other men in the camp, he began, "We have gone over the reason you brought this woman to our camp and under the circumstances it would have been better that she was accidentally shot in the crossfire. The propaganda would have been useful, claiming the Army had killed an innocent woman in their lust to kill our freedom fighters. As it is now, we must make sure she regains her health. Propaganda goes both ways. What do you know of her?"

"She and the man she was with saw our point guard when we were leaving the Dam site. I told you the story last night. By the time I was on the scene we had no time to figure out who they were or what they were doing there. It looked as if they were eating lunch out in the middle of nowhere. There was no identity on the woman. I gave you the ring from her finger. After her attack with her finger nails, I was afraid she might actually use the ring as a weapon. Julio wanted the ring as payment for his injuries, which I think is mostly embarrassment of letting this young woman get the better of him in front of the other men. The ring suggests that she is married, I suppose. I cannot say whether the man at the incident was her husband or perhaps a gentleman friend. I searched her myself when we were no more than ten minutes away from the incident. She speaks English, but my language abilities in that devil's tongue are not very good. That is all I know. As I told you last night Comandante, we gagged her so she would not alert any possible Army patrols, so we did not speak. My first commands to her were in Spanish and all I got was a blank stare. If she speaks any Spanish, I don't think it is much."

"Very well Cesar. One other thing. Are you absolutely sure of the man who was shot? Jorge you said. Are you sure he was dead?"

"Absolutely sure Comandante. I saw him get shot in the chest and fall right in front of me," Cesar said with confidence, remembering the scene in his mind.

"And the companion of our guest, he was not killed?"

"He was hit very hard with a rifle butt. I don't think he was killed. We did not fire shots at him. The Army firing came close to him, but again, only Jorge was hit."

"Very good. For right now, let's not mention any news about the health of her companion. Let's see if the military's media puppets share any information about who he is, and who she is. Then we can decide whether he was killed in the action by the Army, or whether he is going to survive thanks to our unwillingness to shoot and possibly harm innocents. We will not behave like the callous Army in their bloody attack. We will also continue our plan to blow up the Dam. There is enough water in the new reservoir to create much destruction. I believe the Army will not expect the attack, even if they guess what we were there for. I have had several reports that they have patrols out looking for our camp. For now they are looking in all the wrong places. Sooner or later that will tell them where we are as clearly as if they found us. We must strike while we can, because our days are numbered in this soon-to-be famous valley of the butterfly. You know Cesar, some butterflies store a poison that they had ingested by feeding on the leaves of the milk-weed foliage in their larva stage. These toxins provide these butterflies with a lethal weapon. We have been too long in the larva stage of the revolution, but our danger will soon be felt. Keep the men vigilant and keep them away from our beautiful guest. When she is in better health, we will move her back to the cave. Have someone clean it up and put a cot in there, even though it won't be level. It will be safer for her. These men have been away from the natural pleasures of life for a long time."

Louie was beginning to feel strength re-enter her muscles and her head was not aching so she again attempted to sit up. This time she was successful, with the help of an elderly man sitting beside the cot she was lying on.

"Careful, *Señora*. You are still weak," the man said.

As she scooted up to a sitting position, she felt a pain on her ankle. She pulled back the sheet covering her and found her ankle tied by a cord to the front tent pole. Louie looked at the man beside her.

He shrugged and said, "Orders of the Comandante. I would be careful what you say to him. He is fair, but he has little interest in anyone that disagrees with him, even with humor. This is his tent. He allowed you to sleep here and he has remained outside his only place to think and plan away from the other men."

"What is your name?" Louie asked.

"*No importa*, not important" the man answered. He looked at Louie with compassion and he could have been one of Louie's father's business associates from his age and confident demeanor. He wore glasses, had a crisp haircut, and comfortable but clean clothing. His wrinkles and graying hair gave him a distinguished look. Only the hair growing around and out of his ears and out of his nose suggested a potentially different story.

"OK, *No Importa*," Louie said, using his answer as an actual name. "You said last night. How long have I been here?"

"Nearly 24 hours, *Señora*. You arrived very late in the night."

"Does the Comandante have a name?" Louie asked, trying to get this quiet man into a conversation.

"I am sure he does, but that is not important either. He is the leader of the revolution. You are fortunate to be under his personal concern. Some of the men who brought you here are not as interested in your health or your long-term well-being. I cleaned your bloody hands and fingernails last night to remove the direct remembrance of your attack on

Julio, but the camp has heard the story and I am sure he will not forget quickly."

"Julio?"

"The man you clawed," *No Importa* said.

"He attacked us!" Louie said with fierceness.

"*No importa*," *No Importa* said.

"Harold, could you accompany me to the airport?" Diego asked as Harold walked into the Command Post. "I need to leave in a few minutes to pick up Major Zarro. We can go from there to a restaurant in town. The food is much better there."

"Absolutely. At least I would be doing something."

"I was thinking about our recent conversation," Peña began once they were settled in the jeep. "The person we really need to get to know is *Señora* Farnsworth. What should we know about her that would help us ensure her safe return? Any prior military service or background experience in survival? How is her health? Does she take any medicine? Any medications? How about her family? Anything there that the MNS could use as a leverage point? Is her family rich? Are you wealthy? Possibly this was a kidnapping for money as is common in Colombia and parts of Mexico. I apologize for asking these personal questions, but any thoughts you might have would help us in our battle to rescue her and to understand the bigger picture."

"There is no bigger picture than getting Louie back safe, but I know what you mean," Harold began, trying to check his irritation. "Louie is in great shape. She runs and exercises nearly every day. She has a healthier diet than me. No medications, no health problems. Financially we are comfortable, maybe rich by some standards. Her father is a great guy, but not rich or famous. He is retired from managing a grain co-op in Eastern Washington and still does a little farming. My father is fairly wealthy and as I mentioned, he has been the President or CEO of several companies, but certainly not famous. He still sits on a few companies' boards, but other than that and some community and church service, he is retired also. Even the companies he has run are not well known," Harold listed. He then became quiet, looking out the window.

Peña was unsure whether Harold was finished answering, whether he was thinking, or simply collecting his strength to talk about his wife in this difficult situation. Peña had wondered how he would feel in Harold's shoes. "You know, I am professionally embarrassed, and personally just sick about all this, I want you to know that. This has happened on my watch in my assigned area of responsibility. I should have had more patrols out. Maybe I should have not allowed you to travel without an escort from the stockade. At any rate, I truly am so very sorry and I will personally do all I can to ensure your wife's safe return. And," he added with deep emotion, "I will chase these traitor revolutionaries to the last corner of the country!"

Harold wanted to get mad at this foreigner who knew nothing about him or Louie. 'He claims to be embarrassed? Oh brother. That really soothes me,' Harold thought to himself and wanted to yell out. Instead, Harold's thoughts landed on an odd habit of Captain Diego Peña, or lack of a bad habit. Harold had noticed as he had gotten to know Diego that he had not heard a single curse or blasphemy from this young Army officer. Maybe he didn't know any in

English, but then, Diego's command of English was about as good as Harold's. He didn't know if that was from upbringing, being on best behavior with a foreigner, culture, that officer and a gentleman thing, or maybe he simply didn't speak in the way Harold expected a soldier to talk.

"Diego, you are the one always telling me this, but its my turn to say it more for me than you I think, but this is going to turn out alright. I am worried to the point of clinical anxiety and my own words of confidence give me a chill. But when my head is on right, I feel confident Louie is OK and that she will return, and that you will play an important role in this whole thing."

"When your head is on right? Is that another *Norteño* saying?" Peña asked, a little in shock that this near stranger was putting so much importance on him and his role in this terrible situation which had more than a fifty percent chance of turning out really bad for Harold's wife.

"Yeah, sort of a saying. Sort of rewording the truth. The truth is I have a feeling that this is going to turn out OK and that your actions will make it so. I didn't mean to say that to add to your stress, but to add to your confidence. You were sounding more depressed than is helpful. I need you, for Louie's sake, to be on top of your game. That is, to be your best self."

"So, you are a religious person?" Peña asked with some discomfort.

"I suppose you could say that. I believe in God and try to live my religion, if that is what you mean. If you mean I am fatalistic, that I simply turn over all my challenges to some higher being without any effort on my part, than you've got me wrong. I know there are many dynamics in play here. People still have their agency, their freedom to choose. But there are also principles in play that are unbendable. And then there are my feelings. I asked God to help and I believe He will. I have an obligation to those feelings. I have to have faith," Harold explained.

"Faith. Believing is great, but we have a saying here. *A dios rogando y con el maso dando*. It means something like pray to God, but keep your powder dry. I think that references older weapons where you had to load the gun powder. I had faith until my sister Carmen, perfect Carmen, just starting her life, was taken for no reason. I leave faith to the priests and my future in my hands. If we save your wife…" He paused and reconsidered his words. "I am sorry. When we save your wife, it will be because of our abilities and decisions and maybe good fortune. In that you are right, I need to be my best self to help this come out as we hope."

"Hope is a first step to faith," Harold explained with a sheepish grin. "And I believe faith is much more than just believing. Faith includes doing all that we can do. It is action, and that action includes learning principles and then trying to live those principles. That is, faith without keeping our powder dry, is dead," Harold added with conviction.

"What is going on here Harold? It is your wife who was kidnapped by evil men who care little for the lives of others, and you are trying to strengthen me. I hope your faith does not desert you if things don't come out as your feelings have suggested." As soon as he had said the words, Peña was sorry. No, not sorry, just not as hopeful or optimistic as this peculiar *Norteño*. Harold needed a dose of the real prospects for the safe return of his wife. 'That will come,' Peña thought.

Twenty minutes had gone by and Harold was surprised to realize they were at the airport. "Only a few days ago, we arrived here happy and looking forward to a quiet vacation. How things can change in an instant," Harold said more to himself than to Peña.

"Yes, it seems the most significant things in life come quickly and most unexpectedly," Peña said, now lost in his own thoughts.

"Am I to take it you are not referencing the present situation? You seem to be thinking of something else now," Harold said, again surprised at his sensitivity and worried he had alienated Peña with his religious explanations.

Peña turned and looked at Harold with hooded eyes. After a moment, he said, "My parents were killed by a thoughtless act of terrorism in the capital nearly seven years ago. I was just months from graduating from the Military Academy. They never saw their son in an officer's uniform," Peña explained. "That is why the picture after my graduation is only with my sister Carmen. My brother was in Argentina at Belgrano University. It was their greatest desire that I attend the Academy. After their death, it seemed right that I take up arms and serve my country. My uncle, my brother, and I are all that are left of the Peña family. I also have a godfather, a close friend of the family that has sort of become my father. Since the Academy, however, we have not talked much. "

"Then you better find a wife and get going," Harold interjected awkwardly.

"No, I have not had time for my personal life. These postings in the country leave little time for romance." Peña paused and pointed to the trees beside the parking lot. "Here let's wait in the shade over there."

"Just as you say that the most significant things in life come quickly and most unexpectedly, I have noted that opportunity usually comes in the most inopportune times," Harold said.

As they stood in the shade, each in their own thoughts, a voice startled them both. "More visitors my Capitan?" Harold turned and saw an old man with a broom and a large, nearly toothless smile.

"Alejandro! One of these days I am going to sneak up on you and scare the remaining teeth out of your head," Peña said, not really feeling the joviality he tried to portray.

Harold was not sure what was going on, but it was obvious the two men knew each other and enjoyed some sort of friendship. Captain Diego Peña was a very interesting person. 'How come I didn't even notice him when we arrived?' Harold asked himself silently.

They were both surprised again when a young woman turned the corner. She was taller than the old man she was obviously looking for. Peña once again noted her long black hair and large dark eyes to match. Her perfect nose and high cheekbones accented those eyes that almost seemed to sparkle. Harold thought she appeared as a living Latin Waterhouse painting. She was as startled as they were at the meeting.

"Captain, may I introduce you to my daughter Diana?" Alejandro said. "She has come to accompany me. Her mother seems to think I dawdle too much on my way home."

"I am pleased to meet you *Señorita*," Captain Peña said. "I am Captain Diego Peña." Suddenly remembering Harold was next to him, he added, "This is *Señor* Farnsworth from the United States. He does not speak Spanish, so I will introduce you to him in English."

"That is not necessary," Diana said in English with only a slight accent. "I am Diana Costa, *Señor* Farnsworth. I am pleased to meet you," she shared as she slightly curtsied. "This is my father, Alejandro Costa. May I also say that the whole town has heard about the attack on you and your wife. You both are in our prayers. Now if you will excuse us, I must get my father home before my mother comes after us both." With that, she turned, tucked her hand in the crook of her father's arm and walked away with a distant look on her face.

Peña just stood there watching the vacant spot where Alejandro and Diana had just been. He had lived in this valley for nearly a year and this was the first meeting of this girl that he had only noticed from a distance two or three times. And for her to be the daughter of the wily Alejandro, surprising him must be their principle family trait. 'I am scared to death to meet the matriarch of that outfit,' he thought to himself, but the engine noise of a turboprop plane on short final did not interrupt Peña from his thoughts.

"Yes, it seems the most significant things in life come quickly and most unexpectedly," Harold said loud enough for Peña to hear, but he didn't.

Chapter 11
Getting Acquainted

"I TELL YOU FRIEND," ALEJANDRO COSTA STATED for the fourth time that hour, "Captain Za... I mean *Major* Zarro will only bring sadness to this valley. I understand I have no proof in saying that, and considering our history with the man I may appear prejudiced in this prediction, but I am sorry to see him here again."

"It is not my place to judge the officers that command me. My interest is to take care of my soldiers, and follow orders," Sergeant Enrique Hernandez offered as a partial excuse.

"Quique, we have known each other for many years. You know I don't speak ill of any man, even Zarro, but in the next days or weeks, you will not be able to hide behind the convenience of military orders. Life has a way of forcing us to choose our values and the priority of those values. If you choose to obey all orders blindly because you are a soldier, then you have told me your values, as well as your priorities in life."

"Old man, don't try to be too wise," tempered Alejandro's wife Emma.

"That goes for old soldiers too," Consuelo added, playing on Emma's nickname for Alejandro, with orders of her own. "You need to follow my advice and retire. You have dedicated your life to the Army and all they have given you in return is a bad back and a nearly worn out uniform."

"Or is that a nearly worn out body and a bad uniform?" Alejandro joked.

"This old body could stomp the life out of you any given day," Enrique retorted.

"Not if I am faster," Alejandro snapped back.

"Choose our values we must," Emma continued, pretending not to hear their banter. That is inescapable I think, because not choosing is choosing also. And I choose to speak the truth about Zarro. He is an evil man and only interested in himself and his career. That he personally killed our oldest son does not dilute the facts or the credibility of what I am saying. In this Alejandro is right. He will bring new misery to a valley nearly filled with it. The river that refreshes this valley will need many years to wash away the blood he has spilled here already. I spit on the man. I pray for you Enrique for having to deal directly with him once again. Consuelo, you make sure he is careful. Snakes bite whoever is closest."

Enrique and Consuelo Hernandez had been friends with Alejandro and Emma Costa for many years. Together they had weathered many sector commanders. Alejandro and Enrique were not as close, but Emma and Consuelo had naturally gravitated to each other. Enrique had a full life taking care of his soldiers and his other military duties. Alejandro had his job at the airport, his wood carving, and his thoughts. Consuelo came to this valley over thirty years ago with her new husband. She was lonely and lost until the day she met Emma who also helped the medical doctor who supported the stockade clinic when the soldiers assigned to the clinic had other duties. They had been fast friends for nearly half their lives.

"Quique, may I ask your honest opinion of Captain Peña?" Alejandro asked Enrique cautiously. "I am untrusting of any officer that is sent to our valley. He seems to be a fair and honest man, but I only talk with him when he is at the airport. Perhaps in contrast to Major Zarro he appears better than he really is. How is he as a leader and as a person?"

"He is the best Sector Commander I have served with. He knows the men better after these few months than Zarro did after 18 months. He keeps his private life to himself, but he is not a heavy drinker nor has any serious vices that I am aware of. Why do you ask? Are you having problems with him?"

"No particular reason really. He met Diana today and I don't know what he thought of her, but Diana talked about him all the way home from the airport. That is very unusual for her. She hasn't as much as looked at a man since her brothers and Carlitos, uh, disappeared. Now she is curious about a man that could have easily killed her brother if he had been here six or eight months earlier."

Both couples had built a delicate but workable relationship around the issue of the Costa boys. Whether they were working with the terrorists or not neither knew exactly for sure. Where they were, or if either was alive or dead, neither knew for sure. Both understood the other's obligations, but the lack of specific facts had made the truce viable and honest. All four knew that someday the facts may make their friendship more difficult, even impossible, but for now they both suffered and benefited from not knowing.

"I don't think the Captain will have time to get to know Diana, Alejandro. With this recent kidnapping, the entire country's eyes are on our little valley and the one person under the microscope, Zarro or no Zarro, is Captain Peña.

There is another concern besides the kidnapping. What were those rebels doing near the Dam and Power Plant? Was it a coincidence, or were they looking to make trouble?"

"You don't think they were considering some sort of attack on the new facilities do you? They wouldn't stoop that low would they?" Consuelo asked. "That is the single most important improvement this valley has seen in a century."

By some sort of convention established long ago, all serious questions about the military came from Sergeant Hernandez's wife when they were together with the Costas. Even though both couples felt comfortable sharing their own feelings, there was still a wall between Sergeant Hernandez and the Costas when it came to certain military issues. Consuelo provided the natural bridge.

"Yes, and accomplished by their enemies, the military junta," Enrique reminded them and then reconsidered. "I should not talk of these things. I am sorry to bring these dark thoughts into your home."

"The dark thought would not only be the damage to the electrical project, but to the lives and livelihood of many in the valley," Alejandro said. "Not to mention the Madrugada Butterfly habitat," he added as a quiet afterthought almost to himself.

"You know about those butterflies?" Enrique interjected. "That is what got our *Norteños* in trouble. Looking for those silly butterflies. I have lived here for many years and this is the first time I have heard of these insects. Twice in as many days."

"What were they looking for?" Alejandro asked with additional interest. "Just butterflies for a collection?" He thought these were odd *Norteños*. Or perhaps all *Norteños* were odd?

"*Señor* Farnsworth was concerned that no one touch them. He had special boxes for them. Other than that I don't know what his interest was. He may have told Captain Peña. I was just the escort. The *Norteños* seem like good people. These butterflies have brought them great troubles and very possibly great tragedies," Enrique shared, still feeling some guilt for not doing more to save Louie.

"Very interesting," Alejandro said. "If you hear the *Señor* say anymore, please let me know. Those butterflies have been my secret hobby since I was a little boy."

"I'm not sure you have ever grown up," Emma said teasing, but with obvious respect, "and it seems you only have hobbies. It is time to get a job."

"These beans are wonderful, *No Importa*. Did you cook them?" Louie asked. She was surprised at the joy it brought her to call this strange old man by his standard answer to most of her questions. She was also surprised how hungry she was.

With almost perfect timing, Comandante Helicon opened the tent flap just as she was finishing her last bite. "I trust you enjoyed the standard Freedom Fighter's fare of beans and rice?" There was a friendly smile, careful conversation, but that same lustful and menacing look behind those dark eyes.

"My compliments to the cook," Louie replied.

"There was more where that came from. We must get you healthy so we can plan for your return. We are but humble fighters and I am afraid you are bringing too much attention to us at the moment."

"I would greatly appreciate that. I have no interest to be the center of attention in an internal country struggle." Louie did not allow herself to raise her hopes too far. She expected to be there for some time yet until these people figured out how to let her go without knowing their location, number of men and other items she was sure Captain Peña would love to know.

"Our struggle should be your struggle. You are from the United States, no? You were born of your own freedom fighters. You threw off the tyranny of the military in your country."

"Tyranny is the denial of complexity, Comandante. I believe there is more to this fight than I understand. I only want to be released and not cause you or your country additional complications."

"So typical of *Norteños*. No interest in helping the down-trodden, except when it meets their commercial interests. We are a poor country with little to offer, so we are forgotten. No, not forgotten. Never known. Tell me, do you know who Roque Dalton was?" Antonio asked, obviously enjoying this little debate. His men either feared him, or didn't have much interest in the philosophy of the revolution. This woman may not either, but she obviously had a mind and did not yet sufficiently fear him to guard her tongue.

"The erstwhile revolutionary that spent a good deal of his life looking for revolutionaries that would take him in," Louie answered recalling her political science lesson better than she would have guessed under these conditions. "Finally killed by the ERP revolutionaries in Argentina if I remember correctly," she added proudly.

Comandante Helicon was caught off guard. He wasn't sure if she was some sort of CIA plant or simply very unique. He had only discovered Dalton in the last year. "I am impressed, *Señora* Farnsworth. Of course my question was to point out your ignorance of his father's roots in the United States and the important role he played in the revolutions throughout Latin America. Obviously it is I who has underestimated. You are wrong, however. His death was unimportant. It is what he did while he was alive that mattered. I can excuse your ignorance of his important works in Spanish, but his poetic work in English, *Small Hours of the Night*, has guided generations of freedom fighters and along with his other works is what you ought to mention, even celebrate."

"I do not wish to be baited by my captors," Louie retorted. "You may say what you wish and I will listen quietly. You may never know what I think because I am at a disadvantage you see. Speak on if it makes you feel better," she added with as much aggression as she dared. All she wanted was to go home. It was not her mission to debate this tiger in his own den. On the other hand, she felt that she had to push back a little in order to keep them off-balance and unsure of her.

"I see your point," Antonio said. He dropped the tent flap without finishing his thought. He wasn't sure whether to have her killed as a CIA spy since that is why the Trotskyite Dalton was shot. Nobody was sure whether he was or wasn't and he didn't know whether she is or isn't. It would take weeks, if ever, to discover her body and confirm her death. By then the Dam would have been destroyed and they would be in another corner of the country and probably riding the wave of their audacity. Something kept him from giving the order, however. Was it her beauty, her courage, her intelligence? Was it his loneliness? For the first time since his wife's death, he didn't ask for her advice from the grave.

"Put her back in the cave!" Antonio ordered. "This butterfly needs her wings clipped. She is healthy and I need my tent back. We have an attack to plan."

"*Señora* Costa, the doctor is at the stockade and requests your assistance. I am to escort you if you are able to return with me," the soldier repeated just as the doctor had had made him repeat it to him.

"Of course. I can come at once. Is there a sickness among the soldiers?" Emma asked, concerned.

"It is an injured man. The rebel caught in the recent raid. The doctor wants someone to sit with this man while he attends to other duties. The soldiers with medical training are on patrol. That is really all I know."

"Very well. Let me tell my daughter. She is working in our garden. I will be back in just a moment."

Emma traveled with the soldier to the stockade. She knew the stockade well and had helped the doctor many times over the years. She had trained as a nurse in her younger years, but left her training when she married Alejandro. This was a new request, however. She was usually not allowed to get involved in operational medical issues. She questioned in her mind if it really was one of the rebels.

"Is there a danger?" she asked when she arrived at the infirmary. She also wondered why she was being trusted in this situation, knowing the local military authorities knew of her sons' probable (or even proven) connection to the rebels of the MNS. For some reason, both the horrible Zarro and the present sector commander, Captain Peña had not as much as called her or her husband in for questioning.

"He is severely wounded, so there is no physical danger," the doctor began. "Captain Peña has ordered a soldier to guard the exit as well. I am sorry to ask you to help in this matter. It seems the Army wants this man to live at least long enough so that they can speak with him. I didn't know who else to request for support. All of the soldiers that are usually assigned to this detail are out chasing the friends of that one," he explained pointing to the room holding the injured rebel. "I have several other patients in town that need my attention at the moment. I will brief Captain Pena or his lieutenant when I can."

Emma knew the doctor well and knew there were things he was also not saying, but perhaps it would be better if she left those matters unspoken. She settled in for a long and quiet evening. She was glad she had thought to bring her knitting, and a book of Neruda poetry. 'These few hours of care will also allow us to add something to our beans other than water,' she thought.

As the aircraft maneuvered to parking, Diego recovered from his earlier shock of meeting Diana. He was trying to remember the other times he had seen her in his travels outside the stockade, but he had not connected her with Alejandro, an old man of many surprises. 'No matter, I have more important issues to take care of,' he thought to himself.

"Harold, you will find Major Zarro to be professional and a great help in building a plan to reunite you with your wife," Diego said with confidence. "He is here only as additional support to my command. We should be grateful for his willingness to return to this valley." Diego found himself giving this spontaneous pep talk to Harold, but knew it was partly for himself. He did not care for Major Zarro. He also resented the decision from headquarters to send Zarro here. Did his commander not have confidence in his abilities? Did the Generals blame him for the kidnapping? Could he continue to command with Zarro looking over his shoulder? Only time would bring answers to these questions.

Major Zarro was all business. As soon as the plane was parked, even before the turbo-props had stopped spinning, he deplaned like he was a fire fighter on his way to a 5-alarm fire. He glanced around as if he expected a greeting party with a band and a key to the city. He saw Captain Peña and headed that way. His first words of greeting were, "Where is that old man who does the bags? Has he died since I left this cockroach infested valley? Good to see you Captain. Is this our victim's husband?" Of course this was all said in Spanish and Harold had no idea what they were talking about.

"Good afternoon Major. Welcome back to Mariposa," Captain Peña said. "The baggage man has left for the night. He is only contracted to work the regularly scheduled flights. Sir, may I introduce you to Mr. Harold Farnsworth. It is his wife, Louise who was kidnapped. Let me introduce you in English for his benefit." He paused. "Harold, may I present Major Zarro, previous commander of this district. He is grateful you were able to come to the airport to meet him under such difficult circumstances."

Harold put out his right hand and the Major Zarro took it without really looking at him.

"Thank you Major for your personal interest in this terrible situation," Harold said. "I am indebted to you. Captain

Peña speaks very highly of you. Anything I can do to aid your combined efforts, let me know."

Captain Peña translated Harold's statement into Spanish as accurately as he could.

"Let's go," was all Major Zarro said in reply.

An hour later the three men were at the local gentleman's club. Harold actually found the meal hopeful. Zarro asked a few questions of Harold after Harold told his story of the encounter. Captain Peña did the translating. The Major also asked Diego some questions that were left only in Spanish. Diego and Zarro seemed professional, but Harold could also tell there was no friendship between them, no matter how flowery Diego painted Major Zarro's presence. Perhaps that was part of their Army culture. They rode from the restaurant to the stockade in silence. When Harold walked into the Command Post with the two officers, things quickly changed.

"What is this civilian, a civilian from a foreign country no less, doing in the Command Post?" Zarro demanded. "He is not only not to be allowed in this room, he should have a military escort wherever he goes while in the stockade. Where have you been questioning him? Captain Peña, you are in charge here. I expect you to run a tight operation. We do not need any embarrassing comments after the fact from this man."

"Yes sir," Peña answered. He was going to explain the usefulness Harold had provided and his lack of Spanish kept him from delicate conversations, but 'yes sir' was safer and sufficient for dealing with this higher ranking officer. Diego Peña was beginning to form a clear opinion, for the first time, of Zarro. He had always before been his predecessor in command of this stockade. Diego knew it was easy, even tempting, to cast dispersions on a former commander as an excuse for the challenges one faces in the present and for that reason he purposely had not thought much about Zarro. Now he was beginning to think that the real loose cannon in the Command Post was Zarro himself, not the *gringo* victim.

"Where is he staying?" Zarro asked. "I read in one report that he is billeted here at the stockade. I was also briefed that he was a guest at the Hotel *Otra Vez*. Did you see any danger in keeping him at the hotel?"

"Sir, I brought him to the stockade for Army convenience and to have his wounds looked after. I did not want further diplomatic complications if the wounds grew worse," Peña answered, wondering who had briefed Zarro.

"Yes, I see. Very good Captain. It looks like he is doing just fine, however. I think it best he return to the hotel."

"Sir, I would like you to reconsider. I would prefer he stay at the stockade for the time being. Who knows what hour we may need him for questions, communications with the rebels, or decisions on issues concerning his wife."

"You are in command Captain. My comments are not orders. I was not given that authority. But please understand Captain, that I will make a full report of this operation to headquarters. Good night. Please wake me if there are any issues of interest or importance."

Captain Peña waited until Zarro was out of the Command Post and then walked over to Harold who was pretending to study a map on the wall, well aware of the heated conversation even if he didn't understand the content. "It would be better Harold if you didn't come into this room anymore. It would also be helpful if you stayed out of Major Zarro's way. He seems to feel additional stress from headquarters on this operation. He will see we are doing everything possible to win your wife's release. It will be fine." Again Diego found himself in the awkward position of supporting Major Zarro. "Distasteful, but required duty," Diego told himself.

"Oh, he is stressed. My goodness, we mustn't have that," Harold added in mock seriousness mixed with a growing distaste in his mouth. His eyes communicated to Diego that he understood the situation.

Chapter 12
Late Night Interruptions

"THE COMMANDANTE WOULD LIKE YOU TO RETURN TO, er, uh, your previous arrangements in the cave," the man she had named *No Importa* stammered. "I will see that you get a blanket," he added almost apologetically.

"So this is the punishment for having a frank conversation with your boss?" Louie said, more as a statement than a question.

"No. It is for your safety," *No Importa* equivocated. "There is only one entrance to the cave. This tent protects from the harshest weather, but not from the other realities of this camp. You may not feel as comfortable, but you will be more secure," he temporized.

The bravado that Louie had felt just minutes ago was quickly waning. 'The cave again. My nightmare, carved in cold stone and semi darkness,' she thought. A shiver passed through her and she jumped up to try to hide it from her captor. "Well let's go. I wouldn't want to be a burden on the overworked Commandante, with his full plate of terrorizing the countryside and all."

No Importa pursed his lips and held the ropes that wrapped and writhed her wrists as he escorted her to the cave.

"You ever read the Bible *No Importa*?" Louie asked, not really expecting a reply. "There is this passage in Psalms where King David was hiding from his enemies, I forget which, and he hid in a cave. He said something like 'refuge failed me, no man cared for my soul.' That's how I feel about your secure accommodations. Lost, where no one not only knows where I am, but here, where no one knows or cares about me."

Louie was again the center of attention as she and *No Importa* walked through the camp toward the cave. Several men shouted words her way that were not in her Spanish vocabulary. As they reached the entrance to the cave, Julio was standing there with his back to them. Several other men were not far away, snickering. Julio turned around with a wicked grin and healing scratches prevalent on his face while zipping up his pants. The side of the entrance was wet where he had just relieved himself. He added a threatening glare to her list of disgust as she passed him. He spit at her, just missing her face as she bent down to enter the cave. In his own show of bravado, *No Importa* shoved Louie into the opening with enough force that she stumbled and fell to the filthy floor. Louie wasn't hurt, but surprised at *No Importa*'s turn from protector to tormentor. She scooted to the far back wall and curled up in a ball as she listened to the laughter outside. "Just once I would like to enter this stinking cave under my own power! Why did you do that anyway *No Importa*?" Louie shouted.

"*No importa,*" *No Importa* calmly retorted.

Captain Diego Peña was still in the Command Post studying a map of the surrounding hills and mountains considering where to launch several search parties when Major Zarro returned.

"I am glad to see the *Norteño* civilian is out of our hair and that you wisely listened to my counsel," Zarro said, startling Peña. "There is no need to keep this liability on the stockade. Who knows what he will report to his Embassy people if they are allowed to travel here."

"The *Norteño* will not return to the Command Post, but he is still billeted in my quarters Major," Peña clarified.

"He is what?! He is billeted in your quarters? What in the world is billeted in your head? Certainly not your mind! I think you misunderstood the lesson at the Academy that said keep your friends close and your enemies closer. That didn't mean inviting the enemy into your personal life. So you spoke to General Cruz about this? Did you mention you have pretty much given him the key to the stockade?"

Even though it was nearly midnight, sweat was running down Zarro's face and dropping on the map in front of them. Peña noticed Zarro's eyes were bloodshot. Was that from lack of sleep, this tirade, or something else?

"Major, I thought it was the right thing to do at the time. It was either put him where I knew the environment, or billet him with someone else. You know this stockade, we have very little in the way of guest accommodations. The civilian workers overseeing the Dam project were here at the time."

"That is why he should never have been invited to stay at the stockade in the first place. Your poor judgment shocks me, Captain. This…, this arrangement, will change tomorrow. And that is an order."

"Sir, I understood you were here to help and this was still my command. Do you have orders giving you the right to usurp my authority?" Peña asked with equal force.

"I do not need orders. I am the previous commander here and I am your superior officer. I am taking command in this instance," Zarro countered.

"I will relinquish command when ordered to do so through my line of authority. Although your rank is superior, you are a staff officer and not in my chain of command. I respect your wisdom as the former commander here, but your orders hold no weight," Peña added to defer the subject for a moment, "and what do you mean this *Norteño* is the enemy? The last I looked, the enemy is the revolutionary band that kidnapped the *Norteña* woman, and it is her husband that you are treating like yesterday's garbage."

Zarro stared at Peña for a long moment, weighing the words he would share next. With a calmness that caught Peña off guard, Zarro began to explain with surprising earnestness, "Captain, what do you think the October coup that placed the military Junta in control of the country was really about? Do you think it was about rounding up the bands of thugs and idealists that roam the countryside? Couldn't we have accomplished that mission without taking over the political levers of our country?"

Attempting to match Zarro's calmness, Peña replied, "We had to temporarily take command of the political leadership in order to prosecute the war that was thrust upon us. You know the former civilian leadership was constantly changing their minds according to the winds of public perception. We were losing the fight and our soldiers were losing the vision of what this war was about—the survival of our freedoms and way of life."

Zarro offered a placating smile, void of enthusiasm or happiness. "Captain, we have a monopoly of coercive power in our country. We also enjoy a common identity that makes our brotherhood of arms a unified power. If either element breaks down, our nation breaks down. Without a monopoly of coercive power, revolution is possible. Without our common identity, our professionalism breaks down and who knows what kind of changes could occur. We are the doorway that protects our nation. No band of idealists with a few guns will change our true monopoly on power and they have only strengthened our common identity. They are not the real enemy. They are a means to an end."

It was Peña's turn to stare in silence. As he collected his thoughts and was about to counter Zarro's theories, Sergeant Hernandez knocked on the open door and entered. His hastily organized uniform reminded both men of the late hour and the inappropriateness of their conversation in such an open environment.

Sergeant Hernandez saluted and reported to Captain Peña. 'Well, at least Sergeant Hernandez knows who is in charge here,' Peña thought.

"Sir, I apologize for the interruption at this late hour, but I knew you were up and I thought you would want to know right away that the rebel soldier that we captured just died."

Glancing momentarily over at Major Zarro, Peña said, "I thought his wounds were bad, but not life threatening?"

Still only looking at Captain Peña, Hernandez explained, "It appears they were worse than we thought sir, maybe internal bleeding. The doctor has cared for him during the day and we have had an assistant watch over him last night and tonight. *Señora* Costa was with him when he took his last breath. The doctor arrived just minutes ago and confirmed the death. The doctor would like to know if you require an autopsy to confirm the exact cause of death."

"Costa? Why do I know the name Costa?" Zarro questioned aloud. "There is no need to waste time on exactly how this enemy of the state died."

This last comment caused Peña to grimace, but he quickly covered the expression with a neutral countenance that came with years of military training. Sergeant Hernandez continued to look at and wait for an answer from his commander, but asked with his eyes if this was his answer. "Yes, very well Sergeant. Do you know if the rebel ever regained consciousness?" Peña asked.

"I checked with the doctor several times earlier today. The rebel never regained consciousness. He mumbled unintelligently off and on, but those in attendance could not make sense of his words. I don't know if he regained consciousness before death. I think *Señora* Costa would have mentioned something if he had."

Sergeant Hernandez read frustration and disappointment on Captain Diego Peña's face. Peña knew it and let the sergeant assume it was only from the passing of their only link to the rebel group. "Get some sleep Sergeant. It's late for all of us and there is little we can do to coax anything out of the dead. Major, if it is alright with you, I will turn in for the night and we can resume our discussion in the morning."

"As you wish Captain. You are in command," Major Zarro stated.

Sergeant Hernandez waited for the officers to leave the Command Post before turning out the lights and securing the door. He wondered what they had been talking about and also when he would be able to get Captain Peña alone to share what Emma Costa told him about the last words from the rebel. He also wondered why his intuition had told him to quibble for the first time ever to a superior officer.

"We have been friends with the Costa's and you have been the closest of friends with Emma for many years, no?" Sergeant Enrique Hernandez said out loud to his wife after apologizing for his late night return from the post and waking his wife with his undressing.

"You know as well as I do how long we have known the Costa's. About twenty years more or less. Is this just a late night quiz, or is this to get my mind off of how noisily you get undressed?" Consuelo asked.

"Ah, Consuelo, if that were my only imperfection."

"It is the only one that is bothering me at this moment. That and the fact that something is bothering you and it appears to have something to do with the Costa's and you are tap dancing around the issue, Quique. You are quite cute tap dancing in your underwear, however," Consuelo added, trying to lighten her husband's mood.

Knowing that his wife was joking, but still feeling the love behind the comments, he smiled at her and felt whole again for the first time in several hours. He did his best pirouette and fell to the bed. "You are my prima ballerina *Señora* Hernandez," and he gave her a soft and lingering kiss. He forgot about the troubling news Emma Costa had shared with him. He knew he would remember it in the morning.

On the other side of town, but not far from the Hernandez home, Emma Costa also woke up her spouse as she tried to quietly enter her home.

"I thought you were to stay at the post tonight Emma. Did they find someone else to take your place?" Alejandro asked as he switched on the small room's only light.

Looking more exhausted than if she would have stayed up all night, she only squeezed Alejandro's arm as she passed him, heading for the tiny kitchen. Emma was not sure what if anything she should say to her husband. The less he knew, perhaps, the better. On the other hand, she wasn't sure she could carry this burden alone. "The patient died tonight, old man. Another mother somewhere is without her son and without the sure knowledge that he is alive or dead."

"And you carry the burden of knowing about another's son, while not knowing for sure about your own sons," Alejandro added.

Returning to the doorway where Alejandro stood with his back to her, Emma wrapped her arms around her husband and said, "That is no longer the case Alejandro. Gustavo is dead." She felt the muscles in Alejandro's back stiffen and his breathing stop. She held him, not allowing him to move and using him as her support for fear she might crumble in hearing the words for the first time from her own lips.

"Where did you hear this? Did someone at the post finally share the news with you as some cruel form of compensation for helping watch that patient?" Alejandro asked, trying to talk tough to keep from crying.

"It was the patient himself who told me. He began talking clearly during what would be his last hour alive. He told me

many things. I was at his side when he regained consciousness and I became his confessor. In our conversation I told
him my name and he said he knew Gustavo and assumed I
knew he was dead. He began talking in the past tense about
the adventures they had shared and what a great example
of a true revolutionary Gustavo was. He died nearly a year
ago Alejandro. His body lies in an unmarked grave far to
the north in an unnamed valley near the border," Emma
shared in short bursts between sobs she tried to overcome.

They stood in silence for some time, Emma surviving on
short, nearly strangled breathing; Alejandro on long, deep
breaths that took in all the pain, frustration, and helplessness he felt for himself and his family, and letting out each
breath as a sibilation of hope. Long ago Alejandro had
learned to borrow from the future when he was faced with a
present situation where his understanding and strength were
not equal to the task. He wondered if the future held the
understanding he needed this time. "It is good that we know.
That is a burden removed. I only wish I could make sense
of it all—that I could be mad at somebody—that I could
protect Paco and Diana from the pains of life. Isn't that a
father's obligation to his children?" Alejandro murmured.

Emma released her grip on Alejandro's body and turned
him to look at her. Looking directly up into his eyes she said,
"You are the most amazing of fathers. You have taught your
children integrity, to value principles and to be teachable.
There is no one in this entire valley less encumbered with
evils of pride than you. Gustavo lived life as it came. His
fate was to die living."

"No Emma, it wasn't fate. It wasn't bad luck," Alejandro
corrected.

"Then what was it? Perhaps there is someone to blame besides just us. Perhaps there is a target for our grief besides an unmarked grave in an unnamed valley."

Alejandro gently grasped Emma's hand as they walked to their tattered couch and sat down together. He said, "The lesson I am afraid I failed to teach Gustavo was, values guide people's behavior, but principles ultimately determine the consequences of our actions. We have the requirement to choose, but we do not have the luxury to select the outcome. Sooner or later, principles will determine that outcome. Choosing which principles to serve is where I have failed. Gustavo served courage, not consideration—emotion, not empathy—machismo, not meekness."

It was then she told Alejandro the reason Gustavo died and by whose hands. They sat in silence for some time. Alejandro wondered if Emma had drifted to sleep. Then Emma quietly asked, "Old man, where do you find such wisdom? I read my poems of great thinkers from many places and cultures. I find a measure of understanding there. You read little, yet you possess more wisdom than all these poets and famous thinkers. What is the source? What would I do without your love and the support you think you have failed to provide?"

"Sometimes I think your poets shake the tree until there is no fruit and then complain the tree is fruitless, so they have something to write about," Alejandro answered. He knew his emotions were getting the better of him, but he continued. "Nature tells us that silence and space are freedoms that should only be sacrificed when filled with meaning. Most of what people spout is creative noise, not meaning. No, that isn't exactly right. Most of the time it isn't even creative. It is just noise. We get so used to the noise that we don't even recognize it for what it is. The answers are there, but they are sometimes hard to see, like the Madrugada Butterfly. The answers are there, but we need to know how to look, not just where."

Following Alejandro's admonition, they continued to sit in silence trying to make sense of their lives and the tragic death of their oldest child who had so much to live for. Diana found her parents still sitting on the couch, fast asleep in each other's arms the next morning when she got up to take care of her morning chores.

Peña and Zarro parted company shortly after leaving the Command Post. Although there was a vacant officer's room on the post with the bureaucrats gone, perhaps to make a point Zarro checked out a jeep and drove to town, explaining that he would be staying at the *Otra Vez*. Peña let the comment pass and walked to his quarters. His mind was still on the crazy conversation he and Major Zarro had started, but not finished.

"I hope you don't mind, I stayed up in case you had any news or might need my help," Harold stated from a chair at the small table in the living room that doubled as the dining room off the small kitchenette.

Startled out of his thoughts, Peña said, "Oh, thanks for staying up. No good news, but some news. The rebel we captured died this evening. I had hoped we could collect some useful information from him."

"Sorry to startle you. And I am sorry for that person's death. He was vicious in his attack, but I suppose he was somebody's son," Harold said.

"I'm not used to entering my quarters and have some-body greet me. Strange, you are the second person tonight that downplayed this rebel as something less than an enemy of the state. His death may be tragic to someone, but make no mistake, he would have gladly cut your throat if he had the chance." As soon as Peña said that, he felt bad. "Oh, I am sorry, that was a thoughtless thing to say. I am sure your wife is fine. These people are vicious as you say, but they are not dumb. They know they do not need to add the wrath of the United States government to the combative enemies of their little rebellion."

"Yes, well let's hope so. Thank you for trying to sound convincing. I wanted to do some research on the internet about this little rebellion as you put it, but there doesn't seem to be a wireless connection here."

"No, the *Otra Vez* has the only WiFi connection in the entire valley. The stockade doesn't even have a reliable cel-lular connection. My office has one of the only hard-wired connections, along with the one at the Command Post. We are a humble outpost in a humble army in a humble country," Peña explained with no defenses up. "I wish I had other news to give you, but starting tomorrow I will be sending out three additional search and rescue squads to the probable areas the rebels are based. We may know something by tomorrow evening. As far as the revolution goes, it is pretty simple. As I said we are a humble coun-try. Our civilian government attempted to bring us into the modern age which as you can imagine is quite costly. The rich got richer, the poor didn't get any poorer, but the relative deprivation became more visible. Some anarchists from several universities and a few foreigners fomented mostly peasants to revolt. The civil authorities didn't want to disrupt the foreign investment that was fueling our entry into the modern age, like the Elazar Dam and hydro-electric power plant in this valley. Anyway, they went back and forth from a firm stance to appeasement to a firm stance and the MNS rebel force only grew in numbers and credibility. The military had to step in and take control, which we did a few years ago. We had been fighting the MNS for over a year prior to the *golpe de estado*, the coup you would say, no? Within months we had most of the pockets of revolution shut down. There are still a few bands of MNS holding up, licking their wounds. My personal hope was that they would give up their arms and press to join the political process. I am guessing the group that you and your wife unfortunately met is run by a delusional ex college professor who calls himself Comandante Helicon. As his name would suggest, he has a flare for the dramatic, but he's not much of a leader. We really didn't think he would be a threat to anyone in this valley. His popularity is already waning. More attacks that effect locals and his presence would be leaked to us and he would, how do you say, close up shop."

"It is none of my business, but how would this group enter the political process with the military in charge of the government?" Harold asked.

"You are right, it is none of your business, Harold. Let us just leave this point with the fact that politics had to take a second seat in order to save the country. The only institution that could save the country was the military. It was our obligation to act."

"Obligation? Interesting. We are having some of the same conversations in the U.S., whether it is justified to sacrifice social freedoms in order to combat terrorism. The conversation even runs counter to our Founding Fathers' ideals, but maybe this is a new day and we will have to deal with it differently. I don't know… Why is this comandante called Helicon?"

"He calls himself Commdante Helicon, but his real name is something like Martín, Antonio Martín I think. Helicon is the name of a butterfly found in various pockets of our country I think. I heard that it also has some roots in Greek mythology. To be honest, I don't know why he chose this name."

"Interesting. Yes, it comes from a butterfly name. Don't you think understanding the reason for using this name might provide some clues to how he operates and what makes him tick?" Harold asked.

Peña got up and struggled to hold his temper. The previous conversation with Zarro was still fanning flames of frustration. Now an outsider questioning his judgment at this late hour was almost too much. "I think it is time for bed Harold. Several times during this conversation I have been tempted to lose my temper. Our political dealings are our own business. I am sorry you are tied up in them, but simply said, you are an outsider and what and how we do things is our stewardship, not yours. How we conduct our operations is also not up to you or your suggestions. I had forgotten you are a butterfly expert, but that doesn't make us butterflies nor you an expert on our country, or this valley." Exhausted, Peña began walking toward his bedroom. "Good night" he added, to put a period on all the conversations of this evening.

"Here is your blanket *Señora*," *No Importa* said as he entered the small cave Louie was shivering in. It was amazing that as soon as the sun went down, although the jungle mountain camp stayed fairly warm, the cave became uncomfortably cold. "I have also brought you some food, and, uh, this bucket for necessary things." He turned and left, but returned before Louie even moved toward the blanket. "Here also is a candle and some matches. I trust you won't try to burn yourself. You can also feel safe. The guards posted tonight are good and honorable men, with families of their own." As *No Importa* was explaining this, one of the guards called to him in Spanish, telling him, "Don't forget to tell our *Norteña* guest that we don't do room service. If she uses the bucket, she has to carry it. We will keep her safe, but her stink is her problem." *No Importa* began to explain this procedure to Louie and didn't realize he was telling her in Spanish. "If you use the bucket, the guards will escort you to empty it."

Louie, without processing the language shift, since she just also heard it from the guard, said in English, "OK, I got it." As she said this, she realized her error. *No Importa* at first did not appear to register her mistake. After he turned to leave, he turned back, and stared at her. Louie thought her charade was uncovered. *No Importa* then reached into his pocket and gave her a small slip of paper. He turned and left.

Louie just sat there and held her breath, waiting for someone to return, assuming *No Importa* would report to the Comandante that she understood Spanish. Her overheard conversations in the camp would increase her liability if they knew, even tilt the balance to killing her. After a few minutes and forcing herself to breath again, Louie grasped at the hope that *No Importa* hadn't realized he had spoken in Spanish to her. Louie started to reach for the blanket and realized she still held the piece of paper in her hand. She opened it and it read in English, "King David's cave, Psalms 142:4, *I looked on my right hand, and beheld, but there was no man that would know me: refuge failed me; no man cared for my soul.*" Below that another verse was annotated. It read, "*The centurion's servant, Luke 7:6, And Jesus went with them. And when he was not far from the house, the man sent friends to him, saying, Lord, do not give yourself trouble: for I am <u>NO IMPORTA</u> enough for you to come into my house.*" The "No Importa" was capitalized and underlined.

"I thought I named him *No Importa*? Who is this guy? And what is he doing in this camp full of thugs and sickos?" Louie wondered out loud. As she wrapped herself in the blanket and eyeing the plate of cold beans and rice, she thought silently, 'and did he notice he spoke in Spanish and I answered? I have got to get out of here. I can't wait for rescuers which may never come.' She did not allow herself to wonder whether Harold was still alive or not. Louie shivered even though the blanket did feel good.

Chapter 13
Near Escapes

"Mamá, I haven't seen papá this morning; well not since I woke you both up on the couch," Diana Costa said as she entered the house after working in the garden. "He asked me last night after you left for the post to run some errands for him. Oh, and I hope you don't have too many more nights at the post, you look exhausted,"

"What does that old man have you doing today? Surely you have better things to do than his work for him." Emma had decided not to tell Diana about the sad news of Gustavos's confirmed death. She wanted to prepare herself, make sure the time was right, and also figure out what the rest of what she had learned last night really meant. She needed to tell Diana about Gustavo today, sometime, though.

"It is no problem, really. He asked me to drop off this carving of the angel and the butterfly he did last year to Quique Hernandez at the stockade to pass on to the *Norte Americano*. He must be worried sick over his wife's kidnapping. And on their honeymoon I hear. Just like papá to think of others' trials instead of his own. I will bring you some flowers home if I get a chance to go by the river."

"Your papá thinks he has no trials. He is a good man, but a little too quick to think of others when he needs to think of himself now and then. Well, on with you, but you be careful by the river and at the stockade too. Quique is a good man, but some of those soldiers are pretty rough cut if you ask me." Emma didn't like for Diana to go near the Army, or the airport. She wasn't sure why. Maybe it was a fear that somehow those were points of departure and a little foreign. She had never understood the military with their strict way of life, rigid and harsh discipline, and their secrecy—no it wasn't secrecy, it was more life 'apartness' from the rest of society. It was like they maintained a distance because they knew things others didn't and that made them special. They wanted to share what they knew, so in that way it wasn't a secret, but they only wanted to share it on their terms. On the other hand, both the airport and the military were the main sources of money for their struggling family, so she acquiesced to their presence and the necessity to send Diana there when required.

"Everyone at the stockade is on alert, so I am sure it is the safest place to be in the valley right now. And as for the soldiers there, they don't even know I exist. I am years older than most of them," Diana explained.

"A few years older than the conscripts, true. I heard from your father you met Captain Peña, the day the *Norteños* arrived. I understand he is single," Emma replied.

"The Captain? There is another one who doesn't know I exist," Diana said. "With all that is going on, even if he did, he wouldn't have time for even a hello. I am also sure he probably has a sweetheart waiting for him in the capital. This backwater is not where officers look for wives."

"Sure, probably? What do those words mean? And talk of looking for a wife? I just mentioned he was single and to watch out. So watch out!" Emma scolded.

"I will be back in a few hours, in time to help with the laundry," Diana said as she ran out the door before her mother could notice the blush that had surprisingly blossomed in her cheeks.

"Good morning *Señora*," *No Importa* said gently as he stood at the cave entrance preparing to enter. "I hope your night went well. I am here to escort you if you need to empty the bucket."

Louie had slept horribly. At first the blanket offered some comfort, but it proved not to be enough protection from the cold dampness of the cave and no padding from sleeping on the dirt floor. A soldier had tossed in an old cot in the middle of the night. The cot had broken as soon as she tried to lie on it. Just a few more days of this and she was sure she would either toughen up enough to join the Navy SEALs, or she would completely fall apart.

She had finally used the bucket early that morning. She told herself that people used chamber pots throughout history, but it felt dirty and almost violating in the unprotected cave. She remembered reading something about chamber pots in Britain during World War One with the face of the Kaiser on the inside allowing the user an additional satisfaction. Before using the bucket, she drew a stick figure in the bottom that represented these rebels, maybe the Comandante himself. It gave her an instant of control. "The efficacy of defecacy," she had laughingly quipped.

The humor of the situation lasted only a moment. This was not like her to be so coarse, but then, "I have never been kidnapped by revolutionaries in a foreign country before either," she reminded herself. "Still, it is in the hard times that our true character shines through and I will not let these people drag me down to their level. What was it Frankl said? The last of freedoms was choosing one's attitude. Something like that. It always sounded so doable—even if I really never practiced it even in the easy times, but I never realized it would take so much energy. What I wouldn't give for a mattress to lie on right now. Then maybe I could work on my attitude. The latitude of attitude…, OK, enough of stupid rhymes."

"OK *No Importa*, let's get this day started," was all the attitude Louie could muster as she tried to stand up. She grabbed the bucket and was almost overcome with exhaustion, even though her day was just beginning.

"Harold! Time to rise! We will need to be to the chow hall by seven this morning if you want some breakfast. The food line is shut down by seven-thirty," Diego Peña explained from the other side of the door as Harold turned over in bed trying to figure out where he was. "It is six-thirty. You can shower and get dressed. I am going to run by my office and will be back in thirty minutes to pick you up. Are you awake?"

"Yes, I am awake. Sorry I slept in," Harold replied, trying to sound wide awake but knowing his thick tongue made him sound anything but fully conscious. He had been dreaming about butterflies. 'Of all stupid things to have in my head!' he thought. 'Louie is in the clutches of rebel terrorists, injured, maybe worse, and I am dreaming about stinking butterflies!'

Harold pulled himself out of bed and felt his head throb. Diego had told him last night that he wasn't drinking enough liquid. Harold had declined the offer of the glass from the faucet, fearing his constitution wouldn't handle the local water, plus he didn't want to have to get up in the middle of the night and try to find the bathroom. He hoped to get some bottled water to keep with him today and start hydrating himself better. "I need to stay healthy," Harold told himself out loud.

"What's that?" Diego asked from the living room. "Is everything OK?"

Harold hadn't realized Diego was still in his quarters. "Just talking to myself. Sorry."

"Well I am off then. See you in half an hour," Diego yelled and Harold heard the door close.

"How can life feel so mundane?" Harold almost yelled. He wanted to break something, unleash his emotions— something more than just small talk and sleeping in like he had no cares in the world. "This has got to change!" He exclaimed and got up reluctantly. He went about his morning chores of showering, shaving, brushing his teeth, using the bathroom, and getting dressed in clean clothes, knowing all along that Louie probably did not get to do any of those things. Then he knelt in prayer, also knowing that wherever Louie was, whatever her situation, at least they could share this part of their day. It brought some comfort, but he still felt like he wasn't doing enough on his part to change the situation. "It is by grace we are saved, after all we can do," Harold uttered more to himself than to God.

Exactly thirty minutes after Captain Diego Peña had left his quarters he opened the door and found Harold sitting on the couch dressed and ready to go. Diego had stopped by his office to check message traffic. He had avoided the

Command Post, thus avoiding Major Zarro. There was no news, from the early search squads or from General Cruz.

"Let's get something to eat Harold. You look like you could use something to do," Peña said.

"Captain, I could use something more than the comforts of a soft bed and food. I am going crazy being comfortable. I assume there is no news, so what are we going to do to make some news? I am ready to accompany a search team, …anything."

"Let's get some food first. It will be a long day," was Peña's only reply.

It was a short walk to the chow hall. "This isn't the Hotel *Otra Vez*, but the breakfast is pretty good. It is the soldier's favorite meal. I suggest the steak and eggs," Peña said as they entered the small cafeteria-like room.

"Two hundred soldiers eat in here?" Harold asked. "It doesn't look like it could hold more than a hundred."

"The soldiers eat in three shifts, twenty minutes each. Usually we would be forming up for the orders of the day by seven-thirty, but with several squads out and three more going out this morning, I suspended the morning formation. Let's eat and then see the last two search squads off."

They ate pretty much in silence. Diego ate well. Harold choked down his food.

"There are not many places for you to go on the fort. We do not have a library as some larger posts have. As I explained when we met, there is no officers club, but I have arranged for the NCO mess to be opened up for you. There are some books and magazines in the lounge area. There is a Television there. We don't have any channels here, but there is a video tape player with a small selection of movies," Peña explained.

"I don't want movies. I don't want books. I don't want to sit around in an empty room."

"Your only other option is to return to the Hotel *Otra Vez*. The plus is they have the internet in case you want to contact anyone back in the United States."

"I suppose I should talk with Louie's parents. I had hoped to have something to tell them, but it has been two days and I don't want them to hear about this from someone else. Yes, if you could take me back to the hotel that would be helpful. Would it be better if I stay there at night as well?"

"For now you can leave what you brought with you to the stockade at my quarters. Let me go by the Command Post and then I will take you to the hotel. You can wait outside for just a few minutes if that is OK?"

"Whatever works." Harold was already beginning to compose what he would say to his in-laws and his parents.

Captain Diego Peña entered the Command Post and did not see Major Zarro as he had expected. He confirmed that the last three search squads were getting ready to leave and which sectors they were going to cover. "Sergeant Hernandez, I will be taking our *Norte Americano* back to the hotel in town. He is going to talk with his family and let them know about his wife, and his safety. I have nothing for him to do here and frankly with the Major around it would be best if he were off the post."

"Very well my Captain. Major Zarro was in earlier this morning and then disappeared. I assumed he was with you. I will let him know you will return soon if he reappears before you get back." There were unspoken words relayed between them. Neither cared for nor trusted Major Zarro fully. The message was clear: 'I will be back soon—watch him.' 'I will keep my eye on him Captain, but you know there is very little I can do to stop him at anything he wishes to do.'

As Captain Diego Peña stepped out of the Command Post, he almost crashed into Major Zarro. "Captain, nice of you to finally show up. I trust you had a nice long sleep this morning," Zarro said.

"Good morning Major. I am taking *Señor* Farnsworth back to the hotel this morning. I will return soon."

"Very good. I am glad you are taking my advice."

"He has nothing to do here and at least he has the internet at the hotel so he can contact his family and his wife's family."

"I do not think that is wise Captain."

"Not wise to take your advice Major?" Peña asked and was immediately sorry he had said that.

"Don't play with me Captain. It is not wise to have him talk with his family. We don't know what political ramifications that might cause. This is much bigger than a simple kidnapping. This is an international incident between our country and the irritating elephant in our living room—the United States. You should confirm what will be said and even get approval from headquarters before contact is made."

Peña knew that Zarro did not care in the least about the personal issues, but he had a point. "I have thought of that Major," Peña said, even though he hadn't fully thought this through. "Who knows what channels of communication the rebels have either. I wouldn't want any useful information presented to anyone that might leak to the news."

"Good thinking Captain. Could I have a word with him before you take him to town?"

"Certainly Major. I am surprised you didn't see him when you came in. He is right outside."

Captain Peña and Major Zarro found Harold around the corner of the Command Post speaking with, 'what was her name? Alejandro's captivating daughter...?'

"Harold, *Señorita*," Peña said. He wanted to look at the young lady, but he looked at Harold. Major Zarro would like a word with you before I take you into town. *Señorita*, Diana isn't it? Would you excuse us for a moment?"

Diana said nothing. Peña noticed she had a carving in her hands. He guided Harold over to Major Zarro. He would have liked to have said a few more words to Diana, but knew he was needed to translate.

"Good morning Mr. Farnsworth. I trust you had a pleasant night's rest and that the Captain's hospitality, the Army's hospitality has supported you in this very difficult time," Major Zarro said in a very courteous tone. He waited for Diego to translate.

"Thank you Major. I slept better than I wanted to," Harold answered cautiously.

"I understand you will be speaking with your family today. You know it is within our power to keep you from doing so as this is a very sensitive operation. Of course we are an open society, not a police state. I wanted to speak with you about what you should and shouldn't say in your conversations."

As Peña was translating, Harold seemed to feel Zarro's eyes boring into his skull. He did not like this person and could feel the lack of authenticity in his words even though he didn't speak the language—both Spanish and the smug intonation of a soldier used to getting his way.

"Of course our primary interest is keeping our operations out of the news in the interest of the safety of his wife. You could say something to the effect of 'we have done everything possible to rescue your wife and our profession-alism has been outstanding.' The rebels, or terrorists if you prefer, were ruthless and uncaring for your safety or that of your wife. You may also express your gratefulness for our hospitality and support. Do not mention any specifics, times, places, or people by name. Is this clear?" Major Zarro finished with a thin false smile.

Peña did his best to translate this into palatable words to Harold. Harold understood both messages being translated. "Make us look good, make the rebels look bad, and above all cast a good light on the Army and their governance of this country. Oh yeah, and we care about your wife, whatever her name is." Harold just nodded.

Major Zarro, satisfied, turned and re-entered the Command Post. Peña, rubbed his hands unconsciously on his pants and turned to Harold. "Let's get you back to the hotel."

"Captain, I was just speaking with this young lady. Could I have a minute?" Harold said with formality.

"Yes, of course. It was rude of me to interrupt, but I thought it best to complete Major Zarro's mission as quickly as possible." Diego Peña turned to Diana Costa who was just a few steps away. He was surprised Major Zarro had not considered her a security leak and had talked so openly with her so close by.

"Good morning Captain," Diana said as Harold and Diego approached her. "I was sent on an errand this morn-ing by my father to give our North American friend this wood carving. I was going to leave it with someone, but I saw Mr. Farnsworth and decided to give it to him in person. I apologize for interrupting." Diana's English was amazing. It wasn't as polished as Diego's, but it was far beyond his expectations from this assumedly uneducated provincial woman.

"It is very thoughtful of your father to think of me," Harold said. "I don't even know him. In fact I am overwhelmed with his kindness. Would it be possible for me to thank him in person?"

"He is a simple man, Mr. Farnsworth, and a little shy around strangers. I will see what I can do," Diana said. She turned to Diego, "Captain, I apologize again. I will be on my way."

"Excuse me," Diego said, completely forgetting Major Zarro and the rebels and the kidnapping. "Are we talking about Alejandro the cat? I have never seen him act shy."

"Alejandro the cat?" Diana asked, finally looking directly at Diego. It was as if every synapse in Diego's body activated at once, rendering him completely immobile. He was sinking into her dark eyes, while noticing every shape, form and pore of her face. He had really never thought about noses in his life, but he was fast becoming an expert of hers'. Just below her perfect nose were two lips, that were moving, saying something, apparently to him?

"Uh, um, just a nickname I have given him," Diego explained. "He is always sneaking up on me. I have told him he only has a few of his nine lives left. I don't mean it to sound negative."

They had been talking in Spanish and it was Diana who realized they were leaving Harold completely out of their conversation. She turned to Harold, "I am sorry Mr. Farnsworth. It seems my father and Captain Peña have a relationship of which I was unaware," Diana said with a smile that obviously had nothing to do with him. "I must get back home. I have taken too much of your time when you have so much more of importance on your mind than a simple woodcarving by a good but simple man." Diana turned to go.

Harold, not oblivious to what had just been happening, suggested, "Diego, would it be OK, I mean with an army vehicle, to give Diana a lift to her home on the way to the hotel?"

"I am here to serve this people and I can think of no better use of our vehicle. That is if you wouldn't mind riding with us *Señorita* Costa?" Diego said.

"Captain, please call me Diana as I have asked my new friend Mr. Farnsworth to do. Since I will be chaperoned, I accept."

"Please call me Diego;" Diego said simultaneously with Harold who said, "Please call me Harold." Their motivations, however, were completely different. One was being friendly, the other was smitten.

Harold got into the back seat of the Army Jeep, forcing Diana to ride up front with Diego. As Diana stepped into the passenger seat, Diego could not help but noticed her smooth legs and thin ankles. He ground the starter, forgetting to let go of the ignition key. No one spoke during the short drive except for Diana to give some simple directions to her humble home. Diego was secretly elated that he now knew where Diana lived. Diana offered her hand to shake as a thank you for the ride. Diego grasped it and only with a soldier's strength did he let it go again.

Harold hopped into the front seat and they were at the Hotel in less than five minutes. In those five minutes, Harold forgot his mild amusement of watching the sparks fly between Diego and Diana and was once more focused on Louie and her terrible situation.

Louie had emptied her bucket and tried to rinse it in the stream, but it was still disgusting and smelled, as she was sure she did. It also collected flies as they walked back into the camp. So much for ever wanting to live in the days of Jane Austin. 'Give me modern facilities. I can live without Mr. Darcy,' Louie thought to herself as she prepared for what she hoped to be her last day in captivity.

"Ah, good morning *Señora* Farnsworth. Another night with the MNS freedom fighters. Are you ready to join our movement?" Antonio asked Louie as she passed the Comandante's tent.

"Does membership come with a mattress and indoor plumbing?" Louie asked, not sure she should banter with this snake.

"So we are in good spirits! The cave suits you. I am glad," Antonio said. "No, I am afraid the lot of the freedom fighter is hard and alas, no place for a genteel woman. I can offer you breakfast in an actual chair, however. Please, sit."

Louie entered the open tent and sat in the vacant seat. Beans and rice stared at her from the table. A tin plate that didn't look all that clean was placed in front of her. She began to serve herself when Antonio entered the tent and said, "Please let me do that." He stood next to Louie and as Louie looked up to say thank you she caught him glancing at her open collar and her slightly reveled cleavage. She instinctively placed her hand on her shirt and turned away, not bothering to say thank you.

Antonio was flustered and walked to the other side of the small table and ladled the beans and rice onto the plate.

"I apologize for my un-gentlemanly conduct. It is so rare to have a beautiful young lady in our midst."

"To paraphrase Aristotle, 'bad men are full of repentance, when they are caught,'" Louie said.

As quick as a viper, Antonio sprang to his feet and slapped Louie, nearly causing her to fall from her chair. "Do not make judgment of your captors. It is only because of me that you have not been turned over to the less gentlemanly members of our group and that in fact you are still alive! Do not lecture me on manners and proper etiquette on the battlefield." Antonio's eyes smoldered as he dared her to strike back.

Louie stared at her plate and picked up her fork and began to eat, not wanting to provoke Antonio further.

"You smug, arrogant Norte Americana," Antonio began with obvious anger. "You know so much, but really know nothing at all. You think there is so much to be proud of, when in reality all you have is your pride—pride that has eroded the very soul of your nation. You have so many things—your soft mattresses and bathrooms that are bigger than most houses in our humble country. The day will come when we will watch your house of cards fall, and great will be the fall. It will take years, even decades for all to realize you have fallen, but then the wolves will be at your door and you will not be able to hold them back." Antonio's anger was mostly spent but he did not sit down. He continued to glower over her as she ate.

When she finished her food, Antonio asked, "So you may feel intimidated to answer me, but I promise I will not strike back. I want your honest opinion of what I have said. I believe the United States has lost its soul. What is your reply?"

"You are my captor and hold my life in your hands. Why should I reply? Sooner or later I will pay the price and whatever I think is of no matter anyway," Louie answered.

"It is not often, well never really, that I have an educated U.S. citizen in my company. Despite what you think, I am a good person and I fight for freedom from tyranny that our revolution will bring injustice to the sword and be done with it. The U.S., once a shining example of freedom, has sold its place as mentor in the name of security and control of its people. This is what I truly believe. Please, tell me what I have missed in my assessment."

Louie looked at this man she detested, still unsure what to say. Offer him some pabulum and be done with it—risking his wrath for placating, or tell him what she really thought? Her heart told her to be bold. "One of the geniuses of the United States has been getting the rules right so they come closest to mirroring true principles, while keeping unintended consequences at a minimum. To ensure enduring and constantly improving democracy, we must understand and work with, not against true principles. That is, we must get our values and prioritization of those values right. Values determine actions and principles determine outcomes. We cannot legislate morality and ethical living although some in our Congress believe we can. Your communist brothers believe you can. As the saying goes, "when mores are sufficient, laws are unnecessary. When mores are insufficient, laws are unenforceable." Our mores—our values, norms and expressive symbols are what make us one. We must value and nurture a life of principles more than a life of things. In this you come close to the truth—we have become a consumer society where we buy, use, store, sell, dump, and buy new things. I believe we will find our way back to who we really are." Louie waited for an attack or rebuttal, but Antonio was silent. She waited.

"Do the people of your country follow because they are right, or are they right because they choose to follow?" Antonio finally asked.

"I am not sure what you mean," Louie said, fearing this was some sort of trap in their war of words.

"Is the United States really a country of a government by the people for the people? Or is the United States mostly a sham whose true genius is creating a myth that keeps the masses happy as long as they follow your rules?"

"There are always the governed and the government, no matter the system. I think what Abraham Lincoln was trying to do when he said those words was to compare the North to the more aristocratic and slave holding South," Louie offered.

"Are not there different kinds of slaves and more subtle forms of aristocracy? In our country we have a history of *latifundio*, how do you say, peasants and subsistence farmers oppressed by a minority of agricultural and industrial elites. These elites are kept safely in their place by a military that holds the monopoly of coercive power. Is not our revolution a form of government by the people and for the people?" Antonio asked.

"I do not know enough about your country to make a judgment," Louie said. "Perhaps nobody outside of any country can be so fully informed as to pass judgment on what is right or wrong. That has been another blemish of our foreign policy I think."

"Only a blemish, or more of a pariah for the rest of the world? But no matter, I accept your humble thought. A simpler question: Is it not our obligation as a people to fight injustice?"

"Again I plead ignorance," Louie said

"Pleading ignorance, or avoiding an answer for fear it will cost you your life, or at least a quick trip back to your cave?" Antonio bated.

"Probably both," Louie answered.

"I do admire your honesty. So follow through with courage and answer my question."

"From the little I know it seems you are more focused on eliminating the effects of injustice than you are the causes of injustice," Louie replied. "Speaking about the U.S., we need to be a little less concerned about the effects of poverty, injustice, and our other ills, and more concerned about their causes. We can't legislate our way out of our ills—which typically attack the effects. You cannot rebel against the effects of poverty. Take the slums out of the people and the people will take themselves out of the slums."

"A worn out phrase. I am sorry for you," Antonio said. "No one will follow the long-term promise when they need a meal in the very short-term. We will destroy the slums as well as the fine neighborhoods—both of which the downtrodden hate. We will destroy it all, and from those ashes will rise a new people and a new country. We will provide economic as well as physical security for all equally."

"My grandmother used to say that all the world needed to do was hold and love all the little babies, so they will grow to know how to love and nurture others. Nothing more need be done," Louie offered.

"Ah, the wisdom of grandmothers. The problem with grandmothers is, their life has mostly passed and their flames of passion and indignation for injustice burn low or the fire has already gone out. It is for the young mother trying to keep her baby alive that I fight for."

"You didn't know my grandmother," Louie said, "nor her faith in an active God that teaches peace and charity—that is, seeing other people as He sees them. The passion of the young mother is a wondrous thing, but she also needs wisdom. Rushing to a receding future your revolution seems to offer, or harkening to an ideal that leaves the God piece out of the equation will lead to an end justifying any means to get there, and when you arrive, it will be the dogs that you created, at your doorstep that you will not be able to command."

"I think you have, as you feared, overstepped your bounds. I will show you who I really am by not punishing you for your unwillingness to see reality. You are free to go, but if you walk farther than three meters from the camp center, you will be shot, and there are several who would relish that opportunity. Just to ensure your safety, we will also tie your ankles together. You will be able to hobble about, but you will not be able to walk easily, and running will be out of the question. Go!"

As Louie left the commandant's tent, a soldier met her with a rope in his hand. With his other hand he pressed against Louie's leg as he slid it down to her ankles while laughing. Louie shuddered and nearly lost the beans she had just eaten. The soldier tied the rope to her ankles, leaving about six inches of slack between her feet. She hobbled over to a decaying log, sat down, put her head on her knees, and began a silent prayer.

Chapter 14
Escape

"MR. FARNSWORTH?" DIANA INTERRUPTED HAROLD as he continued to attempt to connect to the internet at the corner table of the hotel lobby. "May I introduce my father, Alejandro Costa?"

Harold, startled, turned from his laptop and stood to meet Alejandro for the second time. "*Señor* Costa, it is very good to meet you once again. I wanted to thank you for the amazing woodcarving."

"My father does not speak English, Mr. Farnsworth. Excuse me while I translate," Diana said and then turned to her father to translate Harold's thank you.

"You are the one who is too kind, *Señor*. I do not wish to bother you at this very difficult time. It is hard to be cordial when the heart is in pain," Alejandro said and Diana relayed.

"I am discovering that this is the best time to be cordial, to think of others, and to find things to be grateful for. Normally I am so focused on my own thoughts and my own journey that I don't notice a lot of the world around me. A very bad habit I am afraid. Although I would never wish this terrible event on anyone, I have come out of the orbit around my thoughts and am beginning to see a vast universe that has always been there." Turning to Diana, Harold said, "Sorry, I don't know where all that came from. You can just tell him I am grateful for his kindness."

Diana translated both statements for her father and was surprised at the tears welling up in her father's eyes. What had she missed? A fine statement by the *Norteño*, but to cause tears in her tough old father's eyes?

Alejandro said, "I see we are kindred spirits. There is another reason for presenting you with the carving of the angel and butterfly. I understand you are searching for a special butterfly. Sergeant Hernandez mentioned it to me in passing. I am a keeper of those secrets. This statue also keeps some of those secrets, for all to look at, but for a very few to actually see."

When these words were translated, Harold looked from the statue to Alejandro and back again to the statue. He only saw a wooden carving of an angel and a small butterfly in her hand. He wanted to ask more, but did not want to get distracted from his concern for Louie and his duty to contact her parents, and his. "I am afraid I don't understand, but perhaps when this ordeal is over we can talk again on this subject," Harold said.

"You are right. Knowledge, something we both seek, can become the quicksand of wisdom, *Señor*. It is understanding that builds the bridge over the quagmire," Alejandro offered with a melancholy smile. Diana had no idea what her father or Mr. Farnsworth were talking about, but she dutifully tried to be their bridge, hoping she used the right words. "I will leave you to your day and hope the sun will shine on your hopes. One last thought for you," Alejandro said as a parting gesture of support. "Although the sun shines, often we can't see it, but we can feel its warmth. We can't see it, but we know it is there. God is in the Heavens and our butterfly is in our hand. Both we may not see, but we can feel both."

Harold was speechless as he shook hands with both Alejandro and Diana. They left the hotel and Harold set these thoughts aside as he again tried to contact Louie's parents on Skype. He was eventually successful and of course they were panicked and distraught. They wanted to travel immediately, but Harold suggested they would be of more help staying home in case there was a need to contact the government. The Embassy had yet to send someone to Mariposa, but he expected them today on the afternoon flight from the capital. His parents were equally upset and he promised he would keep everyone informed. His duties done, he turned back to his woodcarving. It was beautiful and for some reason gave him both peace, hope, and something else.

When Captain Diego Peña returned to the Command Post he found Major Zarro talking with, no speaking to, Lieutenant Mendoza and Sergeant Hernandez. It was obvious that Mendoza was under Zarro's spell. Sergeant Hernandez was maintaining the passive face of a soldier. "We cannot be everywhere, but we will use our patrols to push the rebels into areas where we can more easily spot them," Zarro was saying. "They cannot be so far away that they are out of our reach. I want reports back hourly at the most. Make noise, push these buffoons into the open areas where our two-man recon teams will eventually spot them. Then we will have them! We have six squads out and nine recon teams in the field. We must be successful. The world is watching. The Junta is watching. I am watching. We must be successful at all cost."

"Thank you for your, guidance, Major," Peña interrupted. "I am sure we can handle this operation. Lieutenant, Sergeant, you are dismissed. Let's meet at noon to review troop movements."

Both Mendoza and Hernandez made a quick departure. Captain Peña turned to Major Zarro. "I do appreciate your support Major, but I am still in command. You do not have a role in directing the troops of this sector. Please confine yourself to communications with me alone," Peña said.

"While you were off with that pretty skirt in an Army vehicle, someone had to do something to keep this operation moving. I should report you for dereliction of duty." Zarro said with a constricted voice that sounded like he was out of breath. "Do not lecture me on this stockade, its soldiers, or how to run an operation against the rebels that I chased from this sector and your softness has now allowed for them to return!"

"Leadership is more than sitting in the bishop's chair Major. I also don't like the words of your guidance that suggest we will succeed at all costs. The safety of *Señora* Farnsworth is the priority."

"Captain, I thought we had this conversation. Of course we want her safe return. That would greatly strengthen our position with the rebels, our government's position with the United States, and of course personally. But either way, we must defeat these rebels as a means to our end. If a few innocents perish, that is the collateral damage that comes from war, and make no mistake this is a dirty war."

"*Padre mio*, who are you Major?" Peña asked.

"Captain, I am neither your friend nor your enemy. This is very important to the Junta. Our economic plans have not gone well. This kidnapping is a godsend—allowing us to do what we do best. This is so much more important than this woman, *Norteña* or not. You have too many women on your brain. Get into this game now or you will be sidelined."

"I have no intention of executing this operation for all your exterior reasons Major. I will do what is right, for the right reasons and that is enough. I am a professional soldier and only days ago I took the Oath of Brotherhood. I will not run from that. It is you who are already on the sidelines in this conflict. Stay there," Peña said with as much command as he dared.

Major Zarro approached him face-to-face at such a short distance that their noses almost touched. "You are a child Captain. Grow up. You need to learn to trim the sails of your idealism with the winds of reality. We are the power in this country and thus we are duly obligated to save it from destruction. You know this. We have a legitimate obligation to rule because no one else can. Yet even we are not perfect. We need to shore up our support. Success here will do that."

Peña backed away physically, but did not let the conversation go. "So you agree, rule rests on public opinion, on our justifiable and meaningful actions for the better good of all?"

Zarro chuckled. "No idiot. Rule rests on force. Without it, or the threat of it, there is chaos. The common man needs opinion pumped into him like a machine needs oil. The functions of command and obedience—gained by myth, threat, or coercion, gives direction and the meaning you speak of to society. The support we need to shore up is within our own corps. It is power, not moral principles that establishes our legitimate authority. Power kills discord. In that sense power is the moral strength and the legitimacy of our rule. Our only threat is the breakdown of our obligation to rule, from within our own ranks. This military action here in this quiet little valley provides the justification within our ranks for continued rule. With that continued rule, we will have the time needed to complete our mission to get this country healthy and for us to retire as the legitimate heroes, available again when our country needs us. It is really quite simple."

Peña's mind was swimming in these words. Were they words of confirmation, or words of a clever counterfeit argument? Some of what he said seemed to ring true to Peña, who believed that his country really did need the military. The military is the only institution that could hold this concept of obligational legitimacy as Zarro explained it. Where would society be if the military had not stepped in to bring order and security?" Peña shook his head and told the Major, "You are using half-truths to justify power. It is not power that justifies the right to rule. Let's drop this for now. Our philosophical discussions are fine for the officers' mess, but we need to finish this operation and rescue *Señora* Farnsworth. My command stands until I am notified otherwise by my chain of command. Excuse me while I do my duty." Peña left the Command Post in search of Sergeant Hernandez.

Harold deposited his laptop and the statue in his hotel room. He returned to the lobby and asked the desk to get him transportation. One of the town's few cabs was at the door three minutes later. Harold had the clerk explain to the cab to take him to the Costa home.

As the cab pulled up to the humble Costa dwelling, Harold was still formulating his plan. He hoped Diana was there as he wasn't sure how he would communicate with Alejandro otherwise. An older lady walked around the corner of the house wiping her hands. She had a concerned look on her face. Before Harold was able to say anything, Diana walked out of the house. "Mr. Farnsworth, what a surprise. Do you have news? But then why would you be here?" Diana said, getting flustered not knowing the right thing to say.

"Hello Diana. I am sorry to bother you. It is because I have no news that I came by. I wondered if I could speak to your father. Is he at home? And please, call me Harold as we had agreed."

"First, let me introduce you to my Mother, *Señora* Emma Costa," Diana said, regaining her composure.

"It is good to meet you *Señora*. I am Harold Farnsworth. I met your husband and daughter at the Army stockade. I apologize for showing up unannounced."

"It is very good to meet you," Emma said. "Diana has shared with me your meeting. Can I offer you something to eat or drink? We could sit outside on the other side of the house by the garden where it is a few degrees cooler if you would like."

Harold was surprised that this humble lady also spoke English—not as well as Diana, but still he understood her better than the hotel receptionist. He wanted to get to the bottom of this unique family, but that would have to wait. "I would actually like to speak with your husband if I could. Our earlier discussion got me thinking about something I wanted to talk a little more about."

"I am afraid my husband leaves many people thinking, mostly about whether he is crazy or sane," Emma said with good humor. "He is at the airport meeting the flight in from the capital. He should be home in less than an hour, unless he wanders off on one of his adventures. Then I have to send Diana after him."

"It is an adventure I wanted to talk to him about," Harold said. Both Diana and Emma became tense. "Oh, I don't want to put him in any danger, but as you know my wife was taken by a group of rebels," Harold began to explain.

"Yes I heard. I am so very sorry. I see from your bruises and cuts you also met them. I am doubly sorry. Our little valley is usually a peaceful and quiet place," Emma said as she looked at Diana and wondered when she would be able to tell her about the confirmed death of her brother.

"Thank you for your concern. That is why I wanted to speak to your husband. Can I run the idea by you and Diana?" Harold asked.

"I am not sure how two simple women who know only this little valley could help, but if we can we will. Diana, would you bring us some melon. I will take *Señor* Farnsworth around to the garden where we can sit down."

Before they even turned the corner, Harold began to explain his thoughts. "Many must know about the kidnapping of my wife and her simply being in the wrong place at the wrong time. Everywhere I go someone expresses concern. I also guess that no one wants to get involved in my plight because you live here and could face severe punishment for aiding me in my search for Louie—my wife. I have worked in the past with a powerful tool called crowdsourcing. This is where someone obtains needed services, funding, or whatever by soliciting contributions from a large group of people. This is typically done through an online community although we would use anonymous word of mouth communications, rather than from a traditional source like paid employees. Your husband was talking about seeing and feeling and understanding earlier today. It got me thinking that perhaps I could ask for help through the personal communications among the people of this valley. I do not want to insert myself into the political affairs and I don't want anyone getting hurt on my account, but the traditional source of support—the military—is like trying to kill a fly with a hammer. I am concerned they will be successful finding the fly, but also my wife with the hammer. If people passed on any information from many mouths to many ears, it would soon be anonymous. My only concern is, who would be the deliverer of that information to me? Am I making any sense? Would people be willing to take that risk for me and my wife?"

Emma had understood completely what this *Norteño* was asking. She answered with a poem she recited in her native language:

*"Se le vio, caminando entre fusiles,
por una calle larga,
salir al campo frío,
aún con estrellas, de la Madrugada".*

"I think a translation would roughly be: He was seen walking between the rifles, down a long street, out to chill fields, still lit by early stars. It is the beginning of a poem by Machado talking about the death of another poet. It depends on this crowdsourcing you speak of to tell the story—the story of a very hard time in a very dangerous place, and the news of it that traveled quickly and anonymously. We are masters of this."

Harold was dumbfounded. He did not find such wisdom among most of the college graduates he routinely interviewed at his company.

Diana broke into his thoughts, "Harold, my mother sees most things through the eyes of her poets. She is very wise and together with my philosopher father they have raised a unique, but not so unique family. We are not so unique because all people everywhere have deep thoughts. They may lack some level of knowledge about the stars or microbiology, but they still wrestle with the same key issues as some college professor at Cambridge or the Universidad Nacional Autónoma de México. We are only unique because our parents have honed their expression tools to sharper edges than most, often at a great sacrifice. They have studied hard, have spent food money for their personal improvement and their children's education—not in a formal sense, but after a long day and a nearly empty stomach my mother taught me English. My father taught me religion and philosophy. I have one brother who we fear has been killed in the revolution and another who we haven't heard from in many months—products of my parent's idealism they fear, but really the only tragedy is, my brothers will understand their death better than their fellow combatants—they would have gotten involved no matter."

"I am amazed, and I know that shows my own prejudices I suppose. What a wonderful family you have *Señora* Costa. I would not want to impose on you any more than to enjoy this conversation. I had no idea of your family's personal involvement in the civil conflict. Please, forget I even suggested it," Harold said.

"*Señor* Farnsworth, you are not family, but you will become nearly family in the next few minutes," Emma said. Turning to Diana she said, "*Mi Corazón*, I found out last night from the injured rebel soldier that your brother Gustavo is dead, killed in a battle over a year ago in the North of the country. I promised I would tell you today. Our visitor and his own trials have given me the strength."

Diana allowed the tears to flow, but she did not break down. Harold had the feeling that it wasn't because he was in their presence, but because she was just that strong.

"Gustavo was not killed by the Army. He was killed by a fellow revolutionary, a commander; because he was going to tell someone, perhaps the government, of the rebels' plan to destroy the Elazar Dam and the Power Plant. I believe that is what the rebel patrol was considering when they bumped into your picnic *Señor* Farnsworth." Looking directly at Harold, she continued, "You see the Dam is a symbol of the progress the military government is providing our little valley and the country. It is a great project. For the first time we will have electricity in sufficient abundance for lights, modern appliances, and small industry. The destruction of the Dam would not only put those hopes on hold for many, many years, but it would destroy large parts of this valley. People would die and livelihoods would be ruined for several years."

"You must tell the Army," Harold said. "They can put a patrol by the Dam to keep it safe."

"Yes, I need to, but I fear the repercussions on our family from the Army because of our son's involvement and our younger son Paco's probable involvement, and from the revolutionaries who, if they are ruthless enough to consider such an action, would not hesitate to kill us. Diana is just now starting to live. Do I have the right, the obligation to end her life?"

"May I have your permission to tell Captain Peña? I will tell him someone told me at the hotel. Yes, we can write a note and I can tell them it was put under my door. I promise I will never tell a soul where I got this information," Harold offered.

"What is happening here?" Alejandro asked as he entered the garden from the house. Harold stood as Alejandro joined the group. Diana quickly caught him up on the conversation.

Alejandro turned to Harold and said, "A member of your Embassy arrived on the flight today. He will be looking for you at the Hotel. He was escorted by another person. I didn't hear who he was, but he looked Peruvian, or Bolivian," Diana translated.

"I suppose I should get back to the hotel then. Please let me know if you hear anything. As far as letting Captain Peña know about the rebel plans—what do you think?"

When Alejandro was told about the idea of letting Captain Peña know of the threat to the Dam, Alejandro decided he would be the one to tell the Captain. Diana would accompany Harold back to the hotel and then return home.

Louie felt a stiff object, like the side of a knife, push her arm. She jolted to her feet and almost fell over from the vertigo. Her eyes finally focused on *No Importa* and Cesar. "*Señora*, it is time for lunch. Here is your plate. Your favorite, beans and rice," *No Importa* said with a smile. "I hope your nap was therapeutic. You have been out for three hours. I hated to wake you, but you need your strength."

Cesar spoke to *No Importa*, and *No Importa* relayed the statement to Louie. "This is the Comandante's lieutenant. He requires that you come with me outside of the camp, as the Comandante needs to speak with the soldiers on sensitive matters. I have been entrusted with your safety, along with the camp cook and explosives expert, Paco whose food you have so enjoyed. You have eaten his beans, so you can see the logical connection," *No Importa* said dryly. "We will only be gone for about an hour. Eat, and then we leave."

Louie quickly ate, grateful for the opportunity to get out of the camp for something other than dumping her bucket. Speaking of her bucket, that is something else she needed to take care of and she didn't want to go back in the cave to do so. "I'm ready to go!" Louie said moments later.

Paco untied her legs, but put a new rope on her left ankle, with the other end held securely in his hands. He tugged on it to ensure it was tight and also to remind Louie that it could be pulled at any time. They left the camp in the opposite direction from where Louie had gone before. No one spoke. *No Importa* led the way, then Louie, then Paco. About fifteen minutes out of camp Louie asked if she could relieve herself. Paco turned to *No Importa* for translation or direction. It was obvious *No Importa* had not thought about this eventuality.

No Importa directed Paco to retie her rope ankle bracelets and they left the leash dangling. "You have three minutes alone. We will only be a few feet away and our backs will be turned. If we hear any quick movement, we will turn and come after you, no matter your situation. Do you understand?"

"Yes, I understand," Louie said.

"Very well, that tree and bush will provide some privacy," *No Importa* said pointing to some vegetation no more than five or six feet away. Your time starts now."Louie tried to be as quiet as possible, but it was impossible to maintain her dignity. She considered attempting escape, but had no idea which way to run, that is if she could even get the ropes on her ankles untied quickly. Returning to *No Importa* and Paco was embarrassing and like a knife in her heart.

Louie's ankles were freed and they continued their journey for another fifteen minutes where they stopped near a stream that also offered some shade. It appeared this was to be there waiting place for the next few hours.

"Make yourself comfortable *Señora*. We will wait here for a time," *No Importa* said.

Louie sat where she stood. She felt exhausted and they had only walked maybe two or three miles. No sooner had Louie sat that she doubled over and felt violently ill. Pain in her intestines overcame her, followed by a blazing fever and uncontrollable shaking all over her body. She felt nauseous and then the pain only increased. "Oh God, please, help me to not be sick, or at least be strong enough to handle this," she said out loud. She felt completely alone and then she lost consciousness.

She woke several times over what seemed like just a few minutes. All she remembered was *No Importa* putting something cool on her forehead. "You are very dehydrated *Señora*. You need to drink this." Louie awoke once again to see *No Importa* by her side. Louie drank. "Slowly *Señora*, slowly. That is enough for now."

"What happened?" Louie asked.

"My best guess is food poisoning, or perhaps an intestinal infection. It appears the worst is over, but I can't say for sure. You have been very sick for nearly three hours."

"I still feel terrible and what is that smell? Is that me?" Louie asked.

I am afraid it is you, *Señora*. You vomited violently numerous times and you soiled your pants. We have not moved you for fear of causing more violence. If you feel up to it, the stream is nearby and you can clean up just a bit before we head back to camp. The Comandante will be getting concerned. They may send out a search party."

"I am sure they can find us by the smell," Louie said. "Help me up and I will see if I can even stand."

With *No Importa* and Paco's help she stood, but she had to stay partly bent over. She made it to the stream and she collapsed in the water. It was cool and felt wonderful.

"We will turn our backs while you try to clean yourself," *No Importa* said. "Do not stay in the water too long. It will suck all the body heat out of you. You need that heat to give you strength for the walk back to camp."

Perhaps because of her weakened body, or because of the stench, *No Importa* and Paco moved about ten yards away to a small rock outcropping, sat down and appeared to begin a conversation. Louie couldn't hear what they were talking about because of the noise of the stream. Louie rubbed at her filthy blouse, finally took it off, scrubbed it quickly and put it back on. Her upper undergarment was filthy too, but she wasn't going to try to clean that. She did sit in the stream and remove her pants and undergarment and scrub them on the smooth rocks while keeping her lower body submerged. The effort was almost more than she could accomplish. When she was done she crawled out of the stream on the opposite side from her captures. She was tired but refreshed. *No Importa* and Paco were still talking and *No Importa* had just glanced back at her very briefly to make sure she was OK.

Without really thinking about it, Louie stood up and simply walked away. When she was a few yards from the stream the vegetation became thicker and she quickened her pace. She couldn't quite run, but she did her best to put distance between herself and the rebels. Turning toward the sun, she tried to hide her trail. She couldn't hear anyone behind her. She was getting nauseous again, but kept going. She had no idea how long she walked. It seemed like an hour, but was probably less. She could smell smoke and every once in a while she caught what sounded like a voice, or voices. Was it her captors or someone else. The adrenaline rush of fear of being recaptured mixed with the hope of finding someone who could help her gave her the strength to increase her pace.

Louie entered a clearing and could see people not more than a hundred yards away. She was too out of breath to yell. She could hardly keep walking. Then to her right she heard yelling. It was not *No Importa* nor Paco, but she knew it could be other rebels. She had to get to the other people at the other end of the clearing. Then she heard it. Two shots. Was she hit? Her body was so numb she wasn't sure she would be able to tell. Then everything went dark, but felt peaceful. She had escaped.

"Sergeant Hernandez, I would like a word with you," Captain Peña said, mostly for the soldiers to hear. More quietly, he added, "What is Major Zarro up to? He disappears and reappears and then I stumble on him giving orders and directing his own operation. I am not sure who sent him here, what his real orders are and how to keep him from inserting his will into everything I am responsible for."

"I don't know what his plans are or who sent him," Hernandez began. "I checked this morning with Celia and she still has not received a copy of his orders that you requested. Those in our chain of command are strangely silent. He has the Lieutenant in his corner, promising him promotions and glory, and a posting in the capital where his fiancé lives. I don't think the Lieutenant will cause any problems, however, as he has little authority while you are in command. He will sit and watch this unfold. Hopefully he will learn the right lessons and be the wiser for it."

"OK, so what is the report from the search squads?" Peña asked.

"Nothing of significance my Captain." Looking at his watch, Hernandez added, "They are due to report back again in about fifteen minutes. You know, if they find anything, they will call in immediately, so I doubt we will hear any new information."

"I wish I were out with the troops. I feel so worthless..."

Peña's words were interrupted by a corporal. "Sir, Celia sent me to find you. A person from the U.S. Embassy is at your office. He wishes to see you and the *Señor* Farnsworth. Celia sent a driver to pick up the *Norte Americano* at the Hotel."

"Very well, dismissed corporal." He saluted and departed. Captain Peña looked to the distant hills and said to the Sergeant, "The fun never stops does it?" and he walked toward his office.

"Good day, sir, my name is Captain Diego Peña. I am the Commander of this sector. Welcome to Mariposa," Diego said as he entered his front office. "Please, you will be more comfortable in my private office."

"Thank you Captain, my name is Stewart Rigley. I am the junior political officer attached to our Embassy. I brought our RSO, our Regional Security Officer from our Embassy with me. He is in town and will make his way to the abduction site on his own. We do not want to second guess your efforts to retrieve *Señora* Farnsworth, but as you would guess, we have our own reports to complete. Could you provide me with what you are doing and what results you have to report? Also, is there anything we, the United States can do to help?"

"Would you like something to drink, perhaps something to eat? *Señor* Farnsworth should be here soon. We can start our discussion then."

"Some water would be great. Thank you. Is there anything you would like to share with me before Mr. Farnsworth gets here?" Rigley asked.

"We have been very transparent with *Señor* Farnsworth throughout this ordeal. He is as informed as I am. In fact, I have come to consider both him and his wife as personal friends," Peña said. "And I assure you we are doing everything possible to rescue *Señora* Farnsworth. I cannot speak for my country or the Army, but there is nothing I can think of that this post needs from the United States to ensure success of our citizens."

"Have the kidnappers typically asked for ransoms as the FARC and ERP have done elsewhere?" Rigley asked.

"No. That has not been their practice, and I don't believe that will happen in this case. The Farnsworths were simply in the wrong place at the wrong time. Now they are not sure what to do with their prisoner is my guess."

Both heard the jeep drive up to the building and they turned for the office door. The first into the building was Alejandro, followed by Diana, and then Harold. Peña was not sure what this meant. He ignored his own citizens, as hard as it was to keep his eyes and thoughts off of Diana, and said, "Harold, this is *Señor* Rigley, from your Embassy. He has come to offer his support and best wishes. Please come into my office." He wasn't sure what to do with Alejandra and Diana.

"Captain," Harold said, "I bumped into Alejandro and Diana and they have some very important news for you. I think it is a priority over our discussions with my Embassy— unless there is something new to report about Louie?"

"Sadly no, no new news," he said to Harold. Turning to Alejandro, he said in Spanish, "Is this news something to do with the kidnapping? Can it wait until after my meeting with the Embassy official and *Señor* Farnsworth?"

"I will be very brief Captain, but I would like to talk in private if possible," Alejandro answered.

"Very well, let's use the Lieutenant's office. I will be with you in just a minute," he said to his other guests. Once they entered the empty office and shut the door, Diego asked again, "So what is it that is more important than my guests and the kidnapping?"

"They plan to blow up the Dam and destroy the power plant," Alejandro spit out.

"Who plans to do this and where did you get this information?" Peña asked with startled interest.

"I heard it from a friend... No Captain the truth is my wife heard it from the captured rebel before he died. She was afraid to say anything because she didn't want to get questioned. You know we may have a son who is involved with the rebels and we want to stay as far away from these issues as possible. I trust you, so you need to know the source of this information to understand its credibility. The kidnapping of *Señora* Farnsworth was by a reconnaissance party in preparation of that attack. I don't know any more than that. The rebel died after confessing this to my Emma."

"Thank you for telling me this, all of this. I will not put you in any danger. I have much to do, so unless you have anything else to say?"

"Nothing else *Señor*, except that my daughter has also requested to speak with you in private. I know you have many things to do that are very important, but I know she understands that also and would not make this request unless it was very important."

"Of course," was all that Peña could say. He knew he had many more important things to do, but wondered what other revelations were in store for him today. Even a minute alone with Diana was also too tempting to pass up. She entered the office and shut the door a moment after Alejandro left.

"Captain, thank you for accepting my odd request. I assume my father told you about the rebel plot. We thought it best that he tell you alone. What I assume he did not tell you is, I have two brothers who are involved with the revolution. One is confirmed dead—killed by other rebels for attempting to report the planned attack on our valley Dam. We have not seen my other brother for over six months. We assume he is with the rebels also. I tell you this because it may someday come to light and I want you to know on my word that we have no other information and are not in any way involved in the rebel cause," Diana said, nearly in one breath.

"Your father did briefly mention some of that information. Thank you."

Diana took a deep breath and said, "I have two other important discoveries to share. One cannot wait, the other can if it needs to."

"Please, but be brief. This is turning out to be a perfect storm day," Peña said.

"I know I just told you my family, that is my parents and I, are not involved in revolutionary activities. Yet, I have possible news of *Señora* Farnsworth and I can't explain why I have this information."

"Tell me the information and then explain whether you *can't* or *won't* tell me why you have this information," Captain Peña commanded.

"About thirty-five kilometers to the East, earlier today, maybe only two or three hours ago, some villagers near Campo Crespo saw a blonde woman shot and carried away by armed men. I only just heard this news as I was walking back to my home after escorting *Señor* Farnsworth back to the hotel." Diana said. She watched the Captain's eyes as he processed this information.

"We have a patrol in that general area, but they have reported nothing," he said. "Are you sure it was a blonde woman and that she was shot?"

"I can only tell you what I heard. The distance between the villagers and the woman and the armed men was enough that I am not sure they could even confirm with certainty what exactly happened. As soon as the shots were fired, they all ran and didn't return."

"Have you told Harold or your father this?"

"I have now only told you, but I am sure others will hear it soon enough. I told you I couldn't tell you why I know this information. I am not holding any secrets. It was just a strange discovery. I had promised to collect some flowers for my mother on the way home and so I was walking by the river where her favorite flowers grow. I know your time is short, so I will just say, there were many butterflies on the plants, and then there were few. Then there was a man who told me this news of the shooting, and then he was not there. It was very strange and I am not sure I fully believe it myself."

"It has been the strangest of days. It was only a few days ago that the Farnsworth's arrived in our quiet and peaceful valley. I feel like I have lived a month in those days. Some of those moments have been agonizingly long, and a few have been, much too short," he said as he looked at her and blushed. Quickly regaining his composure, he added, "Is that the other thing you needed to tell me if I had time?"

"No." Diana took a deep breath. "Since you speak English, have you ever read the children's book Winnie the Pooh?" Diana asked.

"No. And you are right, I probably don't have time for this discussion," Peña said impatiently. "Lives are at stake. This is not a time to discuss children's books."

Diana continued as if she hadn't heard him. "My mother used to read that book to me when I was young and then I learned to read it for myself when she was teaching me English. In the book, the bear character asks, "Did you ever stop to think and then forget to start again?" I always thought that a silly question. A children's riddle."

"Diana," Peña said, using her first name for the first time. "I really don't have time for this."

She held up her hand palm facing forward as if to say stop. She said, "I have started, and there are two lives at stake so I need to finish," she said and stopped to take another breath. "On my way here with the news of the possible death of *Señora* Farnsworth, I realized something. I have been in a "think rut" my whole life. I have been happy and I have learned much. But I am now miserable thinking of thinking. I will start here and now with my life. When this is over, no matter how it ends--perhaps it won't end--come to me. I am not asking you to consider getting to know this humble girl from a forgotten valley with dust on her shoes and no formal education. I am commanding you with all that sustains my life to come to me."

Too embarrassed now to look at him, Diana turned, opened the door, and walked out of the room. Peña stood there stunned. He simply could not move, or think, or even breath. Then he heard a familiar voice. He turned hoping to see Diana again, but was Major Zarro speaking to him.

Chapter 15
Obligations

"Captain! You are an officer of the Army. I would say go get a room, but it is obvious you just did that! Are you losing the ability to command? You are…" Zarro was saying in a hiss.

"Major, get a grip on yourself," Captain Peña interrupted and sprang to action. "I have important and difficult news and we must act quickly on several fronts," he said as he walked back into his office. He yelled to the outer room, "Celia get Sergeant Hernandez to the Command Post now!" To Zarro, Lieutenant Mendoza, and *Señor* Rigley he said, "I will meet you in the Command Post in five minutes." Looking at Harold he said, "I need a private word with you."

When the three men had left the room, Peña closed the door and began. "Harold, I have a report that there was a possible shooting about thirty five kilometers east of here near a village called Campo Crespo. A woman may have been involved. My information is vague, but it is something new. I don't want to alarm you, but there is a slight chance that could have been your wife. I have a squad in the area and we will have more information soon. Now, I must leave you, considering the danger to this valley if the Dam is damaged. I have much to do. I want you to know your wife is still my priority. Please return to the hotel where I know I can contact you." Peña turned and almost ran to the Command Post.

With his team and guests assembled, Peña outlined the information he had on the potential strike on the Dam and power plant. He redirected two of the search squads, Alpha and Delta squads, of fifteen soldiers each to return to the stockade. The smaller eight-man Foxtrot and Gulf squads were sent to expand the standard security at the Dam and power plant. He turned the security of the Dam and offensive squads over to the command of Sergeant Hernandez.

"I have additional information that a blonde woman was seen in the area near Campo Crespo. It could have been someone with a yellow scarf on their head for all we really know, but shots may have been fired so that makes this very serious. We have Charlie Squad in the area. I am redirecting Bravo squad to back them up. If they make contact they are to accomplish reconnaissance only, unless fired upon. We may need a bigger force in the area and we don't know the condition of their hostage. We don't want to just go in guns blazing. Mendoza, you will travel to Campo Crespo immediately and take command of Bravo and Charlie Squads. That's thirty soldiers. Don't put them all in one place. Remember; do not make contact with the rebels. Report via radio to me within the next two hours. For now I will remain here, but will bring the rest of the company that we can spare to your location when Alpha and Delta squads return here. Expect me to be in place in six hours, at 2100 hours. Major Zarro, anything to add?"

"No Captain," was all that Zarro could muster. His wheels were turning, but not as fast as Peña's.

Mr. Rigley, there is little for you to do at this time, so I suggest you return to the hotel and we will keep you informed as news warrants. I also ask you to not report anything to your Embassy or anyone else until you hear from me personally. Any news could inadvertently increase the risk of our operations and the safety of my men and *Señora* Farnsworth. I have trusted you with this information. Will you trust me?

"Yes Captain. I know how to keep my mouth shut. Good hunting," Rigley said.

"Cesar, are you clear on your mission?" Comandante Helicon asked as he completed his briefing of the attack on the Dam. "It has to be tonight. Waiting any longer will endanger our fighters and we must complete this mission to keep the revolution alive."

"I am ready and so are our men. I had our explosives and fuses checked. We will not fail. By tomorrow, the Dam and the power plant will be gone. The Junta generals will not be able to put this feather in their caps. This will be just another failure of their long list of promises," Cesar said, eager to get this operation finally under way.

A commotion was building outside the Comandante's tent. They both exited to see what was going on. Both expected to see the excitement of the soldiers readying for battle after Antonio's speech and outline of the upcoming attack. Instead he met confusion and even a little fear.

"What is going on?" he asked a soldier who was leaning his hands on his knees and sucking in deep breaths.

"The *Norteña* escaped. The men you sent out to bring her and her guards back after your speech found her and someone fired at her, fearing she would reach Campo Crespo." He took a couple breaths and continued, "We don't think anyone saw us, but they may have heard the shots. The group is only a few kilometers from here. I ran ahead to let you know. They will be here in less than ten minutes. They are carrying the woman."

"Is she dead?" Antonio asked.

"I do not know sir. She is not moving."

Antonio was not sure what to do. "Cesar, should the attack continue or are we compromised?"

"It may be a good thing if someone did hear the shots. It will lure the Army toward Campo Crespo, leaving the Dam even less defended. I think this is the perfect time to attack. It will also be easier to hide fewer men in these mountains, especially if the woman is dead. Leave her here in the camp and let's get on with the revolution," Cesar said with enthusiasm.

"I agree," Antonio said with everything now coming back into focus. "Depart now! We will rendezvous at our abandoned camp where we spent last winter. That is sixty kilometers from here, so don't delay your attack. In and out fast and on your way!"

As Cesar and his demolition team departed to the Southeast, other soldiers were just entering the camp from the West. It felt good to Antonio to see and feel all this movement and action after waiting so long. As the group assembled around the center of the camp, two men dumped the woman's body in the center. She groaned.

"So she is alive," Antonio said. "Was she shot? I don't see any wounds, but her clothes are stained. Is that dried blood? Who shot her? What actually happened?" Antonio knew he was losing his steadiness and took a breath and waited.

"She was not shot. I fired shots in her direction to stop her. We were too far away to catch her before she was close enough to the village that we would not be able to stay out of site and still retrieve her," a man named Dante explained. Antonio hit him viciously with the back of his hand.

"Good job, but not for anything you did right," Antonio said. "As it happens, this will work well into our plans. You would be dead otherwise. Now explain to me what happened. How did she escape? Where are her guards?"

Paco and the man Louie had named *No Importa* stepped forward.

"Ernesto and Paco? You failed me and you nearly failed the revolution. Explain yourselves., NOW!" Antonio ordered.

Ernesto (*No Importa*) explained about Louie getting violently ill and how they let her clean herself up. Paco added, "She didn't get very far and we were about to catch up to her when our brothers saw her from far off."

"As with Dante, you are just fortunate that this unfortunate event plays into our hands. Paco, get out of my site before I change my mind and shoot you. Ernesto, can I trust you to watch over this shriveled up corpse, or do I turn her over to those who would have their way with her?" Antonio asked.

"I will not fail you again, Comandante," Ernesto said.

"Our brothers have already left to restart the revolution. They will blow up the Dam late tonight. We will all be traveling soon. See if she is able to travel. If we have to we will tie her to a tree and leave her here. Perhaps someone will find her. Perhaps she will become part of the forest."

"No!" Louie's subdued voice demanded. "You will kill people and ruin homes and food if the Dam is blown up. You are not saviors, you are destroyers."

In her delirium, Louie did not realize she was displaying her Spanish comprehension, nor that she was speaking Spanish.

"You have just signed your death warrant *Señora*," Antonio said. "You either walk with us when we leave, or I will personally shoot you for your deception, and your dangerous knowledge. You know our plans and I could not allow you to stay here alive. By tomorrow that knowledge will be old news, as will be your usefulness to us." Antonio walked away.

No Importa pulled her to her feet and guided, almost carried her, to his humble tent. "I will be leaving this filthy tent behind happily," *No Importa* said to Louie. "It has protected me from the elements, but I am not a camper and my back will no longer allow me to sleep on the ground. I have prayed for the day that we could leave here. I will either die in the next days, or I will retire from this macho nonsense."

"I am sorry I almost got you killed, *No Imp...*, Ernesto," Louie said. I got out of that stream and just started walking. I didn't actually plan to escape. It almost worked though. That probably would have gotten you killed and I would not want that. Why can't I have my freedom and in gaining it not cause others harm?" Louie said mostly to herself.

"Let's not ask these hard questions. To be, a butterfly must first escape its captivity of the chrysalis. It is now my duty not to just help you out of this camp, but to get you to safety and God willing, to your husband. I cannot stop the senseless destruction of the Dam, but I can protect you from senseless destruction. Now, let's see what your vital signs are and what we can do to give you enough energy to walk out of here."

"I asked this to myself it seems like weeks ago, but it was probably just yesterday: Who are you?"

Ernesto smiled and said, "*No Importa.*"

"That doesn't work anymore. All my secrets are on the table. What are yours? You fit in this camp as much as my grandmother does, and I am not talking about age. What's your story?"

Ernesto cleaned up Louie's open cuts, got out a stethoscope from his pack and listened to her lungs, her heart, and her bowels. He took her blood pressure and looked into her eyes. He pinched the skin on her arm. He had her open her mouth even though the smell of her breath was putrid even to Louie. Finally, he checked her reflexes by tapping on her knees. "I cannot say you are healthy and I have no way of running any actual tests. You may have eaten something days ago that has developed into gastroenteritis, or you ate something recently that was tainted with Salmonella, Campylobacter, or Shigella. I suppose you could have contracted Chagas, Malaria, Typhoid, or have some other exotic parasite, but you haven't been with us long enough for those to develop. For now you should be able to walk out of here with us. I will give you a cocktail shot of vitamin B12 and amoxicillin. I have been saving both for just such an occasion. You aren't allergic to penicillin are you?"

"No. Oh my goodness, who are you? I am going to change your name from *No Importa* to Doctor Who," Louie said in wonder.

"Both names are appropriate I suppose. I am really not important and I am a medical doctor. I used to practice in the capital. That was a few years ago. Hopefully I haven't lost my touch for your sake," he added. "Maybe another day for my story. If you are curious enough, perhaps that will keep you going on our march. I really do wish we had vehicles like civilized revolutionaries, but it is actually quicker to walk then drive on the back roads in these mountains."

Harold returned to the hotel in worse shape than he looked. Could Louie have been shot? Was she lying on a forest floor bleeding to death, or already dead. "No. I would have felt that, wouldn't I?" Harold thought out loud.

"Mr. Farnsworth?" a Hispanic looking gentleman asked him as he entered the hotel lobby.

"Yes, who is asking?" Harold said before thinking.

"I am Tomás Rioja. I am the Embassy RSO, their security officer." He showed Harold an ID card that could have been made with any color printer. "I just got back from looking at the site where you were attacked. Could I interview you for my report? Is there anything I can do for you?"

"Well Mr. Rioja, let me catch you up on a few things," Harold said and began, like tepid water building to the boiling point. "This valley could be inundated with a flood at any moment because the rebels, the MNS I understand, commanded by the one and only Comandante Helicon, plans to blow up the local Dam. I am on the cusp of discovering a secret that butterflies have been hiding for millennia, except their only habitat is about to be destroyed. That is not so important to me anymore, however, because my wife is located somewhere near the village of Campo Crespo and could be dead, or bleeding to death from gunshot wounds. If she is alive, who knows what else she has suffered while I have been enjoying the hospitality of the locals. To be fair, I have never met a people who so very much do not deserve the harsh lives they have been dealt and somehow they just keep striving to survive. No not just striving to survive, striving forward. And then there are the protectorates of these people. There are a few great men at the Army Post, and a few really dangerous ones. The rest are just conscripted and doing their time. Oh, and don't accept room 201 at the hotel because it has no windows and you'll melt before morning. I think that about covers it for your report."

Rioja ignored the venting and said, "I know Campo Crespo! I visited it when I was doing my country localization. It's really out of the way and the roads are terrible. It's almost faster to walk there from here than to go by vehicle. I am not sure you are up for a long hike, and I understand if you don't want to, but would you like to take a drive with me? You can fill in the parts between the lines on the way."

"What was your name again?"

"Just call me Tomás,"

"What are we waiting for Tomás?

As Harold and Tomás walked out of the hotel, they were met by Diana going in.

"Diana, what are you doing here?" Harold asked.

"My father sent me here to invite you to dinner. He said it would not be healthy for you to eat alone tonight. My father knows tragedy and feels for you. I have heard and do not believe any of the rumors about your wife. You have to believe until you know for sure otherwise. She needs that. She needs your strength and your prayers. My father also said he would share with you the mystery of the butterfly you seek, if you would like, whatever that means. If this is only more mysteries created by my father and you don't know what he is talking about, I apologize."

"Diana, let me introduce you to Tomás. He is from the U.S. Embassy. He and I are going on a little outing to Campo Crespo. I would love to accept you invitation to dinner. I could really use the strength of your family right now, but I have a chance to be where my wife might be. I can't pass that up."

"*Señor* Tomás, I am not a security expert, but I am a local. Would it be inconvenient for me to travel with you both? I doubt the villagers will speak to two foreigners, even if you do speak Spanish," Diana suggested.

"I think that would be a great idea if it is alright with Mr. Farnsworth," Tomás said. "You could also fill me in on any local activities and thoughts of the people here in the Mariposa area. It is not often someone from our Embassy gets out to this corner of the country." Tomás also thought, but did not say, 'it would also be nice to have a beautiful traveling companion on this little adventure.'

Harold, surprised to be so observant, read Tomás' thoughts and added, "Diana could also be a valuable liaison with the Army. Her boyfriend is the local commander, Captain Diego Peña."

"Of all the things I have heard today, this was the least surprising, but the most disappointing," Tomás said.

Diana wanted to correct Harold. She was not the Captain's girlfriend, but she hoped she would be and she saw the wisdom of Harold's statement to keep this *gringo* in Latin skin at bay. She said, "We had better be on our way before I change my mind. It would be best to travel the main road to Campo Crespo in daylight. It is only 35 kilometers, but there are places where the road is more like a dirt trail and very slow." Diana almost asked if they could also stop by here home to tell her mother of her plans, but decided not to. Her mother would probably tell her not to go. She would have to disobey her mother and she did not wish to do that.

"Celia, inform headquarters of this information," Captain Peña said as he entered the stockade command offices and handed her a short handwritten report. "I would rather you accomplish this through your informal channels than have Major Zarro or his people at headquarters manipulate any report I make through regular message channels. I will be leaving with the remaining soldiers in the company once our returning squads are resupplied and loaded on the trucks. I will maintain contact via radio for any emergencies. Have you seen Major Zarro by the way? I went to my quarters to change into battle dress and it seems he has disappeared."

"He met briefly with Lieutenant Mendoza in the Lieutenant's office, doors closed, for about five minutes and then they both left together," Celia answered.

"I saw Mendoza leave the stockade and Zarro wasn't with him. I will check again at the Command Post. I don't want to leave until I understand what the Major's plans are. Get that report sent off as soon as you can. If you can get it to General Cruz directly, his eyes only, that would be the best."

Peña walked toward the Command Post and from a distance saw Major Zarro entering that building. "Major Zarro, good to find you here," Peña said. "I am about ready to leave for Campo Crespo. What are your plans? Would you like to accompany me?"

"I am going to stay here at the stockade, so if direct communications with Hernandez fails, I can serve as a liaison.

196 CONVERSATIONS AMONG BUTTERFLIES

You have two bold operations running in tandem and no one to hold the rudder. I humbly accept that duty," Zarro said with his thin smile. Also, while you are gone, I am going to collect the people connected to your surprising information. I knew the Costa name sounded familiar. We have intelligence at headquarters that a Gustavo Costa attempted to take over a rebel cell in the North of the country. He was killed in the attempt. Our intelligence also links this rebel to a family here in Mariposa. In fact, I have reason to believe this dead rebel is related to the family of your local whore I keep seeing in your presence. We may be able to gain further information from them under the appropriate circumstances," Zarro added with a genuine smile.

That smile sickened Peña. "Do not speak of the young woman as anything you know nothing of. Your willingness to go directly to the gutter only highlights your own sick morals. I have spoken to the Costa family and they are innocents in a terrible conflict. Leave them out of this!"

"I am afraid in this situation I do have jurisdiction over your local command. I have been given the power to arrest, detain, and interrogate any suspected criminals to society— that is, anyone suspected of harboring, aiding, or making contact with any revolutionary. That order comes directly from General Cruz's office and as of ten minutes ago is now applicable to the entire country—including the Mariposa Sector. You see, I am much more than a paper-pushing staff officer. I certainly don't want to get in the way of your operations, but you had better not get in the way of mine. That, Captain, is an order."

"What gives you the moral right to sweep up simple and honest people, innocent people, in the name of your own little war?" Peña admonished. "That is not the Army, that is not what you were taught at the Academy, and surely in your heart you know that, as our legal code outlines, people are innocent until proven guilty."

"Those are outmoded words. In a modern war where a terrorist can quickly become the victim in the eyes of a society, it is better to capture or kill all the guilty, leaving nothing to chance. If that means a few innocents are implicated and even suffer misfortune or die, it is the cost we must pay."

"I would rather live in a society where some of the guilty go free if it means never prosecuting the innocent." Peña countered. "Society could never live or survive with that burden."

"There is a weakness in your statement that I cannot live with. You mentioned you just completed the Oath of Brotherhood only days ago. Surely the words are fresh in your mind. You pledged to protect your country from all who would harm her. It is the country that must live, not all of its inhabitants. All the bad and perhaps a few good must be sacrificed at this altar of life."

"We are to protect with honor and virtue a country that is only the sum of its people. When we inflict harm on the people we are only damaging, not protecting our country. You can numb yourself with faulty justifications, but you cannot numb one value and not numb all the rest. You can no longer feel true gratitude, joy, peace, humility, or any other meaningful and worthwhile virtue. You Major, and those like you, are the ones who are weak. You are just too medicated with glory, power, wealth, pride, and fear to know how fragile and depraved of light you are."

"Well, we shall see who is weak and who is strong very soon. You have potential Captain, but it is Will that drives the engine. Good luck in finding the enemy, wherever they are hiding. Now off with you."

Peña left without countering Zarro's words further. He had met other officers that held similar feelings and ideas. They were a small minority, but today they seemed, as Zarro had just said, to hold the rudder of the Army and the government. He had his own ship to steer and he needed to be in Campo Crespo as soon as possible. This war of words would have to wait.

"I have a small detour to make corporal. Start the convoy moving and I will catch up," Captain Peña instructed when out of hearing range anyone else. Peña departed the stockade in the front of the column and they traveled together until a T-intersection just outside of the town of Mariposa. The convoy with thirty five troops headed north toward Campo Crespo. Peña headed south, skirting he town and then turned east to a group of homes just outside of town. He stopped at the home of Alejandro and Emma Costa. He was hoping to see Diana, but also wanted to talk with her parents.

"Alejandro, I am glad I caught you at home," Peña said. "I need your assistance. In fact I need the help of your wife and your daughter. Can I speak to you all now? I am on a schedule I must keep."

"My wife and I are here, but I don't know where Diana is. I sent her to town to invite Harold to our home for dinner. It would not be good for him to eat alone tonight," Alejandro said.

"I do not have time at the moment to explain, but you are in danger. Your whole family is in danger. You need to come with me for your safety. We can't leave a note for Diana. That would inform those that will come for you that you were warned and indirectly tell them where you are. I don't have time, nor do I want to be seen in town, so I can't go after Diana. I am also not sure her safety would be guaranteed simply by the presence of *Señor* Farnsworth," Peña lamented.

"We cannot leave Captain. This is our home and we need to be here when Diana returns," Alejandro said.

"You are in mortal danger. If you ever want to see your daughter again, you need to come with me, now."

"What would anyone want with two old people? We will be fine, but thank you for your concern," Alejandro said. "Is it Diana that is actually in danger?"

"Diana is in danger?" Emma asked as she approached the two men.

"You are all in danger. Major Zarro has made a connection between Gustavo and your family. He plans to pick you all up for interrogations. I am far exceeding my legal bounds, but this is so illegal and immoral, I must. Please, we have to go now."

"Alejandro, you go. I will wait for Diana and then we will leave as soon as it is dark and find a safe place to hide. We cannot leave Diana to Major Zarro!" Emma pleaded.

"You will not get far. The only safe place at the moment is with me. I want nothing more than your daughter's safety, but we must go. The Major may already be on his way. *Señor* and *Señora* Costa, I know this will sound ridiculous as I hardly know your daughter, but I think I love her and right now, the only thing I can do for her is to help her parents. Please, come with me."

Alejandro studied the Captain for a moment. "Very well. I have a warning sign I can leave for our daughter, to tell her of danger. I cannot guarantee she will not decide that it is safest to stay home, but perhaps she will know that since we are not here, she must leave also," Alejandro said. He went to the living room, near the front door and turned a woodcarving of a hawk to face the wall. "Come my *media naranja*." They left without looking back. Peña explained where they were going by the time they were on the North side of Mariposa and speeding to catch the convoy.

Chapter 16
Legitimacy

"Consuelo, are you home?" Sergeant Enrique Hernandez yelled to his wife.

"In the bedroom, my love. I am making the bed that you never seem to sleep in.," Emma yelled back.

"I am afraid it will be another night alone for you," Enrique began as he entered the room. "I have been called out for maneuvers again, starting tonight. I may be gone several days this time. After that though, things should quiet down. That is, if we are able to find and rescue *Señora* Farnsworth. *Diablos!* I can't believe I let those criminal rebels take her. All this would not be if I had done my duty correctly!"

"No cussing in this house Sergeant Hernandez," Consuelo commanded.

Consuelo was no longer as thin and plump in all the places the world defined as beauty. It was a blessing of the deep bonds Enrique and Consuelo had built over their married life that made this woman even more desirable today than on their wedding night. He watched her shake the new sheet and let it fall on the bed. 'What is so sensuous about house chores? Maybe it is the upcoming battle, if there would even be one, that arouses my senses at this odd time,' he thought. 'No matter, I need to be back at the stockade and ready to leave in half an hour.'

"What are you looking at Quique? Have you never seen anyone but your soldiers make a bed?" Consuelo asked.

"I never saw a soldier that looked like you, making a bed," he replied.

"Well come and help you lazy man," Consuelo teased.

Enrique walked to the opposite side of the bed and grabbed the clean sheet Consuelo had just spread over the mattress. "Soldiers are taught to make beds before they are taught to shoot weapons. Sheets should be tight enough to bounce a peso on it." With that he gave a vigorous tug on the sheet and pulled it and Consuelo toward him. The sheet landed crumpled at his feet, Consuelo fell on the bed. "Soldiers are supposed to hold onto the sheet," he said laughing.

"Yes, but as you said, soldiers do not look like this," she said as she began to unbutton her blouse.

"Consuelo, I love you, and you know…, well you know. But I need to be back at the stockade in less than thirty minutes," he said.

"Shhh. No words, soldier. Action! Isn't that what they teach you in the Army?"

Twenty five minutes later Sergeant Hernandez was putting on his battle dress fatigues and Consuelo was again starting to make the bed.

"One last kiss before I am off to save the world," Enrique said.

"You are my world Quique. These maneuvers tonight, are they dangerous?" Consuelo asked.

"Not any more dangerous for a middle-aged man than the maneuvers I have just survived over the last half hour. Don't worry I will be home soon and I will show you how a soldier makes a bed. Nice uniform Chelo," Enrique said, and he was out the door.

"Words are hollow with only burned out meaning," Antonio Martín told Louie Farnsworth. "I used to live with and love words in my former life, but now I have come to realize only actions are real. Especially actions that have no words to describe them."

"In the end, all we have is language and words are the building blocks of language," Louie answered. She had started this march with the single focus of putting one foot in front of the other. Ernesto, her *No Importa* Dr. Who, was keeping a close eye on her, but she had begun to falter when Antonio began walking alongside her.

"How is the prisoner Ernesto?" Antonio had asked.

"She is strong, but she has lost her energy and she is dehydrated still, Comandante."

"Perhaps we should have left her at the camp with a bullet in her. I am not sure she will be much of a bargaining chip after our operations tonight. She is slowing us down and we need to be far from here by tomorrow morning," Antonio said.

"Just let me go and I promise I won't go anywhere or talk to anyone until morning, or whenever you say," Louie begged. "I don't know where you are going. I am no threat to you. Just let me go."

"I would be willing to stay with her until early morning and then I could catch up over the next day," Ernesto suggested. "No one is going to notice or think twice about an old man, and honestly Comandante, this fast paced march is very hard on this old man."

"These are just words, the promises you both make," Antonio said, and thus began yet another debate between Antonio and Louie. This was one debate Ernesto enjoyed because it seemed to keep Louie preoccupied and on pace with the rebel march.

"Words form our reality and define our actions," Louie said. "There was no color blue until the word named it. Other colors were named early in man's history, but blue was a later invention. I don't know what people saw when they looked at the sky, but it wasn't blue. Perhaps concepts associated with blue, like harmony, faithfulness, and confidence were also not fully appreciated until the word entered the mind," Louie said.

"The deaf, dumb, and blind still find meaning in their actions not in their inability to form words," Antonio countered.

"You assume they have no words, because they have no actions to present them. Words are, uh, like data with a soul. That the body is not seen doesn't mean the spirit doesn't exist," Louie said. "Stories are what has transferred meaning from person to person and from generation to generation. Your actions would have no meaning if there were no words to express them, to share them."

"I concede a point or two, but honestly, I tire of your words *Señora*," Antonio began. "You try to hide behind too many of them, but I can see around them, as if they weren't there. You are broken. You have lost, in less than two hundred hours of captivity. Just days ago you entered our camp, yet my soldiers and I have been fighting for not two hundred hours, not weeks, not months, but years! And before us, other freedom fighters have carried the banner. This country has been throwing off the yoke of oppression for two hundred years; many forms, but one master. Until now. We will continue to fight and we will win. There may be a time for words, but not today, not tonight! Esteban, you will stay with her as you requested, but not only you. Julio, you will also stay with her. If she as much as stands without your permission, kill her however you like. You are to leave at midnight and rejoin with us. If she escapes after that the Elazar Dam will already be history. To ensure we are safely far away, Esteban you will stay with her until morning. Tie her to a tree and rejoin us." Antonio strode away.

Louie was overjoyed with her eminent departure from this group of thugs, but now she had her own personal thug to worry about. Julio was the man whose face she had clawed when she and Harold were attacked.

Julio approached her and with a sickening smile said, "I killed your husband, now I hope I have the pleasure to do the same to you, although perhaps more slowly."

Ernesto appeared not to care, but Louie knew he was on her side. She was nearly debilitated with fear though. Ernesto was an old man and she couldn't see how he would protect her from Julio. 'It's up to me to protect myself until I am free to go. What am I willing to do to gain my freedom? Kill him? Worse?' Louie's muddled thoughts continued.

"Could they have known we were coming?" Cesar asked himself. "How? Or maybe this is just increased security because of the kidnapping. That woman! We should have just shot her like the man that was with her." Cesar was not sure what to do. The security was sufficient that he could not sneak through the perimeter the soldiers had established and successfully reach the Dam to plant the explosive charges. He sent one of his soldiers to intercept Comandante Helicon with a request for guidance. For now he would just wait here for further instructions, and hope for an opportunity to get to the Dam. "Elazar, what a name for a dam."

Cesar knew the Dam was named for the tributary, the Elazar branch of the Cambalache River that ran through the Mariposa Valley. The other main tributary, the Certeza was muddy, unstable, and slow moving and thus not a good candidate for hydro-electric power. The Elazar was clear, deep, much of it hewn out of rock over the millennia, and fast moving. It made sense to harness that potential, and it also helped regulate the cyclical flooding of the Cambalache. "But whoever came up with those names? Maybe after the revolution is successful we will change those stupid names. El azar: *fate, luck, chance,* for the powerful river, and certeza: *skill, facts, science,* and certainty for the river that is anything but that. Together they make a river, the Cambalache. And that I can understand." Cesar said out loud to no one in particular. "Why someone used an Argentine word doesn't make sense. We have plenty of words that would do."

"Ah, but Cesar, we don't have the lyrics to the song that the Argentines have," Pepito, one of the more cultured rebels, added in a quiet voice. I was a musician before the Revolution. I used to play this song. There must have been another name for this river before Cambalache. The song is less than one hundred years old. You know the word means Junkshop, or something like that."

"Yes, I know, but I also thought it was *lunfardo,* you know—Argentine slang—for a big mess, or confusion.

Maybe I am the one who is confused," Cesar said. "What I do know is, this country, is a big mess and we are going to clean it up, starting fresh with this valley. Let the water of that Dam join our revolution and wash away all that is bad, and that is corrupted. Somehow, we must get this job done tonight! Pepito, I didn't know there was a song called *Cambalache*. Do you remember any of the words?"

"Sure boss, I could sing you the whole song, but I will whisper it tonight. It is a tango," Pepito said as he reached into his pocket and retrieved a worn and discolored paper in an old leather cover. "I know I've got it here somewhere… Here it is. Pepito whispered the words of a song that told of a messy world that has always known evil of every kind. Verse after verse of sham and treachery, and void of hope for anything better.

"Wow, the guy who wrote that was really fed up or just didn't care anymore," Cesar said.

"I think the author was named Discépolo and I am guessing he cared, or he wouldn't have gone to the effort of writing the song. So, we're fighting the Machiavellians in the name of those they trap, like the song says, right? I mean, we are going to blow up a dam, and I get it, it is the symbol of an authoritarian regime that really cares nothing for the people, but Cesar, how much do we care for the people if we kill some innocents and flood their valley? It's like the song, we may meet in hell with the Army."

"Pepito, we may, and a few people may lose their lives as we may also, but change is brutal. Like the butterfly in its cocoon, it has to fight to get out. It's hard and it is probably painful. If it is opened by someone to make it easier, the butterfly will die. What I don't like about that song is, there is no one of courage willing to do the right thing, no one stands above the Cambalache. We stand above. This is something we must do. The rest of the country will rally to our side and the Junta will have nothing to show for the sacrifices they have demanded from these poor peasants. Now go and see if there is any change to the perimeter security."

Both of the rebels turned and sank to their own thoughts as they continued their wait, stuck in the mud.

Major Zarro's plan was coming together, although the surprising information that Captain Peña had come up with had forced several changes, he could still execute the plan he was sent to Mariposa to accomplish. "Outstanding!" Zarro exclaimed. "Tell the squads their orders have changed. I am in command and will relay my orders to Sergeant Hernandez soon." He paused. "Now, how to deal with Sergeant Hernandez?" he queried aloud. 'Those inept rebels should be ready in thirty minutes,' he added silently to his calculations.

The young soldier whose salary Zarro had doubled was working out well. Lieutenant Mendoza had suggested him and the choice was not surprising. Pregnant fiancé, no money other than a conscript's pay, and a willingness to follow orders without asking questions. "Hopefully Mendoza will prove just as promising."

Zarro picked up his satellite phone and dialed a different number. "Bravo Tactical, Alpha Base," Zarro called to his own command that had more coercive power than the entire stockade of conscripts.

"Alpha Base, Bravo Tactical. In place?"

"Very good. Stand by. Estimate thirty minutes."

"Standing by. Out."

"*Señora* Farnsworth, let's sit down here for a few minutes. This old man's bones are aching tonight," Ernesto said in English.

"Only Spanish old man! She speaks Spanish well enough, and if she doesn't, all the better. One mistake is all I need," Julio snarled. "And you old man, you are not my boss and you are not my conscience, so stay out of my way. It would be easy work to kill you and the *Norteña*."

"I am sorry Julio. Habit. Old men are eighty percent habit and twenty percent bravado. Spanish only *Señora*," Ernesto placated in Spanish. "Julio, I was telling our guest that I need to take a break. Since we have nowhere in particular to go, there is no big hurry." With that Ernesto sat down with a slight groan.

"I don't know about you ancient one, but I would like to get a little closer to the valley to see Cesar's handiwork. Not close enough to get in the cross fire, but it isn't every night we will see a thousand pounds of C4 go boom," Julio joked.

"Give me just a minute then and I will be ready to go," Ernesto said. He pulled his back pack around, got out some rolled tortillas and tossed one to Julio and one to Louie. He quickly ate his and was on his feet. "OK, I'm ready. Let's go. Julio, you lead out and I will bring up the rear."

"Nothing doing Ernesto. I will bring up the rear. I want to keep my eye on our lady friend," Julio said. Ernesto started down the trail and Julio pushed Louie forward and attempted to kick her, but she moved away too quickly.

About ten minutes later Ernesto stopped again. "Julio, I just can't go any further. If you want to see the explosion, go on ahead and we will wait here."

"As tempting as that is, I would rather take the lady with me and we could watch the fireworks together. Romantic, no *Señora*?" Julio rasped. He got up and walked over to where she was sitting. "Better yet, let's be romantic now and make our own fireworks!"

Louie saw Ernesto begin to move forward quietly behind Julio. There was no way Ernesto was going to protect her and would probably get both of them killed. She was not prepared to attempt to run and she couldn't feel anything to grab that might protect her. "Julio, this isn't the smartest thing you've attempted. Come any closer and I promise you I will scratch your eyes out. I will also scream and surely someone will hear me. They may not save me, but they will find you and perhaps that will compromise the mission on the Dam. I will go with you, just let me be," Louie said.

Louie's talk unwittingly masked Ernesto's approach. "Maybe I am tired of walking too, maybe I am tired…" Julio said. He never finished his sentence. Ernesto had produced a syringe that he had stuck into Julio's back. Julio fell to his knees, looked at Louie with glassy eyes and then fell to the ground hitting his face hard on the dirt.

"Well I guess if he is tired, the doctor orders a good night's rest. Midazolam. A sedative in small doses. A weapon of choice for old men protecting damsels in distress when delivered in larger doses. I prepared this before we left the camp, but wasn't sure if I would have the chance to use it. He will wake up in six to eight hours and he won't remember a thing. Shall we be on our way?" Ernesto said.

Tears sprang from Louie's eyes. "Ernesto, you will never cease to amaze me. I thought we were minutes from both becoming part of this forest's permanent landscape. I was preparing to go for his eyes with everything I had—which at this point isn't much. Thank you, my *So importa* Dr. Who!"

"Let's not cry. You are already dehydrated. We should also get walking. I administered enough sedative to knock Julio out, but not kill him. He could wake sooner than I expect." Ernesto pulled Louie to her feet and they began to walk.

After only about twenty steps, Louie asked, "Can you tell me your story now?" She added as an additional incentive, "I need something to keep my mind off of my exhaustion."

"Honestly there is very little to tell. As I said, I practiced as a medical doctor in the Capital. I was married, but my wife left me some fifteen years ago. Too many hours at the hospital I suppose, or my inability to give her children in our earlier years. I was in the hospital one afternoon when a young lady came in with serious injuries from a bicycle accident. In examining her injuries, I discovered she was also pregnant. In attempting to save the mother and the child, I lost both. The woman's name was Carmen Martín. Her husband was a young professor at the University. A witness to the accident said an Army truck had sideswiped her while she was riding her bicycle. It was also possible she lost control of the bike and ran into the passing truck. The young professor tried to get the Army to admit to the accident, but they never did. That young professor is now Comandante Helicon. His loathing for the military and his misplaced obligation to his wife and child's memory keep the revolution in him going today." Ernesto slipped into his own quiet thoughts.

Louie processed all this and asked, "So does he know who you are?"

"Who? The Comandante? No, he has no idea. He doesn't even know I am a doctor. When I came to his camp, I told him I was retired, but had a little medical training and could act as a camp nurse—trying to keep the food safe and minor injuries from getting more serious. Your vitamin shot and the sedative I gave Julio are the first times I even pulled out a needle from my bag."

"But why are you a revolutionary? This is more of a young man's game, isn't it? And you don't seem to be very enamored with the revolution, or am I just reading you wrong?" Louie asked.

"I originally sought out Antonio Martín to tell him of his wife's last days to give him some solace. I saw the need in the camp for some medical support and I stayed, promising myself I would only stay for a few weeks. That has ended up being more than a few months. I act the part when I need to, but most everyone in the camp believes I am just a lonely old man who wants to belong. They neither trust me, nor distrust me. So, I apologize for some of my more brutal acting jobs of pushing you into the cave and not speaking very much to you. In order to do the most good, I sometimes have to appear to do just the opposite."

"You may have been sent to that camp just to take care of me, Ernesto," Louie thought out loud.

"Perhaps, but I hope I was there for other reasons as well. One of my biggest successes was suggesting indirectly the delay of the attack on the Elazar Dam," Ernesto said and shook his head as if he was reconsidering what he had just claimed. "I can't take too much credit, though. I really just spoke with a voice of reason. That caused sufficient turmoil in the tortured mind of our Comandante that he made the decisions to delay. I think deep down, he is also doubtful of this project. The problem with Antonio is, he believes in the revolution, but not for all the right reasons. He has taken irrevocable actions against the State. I and others, you included, have provided him with evidence to the contrary of his beliefs. His commitment binds him to his actions and through these actions to his beliefs that sustain his actions and his involvement in the revolution. He reacts to undeniable evidence of his mistaken beliefs not only unshaken, but even more convinced of the truth of his beliefs. He works even harder to convince others and convert them to his views. This Elazar Dam has become his Moby Dick.

"Are you his Starbuck?" Louie asked.

"No, but I can't really explain why I stayed with the Comandante for as long as I did. Perhaps because I really am a lonely man looking for meaning in his life. You woke me up from my stupor and I now have purpose and identity, and for the first time in a long time, some efficacy. "

"So why do all those men stay with the mercurial Comandante Ahab?"

"They all have different reasons. There really is a need for change in this nation. There is much that is not right and these men are witnesses to many of those wrongs. But I suppose, I could answer by paraphrasing from Moby Dick, 'These men need a good grip; they like to feel something in this slippery world that they can hold on to.' The Comandante provides that for them. You can tell I have thought too much about this. Antonio is certainly no Ahab and I am not a psychologist. I am not really that great of a doctor. You know, that may be a reason I stayed around as long as I did. Perhaps I was trying to pay penance for not saving Carmen and her unborn child. All I know now is, I have a mission to get you safely back to Mariposa. And we are getting close enough to the outskirts of the valley that we should not talk and proceed with caution from here on out."

"Sergeant Hernandez, this is Major Zarro," Zarro said on the radio from the Command Post. "You are to send me one squad presently under your command back to the stockade. I will need those men to accompany me on an intelligence gathering errand under my supervision and directed by General Cruz's office. You can confirm the authenticity of my orders upon your return. Recent information has come to my attention that must be dealt with immediately."

"Sir that countermands the orders given me by my direct commander. I need those men to ensure security of the Elazar Dam and the power plant," Hernandez explained.

"I do not wish to countermand any order. You will just have to accomplish your duties with less personnel. You will still have more than was deemed sufficient before Captain Peña divided his company at both ends of the valley. I will expect that squad back here within thirty minutes!" He didn't add that he considered it a dereliction of duty to leave the stockade with almost no protection. "If the rebels knew that we only had a few cooks and mechanics guarding the sector headquarters, they would attack here, not the Dam," Zarro said in frustration. "Embarrassing the government is one thing. Embarrassing me and the Army at their own house is quite another."

Hernandez was not sure what to do, but Major Zarro was right. His job was to protect the Dam. He would like to have more men to secure the perimeter, but if the Major had new orders, he wasn't sure what he could do about that. It didn't appear or feel illegal, so he sent Foxtrot squad back to the post.

"Cesar, something is happening by the Dam. Some soldiers are getting back in a truck," a rebel soldier reported.

"All or how many? Let's wait and see where they go. It could just be a repositioning, or they could be setting up a trap," Cesar commanded. "Just in case, have everyone ready. The men with the C4 are still in position?"

"It looks like about eight or ten soldiers. Yes, all eight of our demolition team still have their packs on and are ready to go at your command."

They only had to wait one minute and they knew the soldiers were on the highway headed back toward the stockade, Mariposa, or somewhere else. "This leaves an immediate hole on the perimeter that has not yet been filled. Get those men through, now!" Cesar said.

The demolition team, weighted down with one hundred twenty five pound packs of C4, blasting caps and fuses, began moving forward. One of the delays in this planned attack was the secret procurement of blasting caps that used pyrotechnic fuses. They had planned to use match cap detonators, but the concern of stray static electricity or electromagnetic current from the semi-operational power plant could cause premature detonation. There were dangers with their selected detonators as well, but Cesar felt confident the team was well trained and ready for this operation.

It was very slow going and the demolition team was nearly in place twenty minutes later. It was now time for Cesar to create a diversion to get the principle focus away from the immediate Dam area. This was all monitored via night vision goggles of Task Force Bravo, the Special operations team Zarro had brought into the valley clandestinely.

"Corporal, spread your squad out to plug that hole and secure the perimeter," Sergeant Hernandez ordered over the radio. He had watched the eight-man squad disappear over a slight rise and enter the valley floor. They would be back at the base within twenty minutes. More worried about what Major Zarro required of them then he wanted to be, he turned back to his security duties. "It is going to be a long and boring night," he told the night sky. He was concerned that his men would have trouble staying awake this first night of who knew how many nights. 'Hopefully the operations near Campo Crespo will go quickly and either those soldiers will be able to ease the burden here, or the rebels will be defeated and all this extra concern would not be needed,' he thought. "Keep the mobile patrol moving. The party is over. Foxtrot is gone. Keep your eyes…,"

Sergeant Hernandez removed his finger from the transmit button. 'Did I just see a flash of light or a reflection, or are my old eyes playing tricks on me?' he wondered out loud. He stared indirectly, trying to use his night vision, at a dark space about two hundred meters away. Ten seconds later, "There it is again," he said under his breath. "No doubt, something is out there and it isn't the mobile patrol or someone from Gulf squad."

"Is everything OK Sergeant Hernandez or is the radio acting up," the voice on the other end asked. "We are wide eyed and ready for the long night. No worries."

"Stand by. I thought I saw some movement to your three o'clock position about one hundred meters from the perimeter and about two hundred meters from my position. Mobile patrol, advance to your left to fill in the hole left by Foxtrot until we can spread Gulf out. I will investigate the movement. It is probably a stray dog or a piece of plastic moving in the breeze," Hernandez said.

Zarro was unsure who Sergeant Hernandez might have seen as he monitored the movements from the Command Post. 'Foxtrot squad should be back in about fifteen minutes. I expect it would only take another thirty minutes to round up the Costa family and be back here,' he calculated. "Bravo Tactical, Alpha Base. You may have been spotted. Hold your position. I have an errand to run and will be back to the stockade within an hour. Report if you see any movement from our visitors," Zarro commanded and then thought about the importance of having the Costa's back with him before the action began.

"No movement from the main group. A small team moved forward, but we can't see them from our present position. That is why we were moving forward," Bravo tactical reported.

"Then it probably was you the Sergeant saw. I will distract him if I can. You know what to do if any action starts. At all costs, do not be discovered. Alpha Base out."

Switching to the radio, Zarro said, "Sergeant Hernandez, confirm Foxtrot squad's estimated time of arrival at the post."

"Less than fifteen minutes Major. As you may have overheard on the tactical frequency, I thought I saw movement south of the security perimeter. I am moving in to investigate."

"Sergeant, my suggestion is have the mobile patrol check it out so you can maintain full situational awareness. Unless it is an actual attack, which this doesn't appear to be, there is time for the patrol to investigate," Zarro insisted.

"Good call Major. I am just concerned that we have a gaping hole in the perimeter left from Foxtrot Squad's departure. If there was actually an attack, the Dam would be completely vulnerable. I would rather have the mobile patrol fill that hole first," Sergeant Hernandez explained.

"You are the commander on the ground Sergeant. But, is there an attack on the Dam?"

"No sir," Sergeant Hernandez reported.

"I will be out of radio contact while running an errand, that is, as soon as Foxtrot is back here and I feel the stockade is more secure. Keep up the good work! It may be a long night."

Yes sir," Hernandez reported. 'What kind of errand would he be running at this time of the night? Zarro was always a strange person,' Hernandez thought. Zarro was right, there didn't appear to be any rush to check out the odd reflections of light, or whatever it was that he thought he saw. He hadn't seen any more. 'Still, there was something and I am really doing nothing...' he thought.

Captain Peña had caught up with the slower moving convoy about fifteen kilometers outside of Mariposa. "We have about twenty kilometers to go, I estimate," Peña said to his passengers. Neither Alejandro nor Emma had said a word since leaving their house. Everyone's thoughts were on the threat from Major Zarro, the possibility of Diana getting picked up by Zarro, *Señora* Farnsworth's possible death, and confronting the rebels before the potential destruction of the Elazar Dam and the damage that could do to the Mariposa Valley. The Costa's had an additional burden of thought that included the death of Gustavo and not knowing where their other son was.

"I will need to find a safe place to leave the both of you when we get a little closer to Campo Crespo," Peña said to break the silence.

"We don't know anyone in the area, so you can just leave us wherever and whenever it is convenient," Alejandro said.

'Wherever and whenever,' Peña mumbled to himself. He knew they had left their home on a moment's notice, they didn't know what might happen to their daughter, they had a crazy Army officer who they could have considered their enemy, and were probably driving to a battle zone—wherever and whenever. 'I really like these people. How many people like them are there in this valley—in this country?' he wondered.

"If our country is the sum total of its people, we are greater than I ever imagined," Peña said out loud.

Alejandro and Emma just looked at each other.

Chapter 17
Attack

"You three, come with me," Major Zarro ordered. "You four to each stockade security point. Keep your eyes open. You, corporal, you are in charge while I am off the post. Station yourself at the Command Post where you can relay message traffic and keep a situational awareness at the Dam and the Campo Crespo Operation."

"I don't know anything about the Campo Crespo Operation sir," the corporal replied.

"Lieutenant Mendoza is in command there until Captain Peña arrives, which should happen about the time that I will return. There was a report of rebel activity in the area. I expect a full situational update when I get back." Zarro finished and was gone before the corporal had time to digest this and say 'yes sir'.

Seven minutes later, Zarro was following the directions the local National Police headquarters had given him to find the Alejandro and Emma Costa home. It was in a quiet area with only a few houses and very little light. "Perfect," Zarro exclaimed. After sending two soldiers around the back, the remaining soldier accompanied him to the front door. A quiet knock resulted in nothing. A louder knock with still no response. He opened the door to darkness and silence. "Go through the house and let your buddies in through the back door," Zarro whispered. Zarro had accomplished similar raids in other parts of the country and a few had held surprises in the dark, but they didn't feel like this. He knew instinctively this house was empty. After a quick inspection, it did not appear that its occupants had left in a hurry—nothing on the stove, no hot coffee on the counter, no burning cigarettes. Also it didn't look like they had been gone for a long time, as their meager belongings and clothes were still neatly in place.

"Perhaps they were just out, or they were tipped off and were hiding at a neighbor's house," Zarro said. "Soldier, you will stay here. Just sit quietly in the living room and wait. Do not fall asleep. If anyone comes in, arrest them and call me on this radio. I will send back-up immediately. Do not arouse suspicion of the neighbors. Any questions?"

"Sir, who is it I am looking for?"

"An older man and his wife. The husband works at the airport doing menial tasks, so he might look familiar. Also, they have a son and a daughter, about 24 or 25, we aren't exactly sure of ages. It isn't really important you know any more details. If anyone comes in, arrest them. If they fight back, debilitate if you can, shoot to kill if you must," Zarro said with finality and walked out of the house briskly.

A disappointed Major Zarro was back at the Command Post twenty-seven minutes after leaving. He asked the corporal for a situational briefing.

"Sir, Sergeant Hernandez is at his post just below the power plant on the East side of the Dam. There appears to be movement on two fronts. One group is below Hernandez coming toward him and to the far West side of the Dam. The security perimeter hole in the center area is filled in with the mobile patrol as you ordered."

"Very good." Zarro turned to the radio. "Sergeant Hernandez, I understand there are multiple sightings of movement. Confirm visual."

"Sir, no visual sightings. It may just be bored or nervous soldiers. We haven't heard or seen anything for at least fifteen minutes. Probably nothing."

"Very well, keep me informed. I came up empty on my brief hunting trip. Maybe we will all be empty handed by morning."

"Sorry to hear that sir. I will keep you informed." Hernandez wondered what 'hunting trip' meant, but decided if he needed to know, he would be told and with Major Zarro, it might be better not to know.

"Lieutenant, I am officially taking command. Tell me what you know," Captain Diego Peña ordered as he arrived on scene near Campo Crespo.

"Sir, we talked with several locals that saw the confrontation," Lieutenant Mendoza began. "It appeared to them that a *Norteña* was shot and carried away by a group of rough looking men. There are no confirmations and no blood or other evidence in the area of the confrontation. I have Delta Squad attempting to follow the trail of this group. Charlie Squad is still here with me."

"How do the witnesses know the woman was a *Norteña* and even a woman from that distance?" Captain Peña asked.

"They don't. They did tell us that there was also another local woman and a man that looked Peruvian or Boliviano that were asking questions about the incident. They didn't identify themselves and were gone almost an hour before we got here," Mendoza added.

"When was that? When did you talk with the witnesses?" Captain Peña asked.

Mendoza looked at his watch and estimated, "Two and a half hours ago sir, at about twenty hundred hours."

"And nothing new to report since eight this evening? *Gamusinos*! I would say this is a wild goose chase, except someone else is also interested. Are you sure this alleged *Norteña* was carried away? Maybe she is still being hunted," Peña asked.

"It does feel like we are chasing windmills sir. We should hear back soon from Delta Squad." Mendoza offered.

As if on cue, "Mobile base, Delta," came across the radio.

"Report Delta," Peña commanded.

"We are finding multiple fresh trails. We spilt into two groups and they both led to a well-established camp. I think you need to see this. It doesn't appear to be vacated very long. Also, by a stream about one click from the camp has what we are guessing is fresh vomit and blood. We are guessing it is fresh because no animal has bothered with it yet—and it really smells. We left markers so you can make it to the camp in about ninety minutes."

"Very good. Give us the coordinates and stay there. Don't bother anything until we get there. Set up a security perimeter in case someone comes back. We have about forty soldiers coming your way double time." Peña's adrenaline was beginning to flow as he plotted the camp's location and he was ready to leave immediately when he remembered the Costas.

"Lieutenant, take the vehicles with a driver and two soldiers for each, along with this couple I brought along who have local contacts in the area. Follow this dirt road," Peña commanded as he pointed out the route on the map. "I am not sure how good this road is, it may be a path in some places. It will be slow going, especially in the dark, but if you can get through, it roughly parallels our route to the camp. If someone is in the area, they will hear the vehicles and move up the hill. With our main punch on foot, perhaps we will flush them out. This may not be a wild goose chase after all."

Peña pulled the Costa's aside and told them, "You will go with the vehicles. I would leave you here, but I don't have time to find you a safe place to stay and I cannot afford to leave any soldiers behind. You will be alright and we will meet up in a few hours I expect. Sorry for bringing you along, but I know this is still better than you being at your home right now."

"Thank you Captain, we will be fine. I always wanted to be a soldier, now I get to pretend with much more reality," Alejandro said.

"Old man, you never wanted to be a soldier!" Emma scolded after Peña had left.

"OK, it's been thirty-five minutes and that is enough time," Cesar said to those around him. He knew the demolition team needed only about twenty minutes to set their charges. He had waited longer to confirm the troops that left were really gone and not a set up or ambush. Now the demolition team needed a distraction so the fuses would go unnoticed long enough for detonation and to accomplish the escape of the demolition team. "It's now or never," he said mostly to himself this time. "Start the attack!" he commanded. This wasn't really an attack, but a decoy. They would shoot, but not move forward. They would stay as safe as possible and protect their avenue of retreat. As soon as they knew the demolition team was outside the perimeter, they would leave.

The fuses were slow burning, but they only had two and a half minutes before the first charges went off. It would take about five minutes for all charges to detonate due to the importance of weakening key points of the Dam. "C4 is powerful, but not that powerful in the small amount we can bring to the fight. The charges need to build on each other in order to weaken the Dam sufficiently that the water pressure could do the rest. You will need to retreat along the ridge, or you will be a part of the destruction, so keep that line of retreat open at all costs," Comandante Helicon had explained to the entire attack group the day before.

No sooner had Cesar's group started firing, than another attack appeared to start to the West. "*Madre!* Who is that? Comandante Helicon?" Cesar wondered out loud.

Zarro's special forces team was in place to create a secondary diversion by engaging the Western perimeter for a brief time and then retreat. This team was only firing blanks and was taking a calculated risk. Only a few in the Army knew of this team's existence. General Cruz had purposely been kept in the dark on this operation. This team could not be discovered at all costs. They had special equipment and had received special training for unique missions such as this. They could not leave any of their wounded and they could not get caught in the flood that would immediately follow the Dam's demolition. Their mission would only last ninety seconds which was enough time to keep the West perimeter focused while the actual rebels attacked the East perimeter. In short, their mission was to help the rebels dig themselves into a deeper hole—even if it cost a few lives of their fellow soldiers from the collateral damage of the Dam's destruction. But then, that was the rebels doing wasn't it?

"We have a two-pronged attack in progress," Sergeant Hernandez yelled over the radio. "Do not allow a breach of your perimeter! Keep your focus and do not move forward. Our job is to protect the Dam and the power plant, not capture these sons of dogs!"

From a kilometer away from the lights of the power plant, Louie and Ernesto heard the first shots fired and could see some of the tracer bullets. They stayed to the West of the battle as they continued out of the foothills. Neither being experts of the Dam environment, they hadn't realized how close to the West Perimeter they actually were. "It's started," Ernesto said. We will wait out of the way for now. I don't want us to be caught up in that mess.

"Bravo Tactical, collect your spent rounds and get out of there. Your job is done. I will contact you tomorrow. Alpha Base out," Zarro completed as he reentered the Command Post.

While watching the fire fight on the far side of the Dam, something just seemed odd about that side of the attack, Sergeant Hernandez caught movement in his peripheral vision near the Dam. Then he saw it. "Mobile patrol, there are bad guys coming your way from the Dam side. It looks like they may have already planted some explosives. I have a straight shot from here to the explosives. You watch for the rebels. I saw at least two running straight for you."

Hernandez pocketed his radio and ran straight for the explosives. He reasoned they would have a few minutes before detonation, but didn't know when that time had started. He reached the first and was able to pull the fuse. He went directly to the second satchel farther down the walkway and pulled the fuse when he felt someone kick him in the hip. His left leg stopped working. He tried to get up and fight, but found no one there. Blood was coming from his pant leg. He tried to reach for his radio but began to black out. As he laid down, he saw an additional satchel of explosives above him and to his right, nestled in a yet to be connected light fixture. He closed his eyes and tried to roll over just as he heard a massive explosion, followed by another farther away in quick succession. He could feel the cement from the Dam face strike his face and couldn't breath as the dust enveloped him.

"Hernandez, report," Major Zarro commanded. "What is going on?" All he heard was static on the radio. He tried another frequency, but there was still no response.

Cesar saw two and then a third member of the demolition team coming down the hill. They had crossed the perimeter, but were now in the line of fire due to that odd diversion to the West. "That is so stinking weird," Cesar said. There were no more shots being fired from that attack point. "Move back," he yelled. That was the signal to taper down the diversion attack and start extracting from the Dam area. 'One last explosion should do the job,' he thought. He saw two more of his men cut down just as they attempted to cross the perimeter. They had opened up a hole, but they should have been more of a surprise, coming from behind. "So much for perfect plans!" he cursed.

"A total of four, or five explosions," Louie reported to herself. She was now waiting for the Dam to start breaking apart. A single loud explosion rang out and the lights went out everywhere near the Dam. "That must have been at the power plant," she reasoned.

"Yes, it wasn't operational, but it was still connected to the Mariposa grid and provided the lights for security," Ernesto explained. "I wasn't part of any discussions about particulars of the attack, but I would have expected that explosion to happen first."

Four men in black camouflage, painted faces and some sort of goggles strapped to their heads crashed through the forest, almost knocking Louie down. Ernesto, to Louie's left was unhurt. Oddly, the men kept going and didn't say a word. As soon as they appeared, they disappeared.

A final loud explosion turned their attention back to the Dam. It lit up the area for a brief moment. Ernesto saw someone trying to drag themselves out of the way of the impending collapse of the Dam. Soldiers were running toward the small ridgeline to the East. All firing had stopped.

"Someone is alive up there and trying to get out of the way. I think I can pull him to safety. You move to that high ground," Ernesto told Louie, pointing to a small rise to the West. "There isn't any time to run across the entire ravine to where the soldiers are going before the Dam starts to break apart. I will meet you there! Go!" Ernesto demanded.

Soldiers were yelling. Louie was still reeling from the intrusion of the strange disappearing soldiers. She was getting dizzy and was completely exhausted. Feeling no closer to an actual escape to safety Louie couldn't move another step. She was ready for the water on the other side of the Dam. Maybe it would feel as good as the stream earlier in the day—'was that really in the same 24 hour period?' she wondered as she began to lose consciousness.

Sergeant Hernandez had calculated the same reality. He was trying to make it to the West side of the Dam, but had lost control of his arms and legs. Suddenly he was pulled up and was being helped to safety. Then he collapsed again. His guardian angel had just been shot and was lying in a pool of blood. He didn't recognize this old man, but he tried to drag himself and this stranger to safety, but struggled to even breathe. A moment later, two people were with him, trying to pick him up. One he thought was a soldier, Hernandez then considered the possibility that he had died because he was seeing ghosts. He thought he saw the *Norteña* pulling him and the old man to safety.

Louie had watched Ernesto fall down pulling the soldier away from the front of the Dam. She expected the Dam to burst at any second, but she couldn't let Ernesto be a part of that destruction. She was completely exhausted, but pulled herself to her feet, somehow reached the fallen Ernesto, discovered the other person to be Sergeant Hernandez, and began to drag herself and both men forward. As she pulled with all her might and praying for strength she saw dark bodies moving in the partial moonlight. The explosions had ruined everyone's night vision. It was chaos and she calculated that improved her chances of getting to Ernesto without being shot. Then one of the silhouettes approached with his gun raised. Louie almost began to laugh, realizing how close she was to freedom, but now facing a probable one-man firing squad. The soldier hesitated, then dropped his riffle and began pulling Sergeant Hernandez.

"This camp is a ghost town and it feels like the ghosts are still here," Diego said. "It looks like they took some gear, but left most of it behind. That suggests they were traveling on foot."

"Sir, there appears to be a cave that someone slept in, with the letters F-A-R-N-S-W-O-R-T-H' scratched in the dirt at the back end. Is that a name, the name of the *Norteña?*"

Captain Peña entered the small cave and was immediately nauseated from the smell. "Nice work soldier. Have we found the trail leading out of here? They haven't been gone that long. A few days at the longest, a few hours if we're lucky," Peña said as he exited the cave.

"We have found quite a few well-worn trails. We can't be sure which one they left on until we follow them some distance. And we need daylight to really be sure, sir,"

"*Rayos!* So we are back to the wild goose chase," Peña began. "Lieutenant, check in with Command Post and let Major Zarro know we found the Camp and it is confirmed *Señora* Farnsworth was here. We did not find any evidence of a death, but there was possible blood on the trail leading to the rebel camp, so the reported shooting was a real possibility. The rebels left some time ago and we can't ascertain which direction they went until daylight. Have him pass that information on to *Señor* Rigley and to *Señor* Farnsworth. You and your men hold up for the night and we will get an early start in the morning. Let me know if you hear anything back from Major Zarro," Peña ordered.

"Will do Captain. What about the report of the other operatives in the area, the Peruvian and the woman?" Lieutenant Mendoza asked.

"We don't have any real evidence of who they were or what group they were with. Report it, but we won't follow up on that at this time."

Ten minutes later Lieutenant Mendoza reported back to Captain Peña. "Sir, it took a while to raise Major Zarro. It seems the Dam was attacked and there were casualties. Major Zarro could not speak to the damage to the Dam or the power plant. It is a chaotic situation. One of the injured was Sergeant Hernandez."

"Ask Major Zarro to keep you posted. Give me your coordinates and I will come to you immediately. I will leave you with the troops here to follow the trial in the morning. I need to get back yet tonight. Has there been any evacuation below the Dam?"

Mendoza passed on his coordinates and suggested a route to the road. "No evacuation mentioned sir," Mendoza reported.

Captain Peña was furious at himself. He had calculated that this was where he needed to be. Now Hernandez was injured, possibly dying, Zarro was in de facto command, and he was sitting around a ghost camp with nothing to show for it. "I should have been at the Dam!" Diego berated. "If Hernandez dies I will never forgive myself."

Harold had had enough of staying in the car while Diana and Tomás Rioja, the Embassy security officer, talked to the local villagers. His wife was probably nearby, maybe dying, and he was playing the chauffeur. 'And in Mariposa I was just a house guest. All my life I have been the extra piece of furniture! Not anymore,' he thought. They had taken a road that a local villager had suggested.

They were now lost. Tomás had gotten out of the car and climbed to the top of the ridge to see if he could get cell phone coverage. Diana had also gotten out of the car and was standing nearby, deep in her own thoughts.

Harold grabbed the keys from the ignition, got out of the car and tossed the keys to Diana who was startled. She picked the keys up off the ground. It was dark so he couldn't read her expression.

"I am going to walk down this road. You can follow when Tomás gets back. If I come to a fork in the road, I will mark which way I went. I have no idea what we are doing, but I can't just sit here anymore. I have a flashlight, but I will use the moon most of the time. See you when you catch up." Harold started walking.

Three minutes into his walk he was wondering what he was doing in a foreign country, unable to speak the language, alone in a jungle forest, not knowing if his wife was alive or, or something else, and he had no idea where he was or where anyone was really. He felt so puny and weak, so miniscule, inconsequential and useless. Thankfully he didn't feel meaningless. A thought came to his mind. It was a verse from Proverbs in the Bible. Candle of the Lord. Harold flicked on the flashlight and looked around. Dark. Alone. The echo of the words remained in his head. 'Candle of the Lord.' He made a promise to study those words when he got to a place where he could find a Bible. For now it was enough. He took a step forward into the dark, knowing he was not alone.

Diana heard a noise. It was a mechanical sound. It was a vehicle, coming down the road. Maybe more than one.

She ran to the bushes on the side of the road to hide. She didn't have time to get in the car. She didn't know how to drive a car, even if she had time. 'Could the rebels be using vehicles? Of course they could,' she thought. And then she saw the first of four Army trucks—the kind that would carry soldiers. She was frozen in place. She wanted to make sure they were really the Army.

The lead truck stopped and two soldiers jumped out, rifles pointing toward the car. 'They think this is a trap of some sort,' Diana thought. She stood up and called, "Thank goodness you're here, we are lost." A nervous soldier shot a round in her general direction and Diana screamed, "Don't shoot!"

Someone yelled, "Hold your fire!" A search light from the first truck shined in the general direction of Diana. She held her hands high and walked out of the brush. The searchlight found her. It blinded her.

Lieutenant Mendoza held his pistol at Diana and commanded her to walk forward. When she was close enough to see it was one woman, he said, "Keep your hands high and do not speak."

She reached the road and rough hands grabbed her from behind and pushed her to the truck hood where her hands were held behind her and she was quickly frisked. They found the keys to the car.

"Who are you and what are you doing out in the middle of nowhere this time of night?" Mendoza asked.

"My name is Diana Costa and I am with two men, both from the United States. We are trying to find our way back to a main road."

"Right. No one else is with you. Where are these two men?" Mendoza asked with doubt in his voice. Without waiting for an answer he turned to a soldier and said, "Get the Captain on the radio—Oh wait, the radio is at the rebel camp—have them send a runner to catch up with him, tell them our position on the road and that we have captured a suspect person."

Mendoza then shifted his attention back to Diana. "Now, tell me again, where are these men? Or are you broke down and part of a rebel group that is vacating this area?" he asked, knowing he was leading his capture, but wanting to see her reaction.

Diana was now too scared to answer directly. She gathered her wits and said, "I am not a revolutionary. I am a simple woman from Mariposa. I came here to help two *Norteños.*"

A soldier next to Mendoza said, "Lieutenant, this may be the woman that was asking questions in Campo Crespo."

"What are you and your two *Norteños* doing out here, so far from Mariposa?" Mendoza asked.

"We are looking for one of the *Norteño's* wife. She was kidnapped by revolutionaries," Diana explained.

"Interesting you admit to that now. You know a lot about where to look. That is very odd to me. And since you don't have any *Norteños* to corroborate your story, I am going to assume the worst for the moment." Without taking his eyes off of her, he commanded, "Soldier, keep you rifle pointed at her. If she tries to escape, shoot her, in the leg preferably. We will wait until the Captain gets here. Set up a security perimeter in case we have other guests—just don't shoot the Captain."

They waited only twenty minutes and Captain Peña stepped onto the road only fifty meters in front of the convoy, accompanied by one of the soldiers he had brought in his detail. "What do we have Lieutenant?"

"We have a woman we found on the road by herself. She knows about the Farnsworth's. She is in the vicinity of the rebel camp. Just too many intersecting facts to disregard. She says she is with two *Norteños*, but neither are here. She may be the woman that was reported to us that was asking questions in Campo Crespo, but where is the other man? A third man was never mentioned by those we talked to. She also says she is from Mariposa—so what is she doing out here?"

"Thank you Lieutenant. Let's go meet her," Captain Peña said.

"Captain, this is the woman. She says her name is Diana Costa." Mendoza said.

Peña looked at a scared and shaking Diana. "Release her Lieutenant. I know this woman and can vouch for her story, I think. Diana, what are you doing here and what two men are with you?"

"*Señor* Farnsworth and a man from the U.S. Embassy, a man named Tomás Rioja," she said as she began to weep.

"Where are they? What are you doing on this road by yourself, in the middle of the night?" Peña asked as just a little doubt crept into his own mind.

"*Señor* Farnsworth is walking down the road. *Señor* Rioja is on the ridge trying to get his mobile phone to work. I know this sounds crazy and I don't blame the soldiers for being doubtful. *Señor*es Farnsworth and Rioja were going to go to Campo Crespo, thinking *Señora* Farnsworth had been shot, and I offered to accompany them to help out. We found nothing and we were taking this road back in hopes of running across *Señora* Farnsworth."

"Who is this Rioja? Don't you realize that if you found *Señora* Farnsworth she would be with more than a few terrorists? What were you thinking?" Peña was furious.

Diana could tell. She was embarrassed, but also a little angry. "I am sorry Captain, but we thought we could help. We weren't looking for trouble, just information. *Señor* Farnsworth also felt that if his wife was indeed shot and possibly dying, or even dead, he could not wait even one minute without doing something, without being present where his wife was," Diana said, feeling a little annoyed at Peña's insensibility.

"Speaking of being present, come with me," Peña told Diana. He was still upset, but grateful she was here and not where Major Zarro could take her. She followed him to the last truck, assuming he was going to arrest her. Peña was assuming Alejandro and Emma were still there where he had left them when he and the trucks departed in different directions. Dutifully, they were sitting there, fearful, but not asking questions.

"Father, mother? What are you doing here?" Diana screamed when she saw them. "Have you been arrested?" she added with fear rising again in Diana's throat while they hugged each other.

Captain Peña left them to their reunion, even though they had seen each other earlier that same day. Then he checked his watch. It was already twenty-three minutes after one in the morning. No matter. "Lieutenant, let's get this car off to the side of the road. You have the keys? If you don't then push it far enough that the trucks can get around it. Honk its horn. If this Rioja cowboy doesn't show in a few minutes, leave the car with the keys and a note. No, we can't leave him out here. Send a few soldiers up the ridge and find this guy. He is probably lost, so be careful not to shoot him and don't let him shoot you. We need to get back to Mariposa, so find him *pronto*. Our mission is to get back to the stockade. I made a mistake dispatching so much of the company here. Let's hope it isn't total chaos when we get back. We are all needed there as soon as we can get there."

Captain Peña knew he couldn't just leave this Rioja and Harold out in this forest. He wanted his men to hear and understand what the highest priority was—the Elazar Dam, the town, and the security of the sector, not the *Norteña* they had dedicated so much time and energy to find while Sergeant Hernandez, the father figure to many of these young conscripts was wounded, doing their job.

Rioja wandered out of the brush just as the trucks were maneuvering around Rioja's car. "Tomás Rioja?" Peña yelled. "I could have told you, you wouldn't get reception here. We are over 30 kilometers from the nearest cell tower. We will have time for introductions later. Follow the last truck in the convoy. Let's hope we find *Señor* Farnsworth on this road before we get to the main highway."

Chapter 18
Heliotropic Madrugada

HAROLD FARNSWORTH WAS FOUND A KILOMETER DOWN the dirt road. "I am grateful for this experience, even if I didn't accomplish anything toward finding Louie. I did something. I walked in the darkness. I was alone, and then I wasn't," he tried to explain to Captain Peña.

"Harold, the Dam was attacked earlier tonight. We need to get back to Mariposa. I will scold you another time for endangering your life, the lives of others, and possibly complicating the return of your wife," Peña said. He was still more upset with himself than with Harold's foolish idea to go after his wife with Diana Costa and Tomás Rioja.

It was slow moving and they didn't find anything else of interest in the way of the rebel group. Peña admitted to himself that they could have easily passed them in the night and never have known it,"

The morning sun was just hinting at its appearance when the convoy saw Mariposa in the distance. "Heliotropic," Harold said out loud.

"What's that?" Peña asked.

"It is the phenomenon where plants and other organisms turn toward the sun. You know, how some flowers face the sun and follow its path across the sky. It's what this early morning feels like. We were in the dark for many hours, but now we see the sun and it brings new hope to me."

"It's like the butterfly navigation lesson you gave me over dinner what seems like months ago," Peña said. "I will admit, I feel better going toward the heat of battle today, just as I explained then."

"Yes, that does feel like months ago. That picnic by the river with Louie feels like a year ago," Harold added.

"Literature and butterflies are the two sweetest passions known to man," Diana Costa said, quoting Nabokov, one of her mother's poets. Her family had often joked about those lines because they seemed to fit her mother and father so well. Now as she watched her parents in each other's arms, sleeping as best they could, she was grateful for her family and their safe return. "Return to what?" she wondered out loud.

During the long night, her parents had told her of Captain Peña's visit to their home, about Zarro's threat, and his words about Diana that had tipped the scale in their decision to go with him. They also spoke about what this could mean for Captain Peña, getting in the way of the evil Major Zarro. They were grateful, but they also knew values don't always determine the outcome you want. Diana did not mention her words to the Captain, or of her feelings for him. She could not explain them to herself in a way that made sense. Perhaps it would be better for her and her parents to relocate to another valley and simply disappear. "Yes, and Zarro would find us sooner or later, no matter where we went," Diana said softly to her sleeping parents.

"We will find a way," were the words her father had told her the night before, when things seemed the darkest.

Louie Farnsworth was sitting in the military infirmary by the bed of Sergeant Hernandez. His wife, Consuelo was sitting on the other side of the bed, holding the Sergeant's hand.

"I think he is waking," Consuelo said when Hernandez began to move slightly and his eyes fluttered open and shut. Then he settled into a deep sleep again.

Louie sat quietly with her complex feelings, trying to sort out what should have been a joyful return to her husband and to safety. Instead, she found her husband unexplainably gone and her rescuer, *No Importa*, AKA Dr. Who, AKA Ernesto, dead. Major Zarro, when he discovered her at the Dam as part of the chaos, pulled her away from Ernesto and interviewed her, 'no, interrogated is a better word for it,' she thought. She had listened from her interview seat in the Command Post as he took credit for salvaging the attack on the Dam and saving her from the clutches of the attacking revolutionaries. No matter that it was she who had in her clutches the revolutionary who had actually saved her. She would never be sure if Ernesto might have lived had it not been her notoriety that pulled her from him in his moment of greatest need.

Louie had met Sergeant Hernandez's wife when she was called to the infirmary and Louie asked to stay with them since she had nowhere else to go. "I certainly don't want to go to an empty hotel room. I don't feel safe and I don't feel well," she had told Zarro.

"You will be our guest here at the stockade of course *Señora*," Major Zarro had answered. "It would be good for you to be at the infirmary due to the trauma you have experienced at the hands of the enemy of the State," he added as if it was for a public relations press release.

Louie got some sleep during the night, but also spoke with Consuelo. Consuelo had told Louie of her husband's constant berating of himself in allowing the revolutionaries to take her. It was from Consuelo that she first heard that her husband had not been seriously injured and was tirelessly working with Captain Peña to win her release. "How odd that Major Zarro never even thought to mention my husband or his health," she had noted. Consuelo had not said a word in reply.

"*Señora* Farnsworth?" a voice in Spanish asked from the door. Louie had dozed off and for a brief moment thought she was back in the cave.

She answered in English, "NO! I will not go."

"*Señora*, please wake up," the nameless soldier said. "We have news. Your husband has been found. He is well and will be here in about fifteen minutes. He is with Captain Peña."

Louie cupped her face in her hands and began to cry.

"*Señora*, all will be well. You were an angel to me in the midst of the battle last night. How you arrived I do not know, but this I do know—all is well. The night is over and the sun is rising." It was the voice of Sergeant Hernandez who was holding his wife's hand. They too had tears in their eyes.

"We failed Comandante," was Cesar's report over the radio. "Not all the charges went off as planed and several of the larger charges were diffused before detonation. The Dam is severely damaged and could still break. The power plant was demolished. Five of our eight on the demolition team were killed, I believe, although I think we need to assume some may only be injured and could be tortured into giving information to the Army."

"We did not fail Cesar. We can yet finish off the Dam. They would never expect another attack. Let's change our regrouping point to the farm near Campana. It won't be safe for any long period, but it will be a good staging point for a final assault. We will need to see how much explosives we have cached, however. That is our only limitation."

"There were extra troops on the perimeter, but the team managed to infiltrate without detection. A strange thing happened during our decoy attack, however, Comandante. I thought perhaps you had come to the fray. We had some help on our left flank that kept that side of the perimeter focused, allowing some of our team to get out. Otherwise, they would have been completely trapped. No sooner did that attack start than it stopped."

Comandante Helicon was initially furious, then disappointed that the attack was not a success. "It may have been ignorant soldiers who quickly realized their mistake. It may be a sign for us that we continue our attack. I don't know. Be safe and I will see you late tonight or early tomorrow morning." Now he was positively excited about the chance to attack again. "Now I can be present and command the operation! I will be an eye witness to the power of the revolution. Years from now we will mark the day with celebration and speeches and I will be able to say I did not command from afar. I was there."

"Harold, I have some news for you," Captain Peña said, trying to keep a deadpan look. The convoy had just entered the stockade and a soldier had immediately reported to the Captain. "It seems the Dam survived the attack!"

"That is wonderful news, Diego. I can't imagine the tragedy of a dam break," Harold said with some enthusiasm.

"Yes, great news. Oh, by the way, your wife was involved and apparently helped save Sergeant Hernandez's life. She is in the infirmary waiting for you."

"What! My wife is here? You're not joking. She is here?" Harold asked, expecting to hear that he had misunderstood.

"Yes, I will take you to her now if you like."

"Well, I would like to freshen up a bit first," Harold said.

Peña looked at him in surprise.

Harold laughed. "Are you kidding, of course I want to see her, this very instant! Can we run?"

They entered the infirmary and as there were only two inpatient rooms, they were at the door in seconds. Harold walked in barely able to control himself. He was shaking and tears began to fall unrestrained. "Oh, thank God! Louie I can't believe you are here. I can't believe how wonderful…" He buried his face in her hair as they embraced. He looked her in the face and said, "You are the most amazing, beautiful, courageous—and did I say amazing?—person on the planet. I love you so much. Not a minute went by that I didn't pray for you and honestly, at the same time I felt so helpless."

"Yes, I am back. Back from the dead almost, except for a brave man who was the answer to your prayers and mine." She paused, "I love you Harold," Louie said much more subdued. "You sure know how to show a girl a memorable honeymoon," she added with a quiet smile.

"Aghhh, I am so sorry! Sorry I didn't do a better job protecting you. Sorry I didn't get to you sooner. Sorry we needed to try the honeymoon over. Sorry we… No, I almost apologized for picking this place, but that is not true. This has been the most terrible experience of my life and I had the easy side of the equation. But in the midst of all this, I have met some of the most unbelievable people and, well we can talk about all that later. I am just grateful to have you back and well. You are well aren't you? I didn't even think to ask! I promised I would never be so self-absorbed again and here I am already thinking of myself. Sorry."

"OK Harold. Enough apologies already," Louie begged. "One of the things that kept me going was thinking of how brave you were when those thugs attacked us. You still look a little banged up. I didn't even know if you were alive. The rebels reported that you were dead. Luckily they didn't ask my opinion on that one. I would have set them straight."

"I do believe you would have. How did you escape and how did you end up participating in the battle of the Elazar Dam?" Harold asked.

"We can save all that for later too. As well as your explanation of where you and Captain Peña were when I had my Helen of Troy return from captivity moment," Louie said.

"*Señora*," Captain Peña interjected. "Are you being well taken care of? Is there anything we can do for you? It is my fault Harold was away. We had heard rumors of a possible shooting that may have included you, in an area near a village quite a distance from here."

"I have been well taken care of Captain,"

"My name is Diego, please."

"I have been well taken care of Diego. Major Zarro has been very hospitable, but it was my choice to stay here last night with Consuelo and your great soldier, Sergeant Hernandez," Louie said.

"I went out in search of you without the Army's support or Diego's knowledge. He actually rescued me and my companions," Harold interjected.

"I have talked to Major Zarro at length," Louie began, "and would be happy to go over the details of the last week and a half. There are a few things I wanted to go over with you that I felt uncomfortable sharing with the Major for some reason. I think it is you I can trust. First, if it is OK, I would love some breakfast. My stomach has shrunk but I would love something other than cold beans and rice."

"I will hold the chow hall open for as long as you like. Please, come with me. You and Harold have full use of my quarters," Diego said. "Sergeant Hernandez, I will be back to see you in just a few minutes. Don't go anywhere!"

"I will sit on him if he even starts to move," Consuelo said. Sergeant Hernandez was actually feeling the I.V. meds take their affect again and he was dozing off. His wounds were serious, but not life threatening Consuelo knew. It would be hard for the old soldier to stay in bed as long as would be required.

Diego escorted Harold and Louie to his quarters. "I will be back within the hour for you," Diego said.

"Diego, could you stay for just a minute?" Harold asked.

"Certainly, what can I do for you?"

"I would like to offer a prayer of thanks and I would like you to be here for it. No one did more than you to rescue Louie. Obviously she didn't need any of us, but I am so very thankful for all you have done." Harold and Louie knelt down and Diego sat on his couch, not sure what to do. Harold began, "Our gracious Heavenly Father, ..." Diego had never experienced anything like this. It felt good.

After the prayer, Louie said, "Diego, we can talk about all the details of my capture, my days at summer camp, the camp director, and escape, as I did with Major Zarro, but I wanted to tell you in private that the Major is taking credit for many things that he has not been involved with according to what I know—which isn't much. I don't think the Major is your friend, but I am now way out of line, so sorry for speaking so direct about that. Also...," Louie paused trying to get her thoughts together. "during the battle last night, Ernesto and I kind of bumped into these soldiers who were in different uniforms. I don't think they were rebels, at least not the kind I have been hanging around with. They were dressed really professionally and had night vision goggles and much nicer weapons than I saw with the rebels. It was odd. I think they had fired at the soldiers guarding the Dam and then they left just as the fighting was beginning. All they seemed to want to do was get out of there. They hardly even noticed us, even though one of them knocked me over. In the dark they must have assumed we were just a couple of campesinos. For some reason I felt uncomfortable and didn't mention any of this to the Major."

"Thank you for sharing that with me. You will have to explain who this Ernesto is. If I showed you some pictures, could you identify the weapons these soldiers were carrying?"

"Maybe. It was dark, I was exhausted after the long hike back to Mariposa and it happened so fast I hardly had time to think, let alone look at them closely."

"Long hike back? You didn't travel here by some kind of vehicle?"

"No, I got really sick a few days ago, and I was a little delirious, almost escaped, yes, was nearly shot, got recaptured and then walked here, somehow," Louie rambled.

"And then you entered a fire fight and helped save Sergeant Hernandez?" Diego asked.

"It wasn't really like that, but yes, I was there," Louie innocently admitted.

Harold and Diego were both speechless for a moment.

"Helen of Troy was like some Greek goddess, right?" Diego asked rhetorically.

"Only half immortal, and the most beautiful of all women—the face that launched a thousand ships, I believe," Harold added as he took Louie into his arms.

"Oh brother. I know what I look like right now—the face that scared away a thousand ships more like it." Louie said. "Be back in a half hour if you can Diego. I am starving."

"Sergeant Hernandez, can you talk for a minute?" Captain Peña asked. Sergeant Hernandez did not move. "How is he Consuelo? He is a tough soldier, but I understand he was injured in his hip. How bad?"

"He was hit in the hip, but his radio took part of the blow," Consuelo answered. "The Doctor does not think it injured the bone, only the muscle. He lost a lot of blood. He really should be moved to the capital for better medical help, but he refused to go until he reported to you."

"Consuelo, I have actually come with a personal request. I hate to bring you into this, but I don't know where to turn. Major Zarro wants to arrest a family because of their possible implication with the revolutionaries. I have sort of been keeping them with me. I have them in one of the trucks where they have been told to stay, but I can't keep them there much longer. Could you keep them at your home for just the day until I can sort this out? If you don't feel comfortable getting involved in this, I understand completely." Diego knew he was taking a huge risk telling this to Consuelo and that perhaps he was breaking the hermetically sealed brotherhood of the officer corps, but he felt a higher requirement to do the right thing.

"Who is this family? Of course I will help out. I don't want to harbor criminals, but if you say they are innocent, I know that will not hold the weight it should with Major Zarro. I know Quique would feel the same."

"Their name is Costa. Alejandro works part-time at the airport. His wife is Emma. They have a daughter named Diana. Army intelligence has their two sons connected with the revolution. Major Zarro wants to see what information they have related to their sons' activities. I think there older son was killed some months ago," Diego explained.

Consuelo started shaking. She hoped she could hide it from the Captain. "I will get them now and take them to my home. I will do whatever it takes to protect them. You are right. I am sure they are innocent."

"They are in the last truck in the convoy. No one will think twice if you put them in your car and take them off the stockade. Please do so as soon as you can. Major Zarro was up most of the night and I am told he is still sleeping. He left orders to wake him when I returned. I countermanded that order with the excuse to let him get a few more hours of sleep. I need to wake him soon. You can come back as soon as you would like to see to your husband. From what I have heard, he is the true hero of the day."

"Major Zarro," Peña yelled while knocking on the door to the Visiting Officer's Quarters. "Major Zarro. Captain Peña. I am back and looking forward to your report."

A sleepy Zarro answered the door, but he was in very good spirits. "Captain, welcome back! Yes, much to tell. Give me a few minutes to clean up and I will meet you at the Command Post."

"If it is alright, I will be at the chow hall with the Farnsworths. *Señora* Farnsworth is reportedly starving. As soon as I get them settled there, I will go to the Command Post," Peña said.

"Yes, good. Keep her happy. Keep them both happy. This is great news for all of us. I will meet you at the chow hall in ten. Great morning isn't it?"

"Well sir, I was only gone fourteen hours, but it seems the world has changed. Yes, a very good day. After briefings, I am going to need to get a few hours of sleep. For now I will keep going on the adrenaline of all the good news." Peña was play acting and hoped it sounded authentic. He believed Major Zarro cared little for Louie's return and wondered about his interest in the Dam's survival, the deaths of four soldiers, the capture of several wounded rebels, or the serious injury of Sergeant Hernandez, but suppressed those feelings. It was a new day, and a good one at that.

Chapter 19
¡Presente!

"CESAR, IT IS GOOD TO SEE YOU. I AM GLAD YOU WERE able to safely escape," Antonio Martín exclaimed. It seems there were many more soldiers at the Dam than we anticipated. Do you think our surprise was not a surprise?" he asked.

"Initially there were more soldiers, but one group was pulled out, which allowed our demolition team to slip inside the perimeter. Still there were more than we had planned for. And then there is the mystery of the attack on our left flank. I still haven't made sense of that," Cesar said.

"I think it must have been some mixed up soldiers as I suggested earlier. What else could it have been? How many did we lose?"

"Six captured or dead. All from the demolition team, except for Ernesto," Cesar said. "One of the demotion team saw him rush to the aid of a soldier, so he shot him as a traitor. Judge, jury and executioner in less than five seconds."

"I am sorry for Ernesto. He made his choice, and so did fate—at the Elazar, the fate dam," Antonio said trying to raise his own spirits again. "I don't know who Ernesto actually was, or why he chose to fight with us, but I know he wasn't a traitor. We can assume that the irritating *Norteña* is back safely with her husband?"

"No one reported seeing her, but the last in the area was our man who shot Ernesto. As soon as he confirmed Ernesto had been hit, he turned and didn't look back for a couple kilometers. Like all of us, he expected the Dam to break apart at any time."

"Yes, that is the biggest disappointment. I am ready to go myself personally to finish that job. Do you think our men will follow?" Antonio asked.

"Some will fight to the death for you and for the revolution. A few others have nothing to go home to, so they will stay because they have no other options. Together that is about twenty-five to thirty fighters. There are ten others that probably won't—maybe another five on the fence," Cesar calculated.

"That is enough. And if we are successful, we will pull many others our way. Is it doable?"

Cesar thought for a few moments, trying to put the pieces together. "They won't be expecting us to come right back. The Dam is damaged and thus, I don't expect the Army will have many soldiers stationed just below the Dam. There is no power, thus the lighting is out. I think we could get back in and finish the job. What I don't know is, do we have sufficient explosives to do it, and depending on how we execute, it could be a suicide mission. The only place we could infiltrate is the center base of the Dam. They could pull the fuses if we made them long enough, or slow enough, to guarantee our escape. None of our group is fanatic enough to become a suicide bomber."

"Then we will have to find another way. It is life or death for the revolution," Antonio said with finality. "Do you think we could also attack the Army Post in the same blow. The message would be clear. 'We are not beaten and you are not safe, even behind your fortress walls. If we could get the conscripts to start doubting, then we have won another strategic victory."

"I think I am feeling better today," Louie said. She had eaten at the chow hall, not a lot she thought, but enough. She was sick within fifteen minutes. She barely made it back to Diego's quarters. She had been at the toilet, or balled up on the bed for the rest of the day. All she wanted was to keep silent and not move a single muscle.

Just before nightfall, the doctor recommended moving her to the infirmary so he could administer an IV. "She has an intestinal bug I am guessing, or she simply ate too much today. I would need to send stool samples to a lab in the capital to be sure, but I will treat her for the bug no matter. Until then, she should not travel or do anything strenuous. What I am most concerned about at the moment is her severe dehydration. She needs fluids and they won't stay down if we deliver them by mouth. It is very possible she could go into shock, swelling of the brain, seizures, or kidney failure. These could lead to death. "

"I think I actually got some sleep last night," Louie said to Harold. "My first night back I spent in a chair in Sergeant Hernandez's room. It was so much better than a cave floor. Even feeling terrible this bed was like heaven. I have to admit I thought my reintroduction to an indoor toilet was going to be a happier reunion."

"We should have never let you just take up where you left off before your capture. You have been through a lot of trauma and stress. Who knows how long it will take to get you back to one hundred percent," Harold said.

"I would be thrilled with getting to fifty percent, but honestly I have no complaints. I am so grateful to be alive and with you. Did you get ahold of our parents?" Louie asked.

"The guys from the Embassy are returning to the capital today. They wanted to meet with you before they left, but I told them to let you sleep. They sent a message to the Embassy and the State Department is going to contact our families. When I can get back to the hotel I will get on the internet and talk with them. I didn't want to leave you, though. Our families know you are safe. They can wait for my call. They will be OK with that."

"It's funny, you would think that I would want to get on the next plane out of here and never look back, but I am not ready to do that. Promise me that we can do some kind of a funeral for Ernesto. He deserves whatever we can do."

In between bouts of nausea, diarrhea, and terrible cramps, Louie had filled in Harold on her ordeal. Harold in turn had told Louie about Diego Peña, the Costas, and his experiences. They had much to talk about yet, but they felt like they understood the context of their separate experiences that they could at least reference them without long elaboration.

"Major Zarro, thank you for cutting your well-deserved sleep short to brief me on the attack and *Señora* Farnsworth's return. I want to leave soon and inspect the Dam, but I want to understand what happened first," Peña said.

"You may need to speak with Hernandez on the tactical situation. I can speak to the strategic lay of the land and the battle's implications." Zarro outlined the battle scenario as it was explained to him the night before. He then explained the rescue of the wounded and *Señora* Farnsworth. "I think the *Señora* has a fixation on one of the revolutionary thugs as her savior. What is the psychological term for that? Stockholm Syndrome I think. It is like she has this traumatic bonding with one of her captors. She said he rescued her and then even tried to help Sergeant Hernandez. It is like she is trying to make these rebels into people with values and principles."

"Is it possible he really did rescue her? How else would you explain her return?"

"Perhaps. I suppose there has to be the exception that proves the rule. We need to keep her happy, but she doesn't need to put a human face on society's enemy. Before you know it all the naïve do-gooders will tie our hands to the point where we won't be able to prosecute this war to its conclusion."

"Maybe the conclusion of this rebellion will eventually be negotiation, a transition to democracy, and our exit from power," Peña said, knowing he was goading Zarro.

"Have you not learned anything over the last day? These so called revolutionaries, who are really just unprincipled thugs playing a game to take power, they would blow up a dam that was only built for the good of the people they say they represent. Let me explain transition to you. We are the only thing that stands in the way of a transition to chaos or tyranny. We are the minority, but the minority majority because we and we alone have the coercive power to rule. It is our only choice."

"I don't believe that is our only choice, Major," Peña interjected.

"Let me ask you a question: Why does our Obligational Legitimacy exist?" Zarro asked.

"I am not sure it does, but if it does it is because of the breakdown of society, so we had to temporarily step in to bring order so the civilian form of government could get their feet on the ground," Peña suggested.

"No. That is the child's answer. Our Obligational Legitimacy exists to justify establishment and maintenance of rule. Why justify rule you might ask? To bind the military organization together for a task beyond the accepted bounds of their traditional role. Why rule at all? The military perceives the obligation to do so. Why does the military have this obligation? Obligation, as you know from your company officer courses, springs from various sources, both non-moral and moral. Obligational Legitimacy is characterized by an irreducible common identity which must include some type of value or moral considerations. Our Army, all of us, our leaders and our soldiers, perceived a justifiable obligation to establish and maintain power due mainly to moral necessity. Maintenance of Obligational Legitimacy is crucial for continued rule. Although most of the Army is not completely aware of the existence of Obligational Legitimacy, they are aware, as you are, of its manifestations, such as our national security doctrine and how we are organized as a occupier army, not a force focused on external threats."

"I think you are living in a make believe world Major," Peña said.

"Am I? Or are you? Have you noticed how many moderate officers have been retired over the last two years? Have you looked at the new training manual? Elite units with special insignia that have been created. When was the last time you read the final paragraph of the Manifesto that was proclaimed during the coup? Do the lines, '*The actions of the military government are inspired by the necessity of transforming the structure of the state to permit efficient government action to improve social, economic, and cultural structures, and by necessity to maintain a definite nationalist attitude and fully re-establish the principles of authority and respect for obedience to the law in all areas of national life,'* mean anything to you at all?"

"I think it a little odd that a professional soldier has that political statement memorized," Peña said.

"Don't kid yourself Captain. The military became political before it seized power and is now the central political instrument of society. Now we must bend toward the hypothetical imperative. That is, put our accomplishments on display, highlight our mission success not only for society to see, but in order to maintain military unity and thus our Obligational Legitimacy. That is why this *Señora's* safe return and the saving of the Dam from complete destruction are so important to our mission and our rule."

"And thank goodness you were here to highlight those events in the proper light, and to take credit for them in a way that sheds a positive light on the Army," Peña said, shaking his head.

"You can learn the easy way, the hard way, or if you prefer, you do not have to learn your lessons at all. You will not, however, be allowed to sit on the sidelines with that sarcasm for authority and smug self-righteousness much longer."

"If you will excuse me Major, I need to go see how Sergeant Hernandez is doing. It wouldn't look good if the hero of the night were to die," Peña said.

"Not necessarily, Captain. Dead heroes are sometimes more powerful than living ones," Zarro countered.

Disgusted, Peña did not reply. He walked directly to the infirmary.

"Sergeant Hernandez, how are you doing this morning?"

"Much better my Captain. I am finally off those ridiculous medications that kept putting me to sleep in the middle of my sentences. It is not fitting for a real soldier," Hernandez said.

"It is your duty to get well Sergeant, and that is an order," Captain Peña joked. "Now, while we have a few minutes alone, I have a few things I want to go over with you if you're up to it."

"What I am not up to my Captain is just sitting around this hospital like some ugly decoration that my mother-in-law sent me. Everyone is afraid to get rid of me, but no one really wants me around either," Hernandez growled.

"Well, I am afraid I can do nothing for your ugliness, but I am not afraid of you and you aren't useless. Tell me about the fire fight. *Señora* Farnsworth mentioned some odd happenings that took place on the West side of the Dam perimeter. Did you notice anything?" Peña asked.

"Yes I did, now that you mention it. I was about to check it out myself when I was ordered to send a squad back to the post by Major Zarro. We almost lost the Dam due to his shortsighted order, but I guess hindsight is perfect vision."

"So what did you see?"

"At first I noticed some flashes of what I thought was movement below the West perimeter. After the battle began, actual firing came from that area. I thought it was odd, but then I had my hands full trying to play the Little Dutch Boy, trying to put his fingers in the dam."

Odd in what way?" Peña asked.

"It wasn't odd that there was firing—the perfect place to keep that flank occupied so the bad guys with the explosives could get near the Dam. Wait a minute. They had to have already planted their charges. They got to the Dam when the hole was made when Foxtrot Squad departed. Anyway, it was a perfect two-pronged maneuver. At first I just thought it odd that the group to the West wasn't using tracer bullets. The group attacking my position had tracers. Now I know why there were no tracers. They were firing blanks."

"Are you sure? Maybe they just had a different set of ammo, with no tracers," Peña suggested.

"No, they were firing blanks. The flash was different. The sound was different. We had no injuries or casualties in the West flank and no reports of any near misses. Captain, you know the difference between the muzzle flash of a blank versus a live round. Any soldier could spot the difference— maybe not immediately in a fire fight with multiple attack points and then an attack from behind with the explosives crew trying to get away from a dam they thought sure was going to break at any moment. I would stake my professional credibility that they were firing blanks," Hernandez concluded.

"Thank you for your analysis Sergeant. Let's keep that between us for now. I have my reasons. Don't ask. I am going to go visit the Dam site yet today. Anything I should be looking for?"

"Nothing in particular. Be careful. I don't know how safe that Dam really is," Hernandez cautioned.

"A special engineering team will be here in a couple days to assess that. For now we are keeping people away, except for the roving patrol that crosses in front of the Dam every thirty minutes. There is a sort of personal matter I need to mention…"

"If it is about house guests, everything is fine," Hernandez interrupted. "Consuelo and I talked. If it is alright with you sir, we can table that for another time when we have more privacy."

"Understood Sergeant. Thank you, for everything. You have saved the day in many ways."

"That's why I get paid the big money sir," he laughed.

"I need to get back to my office for a while and get caught up before running out to the Dam. Anything I can get for you?"

"A new hip would be nice. Give my best to *Señora* Farnsworth. I hear she hasn't been doing so well."

"She is sleeping right next door to you. I am sure if you use your indoor Sergeant's voice she and the rest of the hospital will hear you," Peña said with a smile.

Captain Peña left the Sergeant and peeked in on Louie. She was sleeping. Harold was not there. "That guy must have been taking lessons from Alejandro, he can disappear at a moment's notice, and show up in the most surprising places," Peña said out loud. He left the infirmary and made a straight line for his office.

"Celia, how are you holding up after all the commotion?" Captain Peña asked as he entered the stockade headquarters.

"I am good sir. Glad you are back in one piece. I have taken care of your admin duties for the day. I have one private message for you from General Cruz." She handed him a hand written note.

"This is in your handwriting."

"Yes, I wrote as the General spoke directly to me. I think that is only the second time I have ever spoken to him. The note I sent him at your request—I verbally read it to his secretary, so he replied in kind on the *secnet*. That's what he called it—short for secretaries' network."

Diego read the note.

Captain, I have not authorized Major Zarro's travel, but it is apparent that my office did. I know nothing of the events you describe. Keep your head low and I will research from my end. I know life may seem complicated for you right now, but oh what I wouldn't give to be a company commander again, doing the Army's job instead of attending these endless meetings and worrying about the price of bread and a liter of gas, or visiting the opening of a supermarket. Keep me informed.

"Celia, please send this note along on the *secnet*. It is an update from the information that Major Zarro sent through official channels. I will have another memo ready to go through official channels once I get back from the Dam." He was walking out the door when he turned to ask, "How is our Lieutenant Mendoza? Keep an eye on his whereabouts for me as best you can. Thanks Celia."

"I haven't seen the Lieutenant yet today," was all Celia felt she should say.

Completing his rounds, Diego stepped back into the Command Post to let the duty corporal know he was going to visit the Dam and to ensure nothing else was happening. Major Zarro met him at the door.

"Captain Peña, I know we don't see eye-to-eye on the politics of the Army, but we need to keep those feelings aside. I have a job to do here as do you. Now, tell me, did you warn the Costa family of my plan to, uhm, visit with them?"

"Major, as you say, you have a job to do and I have a job to do. I need to go inspect the Dam, not worry about your paranoid escapades." He pushed past Zarro and entered the Command Post where he requisitioned a driver, a vehicle, and a radio. Zarro was gone when he came back outside. He made a quick change of plans. Turning to the soldier beside him he said, "I changed my mind, I will drive myself. Let Major Zarro know I expect to return within two hours."

Peña drove out the gate and turned toward the Dam. When he was sure he wasn't being followed, he took a side road that led back past the stockade to the Hernandez home. He figured this was a plausible visit, since he had just talked with Sergeant Hernandez. It was only natural to drop in on his Sergeant's wife in a show of support. This was of course true, but he also wanted to see how the arrangements with the Costas were going. Even this arrangement was only temporary; yet, he wasn't sure of any long-term plan.

"Consuelo," Peña said on the front steps. I just wanted to let you know I checked in on your husband. He is doing well, although he is already getting bored. I came by to see if there was anything I could take to him."

"That is very kind of you Captain, please come in," Consuelo said.

Once in the house, Consuelo walked with the Captain to the kitchen and said, "They are in the basement. I will bring them up. When the military vehicle pulled onto our street I sent them to the basement. I don't know why. It is no safer than the living room or this kitchen." Consuelo was obviously more nervous than she wanted to admit.

As Diego Peña entered the kitchen he was surprised to see Harold sitting in a chair at the table by an interesting wood carving. "Harold, what brings you here? Do you know the Hernandez family?" a flustered Peña asked.

"Yes of course. Sergeant Hernandez was the escort you assigned to us the day Louie and I went looking for butterflies. I am only now getting to know his wife, Consuelo."

"Oh yes. I forgot that."

"Not a great day to remember. I hope one day to forget it myself. I also know the Costa family somewhat. You know that I know Diana, but I have also had a couple of conversations with Alejandro about butterflies. As it turns out, he is a local expert."

"Why am I not surprised," Peña joked.

"Captain, what an honor to see you again so soon," a voice behind him said. It was Alejandro.

Diego jumped. "How do you do that? No one can startle me like you do."

"Like the butterfly *Señor* Farnsworth seeks, some things are not seen but are there." Alejandro said.

Then Emma entered the room, followed by Diana. Peña was startled anew. "I actually came by to make sure this was working out for the short-term. I hope to get all this cleared up so you can return home soon, but first I just wanted to make sure you are all safe." He was talking to the group but only looking at Diana. Everyone in the home did not miss this little slight of their own presence.

"Captain, you don't understand," Consuelo said. "We are old friends. Quique and I have known the Costa Family since before Diana was in diapers. This is like one big party." Diana was still looking at the floor, fearful of looking Diego in the eye. It was obvious to the whole room that the only thing Diego was interested in was just that, looking in her eyes.

"And there is room and food for all of you?" Diego asked, still looking at Diana, hoping she would at least glance at him.

Emma understood the impasse. "*Noia del tram, tens l'es-guard en el llibree I el full s'irisa en veure's cobejat,*" she said.

"Mother," Diana said. She was blushing and no one quite understood why or what the strange words meant.

"I am sorry," Diego said to Emma. "What was that you said?"

"It is one of Emma's poets," Alejandro said. "She uses them to explain awkward moments, or to create them."

"Oh, what language is it? What does it say?" Diego asked as he finally turned to look at Emma.

"It is a poem by Joan Salvat-Papasseit and it is in Catalan. Diana, could you translate it for Captain Peña and also for *Señor* Farnsworth? I am sure you still remember it. It is short and beautiful," Emma suggested.

"Mother, must I? Really? Here? Now?" Diana pleaded.

"It would be an honor if you would," Diego said in English. "Would you like to hear a poem Harold?"

"That would be wonderful. What is the poem about?"

"It is about a shy woman," Emma said.

Everyone turned to Diana and waited.

Diana took a deep breath and began. She had a mental picture in her mind of the old paper copy she had read many times.

> Girl on the tram you've got your eyes in a book
>   and the page blushes on being envied.
> And the conductor wonders if you'll turn the page:
>   just to see your eyes!
> We can see your legs and the stocking so sheer;

and all the tram is you.
But we can't see your eyes.
And your head is bright, tinted by your body of red taffeta,
*   and your handkerchief, back from the wash.*
But we can't see your eyes!
And if I were to get off? -- I'd never know your eyes...
Look now. I've got off!

As she said the last words, she looked up and stared directly at Diego. The room was silent, but full of blushed smiles. Even Harold was overcome with the simple beauty of the occasion. He hadn't understood the conversation which led up to it, but what touched him was that he was here, present, during this intimate occasion. "This would never happen in the United States," he said quietly.

Consuelo whispered, "This hardly ever happens anywhere. I am so glad it happened in my home. I will be able to warm my hands with the fire of its memory for a long time to come."

"I would offer to take you for a walk, but I am not sure it is safe outside for you," Diego said to Diana.

"Alejandro and I had just begun a conversation about the Madrugada Butterfly," Harold offered. "Maybe we can all go in the other room and continue that conversation. Let's leave the girl on the tram with the Captain, before he has to get off. So, Emma, can you be my translator?"

"I am not as fluent as Diana, but I am sure I can handle the basics of whatever fairy tails Alejandro has to share," Emma said as she and the others left Diego and Diana to themselves in the kitchen.

"That was a beautiful poem. So you speak English and Catalan?" Diego asked.

"No, I don't speak Catalan, just poems my mother had me memorize when I was younger. I am sorry if that embarrassed you. It did me."

"Not embarrassing at all. Like Consuelo said, it was an honor to have been here to witness the power of your presence. This isn't completely over. I mean the kidnapping and the Dam attack, and Major Zarro, but I have come to you as commanded," Diego said.

"I don't know what the next command should be except there should be no more commands," Diana said as tears welled up in her eyes.

"That is the wisest thing I have heard all day—a day filled with too many commands. Let's just take this as it comes. I do need to leave and inspect the Dam. I am worried about the safety of those below it. Before I go," Diego said quietly as he took her hand, "Thank you for letting me see your eyes." He lightly brushed his lips on her hand and inhaled as if the air close to her skin was sacred incense, and gently let it go. He turned and left, leaving her in the kitchen alone, but with his presence still lingering on her hand and in the air. Things not seen but are there.

Chapter 20
Cleave

"Cesar, it is good to have you back!" Antonio Martín said. The men look a little shell shocked, but what were we to expect after their first major confrontation in over six months. I have given some thought to your earlier comments. Pick your seven top men and you and I will take the revolution through them."

"Take the revolution through them?" Cesar asked.

"Yes. Instead of the revolution being out there somewhere that we travel to," Antonio said as he waved his hand in no particular direction, "our men need to know the revolution is really inside each of us. Instead of going through the revolution, the revolution must go through us. For that to happen, they need to find meaning in what we are doing. Our revolution is led by men like you and me. We are practical-minded directors and leaders who will produce a new hegemony by means of ideological apparatuses such as education and the media, as Gramsci would have said. We need to take our educator role more seriously. The *Movimiento Nacional de Hegemony Socialista*, 'The Modern Prince' of this country, is the force that will allow the working-class to develop organic intellectuals and a socialist hegemony within civil society. We must develop those organic intellectuals among our own men, or they will see the destruction of the Elazar Dam as nothing more than destruction."

Cesar only nodded. Long ago he had left the deeper thinking to Antonio Martín—his Comandante Helicon. He believed the social and economic status quo had problems and he trusted in others to define the revolution beyond attacking the apparent protectors of what was wrong.

Antonio continued, "Do you know why the Elazar Dam was chosen as a prime revolutionary target?"

"It is a symbol, a symbol of the rich and corrupt trying to lull the common man back to sleep and accept their servitude because now they can have a radio and a television while their children continue to starve," Cesar said.

"That is said nearly perfectly Cesar. Perhaps you will be the mayor of this valley one day after the revolution. But there is more. The vulgar economism that you describe goes far beyond these valley walls. Stanislav Mishin, writing in PRAVDA only a few years ago said something like, It must be said that, like *the breaking of a great dam*, the American descent into Marxism is happening with breathtaking speed, against the backdrop of a passive people. I don't have the article with me, but I remember it because of its reference to the breaking of a dam. Of course, Russia today is no better, but some there still have a streak of the ideal with which to measure the rest of the world. The destruction of the Elazar Dam goes far beyond a revolutionary message to this valley, or to this country. It is a message to the proletariat of the world to throw off their shackles and join the revolution that was derailed because some were in too much of a hurry."

"Comandante, I will let you worry about the rest of the world. I fight for you and for the revolution in my own yard. When do we move on the Dam?" Cesar asked, trying to move the conversation back to the mission at hand. Cesar did not care for Antonio Martín the college professor. He much preferred him as Comandante Helicon.

"Yes, we must break things open so people can see what they don't have, and then they will want it all the more. I have been thinking about how to break things open once and for all. Have you ever heard of bouncing bombs?"

"No Comandante."

"The bounce part is not so important to us, actually. In World War Two, a bomb was developed that would bounce along the surface of the water to avoid nets and other protective devices around dams and other structures. These bombs would then sink and explode underwater. The explosion pressure was more intense because it reflected against the water, plus the water pressure and a thing called the bubble effect greatly magnified the power of an explosion. I think we have been attacking the wrong side of the Dam."

The basic physics of this idea made sense to Cesar. "But where are we going to get this bouncing bomb?" He asked.

"We make it and we deliver it by floating debris. We really only need one brave soul to make the delivery," Antonio explained. "How much C4 and Semtex do we have left in our cache?"

"300 pounds of C4 and 200 pounds of Semtex," Cesar estimated.

"That may be enough. Now the question is, do we have someone that would be willing to deliver it, or will it be me or you?"

"I wouldn't have believed I would say, it feels so good to walk again," Louie said. "It is amazing what a day and a half in bed can do. I could give Twiggy or Kate Moss a run for their money in the skinny department, however. What was the ludicrous thing she said, 'eating doesn't taste as good as skinny feels?' What I wouldn't give for a steak and baked potato with a side of pasta and crème brûlée for dessert."

"Take it easy Louie," Harold said. "You have only been out of the hospital for two hours. Let's get you fully recovered and then we will talk about a visit to Keens's. And you look much healthier than you think, my love. And know, I will always love you no matter what the weight scale says, fat or skinny—just be you."

"Mmmm. I wish I felt better to continue our honeymoon back at the *Otra Vez*. I am afraid the only thing I can do in bed, however, is collapse into deep sleep. Keep up that kind of talk, though. I love it. So what do you want to do after my fifteen minute doctor ordered walk?"

"I will settle for holding your hand and staring at you while you sleep."

"Harold, you are going to win the Husband of the Year award if you keep this up," Louie joked. "Let's talk. I would like that. Over the past couple weeks I have either had to spar with a fanatic, talk to a mystery doctor who didn't want to talk, or converse with myself.

"Well, I have been thinking about a few things I would love to run by you," Harold said.

"Well let's hear it? Your thoughts are one of my favorite things about you."

"Wow, what does that say about my six-pack abs and undying love for you?"

"Undying love is good. We will talk about the six-pack abs if and when they are uncovered from the cute baby fat you wear so well," Louie joked. "So what's your thoughts babe?"

"I have been thinking about the word cleave," Harold said. "I have always thought about it in the sense of the way the Bible speaks about it. You know to hold to firmly and closely, loyally and unwaveringly, eternal. These last weeks have reminded me of cleave's other definition, to divide by a cutting blow, you know like a meat cleaver. The thing is, the one eerily supports the other."

"It is not good for man to be alone, Harold," Louie said with as serious a face as she could muster, but with a smile just struggling to break through. "The experiences over the last few weeks have taught me it is downright tragic for man to be alone," she added, trying to joke again, but now sounding more serious.

"Well, even before the last few weeks I haven't done a very good job of cleaving. I have let work and my thoughts of work—no matter how enduring my thoughts are to you—get in the way of us," Harold said

"I haven't felt that and I knew you were a deep thinker before I married you. It comes with your package. So enough with the apologies and the perceived shortcomings," Louie assured.

"Well, you wanted to know my thoughts and I will try to stop beating myself up. But I want you to know I am going to do a better job of cleaving, and I never want to forget what the other side of cleave felt like so I never become complacent with what a blessing I have in my life with you."

"Captain, I have received new orders from headquarters," Major Zarro said boldly. "These changes impact your status in this sector. I will immediately take command of all operations against the terrorist revolutionaries. This is to include collecting and interrogating suspect collaborators, as well as maintaining security of the Elazar Dam."

"I cannot, I will not release my authority until I receive orders that reflect these changes Major," Captain Diego Peña said.

"Are you questioning my orders Captain?"

"No sir I am not, but until I have orders—and your orders apparently say nothing of your authority over me—I will follow my orders only." Peña wanted to scream. This was so irregular and created a complexity that no one needed at this delicate time. "I will call General Cruz immediately and get a clarification. If I am to be relieved of my command, I will do so with all the support you require. Until that time, I am in command here."

"I have already requisitioned Lieutenant Mendoza to my staff. As I see your duties now relegated to administrative duties, I will leave you with your office and Celia, and the injured Sergeant Hernandez, as well as a contingent of let's say, twelve soldiers. I also authorize you to call headquarters for any clarifications you require. I will set up my command in the Command Post. Once things settle down here, I will see if I can bring you into my command, which is much broader than this small sector, or I can help you find another post more suited to your interests and career aspirations," Zarro said with finality.

For the first time since entering the military academy as a new cadet, a small part of Peña wanted to symbolically break his sword and walk out the stockade gate. The much larger part of him knew he had a duty to the country that was much bigger than the pettiness of Major Zarro. He walked calmly to his office and asked Celia to get General Cruz on the line. Three minutes later Celia told him, "General Cruz is out of the office attending an event of assembled foreign military attaches. He is expected to go home from there. He will be in the office tomorrow morning. His secretary said, if this is an emergency she can pull him from his event."

"No, this isn't that kind of emergency, Celia. Major Zarro just sacked me and claims to have orders to do so. I am now an administrative clerk and you are assigned to me. Could you pass on another message through your channels to General Cruz requesting clarification? I am only asking now. I don't want to get you into any trouble or jeopardize your position here."

"Of course I will get your message to the General. Captain, it isn't my place to say, but you have always tried to do the right thing for the right reasons. This is a complex world we live in at the moment, but clearer heads will eventually prevail. Keep doing what is right and it will all work out. As for me, I am grateful to be assigned to you. Don't forget, I worked for Major Zarro when he was sector commander. I don't speak about past commanders, but I don't need a second t-shirt either."

"Thank you Celia. Oh, I have also been pulled off of security for the Elazar Dam according to the Major. Until I get that sorted out, could you please let the General know that I inspected it and it is in grave danger of breaking apart. I am not an engineer but even I know what a stress fracture looks like. I suggest that the government engineers authorize a release of water to relieve the stress. They can take care of their re-engineering plans after safety concerns are mitigated. Otherwise, their inaction could lead to deaths and crop and habitat destruction."

"I will take care of that Captain. By the way, all of our unofficial correspondence with General Cruz is kept in my purse. I don't leave them at my home or in this office."

"Thanks again Celia. I am going to go see Sergeant Hernandez if anyone needs me."

"OK Captain. Tell him I wish him a speedy recovery. I hope his move to convalesce at home went well. I don't know what the hurry was for him to leave the infirmary."

"The move was the Sergeant's doing. He thought that if he was going to just lie around he might as well be doing it at home. That was his rationale. I think he just wanted to be out of the Nurses eyesight so he could cheat on his doctor's imposed limitations to move around and to be closer to Consuelo's cooking," Peña said.

"I would choose Consuelo's cooking too. Have a good day Captain. Hang in there!" Celia said as Peña walked out the door.

Ten minutes later Captain Peña parked in front of the Hernandez home. "Hello Consuelo, can the Sergeant come out and play?" he asked when Consuelo answered the door.

"No he can't Captain and I out rank you in that department."

"Yes, you do, and it seems this is going around," Peña replied.

"What is going around? Did I miss something in this conversation? Please, come in. Would you like to see my husband, or someone else?" Consuelo asked.

"You didn't miss a thing. Just joking. Yes, I would like to see the Sergeant if I could."

Peña was escorted to their bedroom. He felt a little uncomfortable in this private space. "Sergeant, I thought I would stop by and make sure you are following doctor's orders."

"I don't see any doctor here. I do what I want in my own home sir," Hernandez said. "I am grateful for the company, although it has been nice to have Alejandro around. Have they missed him yet at the airport?"

"Each morning I think, this is the day I sort this mess out and help the Costa family back to a normal life. Then Major Zarro throws another wrench in the works. Today was the biggest. It seems the Major has new orders that are far reaching in their authority and responsibility. I have been removed from my command and only have administrative duties. I have you, Celia, and 12 soldiers to do this job that Celia could handle by herself before lunch."

"And what is it our good Major has been ordered to do?" Hernandez asked.

"Nothing less than saving the world, from what I can see. He has carte blanche in fighting and investigating anything to do with the revolutionaries, including areas outside of this sector. He also now supervises the security of the Elazar Dam. I have come to speak to you about both."

"Sir, who gave him these orders?"

"I have not seen his orders and I have not received any new orders myself. As far as the Major is concerned, he is in charge. I left him no doubt that I will not follow those orders until I get new orders through our chain of command."

"*Rayos*! This is unprecedented, at least since I became a non-commissioned officer. This is a disaster in the making. But my Captain, what can I do?"

"Plenty Sergeant. I will get to that, but first, how are things going with the Costa family here. Do you need money for all the extra mouths to feed? Is anyone starting to get cabin fever? Is there room for everybody?"

"Don't worry about the food. We have plenty. Both Consuelo and Emma are alchemists in the kitchen. They can change beans and rice into steak and eggs, or nearly that. We are fine so far, but Alejandro is worried about the security of his home and if he will lose his job at the airport if he doesn't show up or contact someone soon. Other than that, we old folks are having a wonderful time together. Diana, however, is bored out of her mind. She doesn't complain, but she is having a hard time and I understand she is finding new ways to complicate her life."

"Complicate her life? Is there some problem that I can…?" Diego Peña began to ask in concern.

"You sir, you are complicating her life," Hernandez interrupted. "Not that I can blame you, but with all respect sir, her interest in you is perplexing," he added with a smile.

"Perplexing is an understatement. I have never met anyone like her. I have never met a family like the Costas actually. Am I complicating her life? I don't want to do that you know. For all I know I will be sent to some other corner of the country in a week or two if Zarro gets his wish. Now that Mariposa is the place to be and no longer a forgotten valley, I only seem to be in the way of more important things like sustaining the Junta's grip on power and career progression."

"This is not sounding like the Captain Peña I know sir," Hernandez began. "Certainly the military life is difficult for the spouse, but not for potential suitors. Yes, you could leave soon, but last I heard you are not engaged, you only just met. Have you even been on a single date yet? No sir; I meant the perplexity of the Costa's negative connection with the military. They have a son who was a revolutionary, who was killed perhaps by the military, and another son who may be a revolutionary. I am surprised Diana would even consider you a friendly acquaintance, let alone a potential suitor. And now with the entire Costa family on Zarro's wanted list, that makes you even more suspect, and endangers you as an abettor of collaborators. That is punishable by death for an officer of the Army. That is treason."

"Yes, and I have asked you and your wife to get involved, which massively complicated your lives as well," Peña said.

"We have known the Costas for many years. I would do nothing less for them, but I am not an officer, the commander of this sector. True, what you have done for them is courageous, but we need a plan Captain. We are going to lose at this shell game soon. It is very dangerous trying to con a con man. Major Zarro will figure this out and probably pretty soon."

"I have been trying to come up with a plan since Zarro announced his plan to arrest them," Peña said. "So far I have been lucky, and you are right, neither luck nor hope is a strategy, although I am grateful for the luck."

"And there is one more thing sir. May I have permission to speak frankly, man to man—no rank or military decorum involved?"

"Certainly," Peña said, bracing himself.

"Very well, I now speak as Diana's godfather."

"I had no idea Sergeant, err, Enrique."

"Like I said, I have known her since she was born. I would like to ask your intentions? I know you to be an honorable man, but I have her interest at heart when I ask this. I had no idea you two even knew each other, but Consuelo says she has never seen a relationship like this. 'Magical' was the term she used. 'Magical' doesn't cut it with me. So I ask you, what are your intentions with my goddaughter?"

"Like my non-plan with the Costa Family, I don't really know. She intrigues me, inspires me, and throws me completely off balance. She is beautiful, but with a beauty that goes far beyond appearance. You are right, I hardly know her, but I feel like I grew up with her and that she knows my every secret. Did Diana tell you that it was she that commanded me to meet with her?"

"I have not spoken directly with her about you, yet. I didn't want to fan any flames before I understood your interest and plan. I thought officers lived and breathed plans and strategies. Did you skip those classes at Company Grade Officer School?"

"No, typically your description fits me perfectly. Not so in the case of Diana. I am afraid I have met my match. *Veni Vidi, Diana Vicit*."

"Sometimes not having a plan is a good plan. All those *Norteño* techies who started those companies that I never use probably didn't have a real plan and that kept them open to new ideas and the flexibility to take advantage of new opportunities. That is fine for them, but not for *Sombrita*," Hernandez said.

"*Sombrita*? Why little shadow?"

"Alejandro fancies himself a shadow, a man of secrets and near invisibility—sort of his attempt to not be noticed, and Diana has always been his shadow, so that's what I have always called her. You are the best commander this sector has had in the 20 or so years I have been the Sergeant Major, but that is still not good enough for her. When you have a plan, let me know. Until then, you be careful with her feelings. Do not lead her on, and be a gentleman, or I will break your head to the point that it won't even cast a shadow. Are we clear?"

"Yes we are. Thank you for watching over her. She is a gem that deserves a protectorate like you. Now if you have any ideas for the Costa family, let me know."

"They could use a few things from their home and I am in no form to retrieve them myself. Could you perhaps accomplish a midnight requisition for them?"

"Consider it done."

Chapter 21
Purpose and Duty

Louie Farnsworth had been happy to listen for once to the dinner conversation as she nibbled on her food. Captain Diego Peña had taken them back to the Hotel *Otra Vez* for dinner, although the original plan was to return to the post for one more night close to the infirmary.

"So, what motivates you?" Harold asked.

"Why, do I seem unmotivated?" Diego asked.

"No, to the contrary, you seem very motivated, especially in the face of so much frustration," Harold said. "I have seen in my company that what really gets people going is to be a part of something bigger than themselves. They want to have a purpose—both in the little things of everyday life and in the bigger things—that their life means something."

"Harold, you are getting pretty deep here for a light after dinner conversation," Louie warned.

"I suppose everyone wants to feel like they are more than just a butterfly—here today and gone tomorrow and for what? Butterflies are beautiful, but what are they needed for? Nothing that I can think of," Diego said, taking Louie's caution to Harold as a challenge to engage in this question.

"That's it. We all need to feel, to know, that we are a vital piece of the world, our little part of the world anyway. Without this feeling, people feel empty," Harold said. "I have seen many successful men in the boardroom who feel that emptiness. Here in the Mariposa Valley I have gotten to know some of the poor, at least poor by some economic standards, and the uneducated—again incorrectly measured by short-sighted standards, who have a much better perspective on their purpose and value. They have almost nothing, but they have more self-efficacy and identity than a powerful CEO in Silicon Valley."

"You are talking about the Costa family aren't you?" Louie asked. "He has told me of some of his experiences with the Costas. Maybe they are unique."

"They are unique sweetheart, I'll give you that, but I am also speaking about Sergeant Hernandez and Consuelo. I am talking about the soldier who stayed awake and watched over you when I was ordered to go back to Diego's quarters the night you were really sick. The way people look as we walk down the streets here, versus the look of people on say Park and 57th in New York City."

"Perhaps the events of the past weeks have brought a new sensitivity to your own observations," Diego suggested. "This is certainly a different conversation we are having tonight than the one at dinner your first night in the valley."

"Oh, I hope so," Harold said. "I hope I have improved in that department. But it isn't fair to these amazing people to assign the real talents to me. No, I think the people I am noticing have an instinct that is human, but that many of us have forgotten. It is like the hustle and bustle of my world has forgotten or become numb to part of its humanity. There is an absence of this instinct, or at least it isn't a priority that tells us what matters most. To have purpose requires us to have something we care about most. If that instinct is extinguished we run around like mindless chickens pecking at whatever looks like a seed. Often it is a pebble, a fashionable guru that is the flavor of the day."

"So what is it you do care about Diego? What are your passions in life?" Louie asked.

"My country, the Army, my family," Diego said. "And you Louie? Harold?"

It was Louie who answered. "God, family, and making a difference. Not worrying about being interesting, but being interested in the lives of those that matter to me most, and then interested in those I don't even know."

"This is not a new thought for Louie, as you can tell Diego," Harold explained. "For me this is new territory. I have always thought I was pretty solid in understanding my purpose. I know that I am a child of God, and that He has a plan for me, for all of humanity, his children. The thing is, I am not sure I have really become the plan. I am seeing that it has always been this external thing and I have only checked certain boxes, like life is some sort of checklist. I have filled this empty space with my company, with research, but really these are all such surface efforts. It has been for me, I am discovering, that I have heard the words of godly wisdom, but I have in the end, preferred my own."

"I suppose I have been blessed in certain ways I have never thought about," Diego said. "I am not all that religious, but I do believe in God. I have never sunk into apathy. I have always had hope. And … I have always had duty. But today, my friends, I am wondering about my duty."

"The path of duty is the ultimate path of safety," Louie said. "I learned that in Sunday School. The question is, knowing what that duty is. One of our church leaders said once that in knowing the "why" much of the confusion of what our duty is, fades away."

"My duty has always included a moral code, but I am confronted with others that have no such code," Diego said.

"This is a topic that humankind has wrestled with since we first walked out of the Garden of Eden. I am not sure we are going to come to any conclusions tonight," Harold said. "I am not sorry I brought up the subject, but we can drop it and go on to something more light hearted and easier to get a handle on like how to solve world hunger and achieve world peace."

"Just one thought, since I actually have something to add," Louie said. "It is from one of my favorite authors, Dostoyevsky. He simplified the world into two categories of people. I don't remember him suggesting this, but it is my bet that all of us are part of each, some just have more tendencies to one over the other. Anyway, he suggested something like there are two kinds of human beings. One kind holds each human being as an agent to himself and we should not take away that agency to act. The other kind thinks, or operates as if other humans are objects and that it is perfectly appropriate to use other human beings. What one would hate to do, the other regards as not only the clever thing to do, but the wise and courageous thing to do. One type of person demands fairness and end of abuse. The other type claims ends justify any means and strives to gain power in order to use any means. One type truly believes that we are created equal, that we are in the same boat together, and that here is abundance for us all to share. The other only sees the world as a zero sum game, that is, in order for them to win, others have to lose."

"Thank you," Diego said. "That sounds like, in very different words, what my mother taught me as a child. Not to disrespect Dostoevsky, but I am guessing he got his inspiration from the same source my mother did. There is a plan and although we are all part of it, like you said Harold, we make it our plan, or we vainly try to make corrections that we think are better."

"So Diego, back to the original question. What motivates you?" Harold asked.

"My answer a couple weeks ago would have been duty. Tonight I will admit I do not know what my duty is, so I will say…, I will say that it is love. A very un-macho way to express my thought, but love of country, love of family, and if I can say without feeling like a hypocrite, love of God. You mentioned the Costa family earlier. I have to agree that they are unique, but that every family in this valley is unique and that is why I love my country and why these past few days I have missed my own family."

"And is there a certain person in the Costa family that you are thinking about in particular?" Harold asked.

"Well, Alejandro is an interesting person to be sure," Diego said.

"Yeah right, that is what I was thinking," Harold agreed.

"Oh, I almost forgot. Here are some pictures of some weapons you might have seen at the Dam from that mystery group," Diego said, changing the subject. "Do any of these look familiar?"

Louie looked through the eight pictures. She read the names aloud as she studied each picture, trying to remember, "AR15, FN P90, Benelli M3, M4 carbine, AK47, 4CRS, C8SFW, MP5. Wait that looks really familiar. Especially that long curved part at the bottom in front of that handle thing," Louie exclaimed. She involuntarily shivered at the thought of that night.

"You are sure?" Diego asked.

"Yes, I am. I can see those men like I am watching them in a movie. That is the gun. Why, does that help figure out who they were?"

"Not definitely. Actually, I only added this picture to provide a variety of shapes and sizes. Only a very few would have this weapon in our country. It was certainly not the revolutionaries that you bumped into," Diego said. He collected the pictures and shoved them into his pocket with a distant look on his face.

"Lieutenant Mendoza, you are the tip of the sword of the call to arms the Junta began only a few years ago," Major Zarro began. "The start of the race is always easier. The runners are fresh, the crowd is cheering, and the expectations are high. But the middle of the race is away from the cheering crowd that waits at the finish line. The runners are fatigued. The finish line still feels a long way off. This is where we are today. The path doesn't seem as clear because our enemies, the other runners in this race have raised the dust. But we know what must be accomplished and that we are the right people, the only people who can get the job done."

"Yes sir, I see the way and I am ready to do my duty for God and country," Mendoza said.

"Very well. I have placed the following individuals on the collaborator list and I want them arrested and brought to justice. While you were out on the fruitless waste of time in Campo Crespo, I visited the house of three of these individuals. They were not home. Here are directions to that location. The others are new to the list, fresh from headquarters' analysis of names and probable locations. It may take a while to ascertain the location of these, so start with the Costas," Zarro explained.

"Yes, I know the area. I will take a squad tonight."

"Take just a few men, enough to handle three peasants. We don't want to put too much fear in the people, not just yet. And by the way, Lieutenant, I know that you were only following orders in going to Campo Crespo and I commend you for that, but just remember, I am the one giving the orders now, not Captain Peña. The farther from him you place yourself, the better you will be for your own, uh, credibility, and for your career."

"Yes sir, I understand."

"Good. Dismissed Lieutenant. Good hunting."

When Lieutenant Mendoza was out of the office, Zarro pulled out his satellite phone. "Bravo Tactical, this is Alpha Base."

Seconds later he heard, "Bravo Tactical here. No movement at the Dam and no sign of the revolutionaries. Captain Peña traveled to the house of Sergeant Hernandez and then returned directly to the post. No stops, no detours. He again left the post at 1900 hours with the company of the *Norteños*. All three are presently at the Hotel *Otra Vez* dining in public view."

"Very good. Please keep an eye on the Dam environment. I doubt the Captain can do any harm with the *Norteños* in tow. Give your men some well-deserved rest tonight. This operation will soon be over and it will be back to civilization for all of us. Alpha Base out."

"Consuelo, help me out here," Sergeant Enrique Hernandez said. "You know I think the Captain is a fine man. I have often said he is the best commander I have served. But *Sombrita*, his life is the Army. He is an officer. I have seen him take the Oath of Brotherhood. Family for him will take a distant second place, at best."

"I see something bigger, something more important in his eyes, Uncle Quique," Diana replied. "Yes, we don't know each other. No, we haven't had a talk about this, at least not with words, but I know what I know."

"I don't know. He is also from a professional family. He has told me his brother is a doctor. Both his parents went to the university. Will you feel comfortable in that world? Understand me, I know you are better than him in almost every way, so I am not saying he is above you, but he is different than you. Even in the capital, he is of a different class. Not even women from the university would feel comfortable in his circles."

"Quique, that is enough!" Consuelo scolded. "Circles, class, professional. It's all an invention of prideful people that think they are better than someone else. The only thing you have said so far that rings true is: you don't know. You are putting words in this man's mouth, you are assigning him actions in the future like a prophet. Yes, they are different, but that is the beauty of any lasting relationship."

"Do you all hear yourselves?" Alejandro asked. "You are all talking marriage and families. You might as well be crowning the Captain the next king. You have no idea what is really in his head. Certainly he finds Diana beautiful, as do all the men in town. Diana, you yourself told me that this will take its course, so let it. Don't plan it. Don't create all the reasons it will work or won't work, or if it is real or just a passing infatuation. The Captain practices a brutal profession, but I am willing to let this take its own course. You know what you know, but we will see what we see."

Emma stood up and was about to walk into the kitchen. She turned to the group and said, "Aristippus of Cyrene, on being asked what is the most impressive sight on earth, he said it was the sight of a good man quietly pursuing his course in the midst of vicious people. The poor Captain has many enemies, let us not be found in that camp, no matter our good intentions."

The group sat in silence, staring at Emma as she made her way to the kitchen. "If we were wise fellow countrymen, we would make her Queen," Enrique said.

"Amen," Consuelo agreed.

"And why a queen would ever have consented to marry the court jester is beyond me, but she did, thank God," Alejandro said.

Diana quietly smiled.

Captain Diego Peña was exhausted, not quite regaining the lost night of sleep from a few days before. He pulled up to the Costa home with a mental list of things to pick up. It was dark, but he didn't turn on his flashlight until he was inside the home. A short time later he had almost filled the duffle bag with clothes, several books of poetry and some carving tools. He was trying to remember what else he was asked to grab when a vehicle drove up to the front of the house. He expected the passengers to go to another house, but then he heard a knock on the door.

"*Señor* Costa, please open up. I need to speak with you," the person said. Peña recognized it as Lieutenant Mendoza. He also knew that soldiers would already be circling around to the back entrance.

Louder, Mendoza said, "*Señor* Costa, it would be best if you opened the door. I do not want to invite myself in, but I will if I have to." The door began to open slowly, giving Peña time to toss the duffle bag behind the couch.

"Well, it is about time you got here Lieutenant," Captain Peña said. "Unfortunately, the house is empty. They must be out with friends, or perhaps at church. There is a mass tonight in honor of the Army's heroic work saving the Elazar Dam."

"Captain, what are you doing here? How did you know?" was all that Mendoza could say.

"The day I left for Campo Crespo, Major Zarro told me he wanted to talk with the Costas." Diego paused. "Oh, that's right, you were already on the road. Well, in my new duties as… I don't know what to call myself, Director of Administration? I still have duties at the airport. I heard that Alejandro had not shown up for work, and I also know that the Major wanted to see him, so I thought I would stop by after dinner tonight. I was concerned he might be ill, but I didn't want him keeping the Major waiting. Unfortunately dinner went late with the *Norteños*. I was almost back to the post and had to turn around and come back here. Like you I got no reply and so I came in to see if they were here," Peña improvised.

"Yes, well, what did you find?" Mendoza asked.

"Nothing. They, as I said, appear to be gone."

Mendoza shined his flashlight around the living room, trying to give himself time to think. His flashlight hit the family picture on the side table. It wasn't a large photo, but big enough to clearly see the family. It was also black and white, which actually helped in this dark room. He recognized the family, at least some of the family. "Why did you tell me, it's about time I got here? Were you expecting me?"

"I was expecting someone before I got here. Major Zarro said he left someone here to meet the family upon their return. I wondered why no one was here, but then when you pulled up I thought you might have just been out for food or refreshment," Diego answered.

"Right. Is this the family we trucked back from the Campo Crespo Operation?" Mendoza asked, trying to remember if his gun holster strap was in place.

"Yes it is Lieutenant. I think they were there to help translate for the *Norteño* and the U.S. Embassy Security Officer."

"Why did we not take them to Major Zarro then?" Mendoza asked.

"Major Zarro's plate was quite full if you remember. With the attack on the Dam, the return of the *Norteña*, and our operation just completed, I didn't think it was the best time. In fact, I doubted whether the Major was even interested at this point. I wasn't even going to take them in tonight had they been here. I know *Señor* Costa, and he has nothing to hide."

"That is not our duty, to make those decisions," Mendoza said.

"Lieutenant, that was my job up until a short while ago. I guess it is a habit. I will make a full report to Major Zarro in the morning. You should do the same."

"I will. Anything else you want to say Captain?" Mendoza asked.

"Think Lieutenant. Think, do not just do," Peña answered. "You are an officer, not a dog on a leash. These are times when we must be sure of what we do and what its purpose is. There is no way to do a wrong thing the right way. You are dismissed," Captain Peña said.

"I do not take orders from you and you are not my moral compass. I report to Major Zarro."

"Well, be careful shooting yourself in the foot when you are ordered to do so. It can be painful I hear," Peña said. "I was about to search the rest of the house, I only got through looking around the living room, but now that your soldiers are here, I suppose they can do that. I will wait, in case there is something else I can add for my report."

Lieutenant Mendoza was not sure he had the authority to order Captain Peña to leave, so he didn't say anything in reply. Nothing was reported odd and no hiding Costas were uncovered. "Very well Captain, I will take my leave and I assume that is your plan also?" Mendoza asked.

"Yes, I plan to leave as soon as your soldiers are out. I was the first in and will also be the last out. Another old habit hard to break."

Mendoza turned to leave and Peña followed him. Diego got into his Jeep and waited for Mendoza to leave. Peña turned on his engine and headlights as Mendoza's truck turned the corner. Peña jumped out, reentered the house, grabbed the bag from behind the couch and had his Jeep rolling before Mendoza would have had the chance to round the block. Peña followed Mendoza back to the fort. He put the duffle bag in his quarters, wrote a draft note to General Cruz, and got some much needed sleep.

"This attack will have two fronts," Antonio Martín explained to his twelve most trusted revolutionaries. "In order to get the explosives in place at the base of the Dam on the water side, we will need a diversion. Not the flanking diversion of the last attack, but something much more spectacular. We will attack the Army Post and minutes later, we will launch our attack on the Dam. We will need only three or four people at the Dam. All will share the load of the five hundred pounds of Semtex and C4 if we can't find a vehicle to transport you. One will set the explosives, while one creates the floating debris raft the explosives will be attached to, and the one that will deliver will get into the wetsuit, if it arrives on time. Any questions on the Dam attack?" Antonio asked.

"Not a question, Comandante, but a statement," Cesar said. I will be the one delivering the explosives. I know how to swim and it will be the most dangerous. I cannot send any of our men to do a job that I would not do myself. Most important, I want to make sure it happens. We may not get another chance for years if it doesn't happen now."

"Very well. I will lead the attack on the post then," Antonio said. "We need to be clear what the goal of the attack on the post is. We are going to disrupt operations and shift the focus. Even if they discover our approach to the Dam, once Cesar is close enough, there is nothing more they can do if they cannot get troops out there quickly. I will make sure they cannot. We will rig a car with our more traditional explosives and ignite them with a gunshot. The car will be as close to the main entrance as we can get it without arousing too much attention and with the ability to retrieve the person that will park the car. Within seconds of the explosion, a group of twelve will attack the depot entrance. It will be closed and barricaded, but no matter, this side attack goal is to create confusion of a multiple point assault. One hundred and twenty seconds after the depot attack, the remaining force will attack the front entrance, using the smoke and fire from the explosion to mask your advance. Keep the conscript deaths to a minimum, but by all means protect yourselves. If you see clear enough to target the officers and senior enlisted, that would be strategically desirable. Cease engagement at the front entrance within eight minutes of the explosion. It will take them longer to open the rear entrance for an armored personnel carrier to exit, so cease two minutes later at the rear entrance. The two groups will not attempt to rejoin until we are seven kilometers away, at this point," Antonio said and pointed at the map. "Together we will make our way to this camp. If for some reason this camp is compromised, we will continue to the international border and infiltrate in small groups. We will rejoin at this location back inside the country at this point," Antonio touched a spot on the map that was twenty kilometers to the north of their primary camp option. "Any questions?"

Antonio answered some specific questions and then said, "Good. We will leave this camp for good, day after tomorrow morning. Everyone should be in place by five-thirty in the afternoon. The explosion of the car will be thirty minutes later at six o'clock day after tomorrow. Most everyone should be eating or thinking about going off duty. The sun should be mostly down. Now, get some sleep. We will need to be in top form."

Within thirty minutes, everyone in the camp seemed to be asleep or immured in their own thoughts. Antonio felt more entombed in his familiar melancholy of loss. He thought of his wife and unborn child and as he did every night, he vowed revenge on the Army, on his country, on the revolving world—all that seemed simply not to care, and on love, that demands so high a price. Antonio recited out loud a few words from a Roque Dalton poem. "The butterfly, setting her color on fire, was made of ashes…, without your hands my heart is the enemy in my chest." Strangely, he thought of the *Norteña* that had inhabited his camp for less than a fortnight, but had also inhabited his thoughts since. "How could she know so much of Dalton and his life? She was not an ignorant *Estadounidense*. She always had answers—well not always answers—but she always had something. Something I don't have, or if I do it is still buried deeper than I have gone. First Joaquin Villalobos, Dalton's comrade in the struggle and perhaps Dalton's executioner as the *Norteña* suggested, turned critic of Latin American leftist movements, and now this ghost of a person… They are eroding my own commitment. If I ever have the chance to kill her, I will. Once the body is gone, it will cast no shadow."

Chapter 22
Trust and Mistrust

"Comandante, the detonators have been retrieved from our arms cache," Cesar reported. "We were not able to procure a wet suit, but I don't need one. The water is not that cold and I will be in the water for only an hour or two."

"Excellent. We are ready. We leave by separate paths in just hours, but our destination is the same. Glory for the revolution. Soon the Cambalache River will live up to its name. Chaos will reign for a short time as it did in the beginning of time," Antonio mused.

"I had a discussion with Pepito about the river's name, just before the last attack on the Dam. I never knew Cambalache comes from the name of a tango," Cesar said.

"It was an Argentine word before it was put into a tango," Antonio said. "You know the name I chose for myself when I joined the revolution, as Comandante Helicon, comes from the Greek myths. In Hesiod's Theogony, the origin of existence was water and was called chaos. Interesting, no? I am not a believer in Greek myths, but they often reflect universal principles. In this case, we are the shepherds of the wilderness, wretched things of shame and we know how to speak many false things as though they were true; but we will be the bearers of true things. We aren't perfect Cesar, but we will utter one true thing tonight!" Antonio exclaimed.

"Comandante, you know I am uncomfortable when you express university professor thoughts. My thinking is not so lofty. Yet I have to admit that I feel some connection between our struggle and this place in particular. It feels as if the unwritten history of the future of this place and of our part in its cycle of trouble, judgment, and deliverance are meant to be. The names, the connections, the will to do and fate have come together at this intersection of our country. Our soldiers, like all soldiers on all sides of every battle I suppose, will have to borrow from their futures, of the assumed better times. The destruction is not going to be pretty."

"Let you and I do our jobs and the world will sing songs about this revolution and its soldiers. Our soldiers are only hours from immortality," Antonio promised.

"Good morning Consuelo, may I come in?" Captain Peña asked. He was up early, but he knew he was not too early for Sergeant Hernandez.

"Good morning Captain. Of course. Come in," Consuelo said. "Quique is awake, but still in bed, of course," she said.

"Well, actually, I would like to speak with the Sergeant and the Costa family. The situation is getting more complicated. Here are the Costa's things they asked me to get. May I see the Sergeant first?"

"You know where he is. Go ahead yourself. I will take this bag to Emma. I know she is up. I haven't seen Alejandro or Diana."

Peña walked down the short hallway and knocked on the Sergeant's bedroom door. "Sergeant, are you in?"

"Unfortunately I am in bed still, my Captain," Hernandez replied, "but please come in."

"Sorry to keep interrupting your convalescence. I wanted to run a couple things by you. It is starting to heat up at the post," Peña said. He stepped into the room where Hernandez had managed to sit up and drop his feet over the side of the bed.

"Interrupting? This will be the high point of my day. So what mess has the Major created now?"

"I was at the Costa home last night, collecting the things they requested, when Lieutenant Mendoza and three soldiers showed up with a warrant for the Costa's arrest. It seems they are on some collaborators list that Zarro and his people at headquarters created. We are now officially aiding enemies of the state. No longer are they just friends visiting—even though that was a pretty thin excuse. It has now become really serious—firing squad serious."

"Well that does change things. What proof has Major Zarro of guilt? He can't just put names on a list and all the sudden they are guilty of treason."

"Lieutenant Mendoza didn't really believe my story about looking for the Costas. He also recognized them from a family photo in the house as the people that were at Campo Crespo with me. I don't think he has put everything together, but it won't matter as soon as he reports to the Major. He doesn't know where the Costas are and he has no proof that I know, but it will be difficult for me to visit from now on. I will be under close observation."

"That is no problem in the short-term. Maybe it will give me an excuse to get out of this place."

"I plan to confront the Major on this list and his actions when I return to the post. That may put me in an even more precarious position than your mandatory bed rest. I hope to hear back from General Cruz today also. I may yet be the commander here."

"That would be nice, but I don't expect the General to be overly concerned about our little sector with all that is on his plate. Yes, we had some excitement, but that excitement is over and will soon be old news. You watch your back Captain. Whatever Major Zarro is or isn't, he is an expert operator in this mish mash of military bureaucracy."

"I have another issue to run by you. Do you know of any unit that uses MP5s?"

"MP5s? That is unique for our military. That is easy. Only the Special Tasks Squad has the kind of plug-in to get those weapons. Why do you ask?"

"Our *Norteña* recognized MP5s when I showed her pictures of various weapons. I tossed that one in only for variety. Could it be possible that the STS was involved in the revolutionaries' attack on the Dam?"

"That makes no sense, sir. Why would they be there and if they were, why did they fire on us? That group doesn't get mixed up in a little fire fight. And then, why would they just disappear again with no word of their presence?"

"Unless they weren't supposed to be there, or someone was not supposed to know they were there. The real question is, did Zarro know they were there, if it was really them? I have a classmate that is a member of that unit. Like everyone in that unit, not married, no children, no close family to speak of. Makes it real hard to get ahold of them, but I will see what I can do. Keep getting well. I am going to need you on your feet soon. Now I will let you get some rest."

"Get some rest. Honestly sir, if I hear that phrase one more time my head is going to explode. Go save our Army, Captain."

Peña exited the bedroom and nearly bumped into Diana coming down the hallway. He stopped in time and he cursed himself for it. "Oh, Diana, how are you?" he asked.

"I am fine. Thank you for taking the risk to get our things," she said. Diana was dressed in a loose hanging bathrobe too big for her, probably borrowed from Consuelo. She had no make-up, but then Diego had never seen her with make-up. Her hair was slightly disheveled. 'Absolutely gorgeous,' Diego thought. He was embarrassed to see her in night clothes. Even these borrowed things seemed to accentuate her stunning presence.

"You must be going crazy by now, being stuck in this house. I wish I had better news for you and your parents, but it seems there is now a warrant out for your family's arrest. I think you will be safe here for now. I hope to get this mess cleared up today."

"Thank you for all you are doing for us. The thought occurred to me last night, when I knew you were going to our house that perhaps you have thought that I was so, uhm, forward with you because you would then want to protect us. I...," Diana began to explain with her words trailing off.

"You know it is the other way around. I knew you were in danger before we talked," Diego interrupted.

Diana stood there in silence, studying Diego.

Diego took the silence as Diana's doubt of what he had just said. "Really. What I am doing for your family I would do for anyone in this situation. Of course now it has become more personal," he said with a slight grin. Instead of seeming to convince her or cheering her up just a little, Diego saw tears welling up in her eyes. 'Those eyes!' he thought as he was completely enveloped in their timid stare. "Did I say something wrong? Is there something I can do for you?"

Diego asked, clueless and feeling helpless. "Please don't be sad."

"I'm not sad," Diana replied as the tears spilled over her eyelids and slid down her face.

"Then is it me? I can leave. I can stop bothering you. This should be a professional relationship anyway. Too much going on, too many emotions that can be read wrong, words that we won't want to be held too…," Diego stammered and stopped when Diana raised her hand and put her finger to Diego's lips.

"Shhh. You are trying to solve a problem where there is no problem," Diana whispered.

Diego gently grabbed her hand that was still touching his lips and pulled her to him. He held her as if he would break her with even the slightest pressure. Diana wrapped her arms around his chest and held him much tighter, as if giving Diego permission to hold her equally. He did. And then Diana began to cry softly, resting her head on the lower side of his head. He felt her quiet tears moisten his neck.

"You know I will never wash my neck again," he said. "I wouldn't want to lose your tears."

"If that is the case, I will not get this close to your neck ever again."

"Then I will begin showering five times a day in the chance that I might meet you again." Diego felt her warm body against him. He felt whole, as if a missing limb had been replaced, or a blind eye could now see. "May I ask you out on a date *Señorita* Costa?"

"How, may I ask, are we going to do that? I am a wanted terrorist."

"No, just a dangerous collaborator. I think it is my duty to keep a close eye on you, though," Diego said. "I will figure out a way. Tonight, *Señorita*. I will pick you up at four in the afternoon. An idea is beginning to take shape."

"Four it is my Captain."

"So tell me again about the butterfly conversation you had with Alejandro Costa," Louie said looking at the small white boxes in which the captured, and escaped butterflies were housed. When they had returned to their room at the Hotel *Otra Vez*, they discovered that the box that had originally held the escaped butterfly now again held a butterfly, only it was dead. "It is the butterfly after all that led to the past two weeks. Now that I am healthy enough to fly, do you want to leave this place in the rearview mirror, or still solve your butterfly mystery?"

"I know two things I didn't know before," Harold answered. "First, I think Alejandro actually knows something about the Madrugada butterfly. Second, he doesn't trust me enough to tell me right out what he knows. I told you about the statue he gave me. There is something to do with that statue that is a clue. When I am wise enough I will figure it out, or worthy enough and he will tell me."

"So let's look at the statue again. Tell me what you see," Louie commanded.

"I see a gorgeous woman that is stronger than most any man, holding a statue on her lap. I am suddenly very jealous of the statue."

"OK, let's fix that. Come here," Louie said as she placed the statue on the coffee table in their hotel room. She motioned seductively for Harold to approach her. Harold approached and she pulled him to her until he sat on her lap.

"I am going to break you, Louie, sitting like a babe on your lap."

"You are my babe, so do as mama says," Louie said.

"This is nice," Harold almost purred. "But promise you will tell me when I am too heavy or I cut the circulation off to your legs."

"So, now look at your statue. Tell all the ways you can think of that a butterfly could disappear, or be invisible."

Harold thought for a minute and said, "I can think of four ways, none of which would really make sense."

"Quit being negative and start talking."

"Chromataphore," Harold mumbled.

"What did you call me?" Louie joked.

"Chromataphore. It's where a cell of a plant, animal, or insect can expand and contract by bio-electro impulses, changing its color. Some examples would be the cuttlefish, some frogs, and chameleons. The Blue Morpho butterfly is as close as I have heard of this in butterflies. They get their blue coloring from iridescence rather than from pigmentation. I suppose that is a possibility for the Madrugada."

"But that is more like camouflage, not invisibility, right?" Louie asked.

"Yes, although blending in is being invisible. Another possibility, I suppose, is circularly polarized light. Some types of scarab beetles change colors sort of like a liquid crystal can. Again, it is only a reflective camouflage technique. There are other types of reflective examples, like the Hawaiian Bobtail Squid. It has a light organ and reflective tissues in the skin that consist mostly of proteins called reflectins. Interestingly, these reflectins are created by a bacterium that produces a toxin that causes whooping cough and gonorrhea in humans, but for the squid they stimulate its ability to camouflage with its environment."

"Harold, where does all this info get stored in that head of yours? Louie asked in wonder. Her left leg was starting to go a little numb, but she wanted to keep Harold where he was, so she used the question as a way to adjust her leg as she turned her body slightly to ask the question.

The new Harold was much more sensitive to Louie than he was two weeks ago. "Louie, would it be OK if we switched places?" he asked. "You can sit on my lap. I want the chance to hold you."

Louie was surprised, but loved his suggestion. "Wow, we need to have more of these scientific discussions!" Louie said.

"So the only other ideas I have are light canceling and bending light. They both have big problems though. Light manipulation is very complicated. Some years ago the Georgia Institute of Technology created a prototype device that reportedly was a breakthrough in counter surveillance technology—that is, they could make something invisible to digital camera imaging. It would have been a great application for the movie industry in the anti-piracy efforts, but they couldn't get it to work outside the lab." Harold could tell that Louie was losing interest, so he quickly returned to the subject. "Light cancelling is kind of like sound cancelling. Theoretically, if you could match the high frequency of light at the same frequency and the same phase, same amplitude, same polarization, it would absorb the light. Today's technology can do a pretty good job with sound—like the noise cancelling headphones I like to use when we fly. If we could even get close to making this happen with light, instead of creating invisibility, it would create a black spot of no light. That would be easy to see, except maybe at night."

"So what about the other one, the light bending? Isn't that a Kung Fu movie, Light Bender, or something like that?" Louie asked. She had now snuggled into a very comfortable position and was happy to talk about anything.

"I think that was *Airbender*, which is equally complex, except for Kung Fu masters. Well, the problem with this one is I am not aware of any example in nature. It works sort of like how water in a stream bends outward as it approaches a rock, then bends inward as it passes the rock. Science has tried to accomplish this feat with meta-materials that capture light and bend it around an object as if it wasn't even there. I mean, you could feel the object but our eyes only see what light sends us and if there is nothing to send, we don't see it. This is a pretty cool thing because it would also not cast a shadow."

"Light bending. That is interesting," Louie said as she sat up straighter. "Look at the statue and tell me what you see by the butterfly," Louie said with some awe in her voice.

"I see a butterfly carved into the wood grain that is, curving around the butterfly!" Harold said as he stood up. Louie tumbled to the floor.

"Oh my gosh, Louie, I am so sorry. The new, more sensitive Harold is still working out the kinks. Are you alright?"

"Well, it hurts right here," Louie said as she pointed to her elbow.

"Let me kiss that and make it better, my love," Harold said as he kissed her elbow.

"Oh, and it hurts here," she said as she pointed to her right knee. He kissed her knee. "Is there such a thing as pain bending, because I think it hurts right here." She pointed to her pouting lips.

"I am sure there is and I want to try out my theory of pain cancellation—same amplitude, same frequency," Harold said as he pressed his lips to hers. They didn't get back to their discovery, nor what it even meant for another hour.

"Major Zarro, may I have a private word with you?" Captain Peña asked. It was not quite lunch time and Zarro had the tendency to disappear now and then, Peña had noticed. "I wanted to speak with you about your interrogation list."

"That list is really none of your business, Captain."

"I know some of the people on that list and can vouch for their character and for their innocence of any collaboration or other potential crimes against the state," Diego explained.

They were standing in the Command Post and there were several soldiers there, trying to become part of the wallpaper. "Could we speak about this in private, sir?" Peña asked.

"This war room is sufficiently private Peña. Unlike with some of the people you choose to spend your time with, this is a safe and secure place with trusted soldiers and servants of the state present. That is, ever since I had you eject the *Norteño* from here. So tell me, what is it you want to say? Be quick with it so you can get back to your important administrative duties."

"Very well, sir. Your list of potential enemies includes the Costa family. I have gotten to know this family and they are honest people and have no interest in fostering or fomenting revolution. They have even helped support operations against rebel groups. They should not be on your list."

"Oh, you are saying our analysis experts at headquarters are not as smart as you are? I understand there are two Costa brothers. One was killed as a revolutionary, the other is possibly a revolutionary. Did you know that?" Zarro asked smugly.

"Yes sir I did know that, and yes, in this instance I do have better information than our analysis personnel four hundred and fifty miles away from here and who have never set foot in this valley."

"And what information would you have that we don't have?"

"The Costa killed was killed by revolutionaries because he was trying to warn the government about a pending attack. That information came from a captured revolutionary."

"That sounds like manufactured information and who would trust a captured revolutionary to tell the truth. Why have you not reported this information Captain? What are you hiding?

"We received this information from the rebel soldier that we captured during the attack of the *Norteños*."

"I was told this thug, do not call him a soldier, died without telling us anything."

"That is true, he did die without telling the Army anything. He told the person who was asked by the doctor to watch over him one of the nights we had no medically trained staff available."

"And why did this person not report it? I want to see this person immediately."

"That person was *Señora* Emma Costa. She did report it to me. I did send that information to General Cruz. It must not have gotten to the analysis branch yet. She was fearful that this information would somehow incriminate her and her family," Peña said. He had not wanted to explain this, but he also knew that he would have to.

"So we have the word of the mother of a terrorist that her son was attempting to help the government? This is news indeed. Were there any witnesses? Let me answer that. No, there were no witnesses. This is a fabrication and if you can't see that, I am not sure you are even suited for the administrative details you are now entrusted with. Where are the Costas, Captain? Do you know where they are?"

Peña also knew these questions would come, although he had hoped they would not. "I have them in custody, sir. I will release them when I am presented with a lawful order to release them into the appropriate authority's custody."

"I AM that authority Captain. I want them now and that is an order!"

"May I see your orders Major? I have received no orders from my chain of command that you have any authority here. I have no orders saying you can release me from my duties as Sector Commander. I have not seen anything from you or headquarters that states you have authority to pick up whomever you like for interrogation. As I said, the Costas are in my custody. I am not working against you sir, but my duty is to the Army and the country—which includes its citizens."

"You have just ended what may have been a successful career in the Army. Soldier, arrest this man!" Major Zarro commanded.

Captain Peña turned to the soldier. "You do what you think best soldier, but you may be arresting the legal authority here. Also, I ask both of you to consider—have I done anything that warrants arrest? As the Administrative Commander, as you have labeled me Major, I still do not fall under your command. I have my own needs to hold the Costas. You will have to work through your channels to provide me with actual orders to release them to your custody."

With that, Peña stared down the soldier and turned to leave the building.

"I am the only authority here. Soldier, shoot him if he steps through that door!" Zarro commanded.

Captain Peña turned and said, "Soldier, you are my witness that this officer commanded you to shoot me if I continued to do my duties in accordance with my orders. Major, you are not the authority. The Army exists to defend the ideals of this great country. The Army—including you Major—does not have the authority to replace itself with those ideals. You cannot put your own interests or your idea of Army interests above the values we are sworn to protect." Diego turned again and walked out the door. He figured he had a pretty good chance of getting out of the building without being shot, but he felt bad for the soldier who would have to suffer the wrath of Zarro for not following the Major's orders.

"Celia, may I have a word with you in my office?" Captain Peña said when he entered the building and walked by her in a hurry. Celia followed him with her note pad and shut the door.

"I have just committed treason, according to Major Zarro," Peña said before either had had a chance to sit down. "I need you to get one last message off through your channels to General Cruz. Please tell him that I have been threatened with arrest and that Major Zarro ordered a soldier to shoot me if I left the Command Post to continue my duties. Tell him I have a family in my custody, the Costa Family that Major Zarro wants to interrogate. I tried to explain to the

Major that this family is innocent, in fact they are heroes, and that I requested to see his orders to release me from my command, orders to take over command, and orders to arrest people that fall under my protection as Commander of this sector. I have not been presented with any such orders. Please also express my regret that I have to bother him instead of my chain of command with these details, but my chain of command has been silent on any of these issues. I have not heard from my superiors in over a week, which is odd considering the significant events going on in this normally quiet sector. Finally, I have reason to believe that the Special Tasks Squad is operating in this area. In fact there is evidence they were at the Elazar Dam the night of the attack, opened fire at the Army's perimeter security, but only shot blanks and then left before the actual explosions took place."

Celia had stopped writing and was stunned. "Did you get all of that down?" Peña asked. "I need that to go out immediately. Things are quickly unraveling here and I need some guidance, from someone. If I don't get any answers today, I will take the flight out tomorrow and go to head-quarters myself. I don't plan on knocking on the General's door, but there are some very quiet Colonels that need to start talking."

"I will get this out right away sir. Are you going to be safe until tomorrow?" Celia asked.

"I am going to be fine. There is a slight chance I could find myself locked up, or even shot, but I will be fine."

"Fine and dead don't usually fit in the same sentence Captain," Celia said.

"Nor do deceit and treasured virtues Celia," Peña argued. "Major Zarro has raised the dust and expects that we are now all blind to what is right and we will simply follow his commands. That is not going to happen on my watch, no matter what threats and confusion he creates. That is why I will be fine. Could you get the Farnsworths on the phone for me? They are back at the Hotel *Otra Vez*. The *Señora* is still convalescing for another day. I want to talk to them before they depart our quiet valley. And, thank you Celia." As a final thought, Peña jotted down the words on paper.

Diana Costa may replace Solana Reyes de Cruz

"Celia," he said as he handed her the note, "Add this as the last line of the message to the General, exactly as written here."

"Lieutenant, I want all message traffic between this post and headquarters on my desk in fifteen minutes," Major Zarro commanded. "Tell me what you found at the Costa house last night. I take it they weren't there, or I would have talked with them already. Captain Peña says they are in his custody. I want to smash him and the disappearing act these Costas seem to be playing. If they are hiding, it is reasonable they are guilty of something."

"Sir, Captain Peña was at the Costa home last night when I arrived there. He said he was also looking for them. Then I saw a picture of this family and realized these were the same people that traveled with the convoy back to the post from Campo Crespo. I also think the Captain has a thing for the Costa daughter. She is a looker, but a simple *campesina*, probably without a thought in her cute head."

"Interesting. So that is the woman the Captain has been using Army vehicles to transport and who he has had in the command offices? Lieutenant, you may have just cracked the case on our recalcitrant Captain. He is jeopardizing his career and perhaps his life for a skirt! Send that information off to headquarters immediately. Before the day is over, I may yet have full command of this backwater valley. Funny, when I was here before as the commander, I did everything I could to get out of here as fast as I could. Now this same place will be the trampoline that will make me a Lieutenant Colonel and with the credibility and power that will open the doors of the Junta to my every wish. And you will come along as well Mendoza. Now, get me that message traffic. I need to know what Peña has been saying to headquarters. I have kept his commander silent, but who knows what lies he has created that we will have to undo before we can put him away for good."

"Yes, sir," Mendoza said and hurried from the room. Fifteen minutes later Mendoza delivered the message traffic. "Sir I only see routine traffic here. I don't think he has done anything other than request clarification of his orders."

"As I thought, he talks big in front of me here, but he has no backbone and is afraid to ruffle the feathers of his superiors. It is survival of the courageous Lieutenant. And that is me and that is you. That is not our misguided and spineless Captain. Bar him from further use of the communications system. In fact, bar him from the Command Post," Zarro ordered. "Thank you Lieutenant. I would like to send in a full report on the status of the Dam and Power Plant, so let's plan of making a visit tomorrow. I am hoping the engineer we requested from the capital arrives today. You are dismissed."

Chapter 23
Fissures

"Thank you for meeting me," Captain Diego Peña said to Harold and Louie Farnsworth. "I wanted to talk with you before you left the country."

The Farnsworth's had met Captain Peña in the lobby of the Hotel *Otra Vez*. It was a very public place, which is what Peña wanted. "We aren't leaving until our original three weeks are up and so we still have a couple of days. Family at home wants us to leave immediately, but as crazy as it sounds, we aren't ready to leave yet. That reminds me, I have a favor to ask," Louie said.

"What can I do?" Peña asked.

"Could you tell me what has been done with the body of Ernesto, the revolutionary that ended up helping me escape? I would like to have some kind of a memorial service or something. It just doesn't feel right not doing anything for the person who put his life on the line for me and also for Sergeant Hernandez," Louie explained.

"His body was buried in the city cemetery," Peña answered. "He didn't have any family that we were aware of and he had no funds to cover a proper burial, so for health reasons, he was required to be buried within 48 hours of his death. I can get the information on where his burial plot is located. It most likely is just a number, without a name to help you find that location. If Sergeant Hernandez is capable, he would probably like to attend some kind of appreciation service as well. I won't be able to ask the local priest of this parish to say a mass, as he is still annotated as a revolutionary and our local priest is very conservative."

"That would be great," Louie exclaimed. "Harold holds the priesthood in our Church and he can bless the grave and I would like to say a few words. Nothing fancy, just a parting thank you to a very brave and good person."

"You know Louie," Harold interjected, "maybe Alejandro could carve something for the grave. A wooden headstone wouldn't last too many years in this environment, but it would be nice."

"That is a great idea Harold," Louie agreed.

Captain Peña nodded agreement. "You know, I was going to see Alejandro after wishing you both well. I will also be seeing Sergeant Hernandez and could ask him if he would like to attend a small memorial service. This kind of leads me to something I would like to ask you if it is OK?"

"Ask away," Harold said.

"I am going to share some information with you that I hope won't further complicate your lives. If you would rather not get involved in my little plan, I will stop right here," Peña warned.

"Count us in!" Louie said with a smile.

"The Army, well, Major Zarro, wants to arrest the Costa family as possible collaborators with the revolutionaries. It seems their sons may have been involved at some level or another. That does not make Alejandro, Emma, and Diana guilty simply by association. Would you consider asking the U.S. Embassy contacts that were here to have them send a request directly to me asking for this family to be available for the U.S. Embassy to thank them for their help, their collaboration with the US government in helping you,

Louie, gain your release? If you think that is stepping too far out of appropriate bounds, I understand."

"I think that would be a great idea!" Harold said. "Diana went way out of her way to help the RSO and me talk to people in Campo Crespo, and didn't Alejandro and Emma accompany you in your efforts as well?"

"Well, yes they did, but I actually brought them along because I didn't want them arrested," Peña explained.

"Alejandro has also gone out of his way to present us with a fine wood carving and Emma has served as my translator a couple of times," Harold added. "They have helped us immeasurably in coping with the last few weeks of terrible trials. I will contact them now. If you can wait, with a little luck, we might be able to get a letter via email before you have time to catch Louie up on your new friendship with Diana. I have told her about witnessing the poem recitation at Sergeant Hernandez's home. Let me see if I can make that contact, if you will excuse me."

Harold got up and went straight to the hotel reception desk. Harold and Louie were somewhat local celebrities, which bothered Harold, but in this case it might help him score a quick phone line to the capital.

"Yes, tell me about Diana. Actually, tell me about the whole Costa family. They sound amazing. Like a story out of a Hemingway novel," Louie gushed.

"They would say they are simple people, simply trying to live. They are anything but simple, but they have spent their lives trying to live—that is, beyond survival to finding and making really meaningful lives," Peña began. He wasn't sure what he wanted to say about Diana, especially to this person he only met weeks ago—yet he had also only really met Diana weeks ago.

"They have spent their lives trying to live and I have spent my life living without really trying," Louie continued. "Up until my little guided tour of some of the back woods of your beautiful country, I haven't had many really challenging life experiences. Homesickness at college, a few failed romances, tooth aches." She paused. "I have never even broken a bone. I certainly never worried about where my next meal would come from. I will be eternally grateful for my visit here. It has helped me break down my outlook and understanding to what is really important—something it sounds like the Costas simply know."

"I am not much different than you in some ways," Peña said. "The Costas have taught me a lot about my duty, my obligations, and about life."

"And Diana?" Louie probed.

"Yes, Diana. What is there I can say? I only met her about the same time I met you and your husband. It is really strange that I would be talking to you—a complete stranger just weeks ago, about someone else who was nearly a complete stranger when your plane landed in Mariposa. That I would meet her, and you and Harold and count you as good friends is miraculous. I know that sounds a little, how would you say it—not manly?—for an Army officer, but that is the fact. That I would even be talking to you about this is not the person I was just weeks ago."

Louie nodded agreement. "None of us are the people we were just weeks ago Diego."

"Instead of me proving I am a failure at expressing my thoughts about Diana, would you like to come with me and get to know her yourself?" Peña asked.

"That would be wonderful if it isn't getting in the way of things," Louie said. "Is she with her father? Harold and I could talk to him about the plaque for Ernesto's grave site."

"Yes she is with her parents. You will want to get to know her mother Emma as well. She may be the wisest person in this valley."

"This is Bravo Tactical" the strong male voice announced over the radio frequency. "The Captain is at the Hotel talking with the *Norteños*. We will keep you informed of his travels. I understand he is to be considered a possible threat?"

"That is correct," Zarro answered the caller. "He willfully disobeyed an order and has questioned my authority. I am not sure what he is capable of. What I want to know is if you see him with a young lady. It is very possible this young lady is a collaborator with revolutionaries and the reason he is acting so strange. She may have compromised him as he has undoubtedly compromised her."

"Ha ha. I understand sir. We will keep you posted. Bravo Tactical out."

"May the spirit of the revolution go with you Cesar. If all goes well, we will rendezvous tomorrow evening at the border," Antonio said as he bid farewell to the small demolition team. At least for this attack, the team had transportation and would arrive at the far side of the lake that was created by the Elazar Dam well rested and in plenty of time to prepare for the attack. Antonio was worried about Cesar's strength in paddling the makeshift debris raft to arrive at the appointed time. The revolutionaries watched them leave and knew their turn to depart was coming soon. The two-man team that had been sent to set the explosives in the car left early that morning and were probably ready to drive the car to the post doors. "Not quite a Trojan horse," Comandante Helicon—Antonio, had joked, "but it will wake up Troy!" The men had laughed, but Antonio doubted they had ever heard of the Greek story.

To the remaining revolutionaries, Comandante Helicon said, "It will be our turn to launch our part of the revolution soon enough. Relax and prepare yourselves emotionally for the day that will be remembered as the first page in the book that will be our new country. I am honored to serve with you, and honored to be counted among you at this glorious hour."

"Hello Consuelo, I have brought the Farnsworths to see your husband," Captain Peña announced. "They will be leaving soon and wanted to thank him for his part in bringing the *Señora* home safely," he added as loud as he could without sounding too unnatural, but hoping their neighbors could hear him.

"Come in. Come in. How nice to see you are looking so well *Señora* Farnsworth," Consuelo said.

"Thank you *Señora* Hernandez," Louie said. "I am honored to be in your home."

Diego and the Farnsworths were surprised to see Sergeant Hernandez in the living room playing a backgammon game with Diana. "Welcome my Captain. Oh, and *Señor* and

Señora Farnsworth. Excuse me if I don't get up. I am really not supposed to be out of bed, but I have to keep Diana humble. I am about to trounce her and this will make it two out of three." Louie quietly translated the Sergeant's words to Harold.

"Sergeant, may I speak to you in private for just a minute?" Captain Peña asked.

"Certainly sir. Step into my office. Everyone, could you go to the kitchen and fix our guests something?"

"Thank you for allowing us to use your home as the sector Command Post," Peña said, giving everyone time to exit the room. When they were safely out of hearing range, he began softly. "I disobeyed an order from Major Zarro about two hours ago. I wanted you to know in case you would rather I keep my distance from your home. He ordered me to turn in the Costa family," Peña explained. "I have requested and received a Commendation Letter from the US Embassy, signed by the Ambassador, for the Costa family, thanking them for their selfless efforts aiding in the return of *Señora* Farnsworth. This same letter is going through Army channels and should arrive at the Command Post for the Stockade Commander's attention within the hour. Hopefully that will keep the Major away."

"I am more Army than General Cruz. You know that sir. But my Army is not the Army of Major Zarro, it is the Army of the nation. I know the Costas to be honest and they are not collaborators. They have talked to me about their sons long before any of these issues arose. But all that is secondary to me. I still have my duty, no matter how distasteful."

Peña began to get uncomfortable. "Do I need to take the Costa family from your home?"

"That is the part I was getting to sir. I take orders from you. If you order me to I will protect them with my life. It is an honor to serve you, and I will do that to my last breath as well," Sergeant Hernandez said as he sat up as straight as he could and saluted.

Captain Peña returned the salute. "Now Sergeant, I have one more request."

"What is that sir?"

"I would like to take your goddaughter out on a date. I have devised a way to do so, but want your approval."

"The military life is not what I had in mind for *Sombrita*. I fear for her acceptance with the other officers' wives," Hernandez answered.

"Sergeant, I am not asking your permission to marry her, just to take her on a first date. The reason I am asking your permission is, I want you to be our chaperone, and I want her to act as your nurse. I have a nurse's uniform. We will only go for a drive, maybe out by the lake where we can talk and throughout you will be close by."

"I am allowed to get out of this house? Why didn't you say that in the first place? What are we waiting for?" Hernandez asked. He called the group in from the kitchen. "I suppose you listened in on everything anyway, but the Captain will be taking *Sombrita* on a date, if that is alright with your parents and you," Hernandez asked Diana.

"As long as she will be safe," Alejandro said.

"We have a plan!" Hernandez said formally.

Only minutes passed before Diana returned to the living room dressed in a nurse's uniform and Sergeant Hernandez was in his wheelchair. While Diana had been changing, Consuelo and Emma had persuaded the Farnsworths to stay for *merienda*.

"I love this," Louie said. "A light dinner before dinner. I could really get used to this custom. We would love to stay. Alejandro and Harold have some things to talk about also."

Captain Peña held the door open as Sergeant Hernandez was wheeled to the car by his nurse. Diana was nervous, but played her part. It was the first time she had ever worn makeup and it was to make her appear older and slightly greyed.

"Is this really necessary?" Diana had asked. She was not vain about her looks, but she wasn't happy being "uglied up" as her godfather had demanded, for her first date. Sergeant Hernandez was using the entire back seat. Diana sat in front with the Captain.

"Alpha Base, Bravo Tactical. The Captain took the *Norteños* to the Hernandez home. He was there about fifteen minutes and just left with Sergeant Hernandez and his nurse. Hernandez was in a wheelchair and didn't look too good. He is a good man. Several members of the team know him. I wish we could have waxed that entire group of revolutionaries the other night."

"Bravo Tactical, when I want your opinion on someone or something, I will let you know. You understand the need to let the revolutionaries cause a little havoc. This couldn't have worked out better. I am sorry for Sergeant Hernandez too. Don't forget, he was my Sergeant Major here not that long ago. The engineer should have arrived on the afternoon flight which probably just landed. The Dam will be assessed and hopefully we will be able to close up this operation within a couple days. Then some well-deserved R&R. For all

I care, Captain Peña can stay in this valley and rot. Keep an eye on him, but I doubt he is going to go after his girl with the sergeant as a chaperon. That's the last thing he would want. Alpha out."

"Good afternoon *Señora* Hernandez. Could I speak to the Sergeant please?" the soldier just outside the door asked.

Consuelo didn't recognize this sergeant. He wasn't from this post.

"I am afraid you just missed him. He is with Captain Peña. I believe they were going to drive out to the Elazar Dam. They should be back in a couple hours. Is there something I can tell him when he returns?" Consuelo asked.

"No *Señora*. I am to retrieve the Sergeant Major, and the Captain actually. I assumed the Captain was at the stockade. We came directly from the airport to your home. General Cruz would like to thank the Sergeant for his heroic efforts at the Elazar Dam. Could you hold on just a minute, please?"

The sergeant walked back to the car, a rental that Consuelo now noticed. "Strange that a General would rent a car. Why wouldn't the post send a vehicle?" Consuelo questioned, her doubt and fear rising.

An older gentleman got out of the car and walked to Consuelo's front door. He was dressed in a business suit, but walked like a person in charge and had short grey hair and piercing eyes. As he approached Consuelo he bowed slightly and asked, " *Señora* Hernandez?"

"Yes sir," Consuelo said.

"I am General Horacio Cruz. I was led to believe Sergeant Major Hernandez would be convalescing at home."

"Yes sir, he is supposed to be. He can't even walk yet. Captain Peña wanted to inspect the Elazar Dam and Quique--I mean Sergeant Hernandez—talked the Captain into letting him go as well. He is in a wheelchair and we sent a family friend to go with them."

"That wouldn't be Diana Costa would it?" General Cruz asked.

"Yes sir, it is. You are very well informed General," Consuelo said before thinking.

"Sometimes I am," General Cruz said. "And sometimes I am not," he said more to himself.

"I am afraid there is no cellular service around the Elazar Dam. Do you want to wait until they return? I can send them to wherever you will be," Consuelo offered. "Would you prefer to come into our home and wait for them?" Consuelo wasn't sure how to please the General. She had never seen or talked to a General before, let alone one who was on the ruling Junta of the country.

"I have come unannounced and I have troubled you enough. Please don't pass on to the post that I am here. I want to take care of a few things first. You could possibly help me with three items of information, however *Señora* before I go. I would like to meet the Costa family and I was wondering where I might meet them. Would you have any idea where they might be?" the General asked.

Consuelo was immediately on edge, questioning in her mind if the General was part of the Zarro Army or part of the Peña Army? "What would you need them for sir?"

"I assure you I do not want to interrogate them. I want to thank them for their service to the country and to the *Norteña* that was kidnapped. That is the second thing I was wondering if you could help me with. I would like to meet the Farnsworths. They too sound like amazing people. I assume they are still in Mariposa. Would you know where I might inquire about them?"

"General, would you please come into my home. I think I might be able to help you out. What is your third request? I feel like a genie, granting wishes."

"If you could direct me, I will be on my way. I have disrupted you enough. My other request is directions to the Dam," the General said. "I am in somewhat of a hurry." He leaned closer to Consuelo and said conspiratorially, "No one knows I am here. I am supposed to be inspecting a new bridge in another part of the country and I am supposed to be back in the capital by tomorrow morning."

"I think I can expedite your visit General. Please, step into my home," Consuelo said again, with a smile. The General and the Sergeant stepped into the Hernandez home reluctantly. The Sergeant was a little on edge and held his hand close to his revolver.

"Sir may I introduce you to the Costa's and the Farnsworth's?" Consuelo said.

"I have never been to this side of the lake," Diana said. They had talked little during the drive, neither sure what to say and with Sergeant Hernandez in the back seat they didn't try to make small talk.

"With the lake being so new, I don't think anyone has," Peña said. "The spot I want to take you to see I only discovered about a month ago when I hiked the circumference of the lake. Fortunately this road existed before the lake was filled in last year. Do you know what the road was used for Sergeant?"

"It was an old logging road. I am surprised it hasn't grown over. We used to use it for tactical exercises back when Diana was about ten. I haven't been here since then."

They arrived at a turn in the road and Diego parked the car. "I am going to have to leave you here Sergeant. There is just a little trail to the lookout point. We will be back in a couple of hours," Peña said.

"A couple of hours? You are going to have to carry me on your back if you are gone even half an hour, sir," Hernandez blustered.

"Ok, maybe twenty minutes then," Peña said with a chuckle. "Enjoy the fresh air and sunshine. It is good for you."

"With all respect sir, I will tell you what is good for me, knowing you stay arm's length from my goddaughter." With that Diana bent over and kissed Hernandez on the forehead. Then she walked over to Diego and kissed him on the cheek. Both men were speechless for a moment.

Slightly blushing, Peña said, "OK, let's ditch the Sergeant. What do you say?"

"I will follow your lead Captain," Diana said.

They walked through the brush for about five minutes and then came to a clearing. It was a high point, overlooking the lake. "Oh my, this is beautiful," Diana said. "It's hard to believe this lake wasn't even here two years ago."

"Yes, it is beautiful," Peña agreed, looking at Diana. "Hopefully it will provide electricity, once the Dam is strengthened and the power plant rebuilt. I also hope it will provide fish and water fowl and a way to control the annual flooding of the valley."

"So you asked me here to present a commercial for the military government's successes?" Diana joked.

"No, do you really think that? I mean this does demonstrate progress, progress that probably would have never happened under the previous civilian government. But lately I have been thinking about the costs. You know someone probably lived down in this small valley that is now a lake. The floods were difficult at times, but they nourished the farms also."

"No, I don't think that is why you brought me here. I would not have expected those words from a military officer. I don't know if that means I am prejudice against the military, or if I am simply untrusting of anyone in power. So why did you bring me here?" Diana asked.

"To talk. To get to know you. So you could get to know me," Diego said. "And, I wanted to show you something."

"What you want to show me could tell me a lot about you."

"OK, now I'm nervous," Peña admitted.

"You should be Captain. You have my godfather loading his gun in case we don't come back in a few minutes. You are hiding an enemy of the State. And most importantly, I am guessing this is the first date you have been on in a long time."

"Could you call me Diego?"

"OK, Diego. Hi, I'm Diana."

"I kind of like *Sombrita*."

"Only Uncle Quique calls me that. You would have to ask his permission. So now that we are on a first name basis, what is it you want to show me?"

"It's over here," Diego said as he grabbed her hand and walked her down a short path. They turned a corner and

Diego stretched out his other hand, palm to the side toward some strange-looking trees, without letting go of her hand. "I thought this was magnificent when I first saw it. I don't know if anyone else even knows they are here."

"That, with the lake in the background is worthy of any art gallery in the world, although I have never been a hundred kilometers from Mariposa. How old do you think they are?"

"Ancient, maybe two hundred years old. I took a picture of this and did a little research. They are called Kapoc trees. These are about forty meters tall, but they can grow to over fifty meters. The Mayans in Mexico believed them to be sacred and called them the Tree of Life. They symbolize hope, strength, and rising up. I have never seen one anywhere else in our country and I have no idea how these could have ended up here."

"Honestly Diego, these are amazing. And that they grew together to create a single tree."

"That there isn't just one, but two is like a miracle. That they twist around each other, like they are holding each other up is like a second miracle—maybe why they have survived all these years," Diego said and then he turned from looking at the trees to looking at her and said, "And that I only discovered them a few weeks before meeting you has come to feel like a message. Only because you were so forward with me at the post would I ever consider showing these to you. I don't want you to think I am being too forward, or suggesting anything too serious."

"I am not shy, but I am not a forward person. I have no right to think anything of our , uhm, friendship, other than I am grateful to get to know you. I am an uneducated woman from an almost forgotten valley of the world. You are everything I am not."

"That is true. You understand life better than I do. You quote poetry that would put a literature professor to shame, while I am completely at a loss when it comes to the finer things in life. I know how to manage coercive power. You know how to caress life to its full potential. And you Diana, are more courageous than this Army officer will ever be." Diego took a breath, looked out at the lake and at the intertwining Kapoc trees and said, "And you, dear Diana, have intertwined your soul with mine. I don't know if I can stand alone any longer and survive. You once commanded me to come to you, and I did. Now I am asking you to come with me."

"I am not sure what you are asking Diego. Anyone in the entire world watching our relationship evolve from two seeds to forty meter trees would say we are both crazy. We can measure the time we have spent together in hours. The words we have shared don't fill a single chapter of one book. I am here with you *now* and this now will always be with me. But we are still young trees, saplings my father would call us both. I want what my parents have and that will take time. Time we have."

"We had better get back or Hernandez will be crawling up the trail to find us," Diego said. He wasn't sure what he had expected of this date and showing Diana the trees, but Diana's wisdom had dampened his enthusiasm and hope.

"Diego, thank you for understanding, but you have not understood," Diana said. She leaned forward and drew Diego to her. They kissed, tenderly, and then with more passion. They both felt intertwined, physically and what

Diana thought as spiritually. "This is not the end of a trail, but the beginning."

They shared one more kiss and then reluctantly returned to the car. Diana was happy that they were holding hands as they came into view of Enrique Hernandez.

"The debris raft is ready and the plastic explosives are in the net and attached to the rope," Paco Costa reported to Cesar. "The fuse wire and the rope are fifteen meters long, which should be enough depth. The batteries are already tied onto the raft and hidden with branches. I have got them wired in series, so all you should have to do is attach the fuses to the first battery."

"Thank you Paco. I will connect the battery and the charges will explode within a second or two. I will swim like a fish to the nearest shore," Cesar answered.

"The explosion at that depth should not cause you too much problem as long as you are some meters away, but no telling how long the delayed reaction will be of the impact on the weakened dam and its structural breakup. For that you will definitely want to be out of the water," Paco continued. "I am just a soldier, Cesar. Expendable. You are not. Are you sure I can't be the one to go out on the debris raft?"

"This one is mine. You three need to be the witnesses if I don't make it. Find a place near the Dam and watch. Do not wait for me. I will either be dead, or I will catch up with you at the border. Now get out of here."

The three revolutionaries watched their second in command bravely push off from the shore. He had about an hour to get to the Dam. He couldn't paddle too fast or it wouldn't look like debris floating. It would be a long time in the water, but Cesar had said he was a strong swimmer and wasn't worried. There was only an hour of daylight left as well, so the revolutionaries got back to their vehicle and drove to a predetermined place, a dirt road that led to some high ground, a perfect place to watch the explosion and an easy avenue to make their escape.

"Look, there is another car up here!" the driver exclaimed. "I thought this road led to nowhere and was never used."

"Pull over and let's check it out. Maybe it's abandoned," the revolutionary riding shotgun suggested. "Wait, back up! Back Up! I think there was movement in the back seat. Keep the engine quiet and get out of sight. We can't afford to blow this operation because a couple of lovers report us to the security forces at the Dam."

Paco, who had dozed off in the back seat was also fully awake now. He was the one who had set the charges, the fuses, and the batteries, while the others slept. It would be a long night to get to the border and they all knew they should sleep when they could.

Paco and his two companions got out of the car and quietly crept along the road until they had to enter the brush for concealment. They got as close as they could to the other car and waited for any additional movement, trying to confirm whether or not they had been detected. A minute later two people come out of the woods. A man and a woman. Paco took in a quick breath. "Yes, I see the same thing Paco—an Army officer. So this is what the Army does when they aren't fighting us. Nice!"

The car door swung open and another man inside called out. "It is about time you got back. I was about to come after you!"

The Army officer called to him, "We weren't even gone twenty minutes Sergeant. Relax. We probably have thirty minutes of daylight left."

"It's obvious they didn't see us," Paco whispered. "Let's get out of here before they leave. That's all we need is the Dam security hearing a fire fight, especially on this side of the Dam," he added.

"Wait," the driver and self-appointed leader of the three said. "We are attacking the Dam, right? And the rest of us are attacking the post. I think we have a chance to take out an officer and a sergeant and some low life babe. We are far enough away that I doubt anyone would hear a few shots. We could be heroes for this."

"I get the girl," Paco said.

"Yeah you wish. We don't have time for your sick games. You shoot the officer Paco. You shoot the girl," he told the other revolutionary. "I will go after the Sergeant in the car. Let's get a little closer if we can, but we can't wait until they get in the car. Too many problems then."

"Thank you so very much for your hospitality Consuelo," General Cruz said. "You are right, you did expedite my requests. Would you like a job overseeing road construction for the entire country? I think you could actually get something done. I'm joking of course. I wouldn't wish that job on my worst enemy. And thank you for the map to the Dam."

"I wish I could tell you where the Captain and my husband are exactly, but hopefully you will see them. They are driving a white Ford Falcon. Army issue."

"If I don't find them I am sure I will catch up with the Captain at the Post this evening. You will get the Costas and the Farnsworths to the Post for me? I want some things cleared up before I have to return to the Capital and I only have tonight."

"They will be there. We will leave in about fifteen minutes. We will wait by my husband's office until you arrive," Consuelo said.

"Yes, you would make a great Director of Roads and Infrastructure. Sergeant Hernandez is a lucky man. See you in about an hour."

Chapter 24
Breakdown

NO ONE INSIDE OR OUTSIDE THE STOCKADE THOUGHT twice about the old Volkswagen Beetle parked just outside the gate. These "bugs" had infested most of Latin America like killer bees and kudzu had taken over parts of the United States. One of the MNS rebel soldiers had driven it there as if it was running out of gas or breaking down and it rolled to a stop not ten meters from the main entrance. The stockade was not in the city proper, but there was enough traffic and commerce just outside the compound that this was not significantly odd. The car was not parked inconveniently for any traffic coming and going from the Post, but close enough that an explosion would cause panic beyond just the guards, whose lives were now measured in minutes.

"Five-fifty. Ten minutes to go," Antonio said to himself. Those around him heard the anticipation in his voice. Some shared that sentiment, others were simply scared and hoped to find themselves alive an hour from then.

A single car approached. Five people, obviously not military, were in the car. One had blonde hair. She looked at one of the other passengers, a man with light brown hair. "The *Norteña*. Farnsworth!" Antonio exclaimed. His mind went into overdrive as the car passed through the gate.

"Pepito, you take over here. I am going to go around to the depot gate. I want to see if there is a possibility of gaining entrance to the Fort. I will kill that *Norteña*. It will send another message of our reach and power and as a supreme embarrassment to the Army. You know what to do. Stick to the plan!" Antonio turned and said, "I will take Julio with me. We both have a score to settle with this one." He left without hearing Pepito's reply.

Antonio and Juilo arrived at the Depot Gate attack force location with one minute to spare. "A little change of plans," Antonio said quietly to the armed men who were waiting there. "The *Norteña*, who was our brief guest just entered the fort. Instead of just attacking the gate, Julio and I will attempt to enter, locate the *Norteña*, kill her, exit, and then you will begin your attack from here. Once the explosion and the attack at the main entrance two minutes later, most of the attention will be focused on that area of the post. I want to take advantage of the chaos so that the *Norteña* isn't put in some safer location outside of our reach. The plan calls for the attack team at the front entrance to cease fire and retreat eight minutes after the explosion. Julio and I will be out in six minutes, or we will never come out. So, start your attack then, six minutes after the explosion. Keep up the fight for only four or five minutes and then retreat. This will still provide the diversion Cesar needs at the Dam and we will still be exactly on schedule. Any questions?" There were no questions. Perhaps they are all frozen scared or it was really that simple.

Pepito picked up his rifle and at exactly six o'clock in the evening, he fired four quick shots at the backseat of the Volkswagen. The packed explosives and full gas tank erupted into a ball of flames. Less than a second later the sound was deafening. The stockade front entrance was momentarily obscured. He didn't hear the attack at the Depot Gate entrance ten seconds later, but assumed his hearing was momentarily blocked due to the explosion. He could see one soldier down at the entrance, but nobody else was moving. One minute passed and still no target to shoot at. Two minutes and he began to see some people running, but mostly protected by the stockade walls. He announced the attack and the fourteen men began to fire shots at anything that seemed to move.

Inside the stockade the explosion was heard, but the soldiers were slow to connect it with an impending attack. Most came out of the dining hall wondering what the sound had been.

"Corporal, find out what that was and report back in sixty seconds!" Major Zarro commanded. He had just been reading the Letter of Commendation to the Costa Family from the U.S. Ambassador for the third time. The letter had come through military channels. It had infuriated him. The corporal was back in less than thirty seconds.

"Sir, there was a large explosion just outside the main entrance. One or two guards are down. There has been no further…," and the corporal's words were mixed with the unmistakable sound of gunfire.

"Take command of the main entrance, corporal!" Major Zarro ordered, then turned to the phone and speed dialed Lieutenant Mendoza. "Lieutenant, we are under attack. Take command of security immediately. Get the troops to their posts."

Zarro ran to his makeshift office inside the Command Post. He unlocked a desk drawer and got out his satellite phone. "Bravo Tactical, Alpha Base," Zarro said into the phone almost yelling.

Five long seconds later Zarro heard, "Bravo Tactical."

"We are under attack at the stockade. Large explosion at the main entrance, followed by intense fire. Unsure of size of force and what their goal is. They have our attention. Get here immediately and attack from the rear. We will keep them occupied as best we can from inside. Report ETA to my location. Alpha Base out." Zarro waited for the reply. He was interrupted by a soldier who didn't bother knocking. It was the informant he had used some days earlier.

"Sir, the *Norteños*, the Farnsworths, they are on the post. I saw them entering Sergeant Hernandez's office. I thought you should know."

"Bring them to me here. It will be safer at the Command Post," Zarro Commanded. "What are they doing here now? Is she the reason for the attack? Do they want her that bad? Or, did she bring them here? Was she released with an agreement to help them?" Zarro's mind was running wild with the possibilities, but he really didn't care about the answers. 'I will save her once again and get her out of this country as soon as possible. This will ensure my fast track to Colonel,' he calculated.

Comandante Helicon and the rebel soldier Julio had surprisingly entered the Army facility with little trouble. There had been one soldier who was looking toward the main gate on the other side of the stockade when the shooting began. He seemed unsure what to do. Julio nearly knocked the unfortunate conscript's head off his shoulders with his rifle butt.

"If I had realized it would be this easy Julio, I would have brought the whole group this way," Antonio said. They ran alongside some warehouses until they came to an open area. People were running in every direction. The chaos was palpable. "Look what we have done Julio. The Army is not an invincible giant. They are ants to be stomped on!"

Antonio and Julio saw the Farnsworths at the same time. They were being escorted to another building by a single soldier.

"Now is our chance. Shoot, Julio!" Antonio commanded.

Julio aimed and shot, but missed. He steadied himself, took his time and shot again. This bullet hit just in front of Louie. The group she was running with all noticed the shot.

Antonio saw an old man in the group turn to where the shot had come from and called to the soldier, "There are two men near those buildings firing at us. I think they are trying to hit the *Norteña*."

While Julio took a deep breath and started to let it out slowly, concentrating on his target, Antonio slipped back to an alleyway between the building they were spotted at and an identical building to the right. He ran toward the open area, once again pulling out his handgun.

The soldier next to Louie pushed her to the ground and fell to the ground himself. "We are too far away from cover *Señora*. Stay behind me." The soldier aimed his own weapon and fired just before Julio was able to get off a third shot. Julio fired, but the bullet hit the roof of the building behind the group.

"Come, let's go," the soldier called to the group, who all began running again. Three steps into his run, the soldier went down before the shot was registered in his ears. Julio had been wounded, but was not dead. He began running toward the group in a rage.

Harold grabbed Louie who was now frozen in place, and pulled her up to her feet and toward the building. Alejandro told Emma, "You and Consuelo get to the building. I will be right behind you." He turned toward the charging rebel and felt like a naked matador in the ring with a crazed bull looking for a target to gore.

"I will be your target today bull," Alejandro said. "Here coward! Try taking on a man instead of defenseless women," Alejandro called. As he yelled, he calmly pulled a carving knife out of his pocket. It wasn't a big knife, but used well it could slow down this bull.

Julio the bull, turned on him and saw nothing but red. Julio knew he was losing blood and could feel his body weakening, but he couldn't stop his charge. He believed he would drop this old man and keep going until he could reach the *Norteña* and scratch her eyes out. He would not worry about killing her. Blinding her and disfiguring her as she had done to him would be better.

As Julio reached the old man he had expected to just run over him. Instead the old man pivoted with the nimbleness of a cat and left its claws in Julio's chest. Julio grabbed at his chest and found a knife lodged there. Two steps later he was on the ground, unable to get up. He pulled his rifle to his side and fired, hitting the old man in the shoulder or chest. Julio was not certain as he closed his eyes.

"Alejandro!" Emma cried. She was only a meter away from the Command Post and turned back to help Alejandro.

Harold sprang to action and ran to Emma. "I will get him; you get the other ladies inside the building!"

Harold arrived at Alejandro's side and scooped him up like he was a baby and effortlessly carried him to the Command Post and to safety.

In front of the stockade, Pepito was getting nervous. He was not accustomed to command, especially in a firefight. He called for his soldiers to begin a retreat. He had no idea how much time he had been firing and could not remember how long he was supposed to stay there anyway. "Retreat, retreat!" he yelled. Although the firing was supposed to stop, it seemed only to intensify. Suddenly the soldier next to him went down. 'Where had that shot come from? Behind him?' Pepito surmised. He turned and saw a group of six men coming toward him. They were firing at an incredible rate. "What kind of guns are those?" was Pepito's last thoughts. In a matter of ninety seconds the entire main entrance attack team had been killed or seriously wounded.

Antonio had watched Julio's attack in awe. It was insane, but for Antonio, it was inspiring. He no longer had any fear. He walked to the Command Post and paused only a second before opening the door.

Sergeant Hernandez had seen the car approach, stop, and back up. He wanted to warn Diego and Diana, but didn't want to spook their visitors, if they were someone other than a couple of lovers looking for a private place to talk. "It is time we get back Diego. You need to get down the hill as fast as you can," he called accentuating the action words he needed them to obey.

It took Diego less than a second to process, 'He has never called me by my first name! 'Get Down' rang in his ears. He grabbed Diana and pulled her to the earth with him. As he did a shot rang out and hit the tree behind him. The car was also hit with several shots. A person sprang from the brush and ran toward them firing as he went. Hernandez cursed that he did not have a weapon with him.

Diego pulled out his handgun but the person firing at them fell to the ground before Diego could get off even one shot. Then there was another shot and a man coming out of the bushes to their left also went down. No one was sure what was going on. Then a third man stood, held up his weapon and said, "Don't shoot!" then dropped the gun. He walked forward and said, "Those men are no longer a threat to you Diana." Then another shot rang out from the first man shot before he collapsed again to the ground. The man who had surrendered himself fell without another sound.

"Paco!" Diana screamed.

Cesar heard the shots as he continued to paddle his debris raft toward the Dam. He had no idea what was going on to his right in the hills. He was exhausted. The debris raft was much more difficult to push forward than he had anticipated. The water was a comfortable temperature, perhaps fifteen degrees centigrade he guessed. It felt warmer than the outside air as the sun descended. He had a long way to go yet, so he kept kicking his legs under the water so as not to make a splash, with only his head out of the water. It would all be worth it.

One soldier at the far West side of the Dam security perimeter had heard the shots. He alerted the head of the security detail, who in turn radioed the Command Post. "Gun shots have been heard to the west of the Dam. We do not appear to be under attack, but request support."

"Elazar security, we are under attack. We will not be able to provide assistance at this time. Repeat, the post is under attack. Keep vigilant," the soldier at the Command Post radioed back.

A car approached the makeshift security detail shack. The soldier immediately pointed his riffle at the vehicle and fired a warning shot into the air. The car came to an immediate stop. An Army sergeant got out of the car and said, "Hold you fire soldier. I am Sergeant Pissarro, detached here by General Cruz to look at the Dam. I am looking for Captain Peña. I was told he was here. Can we approach you?"

"Come closer, but I have several marksmen pointed at your heads. Any odd movements and you will be taken out," the nervous soldier yelled back.

The vehicle moved slowly forward and then stopped. Two people got out of the car and walked forward with their hands open and away from their sides. "You are a little jumpy soldier. Do you fire on every vehicle that comes here?" Sergeant Pissarro asked.

"No, but you aren't scheduled to be here. I don't know you. You are in a rental car, and we just got a report of gunshots to the west of us. Considering what just happened a few days ago, I am a little jumpy. Now tell me again who you are before I have these soldiers arrest you." As he said that, two additional soldiers came out of the woods, rifles pointed at the strangers.

"I am impressed soldier," the old man in the suit said. "Who is your commanding officer?"

"Please tell me who you are sir, and why you are here. My questions first."

"I am General Cruz. This is my adjutant for this surprise trip," he said with a smile.

"Forgive me sir if I don't believe you. I need some identi-fication. I have never met a general, but I assume they wear uniforms too. A member of the Junta just shows up without warning? Sorry, try again."

General Cruz pulled out his ID and handed it to the soldier. It looked real and the more the soldier looked at the old man in the suit, the more he looked like an Army officer. "So tell me again soldier, who is your commanding officer?" Cruz demanded.

"Sir, if you really are General Cruz, you tell me," The soldier answered.

"Excellent answer soldier. Captain Peña is your commander. You may have what sounded like newer orders making Major Zarro you commander, but that is partly why I am here. Now, where can I find Captain Peña?"

The soldier lowered his rifle and nodded to the other two soldiers to do so also. He came to attention and said, "Sir we have not seen Captain Peña today."

"Does Major Zarro have you on this high alert soldier?" the General asked.

"No sir, this is routine under Captain Peña. We have practiced this very scenario multiple times. I never expected to put it into practice, especially in front of a general sir. I hope I wasn't too jumpy as the sergeant said. The reported gunshots were not far off."

The General was about to speak when another civilian vehicle approached at high speed. "General, I have to ask you to get behind me and maybe go into the shack. Sorry, but it was all we had time to construct since the attack. I can't believe this is happening again in the same night." The General and his adjutant ran to the shack. Both pulled out their handguns.

The soldier shot into the air once again. The car stopped and Captain Peña jumped out. "We have a wounded man here. I also believe that the Dam is in eminent danger. Radio to Command Post to have them send out additional support, now soldier!"

"Sir, the Post is under attack and we have another guest here that you need to know about."

"A man is bleeding to death in the back of the car. Two revolutionaries were just killed to the West of us. Wait, you said the Post is under attack?" Captain Peña asked.

"Yes sir. We heard the shots and radioed for support. They said they couldn't send anyone. Then this car drove up and…,"

Peña scanned over the other car. The hair on the back of his neck went up. "Who is here soldier? Did you confirm their identity? Where are they?"

"Captain Peña, it is so good to see you again. It has been a long time," General Cruz said as he stepped out of the shack.

"Sir, it is so good to see you! I am surprised you remember me," Peña answered.

"Right Captain. You run a tight ship here but I under-stand our help from headquarters has muddied the water."

"Sir, right now is not a good time to talk. We have a wounded man in the back of our car and I need to get him to medical attention immediately. I am also concerned the Dam is in danger of a second attack. The attack on the Post, however damaging, has got to be a ploy to keep as many soldiers as possible away from here. You may be in danger as well."

"What do you suggest Captain?" the General asked.

"Could I drive you so I can brief you on the situation here in the Mariposa Sector. Your sergeant can drive the wounded soldier to medical attention in town."

"Very well Captain. I hope the wounded is not Sergeant Hernandez. Oh, and how about asking Diana Costa to ride with us?" the General suggested.

Peña was stunned. "Sir the wounded man in the car is Diana's brother. I believe she will want to stay with him."

"Her brother?" Now the General seemed stunned. "Francisco Costa?"

"Yes, Paco is what Diana calls him. It appears it is you who needs to brief me sir."

"By all means let's get him to medical attention," is all the General said.

"Alejandro!" Emma Costa cried again at the wounded man who was lying on the reception desk just inside the Command Post doors. Emma and Consuelo tried to find the source of his bleeding and stop it.

"He is a very brave man. I hope you are able to save him," a voice entering the building said.

Everyone turned to see the soldier who said it and Louie screamed, "NO!"

"YES!" the strange man screamed back. It was Antonio— Comandante Helicon. He pulled his gun to waist level and pointed it at Louie. "I enjoyed our conversations, but they now haunt me. For the good of the revolution, you must now die." Antonio started to pull the trigger, but didn't complete the action. Harold threw a lamp at him, hitting Antonio in the face. It didn't do much damage, but it startled him and gave Harold enough time to rush him. They struggled to the floor. The gun went off and Harold screamed, "No!"

Major Zarro ran through the door from inside the Command Post, weapon in hand. He pointed it at the group. "Everyone keep your hands where I can see them.

I am happy to shoot the first person that makes a move. I don't know who is on whose side here, including you two *Norteños*. Everyone against that wall, now!"

Harold and Antonio did not get up.

Louie cried "Harold, are you alright?"

"Sir, I am Sergeant Hernandez's wife, Consuelo. We have two, maybe three wounded people here. Keep guard if you must, but we have lives in danger. We can sort out loyalties later." She looked at Zarro and then knelt down to Harold and the strange man.

Consuelo turned Harold over and off of the other man. There was blood all over both of them. "I am alive," Harold said.

"Oh thank God," Louie cried and ran to him.

"Aghhh," Antonio gurgled.

"Consuelo, the Comandante is also alive!" Louie yelled.

"Comandante?" Zarro and Consuelo said in unison.

"I am fine Louie," Harold said, "but I am afraid when I turned the gun from that man's hand it went off and fired into his gut. I have never done that before Louie. I have killed a man!" and Harold began to weep.

Oblivious to the present suffering, Zarro asked again, "Who is this man you call Comandante?"

"Comandante Helicon. My kidnapper," Louie said. She cuddled Harold in her arms and said, "This is really some honeymoon babe."

"Antonio Martín, former professor gone bad," Harold added, pointing to the Comandante's motionless bleeding body.

Major Zarro went back inside the Command Post and brought back a soldier. "Get that man to the infirmary and tell the nurse to keep him alive until we can get the doctor here. Top priority."

"What about Alejandro?" Louie asked the Major.

"Who is he and why is he here?" the Major asked.

"He is the man who just saved my life outside this building," Louie said.

"Yes, well we have injured and dying soldiers also. I will make sure he has care as soon as we can get to him. Now, tell me how the leader of the Revolution in this part of the country ended up in the Command Post of an Army installation. Whose side are you on *Señora?*" Zarro asked.

"I am not on anyone's side except these people here, Major. I am not your enemy if that is what you are asking, but I am also not your friend. I will also let anyone I have the opportunity to tell, what your priorities are."

"You will watch your tongue. *Estadounidenses!* You think you can speak your mind with whomever you like in whatever the circumstance. Well, you are in my house and I make the rules. Your life has been spared twice it appears. I have been more or less present both times. You should be thanking me, not lecturing me. We are under siege, so let's continue this some other time." The Major stopped outside the entry way.

"Three times saved Major, and you have been nothing but a distant bystander at each occurrence," Louie called out after him.

"Major, here!" a voice yelled as Zarro walked out to the open compound. A soldier dressed in black ran up to him and reported. "Sir, the threat has been eliminated. We count ten dead and two wounded."

"Thank you sergeant. Another triumph for the Special Tasks Squad. You deserve a rest, but your team needs to get out to the Dam immediately. These soldiers are in chaos and it will take some time to get things under control here. There was a report of gunshots to the West of the Dam. Maybe just poachers, but this could have been a diversion to keep support away from another Dam attack. I can't believe they would be foolish enough to try again, but who understands the minds of fanatics?" Major Zarro walked over to the dead revolutionary, pushed him over with his boot, saw the knife in his chest and said, "Eleven dead, three wounded."

The MNS group tasked to attack the depot gate never saw Julio or Antonio come out. Instead of attacking they simply dissolved into the forest. Some headed for the rendezvous point near the border. Some decided to just go home. A few started the long trip to the capital and a new life altogether. They were less than ten minutes from the bodies of their fellow revolutionaries and would not hear about their deaths for many days. It would take another week for the news to come out that Comandante Helicon had been captured alive. They would never hear about the death of a simple man, a father, a husband, and a friend and brother to many, because it wasn't deemed newsworthy. They would also never hear about the probable death of their brother revolutionary, Paco Costa, because it was too newsworthy to share with anyone.

Cesar finally reached his goal. He sat floating within ten meters of the Dam. He was forty-five minutes late, but there didn't seem to be any added security. He rested for a minute. He could not feel his feet. His hands were shaking. "I have to get control to finish my task. The others have done their best, now I must do mine."

He lowered the explosives that were grouped together in the net. They went down about fourteen meters when all the rope was extended. The fuses were ready to connect to the batteries. "Whatever it takes," Cesar said to himself. He connected the fuses to the batteries and tried to push off. He didn't have the energy. It was all that he could do to get himself back to the debris raft. He pulled himself up onto a log—the first time he had been out of the water in nearly two hours. He rested for a time. "It has never been so cold in the forest," he mumbled to himself.

After a few minutes he pulled the heavy weight up, but could not get it out of the water in order to check the fuses. He let it drop back down. He checked the wiring on the batteries and tried connecting the fuse line once more. Nothing. He decided to rest there and try again when he had more energy. "Just a few minutes of rest," he told himself out loud.

A soldier on the Dam would see Cesar lying on the log debris the next morning. The motionless Cesar had no pulse when the team pulled him from the water. It was only three days later that the Army was sent back to the debris to discover the attached explosives.

No one was ever told that the C4 and Semtex had been purposely miss-wired and posed no threat of exploding. The few that knew put in their classified report that the charges were obviously set by amateurs who didn't know what they were doing.

Chapter 25
Breakthrough Understanding

Two cars had arrived at the doctor's small clinic in Mariposa. Captain Peña didn't want to chance trying to get to the post and its better infirmary due to the reported attack. Captain Peña and Sergeant Pissarro carried Paco Costa in and laid him on the single hospital bed. Then Diego left Diana, General Cruz and the Sergeant and returned to help Sergeant Hernandez into the clinic. The only thing General Cruz had said on the drive into town is, "You have some explaining to do and some decisions to make, son."

"Sergeant Hernandez, you may have saved this man's life," the doctor explained. "Without your first aid this young man would have certainly bled to death. He is not off the critical list, but at least he has a chance. His wound does not appear to have severed any arteries or vital organs. Unfortunately, I do not have all the proper equipment to do a more thorough inspection. We can only hope for the best," the doctor explained to the group.

"Please do all you can, and I know you will," Peña said. Diana had been quiet, but was grateful for the doctor's words.

"Yes, thank you Doctor. Thank you Sergeant Hernandez." The General continued, looking at the Doctor and Hernandez. "Your wife is right, you are a soldier's soldier. It is an honor to meet you. You also are holding a hero's life in your hands." Then turning to Peña he said more sternly,

"Now, Captain, let's find a private place to talk for just a minute. Doctor, may we use your office?"

"Please do. I need to stay with the patient for a while to monitor his vital signs," the doctor answered.

Everyone wondered what General Cruz had been talking about. "Paco, a hero?" Diana thought out loud.

"Captain Peña must have told General Cruz that Paco, a rebel soldier, had saved our lives," Sergeant Hernandez said. "That he may have done so to save his sister's life alone means in a way you have saved our lives *Sombrita*. Paco certainly couldn't have seen me in the back seat of the car and I didn't even recognize him until after you did. He still hardly looks the little pup that used to play in our backyard."

"OK Captain, tell me what has been going on," General Cruz demanded as Peña closed the door to the doctor's private office. Once the door was fully closed, the General added, "I am very proud of you Diego."

The Post was still in chaos, but the shooting had stopped. Only two soldiers had been killed—the one at the main entrance and the one escorting Louie, Harold and the Costas. One other soldier, found near the depot gate, was severely injured and suffering from a head trauma. Major Zarro had already reported the incident to headquarters, although he had characterized it as a major battle and touted his role in commanding the decidedly lopsided victory. He made no mention of the use of the Special Tasks Squad. Of course he also mentioned the capture, after a close shoot-out in the entry way of the Command Post, of Antonio Martín, AKA, Comandante Helicon. As a side note, he also mentioned that the *Norteños* had been on the Post and were safe. He did not deem it important to mention the old man who died in that same bloody entryway. Zarro had ordered that the blood not be removed immediately, so that its stains could permanently remind soldiers entering and exiting the building of the fire fight that had taken place and theirs was a duty to go into harm's way whenever called by their nation.

"Well Antonio, welcome to the hospitality of the Army. You are receiving the finest care we have to offer in this back corner of the country," Zarro said.

Antonio was silent as he stared at the ceiling.

"Your wounds are serious, but you will live. We have not been able to get the doctor from Mariposa out to attend to you yet. It seems the town's people are not in a hurry to be near the stockade at the moment. Once they hear of our victory, I wouldn't be surprised if there was a parade."

"The victory is ours," Antonio said. "We fearlessly attacked at the heart of this country's oppression. That is what the people will remember."

"Right. They will remember that your so-called MNS Army of Revolutionaries was mowed down like grass to the sickle. They will also soon hear that you have been captured and that the revolution has been snuffed out," Zarro countered.

Antonio wondered why nothing had been said of the Dam's destruction. He did not ask, for fear of it still being an active operation and that Cesar had only been delayed. He vowed not to say another word to anyone.

"So, I have decided to let your former victim get the last word with you. She will be returning to her homeland soon. I only wish she had a better memory of our country to take with her than the time spent with you and your thugs. Corporal, bring in the *Norteños*."

Louie and Harold Farnsworth entered the room that only a few days ago Louie had inhabited. "Comandante, I would like to introduce you to my husband, Harold," Louie said.

Antonio turned and looked at Louie, attempting to will his body to leap at her, or to will her body to implode. Failing to accomplish either, he said, "So you have come to gloat at your new freedom and my new incarceration?"

"I forgive you for my incarceration. It wasn't pleasant, but I met Ernesto and that is a memory I will cherish," Louie said. She was clutching onto Harold with more firmness than she realized. Even in his injured state, Antonio still frightened her.

"Ah, Ernesto. The simple old man looking for a place to belong. What did happen to him? Is he free from the revolution also?"

"In a manner of speaking. He died saving my life and the life of a Sergeant at the attack of the Dam. He was a very brave man."

"That is sad to hear, that he attempted to save a sergeant. No matter, the revolution goes on. It was the Spanish anarchist, Buenaventura Durruti that said it best, *We are not in the least afraid of ruins. We are going to inherit the earth; there is not the slightest doubt about that. The bourgeoisie might blast and ruin its own world before it leaves the stage of history. We carry a new world here, in our hearts, and that world is growing this minute. What you think is ended is just begin-ning. That Ernesto gave up does not mean the others will,*" Antonio said.

"Ernesto dedicated his last months of life to you because he could not save your injured wife," Louie said angrily. "He and I both understood that vengeance against a faceless enemy is not a reason for good people to die. And even if you were really fighting for a utopia, ends never did justify the means."

"Ernesto waited upon my dear Carmen?" Antonio asked.

"He was the doctor on call the day your wife was brought into the hospital. I don't condone his misguided servitude, but he was a better man than you will ever be. But I didn't come here to gloat, or to punish, or to find new answers. I came to speak with you because I couldn't believe this opportunity presented itself and I had to take it, for closure."

"My closure? Leave me to my pain and my future glory. Both will be mine because I have willed it. I will fight until my last breath. I am prepared to live with all the energy of revolution in my heart and I am prepared to die," Antonio said.

"I don't believe you. I never did. Even when you had me thrown into that putrid cave and I felt so alone and nearly broken, I knew I was freer than you. Do you know what it is hurricanes are looking for with all their energy and destructive power? Peace, tranquility, quiet, rest. It is at their core—I have been there once, in the eye of a hurricane. It was quiet, I could see the stars, there was no wind, no rattling of its sabers, no darkness. I did not feel puny and I did not feel helpless. At your core, you are just looking for peace. You try to accomplish that by making others feel puny or helpless. You deliver destruction with promises of peace. What a lie. You don't really even believe it yourself. You could have delivered peace to combat the violence. Your wife, a victim of the same kind of indiscriminant violence you tried to create, would have loved that," Louie said. She was spent, completely and felt like collapsing but would not do that in front of what she considered to be the hollow shell of a person.

As Louie turned to go, Harold said to Antonio, "You could have killed Louie at one point and you didn't. Thank you. You came to end your nightmares by trying to kill her, and I nearly killed you. Thank you again, for not dying."

Antonio had nothing to say. He had never heard such an eloquent sentence of eternal damnation as this couple had just delivered. He was done. There was nothing left to say. There was no air left to voice his scream. Carmen had found the peace she demanded from Antonio.

"Wait!" Antonio said with all the strength in his voice that he could muster. "My pants are draped on that chair. *Señora*, please look in the pockets."

Louie walked over and lifted the filthy, blood stained pants. She put her hand into his pants pockets expecting a snake to bite her. Instead she found her wedding ring!

"Thank you," was all Louie could say. She was grateful to have her ring back and it was a last thoughtful act of a doomed soul. She turned to leave.

Louie and Harold had not quite reached the room door when Major Zarro reentered with another man. Zarro moved Louie and Harold to one side of the bed and he rushed to the other side. No sooner did Zarro turn to face the man than he produced a camera and took a picture. Louie had been used. It had been Zarro that suggested the last meeting. Louie had agreed, if only she and Harold went in. "You have broken your promise Major. I do not want that picture published," Louie demanded.

"It is only for Army use, I assure you. You may someday want a copy yourself, once the trauma of this ordeal has subsided," Zarro said.

"I am so done here. Let's go home," Louie said to Harold.

Emma Costa was alone even though Consuelo Hernandez was sitting with her. Diana had not returned from her date with Captain Peña. "They should have been back hours ago. Maybe they were attacked also!" Emma said out loud. She knew Diana was safe with the Captain, 'but then who would have thought anyone, let alone an unarmed old man, would have been killed inside an Army compound?' she thought. 'First Gustavo, then Alejandro. For all I know Paco is dead too. It's just me and Diana. No, it's just me. Diana may one day be *Señora* Peña if I am reading their eyes correctly. No, it's just me.' "I love you old man," Emma said aloud wanting to believe her dead husband Alejandro could hear her. "Who am I going to cook for? Who is going to warm my bed? And who said you could go off on another adventure, and without me this time?" Emma said.

"I am sure Diana is fine Emma. She has both the Captain and Quique to watch over her. They are probably at home already. You have Quique and me also. We are here. You can stay at our home for as long as you like," Consuelo said. She knew her words were little comfort, but they were better than only silence meeting Emma's pain.

They sat in silence in a sterile Army room. Consuelo was tired of the Army. Emma was tired of life.

Louie and Harold returned from their brief visit with the Revolutionary. "You know this is all his fault," Consuelo said. "That terrible man is alive and getting treatment and care while we suffer the results of his twisted idea of bringing justice to this country. I would like to bring him a little justice!"

"He is stewing in justice I think," Harold said. He is in a living hell and it will get worse for him I predict. Alejandro really is in a better place. I know that sounds so empty now that you are left here, but it is true. There is no more suffering for him. I am sure he misses you too Emma, but this time of only grief will pass. There will always be pain, but there will be sunny days and times of joy too."

They all wanted to believe that, but it seemed so far away right now. Harold's words lost power in mid-flight and the overwhelming gravity of the last three weeks of terror and tragedy pulled them to the ground before reaching the minds of those in the room. After minutes of silence, each lost in their own thoughts, Emma said, "*Al fin de la batalla…*" and Louie started translating for Harold,

> *At the end of the battle,*
> *the soldier dead, one came to him*
> *and begged 'O do not die; I love you so!'*
> *But alas, the corpse went on being dead.*
>
> *Two came to him and once more begged:*
> *'Don't leave us! Courage! Return to life!'*
> *But alas, the corpse went on being dead.*
>
> *Then there came to him twenty, a hundred, a thousand,*
> *five hundred thousand,*
> *all crying: 'O so much love,*
> *and to have no power over death!'*
> *But alas, the corpse went on being dead.*

Then millions came round him
all crying together: 'O please stay brother!'
But alas, the corpse went on being dead.

Then every man on earth
came to him; and tears sprang to his opened eyes:
slowly he rose,
kissed the first man; and walked…

"A poem by César Vallejo," Emma completed. "Oh if only it were so for us invisible people, those that the light of peace seems to detour around to avoid."

Captain Peña had given General Cruz a ten minute version of the last several weeks. The General studied the certificates on the doctor's wall as if he hadn't heard a thing Peña had been saying. "We have some serious damage control to accomplish before I leave in the morning. Let's get Sergeant Hernandez in here. We need all the wisdom we can find."

"Sergeant, can we ask you to come in here for a minute?" Peña asked from the door. He wanted to go to Diana and give her the comfort she needed, but duty called. Sergeant Hernandez wheeled himself in and there was barely enough room to close the door.

"There is too much and it is too complex to manage," General Cruz began. "It is hard to pinpoint precisely, but it began about four months ago."

"Sir, Peña interrupted. We have no idea what you are talking about."

"Oh, sorry Diego, err, Captain. I am talking about the beginning of the end of the Junta. Our transition from power began a few months ago. It really is simple. If the Army's monopoly of coercive power breaks down, that spawns the revolution. If our common identity, that is, our will to rule and our legitimacy to rule breaks down, there will be a transition. That has already started. I didn't see it coming, but some, like Major Zarro, did. They have taken up the cause and have manufactured events and processes to help the military continue ruling the country. An outside observer would never see it. We are too good at hiding our blemishes. There is a huge amount of internal strife within the Army today. The little power struggle here is just one of several serious examples of this breakdown. We are losing our professional edge. We have Armies within the Army. We have rogue groups doing almost as they please. All in the name of maintaining power, a power that perhaps we were wrong to assume."

"Sir, I understand your concern and I don't want to be so tactical when you want to think strategically, but what does this have to do with the things we have to solve before you leave?" Peña asked.

"Let's just say there are certain hypothetical building blocks that would shore up our obligational legitimacy to rule," General Cruz began again.

"There is that term again," Peña said. "I have heard it from Major Zarro and it sounds so philosophical or political. It's not the Army."

"It is what the Army has become, and what some are trying to hold onto while others are pushing back. I am sorry for starting my explanation of things as they are at headquarters, but stay with my thoughts for just a minute longer," General Cruz said and then began a lengthy statement that ended with a question. "The Army as the government has some external influencers that include economic forces, external legitimacy, and internal influences such as our relationship with the United States, neighboring countries, the United Nations, the World Bank, etc. I am willing to bet that Major Zarro injects high importance on what the U.S. thinks about how we handled the kidnapping. Am I right?"

"Yes, sir," Peña answered. "It's like it happened just so we could prove we are the right people to rule. He couldn't have manufactured this kidnap, but if he could have I almost think he would have attempted it."

"Yes, magnify that many times over and you will begin to see my world. Now consider challenging internal issues like mission success, mission orientation, Army culture, political culture, political capital, and probably several other things I haven't considered and you will begin to understand our delicate state of rule. We cannot be chased from power—we own the guns. But we can choose to leave power when we see ourselves as no longer obligated, that is, we see ourselves as not the only group capable of ruling. If the Elazar Dam would have blown up or our wonderful *Señora* Farnsworth would have met her end, that would not have removed us from power, possibly only accelerated a transition. In the end it is the military, internally that has to decide to leave power. Thus internally our fractionalization is the target of people like Major Zarro. The military government in Argentina in the early 1980's was already in transition from power when they attacked the Malvinas Islands. Some suggest that attack was partly to shore up internal military fractionalization to stop the transition. I am here to tell you, for your ears only, that Major Zarro has been utilizing the Special Task Squad to support the rebels in some of their operations, without rebel knowledge of course, to make the threat against the country look even more dire—thus highlighting how important we are to maintain societal order."

"You have got to be kidding me sir!" were the first words out of Sergeant Hernandez's mouth throughout this entire conversation. "The facts are there. Captain Peña and I have talked about this, but I would have never have believed he would stoop that low. He has put soldiers in life and death situations, including me, for a political agenda."

"Unfortunately, he has very powerful allies in the Junta and also within my command. His orders to come here, his orders to take command of the Elazar Dam security, the use of the STS, all this was not approved by me, but it left from my office approved. I have some house cleaning to take care of when I get back, but I thought I had better take care of things here, where, as you say Sergeant, soldiers are getting shot at."

"Sir, can't you just rescind those orders? You're here now. Verbally change the orders," Peña suggested.

"Not without ruffling a lot of feathers. You have the blessing of looking at your situation in seclusion. I have to consider many other issues and how this situation will affect them. I am actually considering sending him to a new post that most would consider a promotion, certainly career enhancing. He would oversee all international port security: airports, maritime, and commercial border crossings," the General explained.

"Have we come to that sir? Promoting our problems?" Hernandez asked.

"That is a sad solution to many organizations in modern life, Sergeant. The problem with this specific promotion is, he would still have tangential oversight of arrests and interrogations. That would include the Costa Family. Captain, could we ask Diana to join us for just a few minutes? We could join her in the other room, but the additional information I have to share, is not for the doctor's ears."

"Certainly sir," Peña said. He left the room and asked, "Diana, General Cruz is asking you to join us for a few minutes. He has something to say that I am guessing impacts your family. Doctor, is it OK for Diana to leave her brother for a few minutes?"

"The patient is stable. I can call out if anything changes. Go ahead Diana," the doctor said.

"OK Diego. We should also try to get word to my parents. They will certainly want to see Paco as soon as they can," Diana said. She took his hand and they walked the few steps into the doctor's office. Peña closed the door.

"Thank you Diana. It is a pleasure to meet you and I am sorry it is under such trying circumstances. I know you want to be with your brother. I will make this as quick as I can. I spoke with your parents at the Hernandez home before I came to find you at the Dam. They actually already know part of what I am going to speak to you about. My plan was to join them at the Post and discuss it there. Francisco's—Paco's—situation and the incursion at the Post makes that not possible at the moment. One thing I did not know, but found out when visiting with everyone at your home Sergeant is that you are Diana's godfather and that you also know Paco well. It is very appropriate that you be here," General Cruz said. He smiled as he savored their inquisitive looks. "I am making myself about as clear with this topic of conversation as with the last one I see."

"Sir, the last conversation was crystal clear compared to this one," Peña said.

"Let me start out by saying that there are more levels of complication in what I am going to explain than you will expect and some of that I will not burden you with. I am going to share several items with you that are not to be shared with anyone. Do you understand and agree?" He waited until they all nodded in agreement. "Actually, Sergeant Hernandez, you can share what you feel appropriate with your wife. I actually offered her a job in the government you know. I was joking at first, but I would consider it if she would be interested. We can talk about that later." He stopped again and looked at them. He laughed. "This is more fun than I thought it was going to be. I almost hate to start explaining."

"Sir, you have our attention," Peña said.

"Yes, well here goes," General Cruz said. He turned to Diana and began, "Your brothers, both of them, have served their country, not as revolutionaries, but as implants, agents of the government, in revolutionary circles. Gustavo was contacted while at school and agreed to join. Only a very few know about this program to insure the anonymity of these undercover counter-revolutionary operations. Unfortunately Gustavo was discovered when he tried to pass on information about the potential attack on the Elazar Dam and was executed by the revolutionaries in another Provence. Paco had already been recruited by his brother and was operating in this area. I am so very sorry for your loss Diana, but your brother understood the dangers of the job. He is truly a hero. This much I told your parents, except

I didn't mention Paco to them because when I met with them he was still in place with the rebel group."

General Cruz turned to Sergeant Hernandez. "Do you know why the Dam was not completely destroyed in the attack? It was partly your heroics I know now—thanks to Captain Peña's more specific report. Major Zarro forgot to mention your involvement in the official report. But I digress. The Dam was not destroyed because many of the key explosive charges were set with faulty fuses—thanks to Paco. He risked his life to save lives. Instead of leaving the rebel group, which was the plan, he must have decided that the confusion of the attack allowed him to safely stay longer. The young man out there in the other room is a hero and a big reason, along with you Sergeant, that this valley is not in ruins. No one can know this, however."

"Oh, thank you so much for telling me General. I am grateful my parents know about Gustavo. It has been a heavy burden for them to carry," Diana said. Tears were welling again in her eyes. She looked at Sergeant Hernandez and saw tears in his eyes also. She smiled and gave him a hug.

"Now that Paco is out of the rebel group we will be able to tell them that part of the story as well," General Cruz said. "But there is more to explain." He took a deep breath and continued. "The death of Gustavo was of course reported in Army channels. The specifics were not reported, however, to protect Paco. Unfortunately, Paco and from him to your family Diana, implications were made by some overzealous analysts that your family should be on the interrogation list. I am grateful for Captain Peña's fast thinking. I am afraid that we wouldn't have been able to protect you in the short-term. That is, until we could contact Paco. And you understand our contact with both of your brothers was very sporadic. The letter secretly requested by Captain Peña from the U.S. Embassy highlighting you and your parent's service has been helpful, but only by those few in the Army who are currying favor with the U.S. government. Others do not care. You are still in danger."

"I had no idea you did that," Diana said to Diego. "Thank you." She kissed him on the cheek. Peña blushed in the presence of the General and the Sergeant.

"Yes, so we get to perhaps the most important part of this conversation for the three of you specifically." General Cruz smiled at Diego and then got serious again. Captain Peña and I have exchanged several very confidential notes over the past few weeks. In his last note he mentioned something that got my personal attention. Do you remember what you said?" he asked.

"Yes sir," Peña answered but was not willing to say anymore.

"Does that still stand?" General Cruz asked Peña.

"Yes sir, it does," Peña replied.

"Very well. Diana, there is a way to bring safety to your family and a way for me to help ensure that safety. This is not, however a good reason for you to agree to what will be asked of you in just a minute."

Diego took in a quick breath and Diana noticed his hand started lightly trembling as she continued to hold it in her hand.

"Captain Peña, Diego, had no way of knowing any of what I have already explained to you. He has shared with me much of his feelings of the events over the last weeks. One thing even he did not see coming is the complications of these events on your family. Simply clearing you and your family of any connections with the revolutionaries, as he intended, is not an option as you now understand. My obligation to your brothers, and my respect for your parents and you lead me to this juncture in all our lives." General Cruz turned to Diego and asked, "Would you share with all of us what you sent me in your last note?"

"Yes sir," Diego said. He swallowed. He looked at Diana and said, "Now I know how you felt when your mother asked you to recite the poem of the girl on the tram. I told the General exactly this: Diana Costa may replace Solana Reyes de Cruz."

Diana scrunched her eyebrows and asked, "What does that mean? Who is Solana Reyes de Cruz?"

"May I answer the last part of Diana's question?" General Cruz asked Diego.

"Go ahead sir," Diego said.

"Solana Reyes de Cruz is my wife," General Cruz explained.

"Now I am really mixed up," Diana said. "You want me to replace the General's wife? As what? Is that a secret code for something?"

"It is sort of a secret code," the General explained. "No one could ever replace my wife for me. But now I must ask you to keep one more secret, for a little while anyway, a secret Diego asked me to keep and now I am breaking my promise. You see, I am Diego's godfather. He asked me to keep that a secret because he didn't want special attention or privileges that might come in the Army due to our relationship. The day he entered the military academy was the day we set our connection on a back shelf. I have been proudly watching Diego become a man and a leader since then, but never able to say so out loud. I am doing so today, to you three."

Both Diana and Sergeant Hernandez looked at Diego Peña who was smiling at General Cruz, with additional respect and affection.

General Cruz continued, "When Diego was young he would tell me he was going to marry my wife. I didn't have the heart to tell him she was already mine. And there may have been a few times in his youth when, if he would have asked, Solana might have left me for him."

"If I would have known I had a chance, I would have asked," Diego said. He was enjoying this more than he had thought.

"When I got the note with the statement Diego just shared, I knew you must be amazingly special. He has never said that of any woman. Since I knew your brothers through the circumstances I have just explained, I had to come and meet you in person. Now that Paco is out of immediate danger, it has become clear to me that there is a solution to your family's safety and at least one half of the solution is in agreement." General Cruz stopped talking to let what he was saying sink in for everyone in the room.

Diego Peña turned to Diana, got down on one knee and said, "Diana Costa, will you marry me?"

The room was silent. The three men were looking at Diana. She took in a breath and parted her lips.

"*Señorita!*" the doctor yelled from the other room. "*Señorita!*"

"Paco!" Diana said. She turned and ran to the other room.

"He is trying to speak," the doctor said as everyone came into the room. They all looked at Paco. His eyes were open and he recognized Diana.

"Diana! Oh thank God you are alright!" he exclaimed in a weak voice and then he recognized General Cruz. "Sir, I,

I, I had to protect my sister. She was seconds from being shot, along with two others. One was you Captain. I didn't see the other," Paco tried to explain.

"The other was me Paco," Sergeant Hernandez said.

"Oh my, I didn't see you there Quique. Were you shot? I thought I hit both?" Paco trailed off trying to remember just what happened.

"No, you saved us all son. I was injured in the attack on the Dam," Hernandez explained.

"The attack! It happened? It couldn't have!" Paco said, still disoriented.

"Of course it happened, but I understand you were able to neutralize some of the key charges so the Dam was saved," Hernandez said, smiling.

"Oh, you mean the first attack on the Dam."

"The first attack?" Hernandez and Peña said in unison.

"Yes. The other two rebels and I were just coming back from launching a second attack. A submerged explosion that would have for sure broke the Dam. Not to worry though. I was able to set the fuses in the explosives myself. They won't work. Cesar, the second in command of the rebel group floated a debris raft out to the Dam from the lake side and he was going to set off the plastic explosives from a depth that would have been powerful enough to break the structural integrity of the Dam. So you didn't catch him? How long have I been out?"

"Oh Paco, thank goodness you are alive! I love you so much. Thank you for saving our lives!" Diana said. "Thank you for saving the life of my future husband. Let me introduce you to Diego Peña."

Diego walked over to Paco and shook his hand, but was speechless. Had he heard correctly? Now it was Paco who didn't understand why everyone was cheering and hugging each other.

"Gee I am glad I can bring so much joy into the room," Paco said. Everyone laughed.

"I will explain it to you later big brother," Diana said. She seemed happier than Paco had ever seen her. "Welcome home," Diana added, but instead of kissing Paco, she turned to Diego and gave him a passionate kiss that embarrassed the doctor.

Chapter 26
Transitions

ONCE THE DOCTOR ASSURED EVERYONE THAT PACO was stable and would be fine, General Cruz, Captain Peña, Sergeant Hernandez and Diana left for the stockade. Peña had confirmed by telephone that there was on additional threat of attack. Everyone was surprised by the numbers of deaths and casualties. Adding the two rebels that Paco had killed and his own serious injuries, it had been a terribly brutal day.

"Major Zarro, it sounds like you have had quite a day," Captain Peña said as he walked into the Command Post.

"As usual it seems you were out on a date when you were needed here," Zarro answered.

Peña ignored his remark. Nothing was going to derail his good feelings. "And capturing Comandante Helicon as well. Quite a day for the Army," he added.

"Quite a day for me also. A shoot-out right outside the building and another right here in the Command Post. Thank goodness the Comandante didn't have the same fate as that old man."

"What old man? There was a shootout in the Command Post?" Diego asked.

"Yes, in the entry way. That is where the Farnsworths and the locals ended up. Then the Comandante entered and tried to kill *Señora* Farnsworth. Bad for him, good for us," Zarro said.

"Who were the locals?" Peña asked. He knew the Farnsworth's had only a small group of people they could have been with.

"Sergeant Hernandez's wife and two others. It was the old man that died," Zarro said. He was clearly not interested in that avenue of the incident. "Alejandro, I think somebody said. Did you notice the blood stains from the Comandante still in the entry way? I have commanded that it be left there as a reminder of the importance of our vigilance, and of my battle in the heart of this Post. Great reminder, no?"

"Alejandro Costa? Oh no. Are you sure?"

"Costa? As in The Costa family?" Zarro asked, suddenly interested.

"Where is the body? Where is the man's wife and Sergeant Hernandez's wife?" Peña asked. He had already forgot that General Cruz, Sergeant Hernandez and Diana were waiting for him to bring Major Zarro to them at Peña's office.

"The body is at the infirmary, so the rest of the group is probably there also. I just left there about fifteen minutes ago. The Farnsworths had a photo opportunity with the Comandante. You know, it may have been the Costas who let the Comandante and his rebel soldier, who was also killed, onto the Post. I will accompany you and arrest the woman at least. This is now starting to make more sense. This is the gift that just keeps on giving!" Zarro said.

Peña wasn't prepared to spar with Zarro. His stomach was sick. He knew what he had to do. He didn't wait for Zarro, but ran to his office. Diego found the General talking with Celia who had come in at this late hour for any support she might provide.

"Diana, General. There has been a terrible tragedy. You need to come with me. Celia, could you push Sergeant

Hernandez over to the infirmary? We will meet you there. Consuelo is there."

"Is Consuelo alright?" Sergeant Hernandez asked.

"Yes, as far as I know she is fine," Peña answered. "Diana, could I speak with you for a second as we walk?"

"What is it Diego?" Diana asked. Her voice was trembling.

"I don't have much information, but as I understand it there were shots fired here inside the Post. The rebel commander and another soldier got inside. They attempted to kill Louie Farnsworth."

"Oh no! Is she alright?" Diana asked.

"Yes, she is OK," Diego said. He stopped and turned to face her. "But I think your father was somehow involved and he was shot." Diego couldn't bring himself to say the word killed. He looked into Diana's eyes and only saw confusion.

"Let's go. I must see him!" Diana started running, not even sure where she was running to. Diego caught up with her, grabbed her hand and guided her to the right building. The General was the first through the door, followed by Diana and then Diego.

"Mother!" Diana called out when she saw Emma down the short hallway. "Where is papa? Is he OK?"

"Diana, my child! I was worried about you. I am so grateful you are alright. Sit down here my daughter." Emma guided her to a row of chairs in the hallway. Emma sat down beside her. Others in the large group were silent. "Your father got his dream. He was a toreador in the ring. He killed a raging bull. I was there. I saw it all. He was so very brave. He saved *Señora* Farnsworth's life. Unfortunately, his life was taken. He died in my arms," Emma explained.

"Oh no! No! Not papa. He is the most peaceful and loving person I know. How could this happen?" Diana broke down and began sobbing uncontrollably. She fell into her mother's arms and Emma began to cry softly.

Major Zarro had been watching this encounter. He had just arrived also, having collected several soldiers on his way here. "I am very sorry for your loss *Señora* and *Señorita* Costa. I do have my own questions that must be answered. I will be taking you both into custody at this time. We will sort this all out in due time. Soldiers, arrest those two," Zarro ordered.

"If you do that Major Zarro, I will shoot you right here, right now!" a commanding voice said from behind the group. Everyone turned and saw Sergeant Hernandez holding a pistol in his hands. He was being pushed to the center of the room by Celia.

"You will do no such thing Sergeant!" Zarro said. "These women are known collaborators and have probably earned what they deserve. Soldiers, do your duty! If the Sergeant so much as raises that gun, arrest him as well, or shoot him if he poses a real threat."

The two soldiers looked at each other, not sure what to do.

"Stand down solders," another voice said. It was a quieter voice than Sergeant Hernandez's, but it carried all the more authority. It also carried a volume of sadness that was reflected by everyone but the two confused soldiers and the one who brought them to the infirmary.

"And who do you think," Zarro began. Then he recognized General Cruz. He looked at the others and then back to him to make sure he wasn't dreaming and that the General was still there, in a business suit. "Sir, how did you? This is not what you might think sir. This is a very sad picture, but these women are on the collaborators list and may very well be the reason the stockade was attacked and brave soldiers died," Major Zarro began to explain.

"I am taking command of this situation Major. Another word out of you and I will have you arrested. Now stand there and shut up," General Cruz said. "Soldiers you are dismissed. Out!"

"Sir, I would be happy to brief you on the last few days," Zarro began.

"*Not Another Word, Major.* I will call those soldiers back." General Cruz was actually hoping Zarro made another attempt to speak so he could fulfill his threat. Unfortunately, but fortunately, Zarro kept his mouth shut.

Louie came forward and touched Emma and Diana. "I know this won't bring back Alejandro, but he saved my life and probably the lives of others today," she said. "I will forever be in his debt. I am so very sorry. I have caused so much heartache, so much tragedy. I feel like this is all my fault."

"No, this is my fault," General Cruz said. "I was the one who asked you all to come to the stockade where we could meet. I can't bring back this brave man's life, but I can remind you of this, *Señora* Costa. Your son Paco is alive and waiting to see you in Mariposa. I will also insure the Army has no further interest of anyone in your family."

"Paco is alive? He is here?" Emma asked.

Major Zarro began to leave. "Stop right there Major," General Cruz commanded. "Where do you think you are going?"

"Sir, as I tried to explain. These two women are dangerous collaborators. They are obviously skilled at manipulating emotions to their benefit. And if there is a proven rebel in town, it is my duty to capture him as well," Zarro explained.

Then he threw down the gambit. "And I don't need to remind the General that there are those at headquarters and within the Junta who would want to understand the situation here. Stopping me now will not keep this information from eventually getting into the hands of, uh, clear thinkers."

"Is that a threat Major?" General Cruz asked. He smiled the chilly glare of a lion about to attack a defenseless prey.

"No sir, of course not. I was only trying to explain the reality of the situation. There are bigger issues at stake here," Zarro quibbled.

"Those who cannot see the littleness of some bigger things, usually miss the importance of some of the little things," General Cruz said. "Captain Peña, you are in command here. Please find transportation for the Costa and the Hernandez families to travel to Mariposa to see Francisco Costa."

"Yes sir," Diego said. He turned to Emma and Diana and gently said, "We will take care of Alejandro for you.

Zarro tried one last time to right his sinking ship. "Sir, at least let us hold *Señorita* Costa until this situation is fully cleared up. Some sort of leverage that will ensure that we hold the upper hand."

General Cruz had just been pushed across a line that he knew was coming, but that he had wanted to cross on his own timetable. "Major, why would I want to detain my godson's fiancé?" he asked. Those words stopped everyone in the room again.

"What?" Sir, I think I misunderstood you," Zarro said.

"I said, why would I want to detain my godson's fiancé?" General Cruz knew he had just broken a promise of confidentiality to Diego, but only for a higher good. What he didn't explain to anyone in the room was that he had just made the decision to retire and leave the Junta. He also knew his retirement was an important step in the continued transition of the military away from running the government. For now he would just enjoy the squirming of the Major. "Yes, sometimes it's the little things that bring the most joy,' he thought.

"What is this?" Emma asked.

"I am so sorry to be the one to bring this joyous news to you. It should have been your daughter to tell you and it should have been at a more peaceful and happy moment," General Cruz said contritely. He now felt doubly bad and realized he had been short-sighted in saying what he did to stop the Major's attack of the Costa Family.

"It is the right thing at the right time," Diana said. She reached for Diego, who up until this moment had feared that perhaps Diana would change her mind. After all, the Army had brought nothing but heartache and tragedy to the Costa family, and he was the Army. Diego approached and held Diana's hand and then reached out and took Emma's hand.

"*Señora* Costa, may I marry your daughter?" Diego asked.

"In the midst of a fresh wound, I open my eyes and I am still alive," Emma answered.

"I'm sorry, I don't understand," Diego said. "Fresh wound? Is that a no?" he wondered.

"That's one of mama's poets. It is a line from Octavio Paz, right? But changed for us Diego. What I do know is, it means 'yes,'" Diana explained.

"Yes, Diego. I say 'yes,' as would Alejandro. He had a special feeling about you from the day you arrived here. God bless both of you," Emma said.

Major Zarro left with General Cruz on his private aircraft early the next morning. True to his plan, Major Zarro was given the security position by General Cruz. The next day, the Special Task Squad was disbanded. At least that is what the official announcement said. There were those in the Army who believed that another layer of secrecy and deniability had been cloaked around the unit and that actually it still existed.

"I can't believe it!" Diego told Celia. It has only been three days since General Cruz was here, and now he is retiring. I wonder if he knew that when he made his surprise visit?"

"Perhaps. It will be sad to see him go. The Army loses one of its finest, but you gain a godfather," Celia said. "The office is ready to close. I will see you at the cemetery."

"You have a driver set up to pick up the Farnsworth's?" Diego asked.

"Everything is taken care of Captain," Celia assured. "Just go get Diana and her mother. Everyone else will see you there. I don't know what that lady sees in you, but you make a wonderful couple," Celia said.

"I don't know either, Celia. I am one lucky man. You know, it happened in this building, in Mendoza's office. Diana commanded me to come to her when all the crazy things of the past month were over. I only was able to wait thirty six hours. Now I will have to wait another two months to get married," Diego said. He left the office and the Post as fast as he could and hurried to the Costa farm—really only two acres of ground and a small house. Diego had chosen to wear his formal dress uniform. He hoped it didn't make the occasion feel too military.

"Hello Diana, you look beautiful. Are you and your mother ready for this?" Diego asked.

"I don't know how one ever gets ready for this. Humans have been doing this from the dawn of time, but it is completely new for every individual. I wish Paco could make it, but the doctor demands bed rest for him. I guess there is still a concern of internal bleeding. Mama will be OK. She is so strong. Paco sort of coming back from the dead has made this a little easier for her. I will go get her."

They drove in silence to the cemetery. Emma had decided to have a simple ceremony by the grave instead of a formal funeral at the church. She refused money from the Farnsworth's for a fancy casket and gravesite. It wasn't her pride. Alejandro and she had talked about this long ago. "We come into this world simply. We should leave simply." Alejandro had said. "Have a fiesta afterword if you want, but don't have a formal goodbye."

The graveside service was attended by several neighbors, the Enrique and Consuelo Hernandez, Diego, Celia, Harold and Louie Farnsworth, and of course Emma and Diana Costa. The service was simple. The local priest said a few words, blessed the grave, and turned the ceremony over to the family. Just as Emma stood to say a few words, a car drove up. Paco slowly got out and was helped to the gravesite by the doctor. "The only way I will let you go is if I take you!" the doctor had said.

Emma smiled, nodded, and began, "When asked of what benefit philosophers are to society, Socrates supposedly answered, 'If only this, that if all civil authority were to disappear tomorrow, philosophers would go on living as they always had.' It seems in this Socrates was wrong. Civil society erupted for a brief moment and it took with it the kindest, gentlest, and most caring philosopher I know. Shame on men with power who, unable to reach out and hurt the other, end up hurting the defenseless and innocent. And then they say we owe our allegiance to them. But those with power did not win today. I have lost someone dear. We all have, but I hear Alejandro's voice whispering in my ear. He is smiling and saying, 'Love has no meaning except when proven by sacrifice.' He loved us and he sacrificed for us. He tried like no one else I know to become like his Savior." Emma picked up a flower from the wreath General Cruz had forwarded and tossed it into the grave. "He has won. We are witnesses to his success."

No one else could add a word to what Emma had said. Even in their grief for the loss of Alejandro, they were all amazed at the eloquence and understanding of this supposedly uneducated peasant woman. Paco and Diana looked at each other and despite their own sadness smiled and shook their heads. 'That's our mom,' they both thought in unison.

Almost everyone walked slowly back to the cars. Sergeant Hernandez and the Farnsworths walked a few feet away from Alejandro's resting place. Louie had purchased a grave site just a few feet away for Ernesto. He had no relatives as far as anyone could find out, so Louie felt like she needed to take care of him. "I have been in this country that is filled with the finest people, simply trying to live their lives— simple people like Emma Costa—simple enough to know right from wrong—simple enough to glean the wisdom of the ages out of the clutches of the natural man, and my time here has been far too short. In that time I have been saved from death not once, twice, nor three times, but four times. All four of my worldly saviors are at this very moment within a few feet from me. Sergeant Enrique Hernandez saved me and Harold from being shot by the revolutionaries. Surely without his brave attack when they came upon us, they would have gladly left us dead. Thank you Quique. Here also lies the remains of Ernesto. I never thought to ask him his last name. He saved my life in the rebel camp and eventually helped me escape. In the midst of that escape he also saved the life of you Quique. I will never forget you *No Importa*. We have already honored Alejandro Costa, but I can't leave without saying a heartfelt gracias for all you have done for Harold and me. I am so honored to have known you and to have come to love your wife and daughter. And thank you Harold for saving my life when that wretched man came to attack one last time. Thank you for trying valiantly to dedicate your full attention to me for a second honeymoon in a quiet valley in an almost forgotten corner of the world. But sweetheart, let's not try to do the honey-moon thing again. I just want a life with you. I don't think either of us would survive a third try. And before we go, I want to thank my Savior Jesus Christ for watching over us all throughout this incredible ordeal. Now, let's all go home."

Louie and Harold were scheduled to fly out the next day for the Capital and then home to the United States. They were enjoying one last meal together at the *Puente* Restaurant. "You know, we never did track down the reason for the Hotel's name," Harold said to Louie, Diego and Diana.

"I have no idea, but not knowing is a perfect reason for us to provide a reason ourselves. How many 'do agains' have we been given just this past month? I don't want to become my mother, although I admire and love her, but honestly you don't know what it is like growing up with one parent who answers everything with a poem, and another who has some philosophical answer that takes days or years to decipher. I think sometimes they gave us nonsense responses just so we would have something to do trying to understand their answer. But I would like to answer the Hotel name with a poem. Diana turned to Diego and said,

Podrías decirme otra vez

Amado mio ¿podrías decirme otra vez
Que seamos dos personas que
Van a enamorarse?

Deseo oír la historia antes del
Viento frío entre por la
Ventana y apaga nuestra vela.

Quiero escucharla como si
Yo fuera una semillita que no sabe
Los tormentos o las estaciones.

Then she translated for Harold: My love, could you tell me again … That we are two people … Who are going to fall in love? … I wish to hear the story before the cold wind comes in through the … Window and blows out our candle. … I want to listen as if I were … A tiny seed that does not know about … Storms or seasons."

"Why is it I almost feel like a voyeur whenever you share a poem with Diego? Harold asked. "It is like magic. Is this a Latin thing or is it just you two?"

"It is a Latin thing," Diego said, laughing.

Louie nodded agreement and began her input. "I have another thought, not near as sensual as your poem Diana that I have been thinking about the last few days. Only now am I connecting it with the Hotel name mystery. I am not musical. I tried to play the guitar when I was young, but there was this huge gap between what I wanted to hear from the strings and what actually came out of my efforts. Maybe only a true artist can express his or her feelings through their chosen medium. That is because they know the language. I could barely play what someone else had written, but even then I didn't know the language. That gap for me created a tension. That tension spurred me to change the situation, to improve. I could not master the guitar, or maybe I didn't dedicate enough time. But it is that tension that creates the spark, that delivery of meaning, that passion for life. It creates visions for the visionary and hope for the dreamer. That is what brings legitimacy to our longings and what makes life worth living. Trying again. Your country and its people have taught me that. Trying again is what life is all about. We need to live life like this is our second chance and the mistakes have already been made."

"Nice Louie," Harold said. "But I will go with the poem."

"Yeah, the poem," Diego agreed.

"Do you feel sad that you never got to the bottom of the disappearing butterfly mystery?" Louie asked Harold as they arrived at the Mariposa Airport.

"Not at all. I think I have enough to figure it out actually," Harold said. He grabbed their bags and carried them to the baggage cart. "Thank you again for the lift Diego."

"What butterfly secrets are you looking for?" Diana asked. "I have heard you and papa talk a few times about it, but it sounds like he kept the answer wrapped in some hints that probably weren't even hints."

"Other than picking this place for a quiet attempt at a honeymoon, we came here to find the secrets to the Madrugada Butterfly. A good friend told me those butterflies can disappear," Harold explained.

"Papa loved disappearing acts," Diana said. "He used to tell us stories about things disappearing. He liked to think he could disappear too. I do remember him telling us children a story about a butterfly that could disappear. I just assumed it was another one of his crazy tales." Diana got lost in the memory of her father who had finally achieved the ultimate disappearing act.

"If it is too uncomfortable, that's OK, but I would love to hear the story," Louie said.

"I don't remember the whole story. Maybe Paco does," Diana began. "It was something about a butterfly that believed it was something else. It wasn't as colorful as its butterfly friends you see. At first it thought it was a *luciér-naga*. How would you say that, an insect with light?"

"Oh, a lightening bug," Louie offered.

"Yes, this butterfly thought it was a lightening bug because it could create electricity. But it couldn't make light," Diana explained. "It was a very sad and not so pretty butterfly. Then it thought it was a mosquito, because other bugs, and those birds and animals who like to eat bugs never seemed to notice this butterfly. But this butterfly didn't like to poke things and suck their blood. He thought that was a terrible thing to do. He liked to quietly lie among the flowers, the kind that grows down by the river. One day the butterfly got scared when a bird, an oriel I think you say in English landed near it. It looked like it wanted to eat the butterfly, but then it just hopped away. Unlike its brother butterfly from up in Mexico, the Monarch that makes poisons that hurt other animals, the Madrugada realized it could just think about danger, wrap its wings around its little body and it would disappear. Instead of collecting light, the Madrugada Butterfly could use the electricity it produced to bend light in the opposite direction to light reflecting off of the butterflies that thought they were so beautiful. This butterfly realized it had magic powers and was very special in its own way," Diana paused. "I might have that mixed up, but I think that was at least part of the story. Butterflies that make electricity to bend light is just one example of the kinds of stories we grew up with. No three little piggies, or gypsy queen stories for us."

"That is absolutely fascinating Diana," Harold said. "How could a man with less than a high school education explain meta-machines? If this actually does exist in nature, it would humble the nano-tech community that thinks they have created something nature could not do. Thank you Diana!"

"I hate to be the messenger of bad news, or maybe good news after all that has happened over the last weeks, but it is time to go to your plane," Diego announced.

"Bad news," Harold and Louie said.

"Well Captain, if you will get our bags we will be on our way," Harold said.

Diego's mouth dropped and Louie slugged her husband in the arm. "I'm kidding!" Harold said. "The new Harold thinks about the details, but doesn't get so lost in them that he misses the ones in front of his nose. Honestly Diego, thanks for your patience with me."

"Ah, it seems you have the same ancient flight attendant," Diego noted. It was Diana's turn to hit Diego in the arm. "What?" he asked.

"No one would ever believe that these last four weeks were real, that they happened with barely a mention in the news and little fanfare in its outcome," Louie said. "Someday I'm going to write a book about this. I will change some names and maybe place this in some unknown valley, like Mariposa once was."

"There is much that isn't as it once was," Diego said. "I am planning on retiring my commission. It isn't the same Army I joined when I was a cadet, or I am not the same person I was."

"None of us are the same," Harold said.

"No words can express our gratefulness to know you both. There were times of terrible tragedy. I am so sorry for your loss Diana. But there were times of incredible healing. Thank you." Louie could not get another word out.

Diana hugged Louie and held her hand until the propeller on the door side of the aircraft began to turn. Louie's throat had closed tight and her heart felt like it was going to burst. "I don't want to leave," she said as she stepped through the airplane door that was closing. She walked to her seat, collapsed, and as she opened her hand to fasten her seat belt she realized she was still holding a small note. It was in Diana's handwriting.

We are the stories that define our potential. When stories intersect our potential expands, immeasurably. Our intersection has added new chapters to my story that I never dreamed possible. I hope and pray our stories intersect again someday. Your stories of courage and action are the poetry that is life. Not everyone is a poet, but I have known two, my mother and you.

My father once told me that butterflies live less than one year, but that is not a tragedy because they live a full life , from caterpillar, to chrysalis, to butterfly. Have we not experienced the same? And once the earth-bound caterpillar has wings, it still cannot fly if it is cold. You have warmed my life and I can now fly.

With love, Diana

In This Book

Poems and quotes from others in Conversations Among Butterflies. I provide this to give credit where due and in case you would like to further research the author of the original work.

Public Domain	Quote Used	Author	Notes
Yes	Daydreams have endlessly turning paths going over the bitter earth,	Antonio Machado	From Sobre la Tierra Amarga
Yes	these daydreams are sad playthings for an old man	Antonio Machado	From Sobre la Tierra Amarga
Yes	...Dominant groups in society, including fundamentally but not exclusively the ruling class, maintain their dominance by securing the 'spontaneous consent' of subordinate groups, including the working class, through the negotiated construction of a political and ideological consensus which incorporates both dominant and dominated groups...	Antonio Gramsci	From Prison Notebooks
Yes	A crisis occurs, sometimes lasting for decades. This exceptional duration means that incurable structural contradictions have revealed themselves and that, despite this, the political forces which are struggling to conserve and defend the existing structure itself are making every effort to cure them, within certain limits, and to overcome them. These incessant and persistent efforts... form the terrain of the 'conjunctional' and it is upon this terrain that the forces of opposition organize.	Antonio Gramsci	From Prison Notebooks

Public Domain	Quote Used	Author	Notes
Yes	Aquela triste leda madrugada, cheia toda de mágoa e de piedade, enquanto houver no mundo saüdade quero que seja sempre celebrada. (The dawn rises lovely but ill-fated and full of grief. For as long as heartbreaks prey upon our tragic world, this dawning day should be forever famous and celebrated.)	Luís de Camões	
No	Estoy vivo...' I am alive in the center of a still fresh wound	Octavio Paz	I offer only this brief passage so as not to infringe on any copyrights
Yes	Reference the name of his work: Small Hours of the Night	Roque Dalton	No actual quote
Yes	refuge failed me, no man cared for my soul.'	Psalms 142:4	
Yes	I looked on my right hand, and beheld, but there was no man that would know me: refuge failed me; no man cared for my soul."	Psalms 142:4	
Yes	And Jesus went with them. And when he was not far from the house, the man sent friends to him, saying, Lord, do not give yourself trouble: for I am NO IMPORTA enough for you to come into my house.	Luke 7:6	
No	The last of freedoms was choosing one's attitude	Attributed to V. Frankl in the narrative	
Yes	It is by grace we are saved, after all we can do	Book of Mormon, 2 Nephi 25:26	
Yes	bad men are full of repentance, when they are caught	Attributed to Aristotle in the narrative	

Public Domain	Quote Used	Author	Notes
No	all the world needed to do was hold and love all the little babies, so they will grow to know how to love and nurture others	unknown	I have read something like this, but have not been able to identify an author
Yes	"Se le vio, caminando entre fusiles, por una calle larga, salir al campo frío, aún con estrellas, de la Madrugada". (He was seen walking between the rifles, down a long street, out to chill fields, still lit by early stars.)	Antonio Machado. Poesías de Soledades (1898-1907). El Crimen Fue en Granada	I am actually not sure if this is public domain or not. The English translation is mine.
No	Did you ever stop to think and then forget to start again?	Attributed to Winnie the Pooh in the narrative	Actually from A. A. Milne
No	The song Cambalache is referenced	Attributed to Discépolo in the narative	No actual quote
Yes	These men need a good grip; they like to feel something in this slippery world that they can hold on to.	Paraphrase from Moby Dick which is attributed in the novel	Herman Melville not mentioned
Yes	Candle of the Lord	Attributed to Proverbs in the Bible in the narrative	
No	Literature and butterflies are the two sweetest passions known to man,	Attributed to Vladimir Nabokov in the narrative	

Public Domain	Quote Used	Author	Notes
Yes	The actions of the military government are inspired by the necessity of transforming the structure of the state to permit efficient government action to improve social, economic, and cultural structures, and by necessity to maintain a definite nationalist attitude and fully re-establish the principles of authority and respect for obedience to the law in all areas of national life,	Loose quote from the Peruvian Military Government Manifesto	
Yes	Noia del tram, tens l'esguard en el llibree I el full s'irisa en veure's cobejat,"	Attributed to Joan Salvat-Papasseit in the narrative	
Yes	Girl on the tram you've got your eyes in a book and the page blushes on being envied. And the conductor wonders if you'll turn the page: just to see your eyes! We can see your legs and the stocking so sheer; and all the tram is you. But we can't see your eyes. And your head is bright, tinted by your body of red taffeta, and your handkerchief, back from the wash. But we can't see your eyes! And if I were to get off?—I'd never know your eyes... Look now. I've got off!	Attributed to Joan Salvat-Papasseit in the narrative	
No	It must be said that, like the breaking of a great dam, the American descent into Marxism is happening with breathtaking speed, against the backdrop of a passive people.	Attributed to Stanislav Mishin, writing in PRAVDA	This is a paraphrase, not a direct quote

Public Domain	Quote Used	Author	Notes
Yes	There are two kinds of human beings. One kind holds each human being as an agent to himself and we should not take away that agency to act. The other kind thinks, or operates as if other humans are objects and that it is perfectly appropriate to use other human beings. What one would hate to do, the other regards as not only the clever thing to do, but the wise and courageous thing to do. One type of person demands fairness and end of abuse. The other type claims ends justify any means and strives to gain power in order to use any means. One type truly believes that we are created equal, that we are in the same boat together, and that here is abundance for us all to share. The other only sees the world as a zero sum game, that is, in order for them to win, others have to lose.	Attributed to Dostoevsky in the narrative	This is a paraphrase of a concept, not a quote
Yes	Aristippus of Cyrene, on being asked what is the most impressive sight on earth, he said it was the sight of a good man quietly pursuing his course in the midst of vicious people.	Aristippus of Cyrene	
Yes	The butterfly, setting her color on fire, was made of ashes..., without your hands my heart is the enemy in my chest	Attributed to Roque Dalton in the narrative	
Yes	We are not in the least afraid of ruins. We are going to inherit the earth; there is not the slightest doubt about that. The bourgeoisie might blast and ruin its own world before it leaves the stage of history. We carry a new world here, in our hearts, and that world is growing this minute.	Attributed to Buenaventura Durruti	

Public Domain	Quote Used	Author	Notes
Yes	At the end of the battle, the soldier dead, one came to him and begged 'O do not die; I love you so!' But alas, the corpse went on being dead. Two came to him and once more begged: 'Don't leave us! Courage! Return to life!' But alas, the corpse went on being dead. Then there came to him twenty, a hundred, a thousand, five hundred thousand, all crying: 'O so much love, and to have no power over death!' But alas, the corpse went on being dead. Then millions came round him all crying together: 'O please stay brother!' But alas, the corpse went on being dead. Then every man on earth came to him; and tears sprang to his opened eyes: slowly he rose, kissed the first man; and walked…	Attributed to César Vallejo in the narrative	
No	In the midst of a fresh wound, I open my eyes and I am still alive,"	Attributed to Octavio Paz in the narrative	I offer only this brief passage so as not to infringe on any copyrights
Yes	If only this, that if all civil authority were to disappear tomorrow, philosophers would go on living as they always had	Attributed to Socrates in the narrative	

Public Domain	Quote Used	Author	Notes
No	Amado mio ¿podrías decirme otra vez Que seamos dos personas que Van a enamorarse? Deseo oír la historia antes del Viento frío entre por la Ventana y apaga nuestra vela. Quiero escucharla como si Yo fuera una semillita que no sabe Los tormentos o las estaciones. Then she translated for Harold: My love, could you tell me again … That we are two people … Who are going to fall in love? … I wish to hear the story before the Cold wind comes in through the … Window and blows out our candle. … I want to listen as if I were … A tiny seed that does not know about … Storms or seasons."	Attributed to one of the characters in the novel	From: http:// snowcrumbs. blogspot. com/2007/12 I attempted multiple times over several years to contact this person with no reply. I decided to incorporate this poem along with the other great poems of poets in this book. If anyone knows this poet, please ask her to contact me.

Additional works on sale by this author:

Media in the 21st Century:
Meet-Up or Meltdown in the Meaning Marketplace

Published by Byblos Media, June 2010; 583 pages;

ISBN 978-0-9746003-6-9

Seeds He Planted

Published by Byblos Press, December 2007;

ISBN 978-0-9746003-2-1

Nahum's Story

Published by Byblos Press, December 2007;

ISBN 978-0-9746003-3-8

Upcoming works by this author:

Kitab Kabbani

The story of the search for an ancient book that could change the delicate status quo of the entire Middle East. Writing completed, scheduled for publication in September 2015

Chinese Circus

Six novellas of mixed genres and styles that consider contemporary areas of interest, interwoven into one book. Writing completed, scheduled for publication in December 2015.

For more information check out:
http://www.mike-mitchell.com

Sign up for the author's mailing list here:
http://eepurl.com/bviacf

Or scan the QR code: